The Glowing Inferno of the Burning Floor, the Tower of Living Fire, the Hungry Eyes of Thesian Nobility . . .

Again, heat was strong beneath Tiana's feet and she retreated two paces, running sweat—only to encounter more immediate heat. The fire was everywhere save for this tiny patch of floor. Its diameter was less than the length of a sword. Of necessity, she gave up dignity and danced into the center of that hot but flameless area. They knew what was imminent: the cream of the joke.

Her lips were clenched, while in her mind she screamed, *No, please, no, not this!* . . .

Books by Andrew Offutt and Richard Lyon

Demon in the Mirror
The Eyes of Sarsis
Web of the Spider

Published by TIMESCAPE/POCKET BOOKS

ANDREW OFFUTT
AND RICHARD LYON

WEB OF THE SPIDER

**Part Three
in the trilogy
*War of the Wizards***

A TIMESCAPE BOOK
PUBLISHED BY POCKET BOOKS NEW YORK

Another *Original* publication of TIMESCAPE BOOKS

A Timescape Book published by
POCKET BOOKS, a Simon & Schuster division of
GULF & WESTERN CORPORATION
1230 Avenue of the Americas, New York, N.Y. 10020

ISBN: 0-671-82680-8

First Timescape Books printing December, 1981

10 9 8 7 6 5 4 3 2 1

POCKET and colophon are trademarks of Simon & Schuster.

Use of the TIMESCAPE trademark is by exclusive license
from Gregory Benford, the trademark owner.

Printed in the U.S.A.

In the latter days, at the end of all things, there shall come Seven whose eyes are fire and whose sight is flame. These are the Worldfires. What little there is of good in our tarnished earth they will gather; and destroy all else with fire unquenchable.

—The Visions of Darmosra

Hair of Flame, Eyes of Fire
The Seven watch with flaming eyes
Whilst mortals play a trifling game;
Their souls are petty, fed by lies.
Combatants fall, new warriors rise:
Comes now this woman with hair of flame!

Tiana, Ekron—mighty Pyre!
A mirrored dæmon and Sarsis's eyes;
Soul of toad and cold eyes of fire
Seeking grasp of earth entire!
What matter if a warrior dies?

Ekron and Pyre—wizards warring;
Tiana of Reme, riding higher—
To fall? Pawn of Ekron and Pyre?
Wizards warring, mere pawns sparring!
But to win: those with eyes of fire.

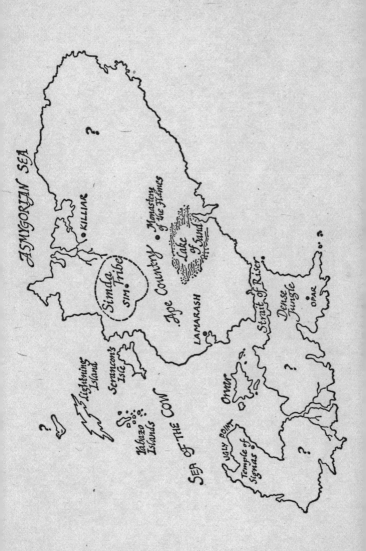

CONTENTS

WEB OF THE
SPIDER

PROLOG

"Tiana, your beauty is a flame and your wit as sharp as your rapier. You have been a thorn in the side of many of the great and powerful. Were I not so far down the lonely path of black arts, I myself might desire you. The world will be a poorer place when you leave it, I, Pyre, who knows that he is supreme, vow by the Fires Which Shall Destroy the Earth that I shall avenge your death."

And I, Tiana, who knows she *is supreme, Pyre, vow that we'd be a marvelous couple indeed!*

The paired day-candles were the color of night. They created eerie shimmers on drapes that seemed parts of a great dark web. The tremulous light flickered and flashed on the great round eyes of the . . . being, who stared at the uncompleted web. He was Ekron, whose soul was that of a toad and whose god was the Spider. He was a wizard and he was at the weaving of a web for the spiderish ensnaring of his mortal enemy. The prize was the world.

The war between Ekron and the wizard Pyre was a dark, dark business like unto an endless nightmare. Often those conscripted to fight its battles knew not what was at stake. Many of those combatants knew not even that they were engaged in war.

Among other things, Ekron possessed a talent—costly purchased—for seeing the future. It was a dangerous talent; dangerous as a knife pointed at both ends. The future, once seen, could not be changed.

One might, for example, look ten years hence and see which of a thousand bottles of wine in a cellar one's enemy would, positively, be drinking on a given night. Thus armed

1

with knowledge, one might contrive to poison that bottle. One might also see too much. Suppose one saw oneself seated at table with one's enemy, forced by circumstance to join in the drinking of that poisoned wine. The future, once seen, could not be changed. One must still poison the wine and must thereafter march unswerving down the years-long road to death.

Thus the deadly game the wizard Ekron had chosen to play, he whose soul was that of a toad and whose god was the Spider.

The ignorant world thought Pyre and Ekron to be the most powerful of black necromancers. Pyre and Ekron knew themselves to be weak compared to the host of dark forces that dwelt beyond human ken. Eyes watched the world, eyes aflame with the fire of jealousy and lust for dominance.

Accordingly the toad-souled wizard contrived to create a situation in which Pyre of Ice must battle such a deadly occult power. Looking beyond the veil of time, which was like unto a web that could be seen through, Ekron saw that this plan would fail. That had been error. Pyre would emerge from his combat with the non-being *Derramal,* who too was *Lamarred,* victorious and more powerful than ever. Error, to have looked forward to that immutable future! Though the plan was doomed to failure, Ekron must carry it through. Yet he saw too an error on the part of his opponent.

Perhaps the effort need not be a total waste!

During his conflict with the non-being, mighty Pyre made one blunder. It served to plant a single tenuous seed for later disaster.

There was the woman. The pirate queen, Tiana, captain of *Vixen.* Proud and beautiful she was, claiming to know no fear and in truth a headstrong adventuress too willful to admit to fear and be curbed by it. She was as vain in her courage as of her beauty. Worse, her wits were as sharp and deadly as her rapier. For reasons of her own, she chose to fight the demon Derramal; the demon in the mirror. Her tactics were so reckless that Pyre predicted her death.

In a moment of vanity he vowed to avenge it.

He swore so, by the Fires Which Shall Destroy the

World, an oath Ekron knew to be forever binding: Therein lay his chance. This was the seed Pyre planted, that Ekron might nurture it into a deadly nightshade. If he could contrive events so that the troublesome woman died at the hands of some invisible dark power, Pyre would be compelled to combat that power. And he would be destroyed.

Ekron sent out his Vision into the future as the frog sends forth its tongue for the hapless fly.

A further look ahead showed him that he would indeed attempt a plan of that sort, using the ancient and pure-evil eyes of Sarsis. And he saw that it too would fail, with both Pyre and the woman—a noble's bastard—surviving. And Ekron cursed. Thus he was doomed to more wasted effort—but he could and did learn from the mistakes he had yet to make.

Now the day-candles, dark as his heart, cast their nervous glim on his web of evil, and now he strove anew, this time with infinite care. For the fly is reckless in its restlessness, and the toad is patient.

A third time he began to spin a web; arranging a circumstance here, planting a seed there—and peering into the future after each action, just far enough to learn whether or no it would bear the desired fruit. Each skein of the web was permanent. No strand could be recalled and spun anew. The prize was the world. The future, once seen, could not be changed.

When at last Ekron had proceeded far enough that he dared look upon the outcome of his manipulations, joy soared in him like a vulture above rich food. Ekron, whose soul was that of a toad and whose god was the Spider, saw in the future that which must mean victory for him and surely the destruction of not only the trifling Tiana but the mighty Pyre as well!

Obliged to carry through with his first two futile plans, he did so with good heart. Never mind Derramal/Lamarred, the demon in the mirror. Never mind the Eyes of Sarsis and that awful bear and even dread Sarsis itself/himself! The forces Ekron had placed in motion had entrapped his enemy in an inescapable oath, and would surely doom him.

And now amid trembling flame-light of his candles

Ekron sat back, and his smile was a hideous sight. For in it was his soul, and the soul of Ekron was a toad.

Of course Pyre of Castle Ice, too, was busy, and his was the knowledge of other matters, other things, and once again the pawns were moved into the game. The war was that of wizards. The prize was the world.

First Strand:

ENTER A SPIDER

"For the crimes of high treason and blasphemy, Tiana Highrider, pirate, you are condemned to be cremated alive at the dawn of the morrow."

As she sat in the darkness of her dungeon cell, the words of the sentence still echoed in Tiana's mind. How dreadfully unpleasant! What an ugly mind High Magistrate Ishcon had!

Still, Tiana felt that she had little to worry about. Men could not be more than men, however they tried. The world was full of males ruled by their loins. The fools always failed to see the strength her beauty concealed. Experience assured her of that fact. It made most men easy prey for Captain Tiana of *Vixen*. Accordingly, during her trial she had dressed as immodestly as possible and postured besides. Throughout the proceedings she had felt the gaze of Ishcon's hot little eyes roaming like spiders over her every curve. Now, condemned and endungeoned, she was nevertheless confident that the High Magistrate would summon her to his privy chamber for a . . . private examination.

At that point I'll simply beat the poor lackwit unconscious and escape.

How annoying to have been condemned for petty crimes of which she was innocent, when she had committed such truly marvelous depredations and offenses against these Thesians! Why, the ships she had cost them last year alone would practically constitute a fleet, and—

Were those approaching footsteps? The prison's guards coming at last to escort her to liaison with the magistrate? *By the Great Cow's Cud, what I'd give now for a lamp and a mirror!*

Since her appearance was most literally vital, Tiana did what little she could, even in darkness. Running her fingers

5

through the mass of her long red hair was a far cry from combing; at best she was putting it in a free-flowing disorder. Some men found that exciting. As for her clothing, her (very) short leggings and sleeveless shirt of green silk were at least still clean, and satisfactorily tight. She knew her emerald eyes were clear if not heightened by cosmetics, and her creamy complexion unmarred—but oh for a mirror!

With a ponderous grating sound, the bolt of her cell's door moved. A crack of light appeared. It widened to reveal the hook-nosed face of Captain Bratch. He grinned through rotten yellow teeth. Probably took up military service when his revolted mother kicked him out of the house!

"Don't git alarmed now," he said, stepping back and gesturing for her to emerge. "The morning is yet distant. We are come to take you to an interview with the Lord High Magistrate. May be that if you earnestly appeal to his mercy, he might change your sentence?"

He has no mercy, Tiana mused, stepping forward. *I know what to appeal to!* She saw Bratch's company of pasty-faced prison guards in armor so ill-kept it showed rust and broken links. She also saw that some secret joke was writ behind their ogling eyes. Then she was surrounded and marching along with them—and a chill sensation ghosted along her spine.

Why does Bratch, a thoroughgoing sadist if ever there was one, come to me with words of comfort and reassurance?

Here, far beneath the city in the subterranean maze that was Dindroom Prison, she had little sense of direction. Still, this twisting path they trod did not seem the right way to the magisterial chambers. Suppose her sense of time had betrayed her? Suppose it *was* already morning? Might not Bratch lie, telling her that she was only going to see the judge, and thus save himself the trouble of dragging her kicking and screaming to the place of execution? Suddenly the prison food lumped heavy in her stomach and her mouth was dry. *Of course I'm not frightened, but still . . .*

"Tell me, Captain," she began, forcing her voice into a tone of casual banter, "exactly what is my execution to be? Lord Ishcon was most confusing. At one point he spoke of roasting me like an ox, I recall. Yet later he declared charmingly that I am to be eaten, body and soul, by some sort of . . . *fire demon?*" She added a tone of jesting incredulity to those last words.

"There are things it is wise not to mock," Bratch sententiously said. "You outsiders do not know. Here in Port Thark, them that dwells beneath the surface are our neighbors. The kind of neighbor a person's wise to avoid." He shrugged, with a little *ching* of mail. "No matter. Soon enough in the Chamber of the Sleeping Demon you will learn more than you want to know."

He all but admitted that I'm really walking to my execution!

Around the next corner a large object stood looming tall —a Chervian Cross! Two long beams of wood were bolted together at their centers to form a great X. A Chervian Cross was about as pretty as gangrene. Tiana could not prevent a shudder at sight of it. The design was commonly used for female prisoners because it displayed them so well. The victim stood more than a sword's length above the floor with her feet resting on and chained to the footrests in the lower arms of the ugly construction. A leather belt strapped her waist to its center, while her arms were pulled above her head and locked in the manacles of the upper section's huge V.

No wonder this band of ghouls has been watching me as if I was a cow going to a roast!

"*Captain* Tiana," Bratch said with the barest hint of a polite bow, "'tis the High Magistrate's order that you be trussed, so he can interview you alone and in safety." He gestured. "If you would be so good as to get yerself upon this nice frame . . ."

And as soon as I'm completely helpless you'll have your fun with me! she thought, with a mild expression on her face and burning rage in her heart. *Only this time the sport is going to be expensive.* She was moving to the cross. She made as if to climb it, then paused.

"I'm stiff after so long in the cell. Give me a boost, would you?"

Though she addressed the request to Bratch, it was one of his men who bent and put his hands together into a stirrup.

Hmm. Only half a loaf.

None of the dozen men in the secure weight of armor dreamed that this lightly-clad young woman could be any danger. Swords and spears were held listlessly. The man who stooped to aid her ascent saw the wrongness when she raised her foot. Naturally he supposed that she was being clumsy, or stalling. In the brief instant during which her kick sped at his neck, his eyes widened slightly. The surprised expression froze on his face as her heel slammed into the side of his neck. He was propelled across the room to strike the wall with a rattle of armor and an ugly *clonk,* after which he crumpled to the floor with his head twisted at a most unseemly angle.

Before his comrades could realize that he was dead she was upon them, hitting, kicking, smashing with elbow and knee and heel. Immediately one was down and spitting his teeth on the floor. Another staggered about with a broken nose drooling blood all down his mustache and chin. Before she could drive the bone fragment back into his brain, a fourth Thesian thrust at her with the end of his spear-butt. He was no experienced fighting man, she saw in an instant, and used that fact to her advantage. All at one time: sidestep with two-handed grasp on the spearhaft and tug and twist and then she *rammed* it.

Mistreated chain links snapped like cord as she drove the head of his own spear back through the rust-weakened armor and into his guts. Tiana felt wild exhilaration. They were so inexperienced, and clumsy and slow in their armor! Her speed and skill might well whelm them all!

Even with the thought the back of her head exploded in pain. She fell, only just managing to turn on the floor to avoid a downrushing spear. A sweep of her legs sent a man sprawling and a heavy boot crashed into her head.

Through pain-swept darkness a voice filtered dimly down to her.

"Kill the leggy bitch and be done with it!"

"Aw—le's torture 'er the way we planned."

"Boy I'd like to get my hands on them—"

"IDIOTS!" Bratch's voice thundered. "If we disobey Ishcon's orders he'll make us take her punishment. What's in store for the fire-headed slut is enough!"

The rest was silence and blackness.

When the fog lifted she was fighting not men but chains. From her vantage point on the huge wooden X-frame she looked down upon a figure in blood-red robes. He stood before her/below her and the bald, age-shriveled head with its deep-set, opaque black eyes was all too familiar.

*Praise be to Theba Who did not claim me once again—
it's Ishcon. I still have a chance. Come to think, even my
pose could not be better for those hot little eyes of his!
I'm just superbly displayed up here to arouse the lust of
this repulsive old scarecrow. And to gratify that lust he'll
have to free me . . . and when he does—ah-ha-ha!*

Smiling in warm invitation, Tiana made her voice softly
submissive. "Your Exalted Justice sir, I am grateful that
you came. Those men were all cursing you and saying
how they'd cut off this and that piece of me! As I said before, I will gladly do *anything* to satisfy you . . . as to my
innocence."

His cold eyes examined her body as though she were a
meat animal. "Girl—do you really suppose yourself capable of seducing the High Magistrate of the Thesian Grand
Court?"

This is not starting well, Tiana thought, but pushed her
face into a smile still brighter.

"Lord High Magistrate, I assure you that no such pre-
sumptuous thought entered my . . ."

Her voice trailed off before Ishcon's annoyed gesture.
He bent close to make a dispassionate examination of her
bare feet. "Astonishingly soft and quite dainty, and still
the soles have good thick callus. Excellent!"

*How churlish of him to mention that—and what's it
have to do with anything, anyhow? It doesn't matter. If I
can't gull this old bone-bag, he'll leave me hanging here
till morning and . . . my execution.* Though tension was
drawing her muscles into tight knots, that thought also
aided her to whisper softly:

"My lord Magistrate has still not told me how I may
please him."

"Oh I'll grant that you're passing fair, *pirate*. At last
month's auction I paid half a thousand gold regals for a
woman not half so lovely as you—but she was easily disciplined and bent! She satisfies. You—you, pirate, are the
reason an entire squad of wardermen won't be fit for duty
for a month—except for those that have to be buried.
Look!" He stooped to snatch a small object off the floor,
and held it up to her view. It was yellow and brown. "This
tooth belongs in Captain Bratch's mouth, not lying on a
dungeon floor!" He bounced the tooth off her bare belly,
drawn flat and taut by her straitened pose on the X-cross.

"Now with an introduction like that, do you think I'd be so lackwit as to attempt treating you as a *woman?*"

Well I'd like to know what else I am, she thought indignantly, but with her hopes of escape so clearly slipping away, Tiana was enduring a very dark moment. Her muscles twisted into tense knots that shone exteriorly with chill sweat. In her imagination she saw the execution. Her execution. Not death in combat, her rapier flashing, but a spectacle for a gawking crowd.

Still . . . if Ishcon didn't come here for pleasure, he must have some business in mind. Of course! I should have realized that at once!

"That rotten tooth is better buried than in anyone's mouth," she said in a bland tone: "even Bratch's. Besides, if I'd had my boots on instead of having to kick him barefoot, his *corpse* would have ten less teeth, along with even fewer brains than he already has."

Ishcon's brows rose. "Hmm! Considering your circumstance, you seem in unusually good spirits. Shall we discuss the arrangements for your execution? It's going to be a major social event, pirate, and some of the details are fascinating, I assure you."

"No doubt. But do we have the time to continue this charade of yours?"

"Charade? Explain." She saw no hint of surprise in his dead black eyes.

"Obviously you want me for some dangerous errand. Steal a treasure or rescue a virgin or take on a wizard, perhaps. I've done all those, as you well know. All this has been a mere ploy to frighten me into working for short wages." She tossed her fiery mane with casual coolth. "Anyone who knows me could have told you that I am entirely without fear, and saved you all this trouble."

Thesia's High Magistrate snorted a quick sardonic laugh. "Oh? Were you never, in all that has happened, even slightly frightened?"

Tiana, whose vanity often shortened her memory, considered only a moment. "No, not that I can remember. Now to business: what is it you want me to accomplish? If it's treasure, we'll of course share it equally." *Let me out of here and asea, swine, and hold your breath till you see me again!*

"My dear," he said quietly, "you've no long while before you go into the flames. That makes your bargaining position a poor one. Too, there is the matter of your crew, including one Caranga, who I believe is your foster-father despite his color."

She had noted how quietly he spoke; now he glanced about the dungeon chamber before he continued. "You know I ordered your crew held in preventive detention until after your execution. You probably do not know that Thesian law provides that a person whose crimes merit his being put to death several times shall be so punished. His family and friends serve as stand-ins during the later procedure. You may change the pronoun to 'her' family, Tiana. Had I not mercifully tried you on a minor charge of which you are innocent—rather than your real crimes—all your friends would also face burning."

"Oh," Tiana loudly said. "In that case we shall consider paying our own expenses out of our half of the treasure." She favored the magistrate with a smile.

Staring, he began an angry reply; checked himself. Most softly he said, "There is no need to shout. Please explain that absurd demand—*softly.*"

I wonder who's listening, she mused, and said: "Why, if I am in a bad bargaining position, yours is worse. You dare not speak above a whisper and jump at shadows. I don't know what so affrights you, but—"

"Girl," Ishcon interrupted, "do you know who rules this world?"

"He who calls a woman a girl risks being called 'old man,' *Magistrate!* My name is Tiana, captain of *Vixen*. None but my father Caranga dares call me girl." After a moment's pause she went on, "No one rules the world. A bunch of kings and such-like hollow-headed men pretend to."

He gestured. At that moment a shadow glided across the floor. Only a trick of the shifting light of these damned greasy torches, Tiana thought; yet Ishcon glanced about and she saw the desperate fury of a trapped animal flicker in his eyes.

"You do not understand and are wrong," he said in a sibilant whisper. "You are better off *not* knowing about the Owner: never mind. I dare not explain. And the 'treasure' is a single object that cannot be divided."

"Oh. Well then I shall settle for a mere half the reward you expect to receive from this business." *The Owner?*

"My reward is staying alive!" he burst out, and quickly

stilled his voice. "I am in a trap and the 'treasure' is my ransom." He sighed. "What I shall do is this. Steal what I need and I shall pay you a thousand gold regals. That is a high wage for a single day's work."

"But not much for a man who paid half that for a pleasure-girl! *Ten* thousand, and we both know that's cheap for your life!" *This is insane,* she thought. *I stand here multiply bound to this awful cross with him looking right into me—and it's I who's doing the strong bargaining! O Tiana, you are indeed fearless and magnificent!*

"Robbery!" Ishcon howled. "You are an absolute pirate!"

A smiling Tiana Highrider nodded agreement.

"Very well," he sighed. "So be it. Now do be silent while I explain my plan."

Tiana looked politely attentive. She managed not to change her expression as she watched him send a furtive glance around the small but high room of dark stone. He began to speak, and he paced tensely.

"To begin with, you must be apprised of two additional points of Thesian law. Our ancient statutes require that if a prisoner escapes sentence, her relatives and friends act as surrogates. Secondly, by time-honored custom, when a magistrate has pronounced sentence, he has no authority to change it."

"What? But then I can't escape without dooming my crew and you can't prevent me from being cremated!"

"I told you to hold down your voice and not interrupt. As I was saying. Only the King may alter sentences once they are fixed. King Hartes has in fact already revised yours." Ishcon permitted himself a moment of strutting self-importance while Tiana curbed her impulse to give him a triumphant "I thought so!" He went on, "I arranged for Hartes to learn of your considerable beauty, you see." *(Hmp,* Tiana mused, *surely he'd already heard of it!)* "Exactly as I expected, he reduced your sentence. Instead of being stripped naked, degraded by thirteen men and a dog and burned alive before the eyes of a jeering mob of commonfolk, you will suffer a similar fate in a discreetly small private ceremony. For the entertainment of the King and his court." He paused, as though expecting an indignant protest.

Tiana said only, "A dog?"

"The advantage to this altered sentence is non-obvious

but substantial, g—Tiana. Such a private ceremony is always carried out in an underground portion of the Temple of Drood on Mount Yazira . . . the Chamber of the Sleeping Demon."

"Demon? What sort of—"

"No one knows and don't interrupt! It may indeed be a demon in an age-long slumber or it may simply be some natural phenomenon—or legend. Of importance is that it is impossible to gain entrance to the Chamber on any pretext, unless one is a dead King receiving his funeral or . . . someone in your circumstances."

Ishcon's pacing had carried him beyond the view of the woman bound to the great X of bolted wood. Abruptly she saw that they were not quite alone. A tiny spider had come creeping into the room. While such a creature seemed unusual so far underground, it scarcely seemed important.

"Perhaps now," Ishcon was boasting, "you begin to appreciate my cunning in arranging this situation. Later I will explain a trick that will enable you to appear to burn, while you escape unharmed. That escape will leave you in an otherwise inaccessible maze of tunnels." Again he was in her sight, a gaunt frightened man in his red robe of office; a man who chewed at his lip and mustache, worried that he might bring disaster by saying too much or too little. "Yes. I *must* give you some background information if you are to do your job. I shall not tell you all— and I admit that I don't know it all. There exists a dark invisible power, Tiana, and it holds this world of ours in an iron grasp. It is a subtle power, for it rules with the bulk of humankind none the wiser. The Owner . . ." He broke off, seemingly biting his tongue as if he might be saying too much. His eyes anxiously scanned the room.

He did not look down. The spider was stalking across the floor. Its pace was so swift and purposeful that Tiana wondered if she should perhaps call it to the High Magistrate's attention. His own uneasy feet meanwhile bore him again out of her sight. She did not bother mentioning her discomfort.

"Now as to the tunnels, Tiana. When Port Thark was first built, the discovery was made that beneath this land's smiling surface the ground is a honeycomb of caves and connecting tunnels. Except for occasional grim incidents, men had the wit to leave the caves alone—until the reign of King Yorg the Mad, a century ago. He desired a prison large enough to hold the populations of entire cities. In his madness he set an army of convict laborers to converting the caverns into a vast dungeon."

The spider reached the base of the wall and began climbing.

"From the start, that project was ill-starred. The workers simply . . . disappeared. As more and more convicts vanished, mad Yorg doubled and redoubled their guards. They too were lost without trace! Toward the end, entire divisions of the Thesian Army went into the depths—not to be seen again."

Though Tiana was listening, the spider was a pleasant distraction from staring at bare stone walls while Ishcon paced. The spider reached the ceiling. With the weird many-legged gait of its kind it began walking across, upside down. Tiana could not take her eyes off the little black creature. Its movements were so purposeful—to what purpose? She supposed that flies might survive down here, even breed in human excrement. But she had seen no flies to feed this journeying arachnid.

"At last, one moonless night," Ishcon said, and paused theatrically. "The horror came out of the ground. The details of what happened are obscure, since few witnesses survived. Fewer still retained their sanity! What little remained of the underground labors became this prison: Dindroom. A word from the dark mind of Yorg the Mad. All entrances to the deeper caves were sealed off and poor Yorg's son, King Yorish, proclaimed that the entire affair was finished and should be forgotten."

While Ishcon spoke, behind her, the spider passed directly overhead. A long silken thread dangled from its tiny black form. It had taken on a grim aspect now, downside up on the ceiling out of the main light of the wall-sconced torches. For an instant she felt the ghost touch of that thread, and then the spider passed from her view. Something compelled her to twist her stiffening neck and strain her back in a futile effort to keep the little creature in sight.

"Now to the importance of all this to us," Ishcon lectured on. "During the Night of Madness a . . . certain object disappeared from the Temple of Sirsinn. It was not seen again until during the reign of Osogar the Incinerator. My ancestor, Prime Minister Marcon, had the misfortune to gamble away most of the money Osogar had entrusted to him for the purchase of . . . suitable young women. Accordingly he devised a means whereby the girls could escape the cremation chamber. Secretly. They were then either disguised and utilized anew, or sold to purchase fresh girls. This procedure for . . . recycling victims worked well enough, although there were occasional casualties. True, sometimes the girls were recovered in a condition that forced their resale at a substantial discount. One wench escaped the chamber of burning, but lost her way in the cave-tunnels. When at last she found her way out, both her figure and her sanity left considerable to be desired. But from her ravings, it was clear that she had seen urk."

Ishcon's voice ceased with a suddenness that was as horribly unnatural as that last word, or sound.

"Ishcon?" Tiana called, twisting vainly, hurting her arms. "Ishcon? She saw Urk? What—Ishcon?"

Silence.

"By the Great Turtle's Back, Ishcon, what ails you?"

The silence seemed . . . loud. Some most unwelcome gooseflesh went wandering over Tiana's stretched form.

Cursing profoundly and with eloquence, she contorted her body. Still she could not turn enough to see anything.

Only when she reluctantly gave it up and faced around did she see the splash of torchlight on the wall opposite, and the shadow. It was clearly the shadow of High Magistrate Ishcon of the Grand Court of Thesia.

He was executing a formless dance in midair with much ugly flapping of his arms and legs. Yet he had no visible support or suspension.

The dance ended with a slight but thoroughly sickening gasp.

Ishcon floated motionless and inert in the air. Except for the fact that no rope was visible, he looked for all the world like a man who had just been hanged.

Second Strand:

THE HANGING JUDGE

Terror held Tiana in a paralyzed silence. She scarcely dared breathe. Back and forth swung the grisly pendulum that had been the High Magistrate. Only one aspect of this eerie murder seemed clear: he had been speaking though fearful, and had been claimed by an obscene death. She had been silent and was passed over. Was death blind but far from deaf?

Was death only waiting for her to make the slightest betraying sound?

Slowly, trying to ignore the icy fingers that clutched at her heart, she looked around. She saw no sign of the spider—which meant nothing.

What am I going to do?

She was still under sentence to the flames. While escape might not be impossible, it would mean betraying her father and crewmen. Without the late magistrate's help and instructions, she would fare no better in the Chamber of the Sleeping Demon than had numberless victims before her. Tiana! A salaciously morbid entertainment for the jaded royalty of Thesia!

On the other hand . . . *There is a treasure.* A treasure desperately sought by some unnamed group of which Ishcon had been a minor member; a treasure in some secret conflict. And sorcery was involved. *Now, on the open market, just how much might I get for such a prize?*

Well, considering that both sides obviously have great wealth at their command. . . . Yes! By the Cud of the Cow and the Back of the Turtle that sustains the world . . . I'll DO IT!

Greed, strong as vanity, pushed aside fear in Tiana's brain and she forgot the fear; indeed, she would deny it hotly. Her mind roiled now with plans and calculations. If 'twas dangerous, what of it? She and danger were old

16

shipmates. No battle was without risk and she was veteran of hundreds of deadly adventures. Scores, anyhow.

All the while a little voice at the back of her mind was whispering that she was doing this not because she would but because she must. Tiana resolutely ignored that voice —but now came a sound that could not be ignored. The tread of big marching feet resounded in the corridor. Coming for her.

Merciful Theba! I forgot Ishcon's corpse! Even if the addle-brains don't suspect me, they'll still just have to question me as a witness. And such interrogation in the matter of a noble's death generally involves . . . persuasion. Dung and pox! No avoiding this one.

Well, somehow I'll just have to bluff my way through.

The guards came tramping into view in tight formation —and stopped dead in their tracks. Every eye stared at the exanimate judge floating behind her. Another moment and the wardmen charged past her in shouting confusion. Ignored, she could see only the elongated shadows dancing on the wall as the play-soldiers hoisted one of their number onto their shoulders to cut the corpse down. She heard curses that rippled with shudders.

"He was hanged by a single strand of—of *spider web!*"

Though Tiana remained quite silent and thought small, all too soon one idiot shouted out, "She must have seen what happened!" and Tiana was instantly the new center of attention.

Captain Bratch stomped around to stand before and beneath her. "Run tell the Prison Commander what's happened . . . and then fetch Kanja the Painmaster!" Staring up at Tiana, the captain added, "You have until he gits back to tell me what happened here, Red. Otherwise you're gonto talk with *persuasion.*" As he took two steps back, limping with obvious pain and displaying the gap of a missing tooth, he finished with, "I do hope you're stubborn! I'm owing you a debt."

"Aww, Captain . . . can't we rape 'er *now?*"

"You owe that debt to your parents, Bratch," Tiana said loftily. "Can't you see I'm tied with my back to the death scene?"

"And 'er legs wide open!" a high-voiced wardman called with exuberance.

"Shut—up—Goatface," Bratch said, but his only reply to Tiana was a very hard look.

Not promising, she thought, and hastily continued: "Naturally I'll be glad to tell you what little I know. Lord High Magistrate Ishcon came in and commenced talking about the weather. How nice a day this is and how we should have a nice crowd for my murder and so on. He was obviously nervous and reluctant to explain the real purpose of his visit. Then he commented on what an idiot you are." She spun the tale on, telling nothing for as long as she dared to stall. ". . . and suddenly the mag. gave a choking sound—*urk,* I believe it was—and I saw his shadow on the wall there behind you. The shadow of a man hanged with a rope—except there wasn't any shadow of a rope."

"You know more than you've telled," Bratch said. "Kanja will—"

He broke off at the entry of a tall man concealed within a hooded robe of dull black. "And Kanja," the newcomer finished for the captain, "will do nothing, Bratch. If you've misplaced your wits, I haven't." The torturer paused while he and Tiana watched anger grow in the captain's face. Then: "Can't you see, *Captain?* This morsel is slated to entertain the *king* this morning. The king, remember? If we were to mar her, our fate would be . . . grim."

Bratch spoke with weary patience. "That just means you'll have to do your work carefully for once, so that she don't show no marks."

Happily watching the growing quarrel, Tiana racked her brain for some lie that might prod them right on into killing each other. *Hmm; suppose I say that—*

Though there was no sound, it was as if a trumpet had blared. Every man snapped into a straight line of straight shoulders, eyes forward. Bratch stood rigidly to attention, right arm up in salute. Kanja bowed low . . .

And out of the dark hallway came a wizened little man. White hair and an obviously uncooperative beard covered a head like a dried apple. It sprouted a bulb-tipped nose veined with purple that matched his ermine-trimmed robe. It covered a thin, twisted body, doubtless a great kindness to anyone who had to look at him.

Every Thesian waited in respectful silence until this man should deign to speak. Presently he was most interested in the X-framed pirate.

"Are you," Tiana asked, "the Prison Commander?—or someone else important?"

His laugh was brief and not quite pleasant. "As it happens, I am the king's uncle, Prince Nired. And I've the power to free you or add to your punishment, pirate." After pausing for a few heartbeats he said, "Which of those I do will depend upon whether you tell the truth or persist in foolish lies."

Tiana nodded. She did like men who did not equivocate. She was used to the fact that they always had to be surly and dramatic about it. In a pleading tone she asked, "I have your word of honor, O Prince?"

"Of a certainty. I am who I am."

Yes, she mused, *a younger brother who always wished he was the elder!* Knowing how much the prince's honor was worth, she was tempted to tell him where he could put his pardon. That, however, would gain her nothing except some pain. If she told the truth, his reaction might be instructive.

"Highness," she said, "I gladly tell you the little I know. The magistrate came in and talked a few scant minutes before he was . . . thus mysteriously slain. About that I cannot be of help, for it happened out of my sight. As to what he said before his death . . ."

Prince Nired was watching, listening with hungry interest.

"It seemed meaningless, Highness. I saw that he had something of great importance on his mind, so important that he must needs talk his way up to it. Without meaning to show disrespect for the magistrate," Tiana said, thinking: *for whom I have nothing but disrespect, alive or dead,* "he seemed . . . perhaps fearful?" (Ah. Nired nodded, almost imperceptibly, and he was most interested indeed.) "I am sorry, but in the short time before his death he dropped only one meaningless hint."

"What?" Nired demanded, and Tiana saw strong emotion in those unreadable dark eyes—and that he was practically dancing up and down to hear more.

"He—he asked me who ruled the world. Naturally I replied such great kings as Thesia's. He said me no! He demanded who *really* rules the world. I did not understand; after all, I am only a poor sea captain. He remarked that—but why go on? As I said the whole conversation was meaningless."

"Let me be the judge of that!" the words practically exploded from Nired.

"But—"

"*Tell* me! For your freedom and a thousand silver regals tell me what Ishcon said!" The prince's eagerness was frightening in its intensity. Kanja and the guards watched him with awe and growing concern.

Deliberately Tiana let the tension build until Nired looked ready to call for a whip. Then, swiftly: "The magistrate spoke of someone called the—the Owner. He pronounced the word with . . . awe?"

At her words utter terror showed in the old prince's features. For an instant he seemed scarcely able to stand. At last his voice came, and it was only a murmur: "He *dared*. The utter fool actually dared to . . ."

As though a curtain had been drawn, his face resumed the appearance of an emotionless mask. To Bratch and his wardmen: "What you men have just heard is to be considered a State secret affecting the internal security of Thesia. Under no circumstances may you tell anyone of this." To Tiana, his eyes showing no interest in her interestingly chained form: "As for you, piratical slut. I shall keep my promise, insofar as the requirements of national security permit. You will wear silken garments and jewels worth a thousand regals of purest silver . . . at your execution. It, of course, will provide your freedom from this world's cares."

Tiana had expected little more from the high-placed swine. In his campaign to wrest information from her, he'd have promised anything. Now that the campaign was ended and he had what he wanted, his promises meant as little as that which he had promised to see to: her welfare.

"Pending that execution," Prince Nired was saying on, "you are to be secured in this room, no one to speak to you on pain of death." He half-turned to gesture at wardmen and painmaster. "All of you men: out of here!"

As they started to file out, Tiana breathed a sigh of relief—and in that moment of relaxation a fine malicious lie came smirking into her mind. While it would gain her nothing, it was likely to give Bratch a bad moment or two.

"Thesians!" she called after them, and at the tone of a ship's competent and confident captain they paused automatically. "If Prince Nired puts me to death to assure my silence, obviously he'll have to do the same to you."

Only the old prince turned to look at her. Though he said nothing, she saw the briefest flash of emotion in his eyes. At that instant Tiana knew that, inadvertently, she had told the truth.

The iron-bound door shut with a rumbling crash. Tiana was left to wonder: what was this dark secret that so frightened Ishcon and Prince Nired, and that a score of men should die merely for having heard *of* it?

Third Strand:
IN A GILDED CAGE

Tiana was trapped within a puzzle murky as a stormy sky during moondark. She had sorted all the puzzle's pieces in her mind without finding any that seemed to link with any other. At last she took a deep breath and tried to quiet her heaving mind. The coming morning was set to be her last. She must look upon it as a battle, as a challenge in which her only weapons were her wits. In what little remained of this night she needed sleep.

And she *hurt*. The muscles in her shoulders and upper back and along her thighs—every one ached and throbbed. Nerves twitched in uncontrollable tics. Her hands, so long updrawn, were chilly. Much effort of will was required to move herself around her fears and her hurts and lower herself into sleep.

The first time she awoke it was to a sound echoing out of the darkness. She knew it had been a tiny, shrill cry of pain. It was followed by fierce little howls and a final groan. A rat had just died. Too much experience had taught her that prisons always had rats. With her bound this way, there was the danger that one might take her for food. Since she was chained well above the floor, the danger was probably minor. Minor, that is, relative to her other problems.

But what killed that rat? A cat would have been much faster. So would any other animal that normally slew rats. The spider, perhaps? *Out there somewhere, watching me, passing the time by killing an occasional rat?*

No, that's silly. I have enough problems without torturing myself with speculations and nightmares. Oh, I hurt!

Perhaps this time her slumber was deeper; perhaps they crept upon her with great stealth. Either way they were close about her before she woke and saw them: three hideously deformed men in livery she knew: Prince Nired's. She choked back her scream and instead began to spit curses at them.

They seemed to take no note. One of them made hand signals to the others. One promptly began to unwrap a package. Deaf-mutes, she realized. *My curses did indeed fall on deaf ears! Nired's not taking any chances that I'll tell anyone else.*

The package opened to reveal a bunch of fat, blood-red flowers. The three horrors looked up at her, smiling. That was hardly encouraging.

Now they take me down from here—and that's when I give them wide smiles on the backs of their ugly heads!

One of them lifted the flowers toward her face. She rejected the apparent placatory offering by turning her head away. For just an instant she strained at her chains. Fruitless and therefore stupid, that. Now she was aware of the perfume. The oddly shaped blossoms bore a heavy sickening scent that was too sweet and seemed almost narcotic. The dungeon room began a lazy spin.

It is narcotic! Oh no, I won't—

. . . let them drug me this way! Got to fight. I . . .

—I'm flying! No! Got to f

Her eyes focused. The dungeon was gone. The dream of flying must have accompanied their carrying her unconscious body. She lay, drawn up, on the floor of . . . a golden cage! The sparkling affair of twisting bright bars and lacy metal filigree was much the sort of gilded prison in which a rich lady might keep her favorite songbird.

It's even the right size. If a woman were a bird, this would be a proper cage to keep her in. A golden cage—shrouded in curtains of pink silk!

The pink drapes denied her any sight of what might lie just outside her prison. She quickly established that they were just far enough beyond the bars to be out of reach. In addition, the bars were not of nice soft gold. They proved to be unyielding hard iron washed lightly in gold. The floor was composed of white stones large as her fists and piled layer upon layer. Now her sore body had a few more sensitive spots. She thought that the floor seemed out of place. She would examine it later. If there was a later. Meanwhile it was frustrating not to see beyond bars and drapes. For there was something there; something strange, that made a sound like the snoring of a giant.

She kept moving, stiffly, trying to work out all the kinks from hours on the X-frame and lying on these lumpy stones.

Directly before her was the cage's only furniture: a stool over which was draped an elaborate white gown, and a mirrored dressing table. On it waited a variety of cosmetics, a comb, an hourglass, and the lamp that lighted her little prison.

By the Cud! These ill-born curs expect me to prettify myself for their entertainment!

So it seemed—and it did not matter. What did matter was that she had no idea how Ishcon's disappearance-from-the-crematorium trick worked. In a short time she must either divine that secret or . . . But there was no use thinking about that. Tiana had never been interested in meeting Theba, and she preferred not to think about Theba's realm: death.

The hourglass was scarcely reassuring. Did it indicate how long she had to live or to make herself beautiful for death? Either way time, like the sand in the glass, was slipping through her fingers and it had become urgent that she search for clues and possibilities.

In the pouch sewn to the white dress she found a sea-green emerald big as a dove's egg, and a note: "Thus Prince Nired keeps his promise."

While flawed, the jewel was still worth the thousand regals, and probably in gold, rather than silver. As for the dress—it was coarse white homespun and badly made at that!

Why, this flimsy thing would last for just about one brief wearing!

A chill ran down her spine with the realization that such was precisely the plan! This dress was to be worn but a little while before it and its wearer were burned to ashes. Frugal Prince Nired saw no point in wasting expensive material and workmanship on such a garment. Come to think, he must have chosen the emerald because it could easily be recovered from her charred remains.

By the Cud this is too much! "Prince Nired," she shouted at empty air and dainty pink curtains, "I might have passed over anything else but this! For this parsimonious insult I vow your death! And by my hand!"

The angry words were all too obviously futile, but . . . what a happy thought! She detached pouch and emerald and set both aside. The dress she tossed aside. The stool did not seem to conceal any interesting secrets. The dressing table, however . . . First there was the inscription engraved along the mirror's round edge:

"Remember the sacred teachings: The Path to Life is never easy but lies through the center of Fiery Death."

One more of those religious mottos dreamed up to try to keep people content in the adversity created for them by rulers and priests, Tiana mused. Unless it was intended as some sort of reminder. *Perhaps Ishcon's ancestor feared a panicky girl and caused this disguised reminder to be laid into the mirror's border?* Perhaps. But what meaning it might hold, hidden, she could not guess. She turned to the cosmetics laid out on the table. They were unusual only in the inclusion of a jar of clear, gelatinous creme loaded with bright silver flakes.

There's enough of this stuff so that I could spread it over my whole body and sparkle like a crystal chandelier. On impulse she smeared some on her off hand. The substance was wet, with a high water content. Cautiously she reached her hand toward the lamp's flame. After an instant's trepidation, she thrust her last two fingers into the fire.

Why, it doesn't—"Ow!" She jerked the hand back and accompanied its vigorous shaking with vehement curses. The pain subsided quickly enough to tell her she had done herself no great harm. Narrow-eyed, she studied the fingers.

So. It did work, if only briefly. *The creme protects from*

fire—for an instant or two. That, for a person in her situation, was good to know.

The table's only drawer opened to reveal a mass of bright red feathers. A little inspection showed her the headpiece and wings of a costume. She was to be a kind of bird-woman? And the feathers felt odd. As though they had been soaked in salt water and dried? She tasted them. No. Something else. Leavening?

Thrust into the lamp's flame, the feathers smoked and refused to burn.

How nice. It's marvelously fireproof—what there is of it.

In itself the headpiece was perfect; strong, with snugging padding like that of a war helmet. Here was coverage and protection for her entire head! Best of all, the eyeholes were fitted with bits of crystal of unusually good glass. The wearer would be able to see even in a raging inferno. The other portion of the costume was a pair of iridescent scarlet wings long as a sword. An abbreviated leather tunic attached them to her back. Beneath a coating of treated feathers, the tunic was designed to fasten snugly in front. Thus it provided good protection for her shoulders.

And that was the costume, in its entirety.

Her own clothing was gone. Nired's gift-gown was too obviously flammable. *Well, what a nice show for them, the gaping swine! I must appear in public with my face and shoulders hidden, my arms bare, and the rest of me stark naked from the tops of my breasts to the tips of my toes!*

Desperately she returned to the drawer, searching for anything more to wear. To her relief, she discovered that something had fallen out to be concealed behind the drawer.

Perfect! She held a pair of shoes, brightly polished black leather with soles of cork the thickness of a thumb's width.

With no further consideration, she began smearing her nudity with the silver-flaked creme. She made sure the coat of gel was even, while she forced herself to work with a deliberate speed. Too much sand had run through the glass. Yet thoroughness was important. Any part of her skin she might miss, the flames would not. At last she slipped into the feathered costume, adjusted it with care, and examined herself in the mirror.

Magnificent!

Peering back at her from the mirror was an exotically

beautiful hybrid: an avian woman. Her face was transformed, sea-green eyes now sparkling amid the delicate mask of dark red feathers with the odd glaze given them by wetted, dried sodium bicarbonate. The brighter crimson of her wings seemed to flap about her like sunset clouds held captive.

As for her body . . . she looked much, turning this way and that, putting back her shoulders and smiling in high satisfaction, *Ah, Tiana, you are* perfect!

Light scintillated from every line and curve of her supple limbs. Had ever a woman been so marvelously constructed; so well displayed that superior shape? Turning sidewise to the mirror, she thrust out her chest and joggled, to watch the silver flecks dance and flash on her breasts.

It couldn't be better. *Those noble idiots will be so busy staring at my anatomy they'll give no heed to what's occurring. 'Twill be easy to pull off that disappearing trick . . .*

Or rather, it might be easy, if she knew how it was effected. With a sudden unease she saw that little more than a cupful of sand remained in the upper half of the glass. In so little time she must learn the secret or suffer the consequences of ignorance. But where to search? Where could some further clue be hidden?

The dressing table held nothing more. Other than stool and table this gilded-prison was empty. Except . . .

I wonder what might be in that interesting ceiling?

She placed the stool atop the table. She climbed precariously up. A moment's close inspection confirmed her suspicion: the ceiling held a trapdoor. With no handholds, it was a poor exit. Besides, it was much bigger than a climber would need. Indeed, it was as long and wide as a reclining woman. An *entrance*, then? Was something lying on this door that was supposed to drop into the cage at some opportune moment? She licked her dry lips. Less than a cup of sand remained to mark her death or escape and Tiana could feel herself sweating beneath her coating of creme. No chance existed of gaining a peek at what was hidden up there—if anything. Tapping gave her the impression that something heavy was resting on the door. Her fingers ran along the crack between door and ceiling and pressed, hard. They came back bearing traces of blood and . . . oil? She whose foster-father was among the best two or three poison-detecters in the world, and who

had worked and worked with her to heighten her own
sense of smell, sniffed.

Pig. A pig recently killed, soaked in oil and set on a
trapdoor ready to drop. *Now where does that piece fit into
this Drood-sent puzzle?*

She glanced down. All but a half-cup of sand had
slipped away. She climbed down to stand a moment,
breathing deeply. Trying to force her mind into clear, calm
thought. Then she realized that in her descent she had
heard a crunch. One of the white stones had crunched
under her foot? No, and she couldn't be so easily distra—
wait a moment.

Stones the size of my fists should not *crunch.*

It had though, and she found and retrieved the broken
stone. It did not require much examination or much application of logic. It was white on the surface only. The
interior was pure dead black. And by the feel of it . . .

*Coal! Whitewashed coal! Someone has furnished this
entire cage with a floor made of coal, and every piece has
been carefully whitewashed. Why? Why go to such trouble?
If they wanted a white floor, why not use white stones?
The only advantage of these imitation stones is that coal
will . . .*

burn. Tiana understood. Her spine went cold, as if icy
fingers caressed her back. She even saw the one way in
which it made sense. What a hideous plan these devils had
contrived!

Since she had no means to relight the lamp, she was
loath to extinguish it. Still, she no longer needed illumination. Indeed, she needed darkness within the cage, so that
she might see out. Putting the lamp into the table drawer
served well enough. In the gloom of semi-darkness, appearances changed. The pink silk drapes were no longer
featureless blanks. Now they were a vertical stage on
which shifting lights and shadows hinted strongly at what
lay beyond.

The several smaller lights she could distinguish were
likely lamps or torches. For a moment she envisioned scurrying servants who placed the lamps and made other last-
minute preparations for the arrival of King Hartes.

The new puzzle was that larger light. A bright, vastly
tall column that shifted this way and that while remaining
in the same place. Behind her dressing table, the silk cur-

tains were dark . . . no. In that direction the floor behind
the drapes showed a dull red glow.

*But it isn't fair! I should have more time! The hour-
glass . . .*

The last grains of sand were trickling away and were
gone. The time of waiting, analyzing, trying to prepare—
was over.

It had begun.

The first sign was a minor commotion. She heard the
rustle of silks, the tread of heavy boots and the slim-heeled
shoes the Thesian women preferred. There was a blending
of soft, cultured voices. Aristocrats. Seemingly they found
their places quickly, for an expectant silence fell. It was
broken only by the soft giggling of this or that woman.
Occasionally Tiana could catch a faint, excited whisper.

*"They say she committed simply terrible crimes. Why
my dear . . ."*

*". . . worse every year. I don't bother to come, except
when . . ."*

*"Do you remember the Salanch sisters? Three of them.
Last year or maybe it was the year before, well, they
were . . ."*

A kettle drum sounded sharply and trumpets blared to
the slaying of all other sounds. Swift upon the trumpets, a
man's voice shouted, nearly as loud.

"My lords ånd ladies, HARTES! King of Thesia, Conqueror of . . ."

"Enough," commanded a quiet, hard voice. "As we are
running a bit late, it is our pleasure to dispense with for-
malities and proceed with the rite. Let us see the victim."

At that imperious command the silken drapes hissed
upward and were gone. The scene beyond her cage was
what Tiana had guessed—and feared.

She was caged at the center of an underground grotto
that was also an arena. Staring down at her from a broad
balcony was homely Hartes in velvet robes of deep purple
edged with lace. About him was the cream of Thesia's
lords and ladies in their lavish finery and flashing gauds.
In the background, hard-faced guards in armor of burnished metal covered by jupons in scarlet and gold—each
with the crown of royalty on the chest. The king's guards,
and no rusty armor among them.

Some of those stern military faces lost their composure
at sight of the center attraction. The avian, naked Tiana

brought murmurs and giggling from the highborn ladies and appreciative muttering from their menfolk.

Tiana stood tall, shoulders well back. *Let the fools gape as they please. My problem is to find a way out of this hole!*

'. . . nice pair, by my ancestors!"

"A trifle skinny, don't you think? I mean after all—*no stomach*—"

If this grotto held a hidden exit, it was hidden from Tiana. How she had been brought here was clear enough. She saw the door at the rear of the balcony. At the front, an iron ladder led down to the floor of the . . . arena. That path was blocked, now. Spiked iron bars like fans shielded the forefront of the balcony. (While she looked, turning, she appeared to be engaged in the display of every side and aspect of her body. She shut her ears to the coarse appreciation of the staring aristocrats and struggled to think clearly.)

The walls of the subterrene arena showed as featureless granite. How could an exit be hidden in their blank faces? *What am I looking at and not seeing?* Everything seemed exposed to her view. The arena floor was empty save for her cage and—the Flame.

Despite the urgency of her plight she could not help staring at such a marvel. What she had seen before as a bright dancing light beyond the drapes was in truth a towering pillar of flame. The jet of incandescence surged whitely up from a hole in the grotto floor to vanish from' sight well above. Behind her mask, Tiana's tongue touched her lips nervously. She had heard of eternal flames, fires that snarled up out of the ground and had burned longer than memory or records. But this monster . . .

Small wonder legend says it's a sleeping demon!

The sound it made was all too much like snoring. Could legend be truth? She knew it would not be the first time that—

"Hey, girl! What are your plans for later? Join me for dinner?"

As she whirled to glance at that highborn heckler, he was rewarded by roisterous laughter from his aristocratic fellows. The obscene reply that formed in Tiana's throat died unspoken. At last the so-called pirate queen saw this arena's least pleasant aspect. Its entire floor was covered with the whitewashed coal. Many coals were already burning with a dull red glow and the fire was spreading inexorably to the rest. The space in which she stood was a dwindling island in a sea of fire.

Despite the mask, the crowd sensed her recognition of this horror. She heard tittering and chuckles. They hushed only when Hartes raised his hand. No less than five rings glittered and flashed on that soft hand.

"Prisoner, we are pleased that you choose not to wear the dress our uncle provided. Such beauty as yours should not be concealed."

"In that case," Tiana snapped, "why not keep your uncle's promise? Set me free!"

"Certainly. Such is the least we can do for one so lovely." And at the king's gesture the cage, a bottomless framework of bars, glided upward until its base was well above her head. "Now," King Hartes declared in solemn mockery, "you are free to go and come as you please."

Oh of course. Five steps in any direction would have Tiana walking on hot coals. The giggles and amused smiles were harder than hard to take.

They'll pay, she vowed, and as if in rage she took up the deceptively pretty white gown and ripped it with violence. *By the Cud and by the Back they will pay, pay; the king, his foul uncle, and . . .* Nired! She had almost forgotten the treacherous pig. A strip of snowy dress dangling from her fingers, she sought his presence—saw him, crouched in the very front row of onlookers.

"My Lord Prince," Tiana called as she moved to the dressing table, "that so-costly emerald you gave me! Would you like it returned?"

"You may," Nired croaked, "keep it for the while."

"Ah, how *kind* the uncle of reigning royalty is! Actually," she said, displaying the valuable big gem briefly before settling it into the strip of cloth, "I mean to fling it against yon stone wall and smash this bauble of treachery into fragments to match your lying promise!"

Tiana whipped the improvised sling up and spun the emerald in an ever faster circle. Nired leaped upright.

"Nay! That jewel's worth—"

"Then take it back!" she shouted, and loosed the big gemstone.

Stone of mocking treachery became messenger of death. It streaked on course, straight and true, to imbed itself in the prince's forehead with an ugly *pock* sound.

For a moment the dog stood there, upraised hand atremble, staring at the world from two eyes vacant and lifeless and a third that blazed bright green in a setting of trickling crimson. Thus for a moment, and then the puppet's strings were cut and life fled. Prince Nired folded up and lay dead, amid a horrified silence.

The island of un-burning coal was now less than six paces from edge to edge. And the outcry arose.

Hartes's shouted command went unheard in the general confusion of screaming courtiers and courtesans. While the panicky nobility tried to retreat, the guards sought to move forward. One soldier, his brain overwhelmed by excitement, screamed that the assassin must be captured, and attempted to climb out of the balcony down onto the burning floor of the arena. His fellows barely restrained him—while another drew back his sword and let fly at Prince Nired's killer. As he did he was jostled by the surging crowd.

The sword went spinning through the air to whistle past her and crash into the table. It fell to her feet with multiple clanks.

Good, Tiana thought, and snatched it up. Its owner was not huge and the sword was little heavier than her accustomed rapier. *Now if I die 'twill be with weapon in hand, as befits the pirate queen and the wonderful warrior I have ever been!* The crawling fire was approaching her from all sides and nearby coals sent up puffs and streamers of smoke. Someone's lovely silk veil fluttered down, became incandescent before it touched the floor, and was vaporized in an instant.

"Yer Majesty," called the guard's commander, whose strife-hardened face was a trifle calmer than the rest. "I can have archers here in a moment to slay this treacherous witch."

Again Hartes raised a hand for silence—and then the other, in its beringed splendor. He looked about at the members of his court. Under the gaze of those agate-black eyes, all commotion died. While heat rose.

"Dear friends," the king said, and the harshness of his voice belied its soft words. "There is no further danger. Return to your places. For all we loved our uncle and mourn his untimely passing, surely he would have wanted these proceedings to continue. A choice criminal is on the fire! Let us enjoy her entirely timely death!"

At that moment the king's gaze met Tiana's, and he winked.

Monster! He was delighted that his doubtless meddling uncle was dead! She had done him a favor!—And abruptly the floor was hot beneath her feet. Tiana stepped involuntarily back from the fire's unstayable spread. Sweat dripped.

"I could cheat you," she called, "by falling on my sword or jumping into the Flame!" She flaunted the sword and sweat flew to hiss on coals.

It hit her then. The Flame. *Of course; I was blind not to see it sooner. My exit is hidden in plain sight—that hole in the floor whence the unnatural Flame jets up! What lies below only the gods and the late High Magistrate know. Still, from what he said there must be some kind of safe cool passageway. I am dressed to survive fire—briefly. I need only jump to be out of this. Here death is sure. Down that hole . . . ?*

"True," Hartes said, brows arched in regal indifference. "However, were you to slay yourself, we should consider that the equivalent of escape. In such case the justice and honor of Thesia would have to seek satisfaction from such of your friends and relatives as might conveniently be found."

Ah gods No! Escape's a leap away and I cannot take it without dooming my father! Eternal Theba, Handmaiden of the Cow and unjealous Ruler of Peaceful Death . . . what am I to do? Surely it pleased You, that time I slew all those blood-sucking nuns who desecrated Your temple in Woeand!

Rumor and old widows' tales had it that once Theba had incarnated, somewhere out in a place called Valley of the Bones. No one had corroborated, however, and only hysterics claimed to have seen Her. Certainly Tiana had not. Nor did she hear any divine answer now. Escape and doom him who was her foster-father and First Mate: Caranga. Remain and become ash, in a most undignified and painful manner. Perhaps she should have fought to keep that idiot Northron, Bjaine, after all. Perhaps she should have tried to entrap the one man ever she had met who was worthy of her. Perhaps . . .

Perhaps . . . maybe . . . might be/might have been . . .

Again heat was strong beneath her feet and she retreated two paces, running sweat—only to encounter more immediate heat. The fire was everywhere save for this tiny patch of floor. Its diameter was less than the length of a sword. Of necessity, she gave up dignity and danced into the center of that hot but flameless area. An expectant hush fell over the watching aristocrats. They knew what was imminent: the cream of the joke.

Her lips were clenched while in her mind she screamed. *No, please, no, not this! In another moment I shall roast like a cow at the feast!*

Amid stifling heat she felt their hot eyes on her, avidly watching every twitch of her shapely, sweat-coated and entirely naked body. To her left, hot wax began to drip from the cage above to fall on the coals and burn with yellow, smoking flame. Seeing this at a glance, she gave it no heed. She was *hot*, and both eyes and brain were affected. Behind her, the dressing table stood on smoldering legs. The cotton dress and then the stool had burst into full flame. She was trapped without possibility of retreat from that swiftly growing new blaze. Save for a circle scarce big enough for both her feet, the entire arena floor glowed cherry red.

They're waiting to see me dance, naked and screaming, across this roasting pit until I'm a living pyre! Well Drood eat me if I don't just show them how fire can spread!

Her sword stabbed into the burning stool. She clamped with both hands and, in a swift backhand exertion, sent flaming stool and dress soaring in among many people in small space: the spectators' balcony. Pieces of flaming cloth dribbled in the wake of that fiery missile.

Most of the packed nobles were in no present danger, although a few, for all their screaming and attempts to move, could not escape the outsize torch she hurled onto them. A gross man, tricked out in countless white-starched lace frills and red velvet longvest, shrieked like a terrified horse. His ornate clothing was afire, and then his beard, while his panicked friends tried to kick and shove him away. A woman who tried to clamber over him became a screaming pyre when her licentiously flimsy skirts caught.

A host of terrified nobles had surged up to the door at the back of the balcony. No one opened it first. Now they were pressing desperately against a door that opened inward. It would never be opened, now. All this their intended victim saw with savage pleasure and a sense of justice they would never have understood. Using her sword as a shovel, she sent a stream of incandescent coal searing up into their midst.

The handsomely bearded fellow who had first jeered at her was knocked over the balcony's edge onto the floor, a few body-lengths from Tiana. The floor there was white, though the whitewash was long since burned away. He became flame. An over-jeweled courtesan screeched as flames leapt up from the lacquered mass of hair piled high atop her head.

"Open the side door!" someone bellowed, and tore down a hanging to reveal such a door. An emergency exit, perhaps.

"No!" Hartes yelled. "The draft will—"

The rest of his warning was lost amid the tumult of voices and screeching metal as frantic hands pulled at the long-unused bronze door. It creaked ponderously open. The majestic tall spire of the eternal Flame quivered, bowed, waver-danced unstably . . . and commenced to laugh.

The thick cork soles of Tiana's shoes were beginning to smoke and stink.

While the Thesian nobility fought their way out past the aged metal door like souls escaping the Hot Hell, the eternal Flame of the Sleeping Demon stood tall and upright as if in defiance of the strong draft. Then it bellied strongly toward the doorway. Bending down, it poured searing yellow into the Royal Balcony. It sought the doorway, roaring in the way of some great beast set free. The sound of its well-fed fury drowned the little screams of the well-fed humans, who were swiftly dying.

Smoke was curling around Tiana's ankles. Awestruck, she watched the roaring incineration of the aristocracy of a nation. The magnitude of the catastrophe whelmed her comprehension. Scores and more were dying in sudden agony. The government of a mighty kingdom was being reduced to ashes amid which a horde of gemstones would twinkle amid melted gold and silver.

Well, she thought righteously, *after the way they treated me, I hope this teaches them a good lesson!*

From her right came the sound of a heavy fall. She whirled to see that the trapdoor had opened to drop a dead pig onto the burning floor. In a trice it was an unrecognizable shape wrapped in fire. Ah—her substitute! Her cue to depart, as countless previous victims must have been instructed. Heedless of injury to her feet, she raced across the incandescent floor toward the towering pillar of the Flame. Her last step was a leap. She dived low, directly into that roaring white column of fire. Pain struck with the bite of a thousand daggers, amid a thunderous roaring.

Next she knew she was through hole and flame and falling through cool darkness. And falling. Deeper and deeper into the earth. . . .

Fourth Strand:
KNIGHT WITH NO NAME

Under an iron sky he rode through a gods-abandoned desolation, a solitary knight on a tiring horse. On this ugly landscape nothing grew save boulders, which seemed to rear menacingly up from land otherwise barren as a hag of eighty. The night would be freezing. Nowhere was there sign of shelter, or food or water for man and mount.

Not that it mattered. He knew his pursuers would overhaul him before nightfall. Now he was too exhausted to curse the blind fate that had brought him into this situation.

What madness, to kill and be killed over a horse!

To cross this wilderness, to survive, he must keep his steed. The savages fighting for a precarious living in this uncooperative land saw the animal as meat to feed their malnourished families. No compromise was possible. They must have the beast. Nor were they concerned about the price in blood and lives.

Once he had broken through their ambush, he had felt safe enough; but no. This race was not to the swift. Endurance must win, and it lay with those more familiar with the terrain. When he sought to stop and rest his horse, there they came, relentless as night. Running barefoot across the stony ground behind him, they were incredible in the literal meaning of the term: not credible. Not believable. They sprinted as if there was no limit on their endurance. Against such pursuit a horse carrying a knight in armor had no chance. They knew what he knew: his fall was but a matter of time, time nearly over.

No. It *was* over. Here he must stand and fight. *Utterly futile,* he knew, *but I'd rather die fighting than running until the running killed my poor horse.* They had their birth and their dignity, both he and the animal.

He reined in and swung off, to give the beast what little relief he could, as long as he could. The wait was not overlong. Their coming was subtle. Perhaps they thought he had crossbow bolts left. Whatever their reason, they stayed just beyond his sight. He heard stealthy footsteps from every direction. Though he twisted his head this way and that and caught flashes of motion at the corners of his eyes, he actually saw nothing.

They were coming. With a murmured apology to his steed, he remounted. The horse grunted. They stood on a flat patch of rock some few yards wide. Beyond this chosen battleground, the irregular terrain provided a great deal of cover. Soon he was imagining a savage crouching behind every boulder, lying in every crevasse and even crevice.

Probably true, he mused. They had him entirely surrounded. *By now they must have seen I've only sword and shield—what are they waiting for?*

All went silent then, a total death of sound. For all he could see or hear, he could be alone in this wilderness. He knew better. As it had so often these past few days, his horse sniffed the arid air in vain quest of the scent of water. Its ears were cocked, all senses striving to be alert.

The laughter grew softly out of the silence. It came from everywhere and from nowhere, and built into a torrent of mockery. The mounted man clamped his mouth. If they hoped to force him into panic and fatal error, they were mistaken. His life was for sale only at a price they would not enjoy paying. He thought, *When they—*and his horse was fighting him for its head, rearing under him, threatening to bolt. He clung to the rein, pulled hard. And he felt his control slipping.

Could it be—"Do you really smell water, big boy?"

Whatever its reason, his mount was in a frenzy. He must let it run, that or be thrown. He dropped the reins and grasped his sword with both hands. Instantly the horse hurled itself into a gallop. As quickly the savages appeared in front of him, rushing to form a wall of spears. The horse raced on, at a dead run. Its need was paramount. It smelled water.

For a fleeting moment the knight saw them, saw the surprise on their sun-roasted faces, saw their long spears wavering in disarray as he was borne upon them at terrible speed. They had not sense or experience to ground their spear-butts in a hedgehog that would destroy horse and rider. Nor could they believe this would happen. Only at the last moment did they vent their yells and start to break. It was too late. Their faces and gaping mouths grew huge and then horse and mailed rider were smashing among them.

Men were howling, dying under hooves while the knight's sword flailed, working mass butchery. For a heartbeat or three the world was a screaming crashing crimson-splashed nightmare. Only briefly did the horse stumble, as it broke a spear that also broke its wielder's arm and stabbed another in the leg. Severed arms and gobbets of flesh, even a head flew through the air like grain before a mad thresher.

Then he was hurtling headlong through them, past them, downhill, and he had to grasp the saddle to stay with his horse. Savages charged in howling pursuit. *Savages?* he mused. *Desperate men, perhaps more desperate than I— they have families whose ribs they can count from twenty paces away.*

By the time he reached the bottom of the slope, his lead was a scant few spear-lengths. One whizzed past on his right; another touched that arm and was deflected with a bang. His mount's mane flew above a neck stretched almost straight out, horizontal to its racing body. Yet when it came to another hill, it had to slow. It had spent much of the false strength gained from thirst and the scent of water. Wiry men encumbered only by spear, stone dagger and breechclout were coming ever faster.

At the summit we're lost. I'll rein in and wheel on them. That way a few more will join me in d—

They reached the summit and no six men could have reined in the racing animal. Its rider's mouth dropped open. Below, a lush green valley sprawled, basking in sunshine and warmth. An utterly impossible fertile island in this wasteland! Bounteous fruit trees reared above thick clover and a colorful sprinkling of wildflowers like gems strewn on rich green velvet.

Had he stumbled upon the garden of some unknown god?

Bent, clinging, he looked back—and saw every pursuer. They were at the summit a few yards back—and they had stopped.

He heard but could not understand the words they shouted at each other. He heard tones of anger and confusion, and he heard the unmistakable language of fear. Fear prevailed among them! None descended after him! A few remained atop the hill, shouting incomprehensible curses after him.

Then they shrank and trickled away like frightened dogs.

"By the Great Cow's Cud," he swore, "what—what is going *on?*"

After they had tracked him so long and so far, relentless as hungry wolves; after he had made them pay in blood, a large red debt; why should they give it up now? Now, of all times, when his horse's legs quivered and victory was nearly theirs? All they had to do was come down into this valley . . .

This valley that was itself another mystery. Off to the right a family of rabbits hopped lazily in tall rich grass, choosing only the clover. To the left a doe and her fawn grazed tranquilly. They only glanced up at the racing horse with sunlight glinting off its rider's armor and helm! Ahead, trees drooped under their burden of ripe fruit.

All this bounty and the savages remain on the wasteland? All this bounty in the very midst of such a wasteland?

An ugly thought surged in: *Is it illusion?—delusion? Could I be delirious and hallucinating?*

With a shake of his head he hurled aside all such considerations. The mystery would not go away, but there were more urgent matters to attend to. To begin with, he must duck and dodge as his mount plunged recklessly among the trees, all heedless of low branches and its careful training.

He heard it. He smelled it. He saw it: a crystal stream! It beckoned his horse and he knew he had to fight to allow the beast to drink what it needed, not what it thought it wanted.

He did. Insanity faded from the animal's eyes. It turned

back to fresh green food. It was happy to be groomed, un-saddled, rubbed, so long as its master did not interfere with its cropping of fine sweet grass.

Once his steed was groomed and cared for—and well tethered, to limit its grazing—the man's own stomach de-manded attention.

Only when he was at last relaxing in the soft grass, armorcoat off, his belly comfortably full and his horse grazing more leisurely; only then did the knight allow his mind to turn again to the mystery of this impossible valley. He sprawled, having decided to retain his leggings of linked chain. His sword was nearby, and helm and mail-coat. The thought eased into his mind that there could be only one reason why the savages refused to pursue him into this lush land and indeed must never come here at all. They had to be terrified of the valley, and with reason. It must be that someone or something most unpleasant dwelt in the midst of all this beauty.

Well, he thought, *I'll face that when I must—fed and rested!* And he collapsed into the sleep his body and brain demanded.

He awoke of a sudden and arose stiff, snatching sheath in left hand and swordhilt in right. There was nothing. His horse, at leisure. A squirrel over there and another over-head; perhaps it had dropped that nut kernel on him. He walked and twisted and wheeled, working the knots out of his muscles. Fruit and rest had restored much of his strength. He ate a little more, and added several nuts, and loosed mailed leggings and linen tights and snug breech-clout in response to nature's call. Then he moved his horse to better grazing.

Despite the valley's beauty and peaceful aspect, he laced up his wool-sleeved, leathern jack and let his mailcoat slide jingling down over his body and arms. Attaching his sword's sheath to its belt, he buckled it on. The while, he held his mouth straight and looked round and about.

If he was going to face whatever danger lurked—must lurk!—in this loveliness, he was as ready now as he would ever be. In mailed leather boots he crossed the stream and ascended the little knoll on its other side. Trees greeted him, in profusion. From a few spear-lengths' distance, a deer eyed him. It looked as though it would suffer even a mailed knight to walk up to it.

And yet to kill in this place, even for meat, seemed definitely wrong.

The knight paced through the green woods. He had wandered but a fewscore spear-lengths when he stepped out into a mossy clearing and saw—for want of another word, he must call it a castle. He stared. How many degrees of incredibility could exist; of incredulousness? Call it pattern: here the impossible always existed, and should be expected.

Certainly that gracious and yet austere structure was the home of a person of wealth and power. Where then were his fortifications, his retainers, gardeners? There was no moat, no defensive walls, no glacis. Not even archers' ports stared, slit-eyed, from those handsome walls. It was as if whoever lived here knew that none would dare attack. That no one would come here at all?

He thought only to walk around this strange castle, to see it from all sides. Walking was easier—and more quiet —when he detached his scabbard and carried it in his left hand, swordhilt profferred to his right. And then he was standing before the building's main entrance: a towering black gate upon whose ivory door strange symbols were carven. Curiosity impelled him to step closer . . .

Slowly, ponderously, quietly, moving entirely of itself, that great door swung open.

Arms tense, hand on hilt, he stared at the dark opening as if it were the mouth of some gigantic monster. The open door was all too clearly an invitation. Or a command?

Despite a feeling of kinship to a fly visiting a spider, he entered.

Could it possibly be more than coincidence that has brought me here?

Walking slowly to quell the jingle of his armor of linked circles of beaten iron, he paced down a corridor wrought of bleak gray stone. It had an ancient look about it, and was oddly chill to the touch. He was never able to see it as clearly as he wished, for the corridor twisted constantly and the source of light was always just around the next bend. It seemed that someone was playing a witless game, walking always just ahead of him with a lamp. Except that, strain his ears as he would, there were no footsteps, no faintest rustle of clothing. Indeed there was no sound or sign of occupancy.

Then he rounded a bend and faced a doorway.

The open door was a massive structure of dark wood carven with strange figures and embossed with a single flame-like design, in cool green jade. Beyond, a black-tapestried room was dimly lit by a few candles whose flames quivered as if in fright. Well they might: the flames were green, a cold green containing more blue than yellow. The knight felt gooseflesh, and drew a long breath to expel it in a silent sigh.

The candelabrum presided over the center of a long ebony table. Its uncertain light carried only a little way. Most of the large chamber was a realm of murky shadows. The intruder did not relinquish his grip on the hilt of his sword. He stared at the nearer end of the table, which was black and highly polished. It was also set for dinner. A single chair of heavy mahogany; gleaming silver cutlery and spoon; bone white platters and aventurine-hued bowl piled with fresh fruit; a crystal goblet and decanter filled with deep red wine; and a large slab of venison still steaming hot from the fire. Its savory aroma drew him like a lodestone.

That did not stop the knight from circuiting the room, peering into shadows. They were only shadows. He saw not even a cobweb. Only then did he doff his helmet and sit at table. Only after he had begun to eat and drink did he notice: at the opposite end of the dining table there stood a tall mirror. Strange that he had not noticed it at first.

Stranger still was the fact that the reflection in the mirror was not his.

"Welcome, Sir Knight, to Castle Ice."

The food turned to lead in his stomach and icy worms were acrawl on his spine. Fear edged his voice: "By the Cud! Who are you?"

Black eyes sparkling with hidden fire, the impossible image smiled thinly. *"That is the wrong question, but I will answer. The world, which little knows me and much fears me, calls me . . . Pyre."*

The name of this most dread of wizards confirmed the knight's worst fears. Small wonder the savages avoided this so-attractive valley! No sane man would enter this place. *Assuming that it truly is the lair of this lord of dark enchantments!* Still, the knight strove to appear unafraid. In what he hoped would seem a relaxed manner, he took another bite of venison and chewed. It was a mistake. Fine meat tasted like pulpy wood in his suddenly dry mouth. Nevertheless he persisted, and swallowed the inert lumps. A sip of wine helped it down.

"And what, pray tell, is the question I should have asked?"

"Why, obviously," the mage smiled mockingly, "the proper question, Sir Knight, is—what is your name?"

"That is for you to ask and me to answer, and I do apologize for partaking of your hospitality without introducing myself. My name is . . . I am . . ."

He had not the vaguest idea. Frantically he sought to grasp at memories that were running out of his mind like water out of a burst bag. He knew that he knew—had known—everything about himself that any normal person knew. And it was fading, evaporating like the memory of a vivid dream that refuses to survive awakening. His name and birth! His family and friends! All his past deeds . . . every recollection of all that made him a man rather than a blank! Vanished! Gone!

"By the Cud, wizard! What have you done to me?" His voice was slurred. The room seemed to waver and spin. *I am . . . but I am . . . I must be . . . Be!*

"Much, and none of it good," the image said, and words and tone were cold and hard as ice. So were his staring dark hawk's eyes, and even his tiny little close-cropped beard of salt and pepper.

"DAMN you!" his victim exploded, flailing out at the chaos that threatened to engulf him. Only after it went rushing from his hand did he realize that he was throwing the dagger provided for his dining. Straight it sped at the darkling wizard's heart. It struck the mirror wherein he sat and smashed it into countless spinning falling tinkling fragments.

The nameless knight was alone.

What have I done? Can I have destroyed even . . . dread Pyre?

Apparently so. If the dread mage had been such a lackwit as to take up residence in a fragile glass, he'd none to blame but himself, except . . .

If Pyre of Ice is truly gone, how am I to regain my memory?

Who am I?

As he reflected on it, his state of amnesia became more

peer cautiously about. Before her stretched a broad and high-domed temple. At one end was a grimly stained altar. Behind it stood a vast repulsive image, dimly and unpleasantly visible in the shadows. *Charming.* She had a feeling of *déjà vu;* the Temple of the Goddess of Death far, far away in sleepy little Woeand.

But no; although those nuns had been dedicated to evil, they had been human. Mostly. At least originally.

Here she could not be sure. Tiana saw worshipers that were only vague squat forms chanting almost in silence before a repellant statue. No, not Woeand; she was reminded more of the ghouls at their obscene worship in the Tomb of Kings in Nevinia. It occurred to her that she had encountered rather too many idiots worshiping monstrosities in dark places!

Some vagrant breeze or puff of air created a trick of light that showed her the face of the image worshiped here. Ugh. The "god" these uglies adored was Death. And to reach the far door she must pass through their midst.

Or . . . over them, she mused, squinting as she glanced around and up. She had after all nothing even resembling a weapon, and could not even see anything that could be broken off to use as spear or club.

The great chamber was hemispherical. Its ophidianly decorated walls converged into a high dome. Monstrous forms of serpentine marble coiled on the walls, their tails at its base, their heads meeting in the ceiling's apex. Thick as a man's body with deeply carved scales that would give her ample hand- and footholds, they were a highway by which she could pass over the worshipers she assumed to be enemies. So she supposed, at least. Little of this inverted well of a room's vastness was truly visible to her.

Tiana backed from the threshold and along the corridor, hugging the side on which her cell was. That way she hoped the carven watcher should not be able to see her. She declined to look at it. With her backside planted against the wall, she drew off her boots, then opened her abbreviated leggings. She folded over each boot and crammed its top down inside the short tights she blandly referred to as "leggings" and which Caranga had dubbed "shorts." When she refastened them at the waist, she had to suck in and was glad she had not eaten in a while—or been fed.

She returned to the temple's entry with a boot dangling

at each hip like a pannier. One always climbed better barefoot, and besides the boots might make a lot of . . . noise. She had just passed her hands over the scales. Her feet would be bleeding in minutes. With a grim face Tiana drew on her boots and started climbing. Her heels hooked just perfectly in the carven scales of stone!

Up she went with the easy grace of an acrobat born and trained—as a thief. She was soon high above the temple floor. Any slip would, of course, send her plunging to splat messily and join the rest of Riser Island's inhabitants in death. Tiana had no intention of slipping.

A more serious source of nervousness was that some section of the stone snake would have weak scales or mortar and refuse to take her weight. Still, what she had seen and left thus far indicated that the thing was in eminently good condition, so that risk was surely a minor one. Up she went, noting that extreme pains had been taken to maintain this snake in an impressively lifelike condition. It must have been carved in blocks and then assembled section by section. Yet she had still to come upon a joint in the statue's long body. In fact there weren't any joints at all. The exquisite attention to detail that made this reptilian statue so lifelike was surely beyond the limits of human craft.

A nightmarish suspicion began to grow in Tiana's mind. Resolutely she told herself that such a concept was scarcely possible.

She knew the feel of a serpent's sinewy strength and bulk and she knew the feel of cold hard stone. Beyond all question this was the latter. She must put absurd doubts and fears out of her mind, she told herself. She had enough genuine problems and things to worry about. *Wasting your time on imaginary dangers, Tiana m'girl,* she thought, *is a sure path to disaster. Just get yourself on up here and over, and down t'other side!*

Thus she argued with and chastised herself, until she was halfway to the dome. That was when she felt the quiver of life in the cold stone. It was not an earthquake. It was faint but unmistakable proof that this thing was alive.

For one moment of terror it was all Tiana could do to hang on. As the initial shock passed, she told herself that it was really all right; the snake might live, but just a little. After all there was no mistaking the fact that it was made of stone. (Stone. *Stone! Keep telling myself that! It is*

stone! If some silly enchantment gives it some bare hint of animation, it's no concern of mine.) That mental admonition failed to quiet the butterflies in her stomach or stop the frozen ones at wander along her spine. Nevertheless she pressed on, steadily up and up, with her teeth and lips set in a determined grimace.

She glanced down. Oh wonderful. The silent worshipers were clustered in the section of the chamber where rested the tail or base of this in-curving snake. Turning back now would be to descend into their midst. She was not interested in presenting them with a free meal: Tiana of Reme.

That hardly matters. Tiana of Reme is not one to go turning back.

So she told herself while she noticed that the nearer she drew up to the serpent's head, its body felt increasingly like cold muscular flesh rather than cold hard stone.

Like it or not—and who could?—it was becoming ever more evident that the tail of this snake was dead stone while the head was very much alive. A gigantic snake, partially petrified and set here as one more guard resembling an ophidian caryatid?—or a stone carving partially animated by a similar but reversed spell of enchantment?

What difference did it make? Who cared? She was now about ten sword-lengths from that huge fanged head and she was clinging to a body that wove to and fro in the manner of feathermoss dangling from a tree in a strong breeze. She glanced down. They were there. They looked tiny. They were waiting. They were hopeful.

I can't stay. I can't go down.

How simple a way to choose! Gently, ever so cautiously, she inched her way onward. Her head hung now as she hand-and-footed it along the underside of a big curving branch. This was no branch. Nor was it stone. The flesh had entirely lost any granitic quality. It had the vibrantly muscular feel of a treebranch-sized reptile. And every few seconds she felt its rumpling heartbeat.

Looking ahead between her arms, she could see the center of the domed ceiling. There the head of her serpent met the heads of a dozen others . . . and praise be to Theba, Cud, Back, Susha, and any others anyplace—they were all asleep!

A few moments more and she was atop the head of her serpent, which was wide as the length of the sword she wished she had. She sat comfortably, mightily pleased with

herself. She was halfway to her goal. The rest would be
easy: all downhill. Once she crossed the gap to the head
of another snake—that one—whose body led down to the
exit from this trebly-accursed building. There was a catch.

The heads did not meet. They were well apart. Even far
apart.

She tried to tell herself that she could jump that far. That
the distance looked greater than it was because of the
darkness and the many, many body-lengths of potential fall.
Long she stared at the sleeping countenance of the prodigious stone-snake while it swayed through the dark shadows. Much she fired her courage. It did not work. At last
she admitted it.

It was simply too far.

What then? Turning back would mean a long, long descent only to become food for the obscene appetites of
those death-worshiping uglies. That left a choice between
two relatively clean deaths: jumping, or staying here until
one of the snakes awoke and ate her. *Hmm . . . but if it ate
me, it would have to . . . hmm!* Why . . . yes. That should
work. Certainly everything else she could think of was
doomed! This nascent plan was considerably less . . .
stupid.

The first step was to wake one snake without waking
the others. Since they were half stone, they were probably
sound sleepers. Her right boot held both her knife and that
strange walnut from Pyre. Therefore she began most carefully removing her left boot.

I'll get only one try at this one. She needed agility that
she could not summon while sitting this way. Still, standing upright would make it far too easy to slip off the reptile's slippery head. As a compromise she rose to her knees.
She sighed. It was no good—and no less dangerous than
being afoot. There was no way she could trim the risk on
this one.

Rising to her feet, Tiana stood precariously while with
all her force she hurled her boot into the face of the other
reptile. Then she fell, groaning—and started getting right
back onto her feet again.

Her aim was true. The boot struck the monster directly
in its closed right eye. Instantly the preternatural thing
awoke. Eyes the size of apples and just as yellow sprang
open and immediately focused on her. Seldom had she
seen eyes reflect such naked uncurbed hunger. The vast

jaws opened slowly, ponderously, as if the stone-snake was smiling in anticipation. They gaped wide. The head was turning so that the enormous mouth was vertical, coming at her like a window-sized door.

Greedy-guts means to swallow me at a single gulp!

She was afforded a fine and unwelcome view of every detail of its glistening stalactites of fangs as it reached for her. Ivory stalactites! She had seen teeth far less clean and smelled breath far worse on highborn members of royal courts!

That did not endear this thing to Tiana of Reme. Flaunting the beauty of her body, she stood erect and proud as the fanged jaws encircled her. Swiftly she squatted. As the daggered mouth snapped shut, she sprang up and out, escaping by a bit less than the heel of her remaining boot. An ivory stalactite removed it. That spoiled her perfect spring, but after a moment of mad scrambling that was all struggle to avoid falling, she was off the stone-snake's head and clinging to its neck.

It turned its head to regard her with one huge topaz eye. As she had surmised, it could not bend in a circle tight enough to reach her. As she had expected, the big ugly eye went dull with sleep, and closed.

I did it! I won! Oh if father had been here to see this one! or *Gray!—or Pyre; arrogant, magnificent Pyre of Ice!*

Glowing with self-congratulation, she slipped rapidly down the snake-into-stone. The hearts of these monsters beat once every few seconds. She had gambled that such a metabolism wouldn't allow the creature to close its mouth fast enough to catch her. Pure cleverness, she delightedly thought, had again won a brilliant victory and saved her.

Despite the renewed swelling of her ego, she descended to the floor as stealthily as possible. There was no point in celebrating her latest triumph at dinner—not when she was the main course! She did not even drop the last few feet, but eased all the way down. For a long moment she stood on that stone floor, staring back into the temple. She could see the doorway of the corridor of cells, but she could not see the worshipers or, far more importantly just now, her left boot.

Well, with the heel bitten off the right, my feet are almost level!

The door that meant escape from this temple of horror was before her. Swiftly she slipped out of the temple—

and onto an open plain. She drew in several long breaths of real outdoor air with unusual pleasure while she looked about, examined a couple of scratches, and noted an unmatched pair of tears in her clothing.

A few hundred paces away she could see the white marble building that glowed as if it somehow housed sunshine. She would wager her life against a single copper coin—Bashanese, even—that what she sought would be found in that building.

She was on an island where perpetual night was maintained by arcane means. Why, then, had the Owner created a pocket of sun-brightness in the midst of that night-dark? Given: the isle's inhabitants could not abide light and the owner used illumination to prevent untrustworthy minions from stealing his edible human property. Given: a building that was obviously very brightly lit within, indeed. Deduction: anything housed in there must be extraordinarily valuable! In that case it was surely just what she sought: the secret of the Owner's vulnerability!

Her goal was in sight. She had gotten herself here, escaped, won her way past worshipers and stone-snake guardians and no one the wiser—

"Greetings. Did you lose this?"

She whirled to see a squatty little figure swathed in a lot of black robe. It stood beside the doorway. It was holding Tiana's left boot.

22nd Strand:

WEDDING AND FLAMEDEATH!

"You, my dear," it whispered softly, "were only half clever. When your boot fell from the ceiling my attention was attracted. Naturally I concealed my discovery from the others and came out here to meet you."

Why "naturally," Tiana could not be sure, but . . . "Since you kept my escape a secret," she said in a level

voice, "I presume you are no friend of the Owner. Are you interested in . . . an alliance against a mutual enemy?"

Tiana knew she had stumbled onto luck. Whether it was very good or very bad depended upon this unknown's answer. If the presumed vampire was willing to cooperate with her against the Owner, she'd have moved much closer to victory. If, on the other hand, she had guessed wrong and/or it did not want to be friends . . .

"To take your questions in order," it purred softly from within the all-encompassing black, "yes: the Owner and I are enemies. Indeed, here on Riser every single entity is enemy to every other. The social order is basd on compulsion and fear, you see, cooperation being a thing unknown."

Back of the Turtle, Riser Island is even worse than the situation aboard a Narokan ship! "Then—what do you want of me? Only to return my other boot?" With that query she bent a little rightward to pat the boot she still wore. It seemed a normal enough gesture.

"I hunger."

Several swift motions blurred into one and Tiana stood in a fighting crouch with her dagger drawn and extended before her. She sincerely hoped it served her better than it had that Sarchese sailor she had it from.

At first the squat black figure did not seem to respond. Slowly then it began to *unfold*, like a deadly nightflower blossoming. From out of the collapsing robes stepped forth a tall, slender figure! It was female. Though twice Tiana's height, its body was in the same superb proportions.

Tiana gasped. This female demon wore a tight shirt of green silk and short-cut leggings and her head was crowned with long fiery hair! Tiana was staring at her own enlarged mirror image, complete in every detail—even to the dagger in its right hand and a bare left foot. Yet the image was fiendishly distorted. The Tiana-green eyes glowed with unnatural desire. Smiling red lips bared sharply pointed teeth. The hands were shapely paws worthy of a lioness.

There were no words between them now. There was instantaneous battle.

Sensing that her one hope lay in bold attack, Tiana sprang with her dagger lunging at the other's stomach. It was a hand's breadth from its target when the demon's blade swept up. Iron rang on iron. Thrown back and aside,

Tiana ducked beneath her double's return stroke and cut at its bare ankle.

Even as the red of first blood stained her blade, the world seemed to collapse on Tiana Highrider. Her demonic opponent had fallen on her.

Crushed beneath its greater weight, she struggled frantically to get her knife back into play. She succeeded in squirming partially out from under. She was sitting up, blade coming up for another thrust or swipe, when the demon seized her. With a paw-like hand on each of Tiana's shoulders, it threw her to the ground with shocking might. The demon followed. Though Tiana struggled frantically, her efforts were futile. Her own magnified image perched upon her, knees buried in her stomach, a hand/paw on each of her forearms to hold her arms prisoned against the ground.

"Now, my pretty tender one," it murmured in tones as sweet as poisoned honey, "if you will but relax, you may enjoy this nearly as much as I will."

The crimson mouth, redder than blood, smiled in an uglier displaying of those pointed teeth. The demon bent. That loathsome mouth lowered toward the pulse of Tiana's throat. Tiana fought with all her strength to raise her dagger-arm.

No use. *But it isn't fair! After all I've done, all I've accomplished, to be caught because of a boot I had to use and then—No!*

No use. She simply did not have the brute strength necessary and . . .

Abruptly the demon's grip went limp. Tearing free, Tiana's arm flashed up to bury the dagger in what she hoped was the monster's heart. Shoving and dragging herself out from under her dead double, Tiana exulted.

"Monster, you should have known better! A great warrior such as Tiana is not . . ."

She silenced herself on discovering that her opponent's back bore a fresh sword wound that had obviously been its bane. She had stabbed it after its death. How . . . who . . .

A sword still dripping blood in his fist, the Gray Knight was leaning casually against the wall. In soft relaxed tone, he spoke. "You know, if you had waited for me as we agreed you'd have saved yourself a deal of trouble."

"I was managing perfectly well by myself, thank you!" She showed him her back, scrambling to recover her lost boot. "I hope you remembered your promise and brought me an effective disguise."

"Unfortunately," Gray replied blandly, "that's impossible. It develops that nothing less than the spell I am under has any chance of deceiving the inhabitants of this island. I *have* found a good hiding place where you can wait while I tend to the business at hand."

She stared at him. How could this lackwit male possibly imagine that he could get along without her! On the point of railing at him, she felt a surge of some inexplicable feeling, and spoke softly.

"Don't go all arrogant on me, Gray. We work together."

"I am merely being considerate, believe me. I am disguised and you are not." The shoulders of that nameless, faceless man shrugged. Then he squatted to wipe his sword on the pile of black robes dropped by the demon.

"Those robes!" Tiana cried, pointing.

He picked up the apparent mass of black fabric that had covered an apparent toad-like form and had somehow concealed a giant version of Tiana. Now she saw that what Gray held scarce contained enough cloth to make a shirt or tunic.

"Perhaps if I crawled . . ." she said, in a desultory little voice . . .

She was grateful that he did not sneer and glad that he did not dignify her wishful thinking with a comment.

"There has to be a way!" she said. "Don't forget what business brought us here—*both* of us!"

"I'm not forgetting," he said quietly. "The Owner, we hope, is vulnerable . . . somehow, in some secret way. We are here to steal that secret."

"Aye! Together! And of the two of us, I'm the skilled professional thief while you're merely an aristocrat! You don't even know your name, much less the location of what we must steal!"

"What's all this noi—oh, now you are a pretty morsel!" That from the black-robed thing that emerged from the temple. As it leered at Tiana, Gray stuck it through the back. All the way through. When he withdrew his sword, robe and occupant crumbled into nothing much. Tiana kicked the door shut. Sorcery, animated corpses, enemies that vanished on being slain did not even faze her anymore. She did wonder that her demonic image still lay where it had fallen.

Again Gray wiped his sword on the bit of black cloth it had worn. Tiana was glaring at him, ready to explode if he dared patronize her.

"All you said is true, Tiana," he said quietly. "But I can't transfer this spell on me, to you. You must agree— hush!"

At his gesture for silence, she heard the tread of approaching feet. The ceremony must be over. Those death-worshiping squatty somethings in the black robes(?) were about to come marching out of the temple. Tiana and Sir Gray were caught in the middle of wide-open space. Trapped with no hiding place in sight.

Throwing back his long gray cloak, he bent and gestured. She was to climb on his back! Frowning, Tiana went along. Scarcely had she done so when he tossed the cloak over her—and the door opened. Black misshapen figures began to file past them.

This is absurd, Tiana anguished. *This disguise is a trick that wouldn't fool a child! And even if it works, they'll still see us standing over the corpse of one we just slew!*

One by one the dark forms went by, single file. None paid any special heed to Tiana-surmounted Gray. The fresh corpse they walked around as if it were a commonplace. Apparently murder on Riser Island was of concern only to slayer and victim.

The last figure in the line passed and gestured as if expecting Gray to follow.

Still carrying Tiana pickaback, the Gray Knight walked forward and fell in at the end of the line.

"One catch," he whispered, "to this See-The-Expected spell. One is then obliged to *do* as expected."

Oh, wonderful, Tiana mused. *I hope our fellows don't start eating somebody! And damn Gray! If he'd thought ahead, he could have cut eyeholes in this cloak so I could—* Just then she discovered the nice convenient arrow-hole Gray hadn't bothered to repair. After a moment's squirming she was able to peer out. Soon she whispered, "I hate to mention this, but that monster we killed has just risen. It's . . ." She broke off to stare as her demonic likeness folded itself back into a squat form wrapped in blackness. It looked like an animated sack of grain, in whaleskin.

"I suppose," Gray said in a tone suitable for discussing the weather, "that we should have expected that. We must have been lucky to catch the thing in a state that made it even temporarily vulnerable to ordinary weapons."

"Oh, wonderful. A Thing? What is it?"

"A thing," Gray said equably, and paced on behind the others.

Tiana hardly heard. She was watching their reanimated victim approach them. As she stared in horror, it took a place directly behind them and marched along as the tail of the file of . . . things. After a few paces, it spoke in a voice that might have emerged from a deep grave.

"That runaway girl . . . how did she taste?"

Gray's voice was amicable: "Are you assuming that I struck you from behind and devoured that woman?"

"Of course. It must have been you that struck me and she is not here. Certainly you didn't let her flee. Therefore, ergo, and was she tasty?"

"Perhaps," Gray said, without turning. "Is it of any great importance?"

"Oh no. It would have been pleasant to have had one last meal before the Rite of Termination, though. But no, it does not really matter."

Sacred Cud! Did that thing just tell us we are in a procession of death-worshipers on its way to the ultimate religious experience—death? We're trapped among them! Forced to go along with them to their suicide! Drood's Arms and Dung! Here I've finally found the best man I've ever seen—uh, not-seen—aside from Pyre and Caranga . . . and instead of a lovely romance we're about to be roasted like those Thesian nobles! It's just not fair! Why is it one works so hard and these things happen? Isn't there fairness anywhere?

She pressed her lips to Gray's ear. "Can't you think of some excuse to get us out of here?"

"I don't think a call of nature would suffice, Tiana. They probably don't experience such urges. But—yes, *I* could, if I were alone. Unhappily the disguising spell only covers you the way it does my clothing. To get away with what we have to do, it would have to cover you the same way it does me." He squeezed her crimping legs. "Much as I regret saying it, my beloved, it appears that we're doomed."

He said that before, and I had to do something. "Then stretch the spell to cover me fully!" she burst forth, knowing it was beyond his ability. Before he could say so, she was seized by a brilliant inspiration. "Gray! Man and wife sworn each to the other form a mystic One! *Darling*— marry me! Quick! We're cattle walking to the executioner!"

She bit her lip. Cud and Back and gods, what words! Worse—had she spoken too loudly in her excitement?

Apparently not. She had *merely* said that which she had never expected to hear herself utter, even to the one she respected above all and who was thus most worthy of her —that damned Pyre. The long line of grim marchers gave no sign of having noticed anything. Which meant little, she thought, for she could expect no warning from these doom-bound creatures of black.

"Cling with your legs," he muttered, and she felt the shuffling under his all-covering cloak. His hand came onto hers, and placed it on the hilt of his sword. Her stomach trembled and she clung with legs and one arm. *Marriage! Me? I'm so young and innocent!* . . .

"I," he murmured, "who knows not his true name or visage but accept willingly the name Gray, a knight, take thee, Tiana, to be my wife and upon this sword I vow and swear . . ."

He paused and Tiana began to say her part of the vows. From behind them the slain thing said, "Does something ail you?" Spell of disguise or no, the undying monster's tone indicated clearly that it was suspicious.

"Merely indigestion," Gray drily answered. "Can it be true that we actually go to final, ultimate termination . . . real death?"

"You know that it is. At last!"

Tiana shuddered. She felt no different, but knew that in at least a halfscore nations of the world, she was wed. Then Gray surprised her; he made an addition to his swearing.

"And if you die while I live by any causes other than natural, I vow by the Flames Which Shall Destroy the World that I will avenge your death, Tiana my beloved wife."

Tiana was deeply shocked. Nevertheless, she uttered the corresponding oath. As the words left her lips it seemed that a veil closed about her; as though she were suddenly fully, concealingly clothed. Was it possible?

"My husband," she whispered, "it seems to have worked. I *feel* it. But could you not have used some lighter oath? All know that the consequences of swearing by the World-fires are always unpleasant."

ute females was locked up lest they be got at by some untrustworthy minion. This was an island of vampires. Once
she left her cell, any who—or that—met her might regard
Tiana as a convenient and free meal.

Better that than stay here to be fattened for the Owner.

Stealthily she slipped from the cell. She was in a narrow
corridor lighted by infrequently set and smoky torches.
Their yellow flames showed a seemingly endless corridor
endlessly lined on both sides with doors. Cells, Tiana assumed, identical to her recent abode. There were many
more such cells than would be required to house a hundred women and girls. She turned to look the other way.
The corridor opened into a dark, cavernous room.

*Now why take the trouble to light torches after locking
us in?*

The answer came to her at once: the torches were additional protection against theft of human property. Riser
Island's inhabitants could not abide light. Illuminating the
corridor should keep out intruders. In that event, Tiana
was in a place of relative safety. The problem was that to
continue her escape/exploration she must cross that great
hall of midnight.

Well, she thought, in a mental shrug. Tiana's will was
forged on some preternatural anvil and despite circumstances of fearfulness or worse, she tended ever toward
calm and inflexibility of plan. True, at present her "plan"
consisted only in getting out of here and finding Gray.

She was just starting to take that first step when she
felt . . . observed. With a hard swallow and a sensation
of tension, she turned back.

She had noticed that each cell door bore a crudely
carved head, but had given little heed to the fact. That
had been an error. The carving on the door of her vacated
cell had eyes. They were watching her. Now Tiana stared
back, and her nape prickled. Though it was but a poor
likeness of a head roughly hewn into the dark wood, there
was a mindless evil in those sunken eyes—and they saw
her. Tiana continued to return the stare, gnawing her lip.
She was reminded of a guard dog baffled by a situation
beyond its training.

Trained to watch for intruders but not departers? She
could not know. She could move along before it made up
its limited mind. She did.

At the threshold of the cavernous hall she paused to

mounted on one-legged horses. Perhaps by occult means they could become an actual fighting force. Perhaps they were mere perverse decoration for the vast hideous mausoleum behind them. That obscene structure, she little doubted, was the palace of the Owner.

Then she saw no more. She and the others entered the squat building of black stone. The structure's angles and proportions were faintly wrong, as though it had not been constructed but instead had grown like a huge stone cancer. Her smiling chamberlain rushed Tiana blindly through the inky interior of the place, to her "Royal Apartment."

It was of course a pen of the sort used for housing cattle awaiting slaughter.

She sat in dank darkness. Gradually her courage returned. She did not, could not believe that she was doomed. But if she was, what of it? Every warrior must someday fight a last battle. No one man, god or demon could treat her with contempt without paying heavily for the error. She sat. She stood and flexed, swung her arms, rolled her neck, sat. She tried to tell herself that there was no way Gray could get to her swiftly. She must wait. She waited. In the dark world of the dead, there was no sound. She waited in darkness and silence. When she began to grow chilly, she rose and again exercised. Her stomach snarled. How much time had passed? She waited.

She could not control rising impatience. She worried for Gray. He placed such great reliance on that See-The-Expected spell. What if it should fail him? What if his illusion was whelmed here in the abode of the Owner, a master of illusions? The Gray Knight could be dead! Or—a pleasing thought—he might be a captive in need of rescue. If that were the case, how foolish and time-wasteful for her to continue waiting for him!

Her patience was hardly without limits. Indeed it hardly existed. At last it was exhausted. She convinced herself that she had *decided* there was no use waiting longer. Out with an eardrop! Though her mouth was still rather dry, she found the lock of her cell and began to pick it. It yielded almost immediately. With the door open, she could see why: the lock was not intended to keep her in, but to keep others out.

That was distinctly unencouraging.

It appeared that the Owner's personal property of trib-

and more intolerable. He knew he was a man of rank and position. A man born to a life of great responsibilities and sacred duties. Death relieved a man of his obligations while it joined him to his ancestors. This . . . this obscene fate . . . robbed him of his forebears and made him an unconscious traitor to them and his land.

And family? *Have I a wife?—children?*

All recollection was gone, but it seemed probable. His hands were not those of a boy. Certainly there were more tasks in this world that he must perform. If . . . He stopped with a burst of laughter at himself and his fears. Usually there was no great problem in learning a stranger's name, even though he might refuse to disclose it. *Why should it be any harder to learn my own?* Ah. Almost he smiled. Obviously the first step was to take a look at his own face. He peered into his wine goblet.

The image looking up at him was that of . . . Pyre!

"As I was saying," the wizard said blandly as though nothing had happened, "I have indeed done certain quite harsh things to you. In addition to arranging events so as to bring you here, I have robbed you of your own memory. Too, I have placed a spell on you whereby . . . but you will discover that in due course."

"But *Why?*" he demanded, scarcely noticing the threat in the wizard's final words.

"Can you believe that I deeply regret it," whispered the image in his goblet with no small hint of mockery; "that I took this extreme measure out of necessity?"

"Necess—my name, all my memories? *Necessity?*"

"Dire necessity."

"No! Damn you no!"

The image shrugged. "Very well; in that case I'll not bother saying those things. Instead I shall tell you that I require you to run a rather dangerous errand on my behalf. If you succeed, I vow to restore your memory and treat your every problem as though it were my own."

"Swear!" the knight burst out. "You—by what can you swear?"

"Why, whatever oath may please you, of course," the wizard glibly replied. "Most western folk believe that the world was created by a Great Cow and is sustained by resting on the back of a Great Turtle. Accordingly they swear oaths by the Cud and the Back. On the other hand, the Narokans believe that a Great Spider created and sustains the world. Thus they swear by the Spinning of the Web. Few swear seriously by the dark lord, Drood of the Thousand Arms. Now again, in the southern lands people sw—"

"*No!*" the knight shouted. "I'll accept no such light oath. Swear instead the Third Oath, mage. Swear by the Worldfires—the Fires Which Shall Destroy the World!"

"That is impossible." The mage's tone was calm and final. "We both know that swearing by the Worldfires will always bring unpleasant consequences. That mistake I have already made, and bitterly regret." After a moment of seeming reflection, the mage continued, "If you must have a strong oath, why then I do solemnly swear by my power."

Taking a deep breath, the knight let it out slowly. Much as it galled him to be made the wizard's cat's-paw, it had happened. He had nothing to gain by expressing his anger. No, this was a time for making the best bargain he could. He tried for a little more:

"At least tell me some part of my name."

"Hmm," Pyre said musingly, "for longer than you can imagine, you have traveled a solitary road, twisting through shadows and twilight. Accordingly then . . . I dub you the Gray Knight."

The irony that rode the wizard's tone was maddening. Angrily his victim snapped, "And what is this footless quest on which you'd send me?"

"Unfortunately I am subject to certain . . . occult limitations, Sir Gray Knight. I may not tell you the answer to that question."

"Are you mad, wizard? How can I perform a task when you can't even tell me what it is?"

"Very simply. That which I cannot tell I can show. Pray direct your gaze upward."

The knight did. Again, he felt that what he saw had not been present before. Hanging from the center of the ceiling by a fine thread was a . . . something. A round bit of crystal small as a robin's egg. Staring, he saw that it was multi-faceted and not quite still. Each facet was a bright flash above the light of the candles, and the facets were of different colors.

Seeming to whisper in his ear, Pyre said, "*Look*. Look deeply. See rainbows aspin, round and round . . ." He continued to murmur and gradually his voice faded. It became an auditory blur the Gray Knight heard and understood without consciously noticing. All his attention was absorbed by the rotating sphere of many-colored lights. It was beautiful. And it was more than that.

Each bright facet of the turning crystal seemed to offer a fleeting glimpse of a . . . a scene; some strange new world *within.*

An iron gray sky above a dark, storm-troubled sea . . .

Mountains like the teeth of some awesome giant . . .

Trees . . . the tops of trees . . . no, of gigantic plants, bushes . . .

These and more he saw, almost as though each of the crystal's thousand facets had become one of his eyes.

Almost?

Could it be real? Could he actually be seeing the world thus, while flying above it—*flying? Wait! What's happened to me!*

Rather than the arms and legs and the body of a man he had wings and six multi-jointed black legs, all furry, and the body of . . . a fly!

Small wonder everything about him looked enormous. He was shrunk to the size of a tiny insect. *Blast the wizard! May Drood grasp him with every arm! It's true he said he would show me something—but this!*—He put an end to that mental yammer, to think more carefully. He was a fly but he had his own brain. Cold, callous though Pyre was, he had hardly transformed him into a fly merely for sport. There had to be some purpose.

What purpose? *There is little a fly can do save observe. If one is supposed to be a spy, one could hardly ask for a better disguise. Surely I will be restored to normal once I . . .*

While the wind was but a gentle breeze, he was not flying as fast as it blew against him. Steadily it was carrying him out toward that dark sea. For a fly, that meant death. Death in this strange form would be as final as in his own. *Wouldn't it?* Trying to fly faster proved futile. It wasn't that he lacked strength; his new body apparently had only one speed. He was not gaining. All his efforts into the wind succeeded only in being blown less rapidly. Behind him he could detect the splash of a storm-angered surf, and the dreadful sound was drawing nearer.

Abruptly he folded his wings and dropped. Now he was a small hard object too heavy for the breeze that defeated him when his wings were spread. His fall seemed a vast drop into a rock-strewn canyon. Scant moments above the jutting stones he unfurled his wings and came into level flight just above the ground. Here the wind was much less forcible.

I did it! At this altitude I can hold my own—even gain!

For a moment he congratulated himself on his cleverness. Then he realized. His "cleverness" amounted to no more than what a dumb animal—or a dumber insect—accomplished by instinct. He was only a successful fly.

Ahead was a pathway, a long winding trail full of odd twists and turns and seemingly trod by innumerable feet. He flew it. At its end a dark outline rose against a sky lit by a moon like a grinning silver skull. A little cottage made of crude lumber, crudely. Old and many times overgrown with ivy. Rather in need of care and repair. And yet, as he approached, he had the sensation of *Trespass,* as though he intruded into the abode of gods.

Wondering what blasphemy the wizard had conjured and tricked him into, he buzzed through the one lighted window. The cottage's single room was illuminated by a single flickering candle. Here three women toiled; slowly, painfully slowly, they were weaving an enormously complex tapestry. Old they were, gnarled and deformed by the great weight of incalculable years. And they were *blind.*

Each strand of the infinitely diverse pattern their fingers found by memory, reaching to a thread's last location and drawing it to its next needful place. The entire tapestry, strange as it was, was still all of one piece; in its way it was a consistent whole. Some instinct (?) told him he must look for that which was out of place.

He did. He soon found it.

The floor showed wet prints, Evidently a large toad had recently come this way. There it had entered, to hop over the floor thusly, and there it had stopped to sit motionless just beyond the area where the three sisters labored. There was no logical way in which he could divine the toad's purpose. Yet with an uncanny certainty, he *knew*.

The toad had come here with purpose. That purpose had been to bring something. It had spat that something out onto the floor, and for an instant the man-into-fly could almost see it happening: the toad vomiting forth a shining, hairy black sphere that unfolded eight legs to become a spider . . .

(How do I know this?—I know it.) Yes. There, entangled among the many strands of colored threads, was the shining silver strand spun by a spider. And there, too. And there. And . . . many places.

A toad had brought a spider into the house of the three sisters. In their blindness they had not known, while it spun its web in among the threads they wove. Unknown, unsuspected, sinisterly, a spider web was being woven into the great tapestry.

This has to be what Pyre meant for me to see.

What it could mean, though, he could scarcely guess. Now was a time not for thinking but for leaving this forbidden place while he still might. He flew out the window —and was in total darkness and confusion. A fierce wind pummeled him. Again the roar of the sea was menacingly near. Hurled onward, he struggled to control his wings. To no avail. There was no response. It was as if they were no longer there.

Instead he raised his entirely human hand and found it clutching a rein—the rein of a galloping horse.

I'm back! I'm a man again! Riding—galloping directly toward the chaotic sea. It and its cliffs were some little distance ahead, and he reined in. His horse—his own horse —halted a dozen or so paces from the edge of the precipice. There he made the beast stand quiet as he sat and pondered.

For all that accursed wizard cares, I could have ridden into the sea! What can his game be? First he swears there's some urgent mission I must carry out. Next, instead of explaining, he gives me a bad dream. Now I'm tossed out of his damned unnatural valley with no idea what I'm to do and no way to find my way back and ask the bastard.

He gazed about but was able to see little in the dim light of stars. The air was alive and thick with the scent of brine, and only a little of grass and trees. He was a long way from the valley of Castle Ice.

Now what, by the Great Cow's Cud, does that absurd mage expect me to do? (Not, of course, that I'd do it. Just to spite the insufferable swine I'd—) Hm. *That might be part of the explanation. Knowing I wouldn't obey his commands, he keeps me in the dark as to what he wants of me.* The Gray Knight's shoulders rose, amid a little *ching* of mail, in an angry shrug.

*However it lies and however it falls out, the fact is I
must tend my own affairs as best I may. And can!*

That presented no small problem. There was no sign of
human habitation . . . wait! The shifting wind now
brought him the odor of smoke!

"Let's go find it, uh, horse."

A few minutes of riding upwind brought him over the
rise. Below, he saw the fire. It was tended, a cheerful blaze
dancing in the midst of an armed camp. A dozen long
ships were beached in a hidden cove.

Northrons! Lawless savage raiders out of the Northlands where only they went. Far safer, surely, to brave the
hostile wilderness than attempt to talk his way into the
good graces of such men.

So he rode slowly down into their encampment on the
strand.

Just what he would say to them the Gray Knight had
no idea. Nor, as it happened, did it matter. The first of
the raiders to see him, a bear-sized man in a winged helmet, leapt up and ran, shouting to his companions.

"He comes! The warchief the wizard promised to send
us has come!"

Fifth Strand:

IN THE HALLS OF HELL

She was falling headlong through empty space dark as
midnight. Abruptly the fearful brilliance of the Sleeping
Demon was above her. And below her . . .

*Gods no! I'm falling into another fire! A pool of burning
liquid!*

The bright red wings still clung to her back. Though she
fervently wished that they might lift her in bird-like flight,
naught happened save that the wings flapped in the
rushing air. They slowed her fall by some little measure.
Now the burning water was directly beneath her. Within

that roiling fury she saw another bird-woman rushing up to meet her. They met with a mighty splash.

Semi-stunned by the impact, Tiana hung onto her breath and had no time for thinking. Her first clear thoughts came after she had stopped swimming and began wading, spluttering, out of the pool. Now she realized that what she had seen as another fire was simply the reflection of the blaze she had escaped. The other bird-masked, winged woman was also a reflection—hers.

She collapsed to lie exhausted and panting at water's edge. Slowly she sorted out events in her mind. Putting them into order was rather more difficult.

High Magistrate Ishcon's crematorium-disappearance trick had worked well enough, if not exactly as planned. No doubt the plan was that just before the dead pig dropped onto the fire she was—somehow—to have made a thick cloud of smoke. That way she could have exited, leaving the pig to flame stenchily up in her stead, with no one the wiser.

Well, no one was the wiser. And the nation of Thesia was fresh out of ruler and high nobility.

Actually, she now knew, not she but a misfortunate coincidence had doomed them. Any fire must have oxygen, and a chimney. The long-dead designer of the arena had made an error; he had provided a secondary exit from the spectators' balcony that was a better chimney than the one normally used by the Eternal Flame. The "Sleeping Demon" was wide awake—and well fed.

The stage was set for today's happenings long before my birth!

Should she be suspicious of such a coincidence? She knew full well that Other Powers sometimes interfered in human affairs. Slowly and rather reluctantly she dismissed the concept. There was nothing she could do about it, and there was much else that needed doing. About her lay a strange underground realm. Every surface of the rocky cavern glistened with a pearly luster. Once again she had the feeling that she was beyond the pale of normalcy. She had spent all too much time in such places and situations, and fighting such enemies.

It's almost as if I'm inside some enormous oyster! Tiana thought, and laughed at the conceit.

The pool into which she had fallen was a stagnant tributary of a rushing stream. Water surged out of a cleft in the wall of jagged stone. It swept along this cave's floor for perhaps a dozen paces. Thence it rushed into a hole. Amidst froth and foam and hollow gurgling sounds, the sparkling water whirlpooled down out of sight. She gazed upon a scene of considerable beauty—cold, hard beauty that could be infinitely cruel.

Some time ago, as Ishcon had told the tale, a girl had come here as Tiana had. Losing her way, she had stumbled upon some signally important object—the unknown treasure Tiana was come to steal. Logically, that girl's becoming lost seemed to indicate a right and a wrong way to leave this noisy chamber. Tiana looked about for them. She found only a single exit. Opening on her right was the mouth of a tunnel wide enough for three men to walk abreast—and blacker than her foster-father's face. She must go into that blackness. It was that or stay here till she starved.

First she stripped off the bird-woman costume, which was now merely clumsy and uncomfortable. Since she could not make a torch from it or anything else this bare cavern offered, she tossed the silly gear aside.

She was glad for the sword. Staring into the yawning darkness ahead, she hefted its comforting weight. She tried to put facts in order and make some semblance of a plan.

I mustn't become lost. If I did I could wander far from this place, and I'd wager that what I'm looking for is nearby. No, the thing to do is make a systematic search. Hmm . . . I'll start by going down the tunnel for a reasonable number of paces, turning right at every branch. If I don't find anything, I'll come back here and try again, with leftward turns.

That seemed sensible, and anything that seemed sensible was comforting. Ancient legend had it that here in Port Thark, the partition separating the world of humans from the nether-realm was thin. She was about to enter a tunnel far below the surface. Such passages were reputed to lead one out of the normal world into . . . where no human ought enter.

That's all it is, she told herself hopefully. Legend! Empty tales told by fools! The pearly appearance of this cavern is a bit odd, true. I've no doubt there's a rational explanation, though. Because of such queer appearances and the fact that a few idiots manage to kill themselves by their own incompetence . . . men even more idiotic have made

up all sorts of childish horror stories about these caverns.
That's all.

Though she ardently assured herself that this domain
of dark-wet held no supernatural dangers, the cold feeling
stayed on in the bottom of Tiana's stomach and her mouth
stayed dry as the cork shoes she also discarded.

She set forth anyhow. Naked as the day she was born,
except for the unfamiliar sword. She would just see what
demons the darkness held!

(On second thought she went back and had a nice
drink.)

Since she wanted to hear before she was heard, she made
her way on the stealthy feet of a thief. The tunnel wound
as if laid out by a lovesick worm—a big one. For the first
little bit of her trek, there was light. The pearly luminance
from back in the cavern echoed in rainbows off the tunnel's smooth walls and cast ghosts of colored light ahead
of her. She crept on and the tunnel wound. Presently all
light died. There was only the darkness, and the seamless
smoothness of the tunnel through rock.

Only after a seeming long trek did she reach the first
branch. She turned right in accord with her plan, which
was better than nothing. Thus far she had heard no sound.
Nor had she come upon any hint that she was not entirely
alone in velvet, almost palpable darkness far beneath the
earth. Some of the world's religions, she knew, condemned
the evil dead to Drood. Some claimed that His domain
was a warren of shining halls where the ghosts of the
damned wandered in utter desolation. (More to her liking,
others said that the dead went to Theba, Who fulfilled
their fondest wish, forever. Also relatively pleasant was the
Ring concept: that death was only the beginning of a new
life, in a new form. That supposedly explained geniuses
and those strangelings who seemed to be born with sorcerous lore and ability. But Tiana wasn't very religious.)

After a long and twisty distance her gliding foot came
down on—nothing.

Had she been walking without such caution she would
certainly have pitched over and fallen . . . how far? How
long? As it was, she wrenched her back and cursed—
quietly. Feeling first with her hand and then with her
Thesian sword, she discovered that the hole was apparently a chasm. The vertical shaft was deeper than she could

reach. Worse, it extended to both sides of the tunnel and was wider than her reach.

That did not prove overmuch. It could still be that the hole was no broader than an easy jump with the tunnel continuing beyond. *A candle would be nice. Just a candle's stub. . . .* It was equally possible that the hole was but a thumb's width deeper than her reach.

Um-hmm. And this hole might go all the way down and come out in Zugaboogatooga, and be wide as Lake Whatever-it's-called up in Collada! The point is, how do I find out short of jumping?

The obvious was to toss a pebble and count until it hit bottom, and toss more until one hit the other side of the gap, if one did. The problem was that this faultless tunnel contained no more pebbles than a ship's deck. It occurred to her that one thing was sure; it was a poor idea to assume this path was a dead end, without making certain! She had business down here!

Thoughtfully she ran her fingers along the wall. She found only that same uncanny smoothness of entirely faultless, mirror-polished rock. Nowhere could she chop out so much as a shard without ruining her swo—wait a minute!

Almost an arm's length above her head there seemed to be some sort of depression in the cavern wall. Yes, and it felt pretty good-sized, too. She pushed the sword into it, moved it with a series of clicks. She pushed it in and let go. Only a clink. Though the best handholds she could find on that slippery stone were poor indeed, Tiana contrived to get herself up and into the niche. She put her hand on the sword right away—and something else.

She had company.

A long-dead body by the feel of it, mummified by time and some property of this subterrene domain. The late High Magistrate had mentioned that some of the victims who used this escape route were not seen again. Gooseflesh made Tiana shiver. *Chilly down here,* she thought. She continued her check-by-feel. Judging by small bones and long silky hair, this had been a quite young girl who . . .

Tiana froze motionless despite a new wave of gooseflesh, and she fought not to scream. The grim task of inspecting a dead body meant little to her kind of person with her experience. But this one's face was missing!

Though her back was acrawl with worms, she forced

her hand back to feel again. Her first impression was correct. From forehead to chin of the mummified girl was—
nothing. The face gone. Bones intact, but with the same
pearl-smooth feel as the tunnel walls.

What this grisly fact portended she could not guess.
Further, Tiana hoped devoutly to depart this place without learning. She started to leave the niche. It was then
she noticed the slight breeze . . . cold. It was seemingly
wafting up from the pit. While there was no sound, no
other hint that anything might be coming, Tiana needed
no second warning. With swift silence she moved over the
mummy and into the deepest region of the niche. There
she waited unmoving, scarcely breathing.

The cold grew.

Something was coming.

It kept coming. An awesome Presence that was the more
dreadsome because it was invisible to her senses. Thoughts
dripped from it like bits of flesh falling from a decaying
corpse. *It was hungry.* It had only recently come to this
place and was wandering about in search of food before
going deeper to join others of its kind. Its *hunger* was vast
and unnatural, obscene in its intensity. That *hunger* was
a palpable force that beat at Tiana. If it sensed the paralyzed woman, its thoughts gave no hint. Yet it was coming
ever closer. But a little closer, she knew, and this cold
thing would feel the warmth of her body. It had to, something that radiated such cold. And with such *hunger.*

Flight and fight would be equally futile against the
power she sensed.

What then? Submit, as this poor dead girl had so long
ago, to one of this *thing*'s ghoulish brethren?

With slow reluctance the thing halted its advance, knowing it was close to the boundary it must not cross. Tiana
felt it turn and begin to slip away, leaving behind thoughts
of hatred that quivered in the air. She felt hatred, and its
name. *Paramane.*

With no little speed Tiana quit this place where she had
met horror. Back she hastened to the branching point in
the tunnel. She turned right, along the fork that previously
would have been left. It soon showed itself more promising: she saw the shimmer of a distant light. She did not
let that interfere with her stealth. A few moments later
she rounded a corner to behold a lamp. No; it was the
reflection of a lamp in the walls' mirror-like surfaces.

Here the tunnel came to a dead end in a round alcove. A massive block of black stone occupied the center of the chamber. A single lamp, reflected many times in the walls, filled the chamber with shadowless light. Except that she must correct her perceptions still again. All the lamps were reflections, with no original as source.

Someone possessing deep occult knowledge went to a lot of trouble arranging this . . . repository.

Presumably the reason was the object resting atop the black stone altar. The square box of ebony with burnished silver trim resembled a jewel box. On two sides of the small casket, bands of silver were attached to the black stone by means of hinges. Each band looped over the box to be fastened to the stone on the opposite two sides. The latch pins, also, were of silver.

Tiana had no doubt she had found the treasure Ishcon had wanted. To take it, she must pull both pins. That had been made more difficult; each pin was attached by fine chains to little silver bells.

Why did someone go to all this trouble? What was the purpose? *I can draw those pins without the slightest sound. Any thief worthy of the name could.*

Why all this elaborate trouble, fittings of precious silver and shadowless, never-failing light? All were useless for keeping a thief out. Very well then. They appeared well suited to the purpose of keeping something *in;* to force whatever was in this black casket to remain inside. That was not only shuddery, it hardly seemed to indicate that this apparent jewel box contained jewels. She had descended more than halfway to Hell to steal what grim . . . treasure?

Time enough to worry about that later, Tina mused practically, *when I am selling this prize!*

She set to work on the latch pins. They yielded as expected. Presently the box was hers for the taking. Now she hesitated, leaving it undisturbed.

For all my caution, they—whatever ghastly beings are master here—might know if I move that box. That would put me into a race to reach the exit before they catch me . . . and I've no idea where the exit can be. There was only one clue: the exit was not also an entrance. Otherwise Ishcon would have used it. Tiana raised an eyebrow. *Perhaps . . .*

Abruptly Rage lanced into her mind and came boiling

up out of the ground. It or they were coming. No matter whether she had accidentally moved the ebony cube. It mattered now only that she must flee that rage and *hunger*.

Tiana snatched the head-sized casket and raced away.

Distances that had been long when she walked them step by careful step now dissolved beneath her speeding feet. At the branching she bounced off the opposite wall and the dancing blots of light she saw were behind her eyes. She continued almost without slowing. Her chest hurt, both exteriorly and within. Ahead now was the light of the cavern of her arrival. Behind was *hunger* and nameless rage baying in hellish silent fury.

As she came bursting into the light, *they* were closing behind her. She felt that dread coldness at her back. Without a backward glance she made for the water's edge and hurled herself in.

If this was suicide, it would also be a far cleaner death than what lay behind her. She had time for a single deep breath before the vortex pulled her under. She was swept swiftly down and away by madly rushing waters.

Scarcely had the cavern lights disappeared behind her when new light was visible ahead. Tiana was tossed, thrown, and sent tumbling through the air and blinding bright sunshine—only to fall back into the water with a painful splash.

Awkwardly she fought up to the surface. Treading water, she blinked and jerked her head to hurl off water. Her hair stung her face as its wet strands snapped. She managed a grim smile of triumph. Though her sword was lost, her piratical instincts held; she had managed to retain her grasp on the black box.

Now she saw the waterfall above. It came jetting whitely out of a cliff of black stone to cascade down into the blue lake where it had deposited her.

Why, this was Cave Run Falls on the other side of Mount Yazira!

For a moment she pondered the geography of her adventures. It seemed twisted, but she put it aside in favor of other problems.

She was naked and unarmed and it was a long, long walk back to Port Thark.

Sixth Strand:

KNIGHT WITH NO FACE

A dozen longboats skimmed a calm sea bright and sparkly with dawn. At the prow of the first stood a man in leggings and coat of linked chain the color of slate. Over it he wore a cap-sleeved surcoat that fell past the knees and was slit on either side past the waist. Its loosely woven white was broken only by the small design embroidered on its chest: a single tongue of flame, in the cold green of aventurine. The surcoat—to protect an armored man from the sun—was girt by a belt wide as his wrist. From it on the left a sheathed sword hung to the heel of his armor-studded leather boot; on his right hip was slung a dagger long as his forearm. He wore no helmet, and he was not called the Knight of the Green Flame.

He was the Gray Knight, and he was pondering the tangled affair into which he had been thrust.

These men from the Northlands hated the Narokans for good and ancient reasons, which were renewed all too often in blood. When Pyre offered them a warchief, a man to lead them against Naroka's impregnable capital of Shamash, they eagerly accepted. All assumed that from the great wizard would come no normal man! The moment Gray, marked with Pyre's sign of cold flame, rode into their camp, they had known he was the promised nigh-fabulous combat leader. That, or he was an enemy or a spy. Either must be killed.

It was not a situation that yielded any sort of choice to a prudent man.

Though how I am to accomplish the impossible tasks that cursed wizard keeps setting me, the Gray Knight mused dolorously, *is a total mystery.*

It was a mystery he knew he must not share with his followers. He shook his head, now bare to the sun. There were far too many mysteries. How, for example, could this morning find him a few hours' sailing from Shamash on the far southeastern coast of the main continent, when last evening he had been thousands of leagues away, at Castle Ice near the far northwest coast?

Did all that really befall me?—or was it an ensorceled dream?

What matter? Whether the past was real or illusion, his present with its problems was all too real. Before long he must investigate. He must learn what—if any—arrangements the wizard had made for this seemingly suicidal attack. Just now he had time enough for something a gentleman must do daily: shave around his beard, and trim it.

"Hey!" he called, and the nearest sailor looked alive. The man had a yellow-orange beard that looked untrimmed since the birth of Pyre. "Is there a mirror on this ship?"

The big Northron bore the marks of years asea and many battles. Yet he replied in a timid tone, his watergray eyes never looking directly at the Gray Knight. "Yes sir! The Great Wizard, Runemaster Pyre, left a chest of things for you, sir. I recollect him saying it's got a mirror in."

The seaman gestured toward a big iron-bound strongbox, black and covered with indistinct, somehow rather disturbing figures. The Gray Knight ignored it. He moved instead to his saddlebags. No doubt he would have to look into the mage's enchanted glass—where Pyre perhaps lurked, smirking?—but not, by the Cud, before breakfast.

His small black beard was streaked with gray and close-cropped so as to cover only the area of his face immediately below his mouth. He was hardly surprised to find soap—and Tashol soap at that—and even a bone-handled noble's razor of exquisite sharpness, and a fine mirror. All these were merely what one would expect to find in the baggage of a gentleman. The odd aspect was that none bore any coat of arms or other identifying mark. The same was true of every other object in the bag, and the bags themselves. When Pyre robbed a man of his identity, the darksome mage made a thorough job of it! He provided good servants too; here came a strapping Northron with shaving water.

At least the mage can't keep me from seeing my own face, Gray mused. With his throat and cheeks washed and soaped anew, he lifted the bright razor and peered into the mirror. His reflection was only a blur.

By all the mud on the Great Turtle's back—now *what?*

The mirror was faultless. It showed sharp, perfect reflections of every object he held before it—except his face. A sudden thought made him try looking at his reflection in the smooth surface of the razor, and next the flat of his sword. Both showed him no face; only a blur. The problem did not lie in the mirror, then. In . . . what?—his eyes? Somehow he could not focus on his own reflected image. His heart beat too rapidly and he had gone warm. This was maddening. How could the wizard steal a man's very face? Gray seized the man who had brought the basin of water.

"Is there a man aboard who can draw, make charts; that sort of thing?"

He had thoughtlessly spoken in such a harsh manner to a sea-wolf from the cold continent or big island known only as Northland; a lawless barbarian who took his living from people he saw as soft. Absurdly, the Northish wolf acted the sheep. He shifted awkwardly from one foot to the other, his eyes directed at the deck.

"Ahh, well, sir, ah, the lad Cormer has a talent, uh, if you . . ."

"Look at me when you speak to me, man!"

Slowly, reluctantly the seaman raised his head. When his eyes reached the level of his warchief's face, they went visibly out of focus. "Uh, sir, it ain't anything I can explain, but looking at you bothers my eyes. Sir."

"Then go back to your duties!" the knight snapped. "Ah! Wait. D'you think there's a bale of good gray cloth aboard? Cotton? Woolen?"

"Well, ah, probably, sir. Bjork, he'd know. I'll send him to the warchief, sir."

"Don't bother. I haven't time to talk with him. Got to keep my mind on tactics, the full big picture, you know." *Stop blithering,* Gray told himself. "Go to this Beyork. Tell him if there's good gray cloth aboard, I want a cloak of it, and a new surcoat, too." He saw the Northron eyeing the obviously new surcoat he wore. "White's hardly the color to go wearing into battle, is it—what's your name?"

"Skiller, Lord."

"Get to it, Skiller." And Gray turned away without giving Skiller a chance to say anything.

So. It seems I have underestimated Pyre. The dark wizard used a lot of care to rob me of all identity, to make me nameless and faceless both. Why? What great enigmatic purpose lay behind Pyre's actions? Surely he'd have gone to no such lengths if it weren't extraordinarily important.

Much as he chased thoughts around his mind, he found no answer to the riddle. Nor could the Gray Knight draw any sure conclusion save that his belly was empty, and grumbling about it.

"Warchief?"

He turned to face a man built like an oak. His knotty calves were the size of a big man's thighs and he wore enough bronze-hued beard to house a raven or two. For all that his nose was little more than a button and his sky-hued eyes were carefully gazing just past Gray.

"Are you Beyork? I told Skiller that I—"

"Nah, Warchief. I'm Blaze Blazetop. This is my ship, *Firebird.*"

"Oh." Gray had forgotten. He had met this man last night—along with eleven other shipmasters and their High Leader, who was on the ship with the red sails. Gray felt he lost nothing by saying, "Sorry, Ship's Master. I am naturally preoccupied, and met too many new people last night, in the dark. You can't look at me either, hm?"

"It sorta hurts the eyes and the head, Warchief. You ain't a demon, are you?"

"I am definitely not, Blaze. And I was just going to prove it by looking for some breakfast. Come along?"

" 'Course, Warchief. We do got gray cloth aboard, but we've got better, in finer colors." The two were moving aftward.

"I've no doubt. I am the Gray Knight and have no other name—as far as anyone is concerned, you understand. Gray is what I want to wear. There is someone aboard who sews?"

"Oh a cloak's no trouble, Warchief. You just say whether you want 'er square or round, and Bjork cuts out a great big square or circle. Then he cuts a nice hole in it, off-center, and hems it up. That's it."

Of course, Gray thought, *but I don't want to wear this accursed surcoat that is a "present" from Pyre!* "And this?" He touched the surcoat. "One just like it, with longer sleeves, perhaps. About to the elbows."

"Well, we don't wear 'em, Warchief, and we don't wear armor's good as yours, either. Probably be a good idea to let Bjork borry that one to measure by."

"Of course," the Gray Knight said, but sat down to eat first.

Wearing a light cloak of pale brown and "fed" on leathery dried beef and wooden rolls washed down with watered beer, the Gray Knight turned his attention to the chest containing Pyre's gifts. He opened the polished ebony casket to reveal several drawers. The first held maps, charts, forged letters and the like; the common coinage of intrigue. Some of these rather explicit tools seemed to call for actions only an invisible man might take. Examining them, he realized that Pyre had planned this raid long and well. Some aspects of the plan were clear—and brilliant. Others may have been brilliant, but remained baffling puzzles.

He moved on to the second and largest drawer, which bore the label "Bad Dreams for King Ormul." Inside floated a soap bubble . . . or rather several soap bubbles, each within another within another.

As he closed the drawer he frowned. That wasn't possible! All the bubbles could not be inside each other. Obviously, logically, one had to be the outermost. He eased the drawer open, and had an idea what Skiller and Blaze had meant about getting an eye- and headache. He closed the drawer. Best to leave that well alone, for the present.

The next drawer was labeled "A gift for my enemy Ekron Toad-soul."

In it was a blue stone the size and shape of a hen's egg. A gemstone, burning with some internal fire like a great unnatural eye. Gray gazed narow-eyed at it. The war between the wizards Pyre and Ekron was old and legendary. This handsome "gift" would doubtless provide little pleasure to its recipient. Nor would presenting such a gift be a simple task.

How in the name of Drood's arms is it to be accomplished?

Gray sighed. Speculation was futile. Still . . . if Pyre had arranged the tools of this dark mission in logical order, the second drawer's use must precede that of the third. Or pave the way for it, lead to it? Probably; the nightmare for the King of Naroka was to be used in some manner to facilitate delivery of this malign gift to Ekron. Odd; the stone had the look of being a present such as Ormul would like to hand his lady queen!

This third drawer also held a jar of goose grease, just rancid enough to be mildly unpleasant in close proximity. Whatever was he to do with this?

The several other drawers would not open. It was not that they were stuck. This inanimate piece of wood, Gray definitely felt, was not willing to let him open them. Much in the presence of sorcery, he had to accept that. Perhaps the chest was right. Peradventure those drawers held items he would not need during the coming raid, but after. He would remember and check—assuming he survived.

Then where's that accursed mirror?

Though he did not relish another interview with the mage, he had to learn what he had planned. Looking again at the chest, Gray spotted the slim topmost drawer. He had overlooked it. Doubtless he should have examined it to begin with. He tugged it open with ease.

Within rested the promised mirror. Nor would it be breaking; it was of electrum, and butter-finished. He withdrew it, stared at it. He saw the blur, and ground his teeth. *Nameless and faceless, I—and where are you, enchanter, pox take you?*

Pyre appeared, and spoke hurriedly.

"The purpose of this message is simple: to tell you that my powers, while great, are subject to certain arcane restrictions. Because of this, Gray Knight now Warchief, I can give you absolutely no help of any kind, not even to answering the simplest question."

The mirror was of electrum so that there could be no possibility of its being broken in the hands of the Northmen. In that case why did it now become merely a piece of ugly rusted iron?

Seventh Strand:

HOUSE OF THE HAG

She lay at the edge of the sparkling blue waters only for a few moments while she caught her breath. She was bone weary, but her curiosity gave her no rest. The mysterious treasure in the box—what was it? Why was it so vastly important?

And above all—how could she sell it at the best possible price?

Despite her eagerness, Tiana did not forget caution. Such things were often guarded. More than once she had gained a treasure only to be forced at the last minute to battle creatures most people did not know existed. Demons, a lustful lamia. Serpents working in concert. Spiders working in concert. Those ghouls in the royal tombs of Nevinia. The horrid bear acting for Sarsis. Seeming myriads of armed men. And now?

This sort of container was to be opened respectfully and only after most careful examination. The ebony was covered with silver inlay resembling the bars of a prison. To open the box—or perhaps to unleash whatever lurked inside—she need only remove a pair of silver pins. The black wood showed little scratch-marks, evidence that various others had raised the lid as she was about to do.

She, however, had stolen the box out of a specially designed room, a room so lighted that there could be no shadows. Tiana was about to open it in ordinary daylight. What difference might that make?

Tiana me girl, you're starting to worry as much as your father Caranga!

Two quick tugs removed the pins. With her hand poised on the lid, she stopped. An extra measure of caution might be called for. Breaking a branch off a nearby tree, she

stood well away from the box. Then she used the stick to
lift the lid.

*On an island surrounded by dark and storm-troubled wa-
ters stands the dwelling place of one known as the Owner.
Within those somber halls is one room that is ever bright
as the morning. From a domed ceiling of clear blue the
image of the sun shines down. It is more brilliant than its
natural counterpart, but moveless. The floor of this room
of brightness is a great map that shows all the nations of
the earth. Each is drawn in fine detail.*

*At the edges of the room, shadows lie beyond the light
of the surrogate sun. There many eyes stare without rest.
Long have they watched this image of all the world. Long
have they seen no change. Their vigil has gone unre-
warded—until now.*

*It has come, many voices shout in perfect mindless ac-
cord. Tell the Master that it has come, near Cave Run
Falls in Thesia!*

Apparently nothing had happened when Tiana opened
the box. She approached it cautiously, and peered within.

Something ivory-white grinned up at her. A human
skull. *Charming,* she mused, thinking of her first foe in
this long war of wizards. The skull's jaws were wired shut
—with silver—and she saw the engraved plate. For a moment she was sure they were in old Narokan. Then they
were not, and were very clear to her.

*Adventurer: This is the skull of one called He
Who Sleeps. His jaws are bound that he may
not wake. Unbind them not, unless you would hear
what He Who Sleeps will say.*

She glared angrily into the casket. Had she gone through
all these perils only to gain some mere piece of mum-
mery—a trinket used long ago to gull the superstitious?

Worse, any occult importance this object might possess
was not likely to help her sell it. At best . . . Without

thinking she had moved the box so that the sunlight struck
at a different angle. It entered through the empty eyeholes to illuminate the interior. Tiana's eyes widened, then
squinted. It was as though a fire had flashed alight. Dazzling red brilliance spilled from every crevice and opening.

*That's a ruby in there! By the Great Cow's Cud, a per-
fectly huge ruby that completely fills the ugly thing!*

Swiftly she lifted the skull to the light. She looked at it
from every angle, desperately eager to be sure that she
was right; that she had indeed gained a fabulously valuable
gem. Had a rock lain handy she might have smashed the
ivory shell to get at the jewel. As it was she paused to
think.

The skull was whole and seamless. How had such an
enormous gemstone been placed in such a container? By
arcane means, obviously. Such means usually served fearsome purposes.

*Perhaps I'd best learn a little more about this before I go
for the stone.* Reluctantly, she returned the skull to the
silver inlaid box of ebony, and shut the lid.

*The shadow had disappeared from the world-map in the
House of the Owner, amid the disappoined sighs of the
watchers. They had hoped to gain sight of the forces the
Master was sending to do their work.*

Being richer than all the world's queens did not, Tiana
reflected morosely, change the fact that she was naked,
hungry, unarmed, and a long way from her ship. *Vixen*
lurked somewhere far downriver, assuming Caranga's patience held out.

Still . . . some luck's with me, at that.

Fish could be caught in this lake only in autumn. When
the bluegill came surging downriver, men were here to
meet them. For the present, their little village was de-
serted. Nice of them to leave this small, entirely service-
able boat. And how fortunate that compunctions about
stealing were not part of Tiana's makeup!

She considered, teeth in lip. Were she willing to spend
the time thoroughly searching the abandoned village, she
might well find something to wear and a bit of preserved
food. Yet she listened to her instincts, which now suggested that such a delay would be a bad risk. Best she keep

moving. Certainly this damned box was valuable to those she'd left behind.

Tiana pushed off.

After most of a day spent in negotiating the swift and often treacherous river, she was weary of arm and sore of bare bottom. Without joy she watched the sinking of the sun, crimson against the forest's deepening green. Now she tried to decide whether night-boating was worth the risk. This river was—

Green eyes narrowing, she looked about and sniffed. *Smoke.* The wind from downriver carried its unmistakable odor. Now she could discern traces, wafting above the tree-line.

Farmers burning their fields after harvest? Hardly likely, in early summer! No cooking fire plumed up such smoke and odor, for all her stomach's hopeful rumbling. Her jaw hurt and she stopped clenching her teeth. Something here boded ill, and she dared not not-discover what it was before she continued.

Heading into shore, she pulled the boat up onto the mud bank. With branches from leaning trees she hid the small craft; a large leafy branch served to erase the marks of her passage and labor from the mud—and stingingly abrade her bare thigh. Perhaps she should also hide the ebony casket. After all she'd endured to obtain the thing, she was loath to part with it. She told herself it was better strategy to keep it with her.

It was, after all, treasure and Tiana was, after all, Tiana.

Having taken all the precautions she could, she entered the forest, with stealth. Bare buttocks long seated in the boat objected to this resumed use of their muscles.

The trouble with being a woman so perfectly built as I, she thought, *and walking naked this way, is this accursed jiggle-joggle!*

She was approaching more than smoke, she soon knew, for everything that went into fire left its imprint in the air. The captain of *Vixen* sniffed, considering. Ahead was no fire of grass or trees, but of seasoned lumber. Little undertones of odor told her of other things in the flames, some unfamiliar. Not all; she recognized the scent of burning flesh. Her stomach snarled and she damned it for its cannibalistic leanings.

She came upon a path that wound its way through the

forest, apparently leading toward the source of the smoke. The easier walking along the trail would save her bare feet from stones and stubs, and her skin from whippy branches, thorns and burrs. Nevertheless, she grimly chose to walk parallel to the path. Naked or no, she'd be ready to dive into a clump of bushes. The signs were all too clear that she was not likely to like those she might meet on the trail.

Tiana could not imagine who such might be. No savages peopled this part of the world. Thesia was hardly at war with any of its neighbors—having conquered and enslaved them all.

Reaching the top of a small hill, she looked down to see what she'd feared: a small farming village. Fields of growing wheat surrounded the burning ruins that had been a cluster of a dozen or so houses. If humans survived, she saw no sign. All too likely the men had bravely and foolishly hurried right out to be slaughtered by experts while the women and children remained inside to be burned alive, after a bit of use.

Barbarian attack? Those Drood-damned swine from the hill-country?

Tiana, it is not your affair, she told herself, at the urge to make the villains pay—an impulse all the stronger because she could see them clearly.

Below, not fifty yards away, a small hut nestled cozily to the forest edge. Smoke—honest smoke from a cookfire —poured from the hut's stone chimney. Men in steel-studded leather jacks and the horned helms of Thunlander Light Cavalry milled about outside.

They've spared some poor woman to use and kill later— after she's cooked dinner for the murdering monsters!

For all her mounting anger, what Tiana saw was disturbing in another way. These were the swine King Hartes had hired to help oppress their own countrymen! Why had they suddenly broken peace with their employer's kingdom? Could it have anything to do with her black box? Something important was afoot. It was something Tiana didn't understand, and that was a situation Tiana could not bear.

She understood the sound behind her: footsteps.

Someone was approaching, and who but an enemy? She nodded, considering. Aye; she saw no horses below. A raiding party of this size would leave a man behind to mind the mounts, and in the cavalry it was the horses that ate first. The one approaching must have watered and fed them. Now he was returning to join his fellows for dinner. Tiana pressed close against a huge tree—a scratchy one.

If I kill him as he so richly deserves, I can steal horse and sword—perhaps even armor—and be away before those other scum miss him!

From around a bend in the trail he appeared, a shortish, wiry youth with a city-bred cunning written on his weasel's face.

A street-tough joined the army. And praise Theba—he's just my size! she thought happily, and amended, *Well . . . maybe a bit slight in the chest—*

The young horse-soldier walked with eyes alert and sword at the ready. Nevertheless the thought did not occur to Tiana that such a formidable young man should not be assaulted by a stark naked woman without weapons. Vanity and pride were not always conducive to good sense, which was why she had to be clever and strong as well as swift. Confident of those qualities, she sought the most direct way of dealing with this situation.

Quickly she set down the box. She had to look only a little before she found a nice large pine cone. Wagging her shoulders with both hands behind her as if flirtatiously flaunting her nudity, she stepped out onto the path before the youth. Rather than smile, she adopted the subtlety of a coolish, arch look.

"And to think I thought all cavalrymen were old and ugly and bowlegged!"

The sight of so fair a woman, with her beauty so completely revealed, would have painted a frozen stare on the face of any man. This one's astonishment was compounded by Tiana's words, and she added more.

"I have something *for* you-u-u . . ."

His sword arm quivered down. Eyes bulging, he asked numbly, "Wh-at?"

"This!" And she slammed the pine cone full into his face.

A stone would have been a lot nicer, but the knobby-knurly thing was a good start. In the instant that he was blind and mazed with shock and pain, her left hand caught his sword arm. She yanked him toward her while her knee rammed up into his crotch and the point of her elbow slammed into his neck. Another such blow, harder and better placed, rewarded her with a snapping sound. His sword flew from a jerking arm. The soldier, his head now hanging at an ugly angle, no longer breathed. His body partly pivoted, trying to fall, and Tiana released his wrist. He fell.

There. Swift and easy as a cat slaying a rat! He probably never had a mother anyhow.

Though there had been but little sound, Tiana was hardly pleased to hear a shout, all too near. "Kerreas! What happened?"

Damn them! They sent more than one with the horses. Now where did this uncooperative wretch drop his sword?

Another voice: "Mayhap something's amiss? Kerreas?"

The speakers were some distance down-trail, following Tiana's victim. She was trapped between them and the main force at the end of the path, down the hill. Then—

Ahhh! She retrieved Kerreas's sword, though at cost of having to pluck it from a thornbush that tried to eat her arm. *Now to slip away from here without—*

A man came dog-trotting around the bend in the path. His mouth sagged at sight of the naked young woman standing over his apparently dead comrade. Rather slowly in his shock and indecision, he began to raise his crossbow.

"Shoot her, quick! Loose, Kensh, before she gets away!" That from a man behind him, and then there was another, goggling:

"Who liked Kerreas anyhow! Surrender, girl, and we'll show you a great good time!"

"Shoot her, Kensh! Stick an arrow right in her gut!"

"J-just a *girl?* And *nekkid?*"

The sword in Tiana's hand, by the feel of it a well-balanced weapon, rose high above her head. It flashed at the crossbowman. In a continuation of the same violent movement she was wheeling away without waiting to see how well Kensh loosed his nasty quarrel while wearing a sword in his gut.

She bolted at a dead run, still—damn them—naked.

Like a horribly angry bee the crossbow quarrel *screeed* past her head to disappear into the leafy forest. She kept moving. *If I can get past the main squad before all the noise stirs them up, I'll make for the village. It's not burning so fiercely that I can't get through, and they're apt to*

*go around rather than follow. Then I can—oh dung! I can
burn my feet, is what! Well—*

The trail widened into a clearing. There, in perfect semi-
circular formation, stood Thunland soldiery. They faced
her with leveled cavalry-spears as though she were some
hunted beast. Tiana was given the choice: stop running or
impale herself. Tiana stopped. Even then her swift-moving
gaze was picking out the man whose copper-chased helmet
indicated rank.

"*Captain!* These men tried to *rape* me!" she cried, gesturing at her pursuers just as they came into view. "They
couldn't agree who'd be *first,* and—"

She paused, frowning as she looked back along the trail.
The crossbowman was unmarked, while the bald spearman
bled from a sword-cut that had laid open half his face.
Hmp, she thought, *that stupid sword must have been poor-
ly balanced at that!*

"—and *this* man," she continued, pointing at the spearman, "slapped Kerreas, who hit him with his *sword,* and
then these *other* two fell on Kerreas and broke his *neck.*
Oh it was *horrible! I ran,* and—"

"Captain Ashina," the crossbowman interrupted, "this
flame-haired slut is lying."

"A *natural* flame-haired slut, too," one of the men with
the captain said.

"She's the one killed Kerreas, poor boy," the crossbowman went on. "Broke his neck the way a wolf kills a rabbit."

Tiana's voice was an incredulous little squeak: "Me?"

"Aye," the spearman put in, "and it was her what cut me!
Throwed Kerreas's sword like a dagger 'r a spear, she did,
and . . ." The fellow's voice trailed off at the expression
on his captain's face. Ashina looked as if he had just eaten
a green apple. With a worm.

"I'll pass over the murder of your fellow soldier Kerreas," Captain Ashina began in a dangerously soft tone,
and his droopy broad mustache twitched. "He was a snotty
little snake and probably earned worse, years ago. He's
small loss. BUT—" and his voice rose to challenge thunder
—"troops who forget their orders because of rut and then
lie about it afterward are of little use when they're whole,
and NONE when they're wounded!"

He stopped. His words hung in the air as a dreadful
threat.

"Aside, m'girl," he murmured, giving Tiana's flank a slap as he passed her. "You think I'd believe that this lovely slip of a girl with her genuine red hair and pretty—her pretty form BROKE THAT GANG-BOY'S *neck?*"

"Captain, I swear by the mud on the Turtle's back—"

"Miscor, you've got a bad cut there," Ashina said. "But I think I can stop the bleeding for you."

Like a striking viper then the captain's sword-arm flashed, and the bald spearman crumpled to the muddy ground. The bleeding from his face was most effectively stopped: scarlet poured copiously from his slashed throat.

"As for you two," Captain Ashina snarled at the others, "the next time we have a really nasty job needs doing, it's yours! Now go stuff your lying bellies." With his soldiers thus accounted for, the youngish captain turned back to Tiana. "My dear, we were just having dinner." He gestured toward the hut and smiled in a display of large teeth beneath the bushy-droopy sorrel mustache. "Would you care to join us?"

Tiana returned the mock courtesy by smiling right back. "Really I'm not hungry—but if you insist," she said, noting the twitch of his sword, "I'll keep you company. Would you perhaps have a spare tunic?"

Even at this distance she could smell the stew acooking, and Tiana's Caranga-trained nose told her something most interesting. Her stomach growled and she ignored it. Fasting would do her a lot of good. Lots of philosophers said so.

"Afraid not," Captain Ashina said, and several men sighed in relief. It would be criminal to cover this lucky find of theirs—and besides, they'd just have to rip it off later, anyhow. How many times would twenty go into one?

Tiana kept her eyes sweetly wide and her head high while Captain Ashina ceremoniously ushered her toward a smallish one-room structure of braided kinkoo branches under a roof of thatched straw. Around the edges of the roof were woven bright serhawk feathers and within the thatching—though sharp and knowing eyes were required to note them—were the birds' white skeletons. Tiana's vision was sharp, and she knew more about this place than these stupid murdering Thunlanders did. Surrounded and close-watched by helmeted soldiers carrying sharp weapons, Tiana thought it politick to accompany their captain.

Before the hut, a cooking fire danced under a black iron

pot big as a cow's head. The Thunlanders apparently saw nothing strange about the fact that the smoke swooped straight into the hut and up the chimney. Beside the suspended kettle, slowly stirring its contents with a long wooden spoon, stood an old woman, a crone innocent of teeth. Her time-ravaged face was twisted and ugly beyond even its obvious years. The perfect witch of the woods, Tiana mused, as the woman raised a brown, gnarled finger to level it at her.

"Would you like some of my stew, dearie?" she asked, croaking like a raven or a serhawk on the wing.

"Oh, no thank you."

"Claims not to be hungry," Ashina said, letting one hand stray to his guest's backside, "but I'll have some."

Tiana tried to be unobtrusive about edging away from spidery fingers. As their captain knelt to retrieve his trencher from the ground, one of his men muttered:

"Best have her eat some more, to be sure she's added no . . . spice."

"Oh you suspicious soldier-boys," the crone said with a horridly toothless smile, and downed a generous spoonful of her savory stew. Ashina, satisfied, let her fill his plate.

"Girl," he said between mouthfuls of meat, leeks, herbs and gravy, "as I am sure you appreciate, you find yourself in a delicate position."

"Yes, I'd certainly appreciate something to wear. Even a dishcloth?"

"Cooperate like a nice girl," he said, ignoring her words, "and I'll deal kindly with you."

"A *nice* girl," one of his men muttered. "Who needs a *nice* girl?"

"Otherwise," Ashina said, favoring Tiana with a wolfish grin while gravy dripped from one mustachio, "I shall have to follow my orders."

"Dearie," the old woman interrupted, "do try my stew. I'm sure you'll love it. That little belly of yours looks like it would welcome good meat."

Tiana ignored the proffered bowl. Instead she took the spoon from the crone's clawlike hand. Raising it to her mouth, she sniffed, and touched it to the tip of her tongue. Eyebrows sweetly arched, she returned the spoon.

"For what it is, it is very well done, mother. An excellent choice of seasonings. But—thank you—it's not to my taste. You see, I've—"

"Enough," Ashina snarled. He sat down. "Girl, I said—"

"Captain, I am no more girl than you are boy, as I'm sure you can see." And Tiana stood with her shoulders well back. Someone snickered. It was not the captain.

"Look here trull, are you going to be a cooperative girl, or—"

"Captain, why don't you let me—"

"But Cap-tainnn," Tiana said, interrupting the drunk-looking soldier. Her eyes were wide in innocence and her arm was amove as if aimlessly, the better to jiggle her bilobate chest. "I don't know what you *want*. How can I help *or* hinder you in carrying out your *orders*, when I don't know what they *are?*" As if idly, she rubbed one shapely hip.

"My troopers and I," Ashina said, his words ever so slightly blurred, "are part of a very large force combing this countryside."

"Oh my."

"Yes. This morning all the border garrisons—our fort's only a bit to the east of here—received double star orders. That's decimation for whichever unit obeys least promptly. We were to ride west and search for some Drood-sent black box, and kill all we meet who object to search . . ."

"Oh how *awful!* And such *nice*-looking horse-soldiers, too. Oh I *assure* you you are welcome to search *me*, Captain Ashina!"

Men laughed. One volunteered, though in a strangely weak voice, considering the nature of the task he requested.

". . . first questioning," Ashina went doggedly on as though focusing only on the words he had to get out, "under torture, you understand, any who might have knowledge of the Drood-damned ebony box. It's stolen property, you see. *But*. You can most assuredly be cooperative in other ways, and maybe on the morrow we can find you some nice clothing."

"She KNOWS!" This from the hag, in a raucous hawkish shout, while she aimed her long spoon at the naked redhead. "She's the one! I have the Sight and I know!"

The last standing man sat down, rather suddenly. Tiana tried to look fresh and innocently uncomprehending while Captain Ashina glanced back and forth from the time-deformed old woman to the gloriously well-formed and naked young one. Confusion clouded his eyes—or something did. It seemed to be glazing them, as well.

"Wha's this—" Ashina began, and gave his head a hard jerk as if assaulted by mites.

Tiana kept her eyes wide while she addressed Ashina of Thunland. "Now let me see if I understand you," she said in a calm sweet tone. "If I cooperate, meaning play the whore to this gaggle of armored lovers of yours, I may get a whole big reward of something to wear. If I don't, then you rape me, and second you torture me to death. Is that about it?"

"Yessss," a man muttered low. Strangely, his eyes failed to brighten.

"Aye, girl, you've got it," Ashina mumbled, the words falling mangled from his lips, which seemed to have gone lazy. "But what the hag just said—"

"Witch," Tiana said. "Witch, not hag. But it doesn't matter," she went on equably. "Thank you all the same, but I'd prefer just to be raped."

"What?"

"You heard me!" Tiana stood with legs well apart and hands on hips. "I said it will just have to be rape. And, Ashina my baby-burning friend, it's your place to begin the horrid deed. Up up man, I'm waiting!"

He started up, but fell back onto his buttocks. "I— I don't feel well . . ." His eyes strayed their glassy gaze in the direction of the crone.

"Well come come now! By my count, there are two-and-twenty of you," Tiana snapped. "Surely among so many brave slaughterers you can get up the manhood for such a task!"

"Quarmos," the captain snarled with a gesture in the general direction of a slouching trooper, "give the fire-haired slut what she wants! Kensh—fetch that hag over here."

As the first hulking oaf commenced to rise from the fallen tree whereon he sat, Tiana's foot flashed out to catch him full in the face. He went tumbling backward over the great log. Kensh had started for the old woman; spinning completely around, Tiana slammed her forearm across his back just above the buttocks. A cry burst from the cross-bowman while Tiana snatched out his sword.

"I'll take this slut," a full-bearded hulk said, starting up.

"I only had two this afternoon: Virgins. What fun are they?"

"Oh, I'm so glad you said that," Tiana said, and drove Kensh's sword into the man's mouth. Another was rising; she kicked him backward.

"Next!"

What followed was hardly a fight. Those troopers who retained strength to rise, rose; Tiana knocked them down and kept them down until the poisoned stew had finished its work. Ashina drew dagger and Tiana kicked his arm so that he slashed his own leg. As she raised her sword, the old woman called out.

"No! He's their leader," she said, weak-voiced. "Mine! Must be mine."

"Yours," Tiana said, and waited.

She had not long to wait. The last of the Thunlanders to succumb was Captain Ashina, who managed three last words though his face had gone the color of ashes.

"I—don't . . . understand . . ."

"True enough," Tiana said, and she spoke on swiftly, to send her words with him into the darkness. "You understood nothing of the people you butchered, butcher. Had you eyes to see, you'd have known this is the home of a Thesian hawkwitch, a woman who'd go to any length to repay you. She has."

Captain Ashina may or may not have heard the last few words; he was gone off with his men and their victims. Tiana glanced around without seeing the old woman. Knowing the hag had not departed, Tiana peered into the hut. Aye, the hawkwitch lay on a blanket in the darkest corner.

"Mother," a pirate asked gently of a witch, "they are yours. Is there an antidote I can fetch you?"

"Nay, child. It is better that I die. For the vengeance I owed, and took, it is a small price."

"The vengeance is taken. Tell me—why did you seek to betray me to our common enemy?"

The reply came drifting from the shadow-splotched darkness in a voice labored, as though the woman fought back death to speak her final words.

"Because it was your fault, your doing; all this evil. When I saw you, I knew. You have the casket. You meddle in something forbidden to humankind, girl . . . Tiana, pirate! Send the box with me where I go, else all the

Powers of the Earth and the Hands of the Sea and Jaws of the Water and even the Eyes of the Sky shall rise up against you, and your only true ally be Facelessness and Illusion!"

"But," Tiana began to protest, and held her tongue. She knew better than to argue with the dead.

The sun had died, leaving the sky to a red, ill-portending moon when Tiana rode from this village of the dead. Mounted on the best of their horses, she was clad and equipped in such of their clothing and weapons as suited her.

Behind her the witch's house burned, a funeral pyre whose crimson and smoky flames added to the sky's forbidding omen.

Ashina and his men she had not touched. They were two-legged jackals; let their four-legged kin tend to them.

Eighth Strand:
DREAM-TRAP

Bearing King Ormul's supper tray, the servant walked the palace's marble corridors without one of the numerous guards giving him a second glance. His face? Did servants have faces, identities? A servant was merely a servant. No one noted that this man walked with the spear-straight bearing of a warrior.

The fat soldier lounging outside the king's bedchamber only mumbled, "King's already abed." His gaze never rose from the crimson carpet.

"Yes," the servant answered mildly. "Still, he cannot sleep and would eat. Pardon me, General." And he passed through the doorway and closed the heavy portal after him. The fellow stood for a moment, breathing slowly while he relaxed tension-knotted muscles.

The Gray Knight's scheme was working exactly as he

reasoned—or rather guessed—that it should. At first
glimpse those Northrons had seen the warchief they expected. When he donned the clothing of the ship's cook
and served dinner, no man was any the wiser. It followed
a form of sorcerous logic: since the wizard's spell prevented anyone from truly *seeing* him, those who looked at
him supposed he was whoever they expected. It was better
than invisibility, and apparently less dangerous.

Now it was time to see whether he had guessed right
about the rest of Pyre's magic. Here, in the bedchamber
of the king of Naroka. Ormul, ruler of an infamous land,
snored within a richly-sheeted bed. His homely face was
sickeningly peaceful. Gray lifted the cover off the tray he
bore.

"*Bad dreams, Your Majesty,*" he said, noting the emergence of the bubbles-within-each-other. While he watched
the sorcerous bubbles float around the room, he tried to
understand how each of them could possibly be on the
inside.

Perhaps he was looking at it awrong. The truth—no
more possible—was that he, the king, and all this silk-
draped bedchamber were inside all of the strange bubbles.

The first bubble shimmered every fulgurant hue of the
rainbow and burst into nothingness.

Gray opened his eyes, blinking as though awakening
from sleep. Clad in light armor, a sword in his gloved hand,
he stood in some strange sort of . . . jungle?

Sacred Candence no! I've fallen into Ormul's dream!

Ormul of Naroka, looking down upon the Games of the
Snare, smiled in the confidence of his power. Seated with
their heads beneath his feet were the lords and Powers of
Naroka, as well as the kings of several lands. This was
the day when the great and powerful humbled themselves
before him. The Games of the Snare comprised the High
Celebration. This demonstration of Narokan power displayed their cunning and skill in the setting of traps.
Those privileged to attend were people like jewels; beautiful, sparkling of wit and attire; polished hard, without trace
of such soft weaknesses as compassion. At the king's right
foot sat Baron Tarnok, in blood-red robes trimmed with
what appeared to be pearls. They were not pearls. They

were the eyes of those who had once thought themselves the baron's friends. The High Priest Hogrith sat at his king's left foot. He was bare to the waist that all might admire his young handsome body. It was the result of nameless ceremonies, this false appearance of a man who was in truth centuries old.

Directly before Ormul waited an empty space. The wizard Ekron had not deigned to come. His place continued reserved.

The victim of the first and simplest event of this festival was already in the arena. A tall, hawkfaced man with black burning eyes set in a bony face, cleanshaven except for the small gray-streaked black beard on his chin. Ormul stared at the fellow's intensely erect, prideful bearing and decided he was—or had been—a noble from one of the western countries.

Now that he bore the mark of the Spider on his forehead, he had no rank save that of King's Victim.

To his right Gray saw a high blank wall. In all other directions spread jungle verdure. Plants of many different kinds grew in patterns too regular to be natural. Above he saw only blue sky shot with clouds like snippets of cotton. Yet, if he were to believe his ears, many people sat up there and mocked him with quiet laughter.

Some optical trick that allows them to see me while I see only sky?

The seamless wall abruptly opened and ended his speculation. Beyond the opening, he saw the streets of Shamash. A voice whispered then, from everywhere and nowhere.

"Stranger, know that you are King Ormul's chosen victim in the Games of the Snare. The contest is completely fair. You may win your freedom and safety simply by escaping this arena. The way of escape is open before you. However . . ." The voice paused, doubtless relishing the words. *"The woman you love is captive in the center of the jungle. Should you desert her, she will die—quite horribly."*

Expectant silence fell. Gray *felt* the host of hidden eyes watching him intently. In this high religious ceremony it was vital that the victim enter the trap voluntarily, just as the fly entered the spider's web.

Gray hesitated only for a moment. He was hardly obligated to rescue a woman who was only part of a dream!

Still, the project seemed to involve no danger. And she might hold a clue to his lost identity.

(As Gray went striding along a clear trail into the synthetic jungle, Ormul smiled broadly. He bowed ever so slightly in acknowledgment of the polite applause of his nobles. He knew they dissembled; they were not overly impressed, and he cared not a jot. This young foreign nobleman who walked so tall and straight with pride in his every move . . . obviously he was a victim brave enough for fine sport. What was to come would be a delight!)

A mosquito bit Gray.

He swatted it, scratched—and stopped short.

The sting and irritation were just as real as any he had ever felt. *O Candence Eternal! If in this supposed dream the insects bite in earnest, will death not be just as authentic? Damn! I had this same problem when I was a fly. Logic insists that an illusion, no matter how vivid, has no power to harm me. Still I can't quite make myself believe it!*

Fear strove to creep over him, and it was too late to ponder philosophical points. Ahead of him spread a clearing as if by magic. Even the grass looked tended. Here was a woman beautiful as any he had ever beheld. Hair like flame and eyes like emeralds. Even with most of her body concealed by some flowering plant, she appeared most shapely indeed. Marvelously shaped breasts were bare to his eyes, and the languid lips were beyond attractive. She was the woman of a man's dreams . . .

Softly, tenderly, the captor-flower's many white blossoms were caressing her lovely nudity of pearl and pale bronze, stroking the smooth skin. And drinking red liquid from her.

Identification seemed to pounce into his mind. A demon-flower!

As he rushed toward her, the sight of him roused the plant's victim. She screamed a warning. That and the slight rustling to his right spurred Gray to spring aside, barely avoiding the second demonflower and nearly falling as well. Like a striking serpent its tendrils whistled past him to seize on empty air. In that instant it was uncoiled and vulnerable, and he seized that fleeting chance. Before it could recoil he was at the plant's center, hacking the main trunk with mighty sword strokes.

Dream? Hardly!

By the time the plant could snatch at him, its trunk was

half severed and rivers of sap were spurting onto the
ground like green blood. Its tendrils tightened about him.
With waning strength it struggled to pull him off balance—
while his sword swiftly hewed away its life.

He stopped only when the little sap that remained in the
floral monster was slowly dripping from innumerable
wounds and its leaves were withering to a yellow-brown.
The sense that all might be only a dream had been swept
away in horror and cold fury. Gray exulted in his destroying such a thing of evil. It was almost a happiness in a
miserable man with no name or face.

Its twin, however, was much larger. It held the girl im-
mobile in its obscene embrace. Weakened by loss of blood
and drugged by its narcotic perfume, she nevertheless
struggled valiantly. Her eyes widened at sight of the approaching man with the raised sword. She commenced
shouting. Blurred incoherent words tumbled from her
mouth like a storm-driven stream.

Warily he circled the monster, knowing that the same
tactics could not prevail against this more powerful foe.
With his entire mind focused on the problem, he scarcely
noticed the shouts of the object of his rescue attempt. Her
voice had become harsh in her anger that he was not heed-
ing her advice.

Pacing just beyond reach of its tendrils, he was taunting
the demonflower by holding tempting food—himself—just
beyond its grasp. He sprang at it and leapt back just as
swiftly. He allowed it to catch nothing but the edge of his
sword. Again and again he played that potentially lethal
game of catch-me-if-you-can. Each time he eluded the
sentient green limbs while leaving wounds in them. From
some of the cuts sap poured in a steady flow. From others
it spurted gratifyingly. There was no mere dripping.

Like an animal, the plant learned. It ceased to respond
to his challenges. When Gray stood motionless, easily within the wide circle of its reach, it drew itself into a tight
defensive position. The blossoms clustered more tightly
about its victim's naked body. The sucking noise grew
louder.

Before such horror to whelm a man's reason, the coldness in Gray's mind only grew. In the back of his consciousness, doors opened. Dark knowledge spilled forth. He
stepped back, his eyes fixed in concentration.

There was for all things a Word that revealed the

internal logic of their nature. The man who could discern that Word was master of all things. He looked at the plant. From some of its wounds sap flowed steadily. From others it spurted. The comparison of flora to fauna was obvious. He saw it, recognized it, and *knew*.

The nameless knight rushed his foe in seeming berserk fury with his sword held high in a two-handed grip. Coil upon coil of enwrapping green could not halt his inward rush. Even as he was lifted off the ground, he struck. With both hands and all his strength he drove his sword into the ground at the base of the demonflower. Preternatural cunning aimed and directed his blade. It pierced the horrid thing's heart and brought a single intense convulsion. Torrents of green fountained up, the arterial vital fluid of a plant. In an instant the demonflower was limp and withering.

The captive's fury was unabated by victory. She continued to beat upon their dead foe. Grasping her arm, Gray had to drag her away. She was shuddering and panting. He forced her to run, practically dragging her down the jungle trail. His ears were alert and his sword poised to meet new dangers.

There were none. In but a few minutes they were out of the jungle maze. Before them yawned the hole in the wall of the arena. They ran to it, and through it . . .

High in the Royal Box, Ormul looked down and smiled as the web fell over the King's Victim and the redtressed woman. It was swiftly evident that the man's sword could not cut the strong and sticky network. The woman's intense struggles were equally futile.

As Ormul bowed, a wave of cheering burst from the spectators. At the king's right foot Baron Tarnok shouted in jubilance:

"They are taken, Your Majesty! They are all three well taken!"

King Ormul heard without really hearing the words. His mind was filled with pride and his gaze was fixed upon the Royal Spider. The king's pet monster was coming on hairy legs for the people who were its dinner. Ormul deemed it fitting and proper to begin the Games of the Snare by feeding this earthly manifestation and substitute for Naroka's deity. The first event was coming to a perfect conclusion . . .

Only now, much too late, did His Majesty re-hear Tarnok and see that there were indeed three figures caught in the web. The warrior, the woman—and a man in a black robe, as broad of shoulder as the warrior and just as tall! His black eyes brooded from a sharp, angular face. Ormul looked into those eyes, and screamed.

Yet the King of Naroka sat helpless in his finery, for there was nothing else he could do.

The robed man walked through the web. Where it touched his black garb it smoked and fell away as though the man were made of flame. For all its size, the Royal Spider was no wiser than its smaller fellows. It threw itself confidently upon the stranger and fell away a charred ruin.

The warrior and the woman followed through the hole, but this Ormul scarcely noticed. A cold wind was blowing from the man in black. Ormul's nearest nobles, retainers and advisers stiffened, froze, and fell to shatter like glass figurines. More and more of them, and more, and all . . .

Ormul was alone.

Everything around him faded. The robed man's face was enormous, now. It filled the entire area of Ormul's gaze. It filled the sky above him, and its voice thundered down.

"My enemy Ekron Toadsoul spins a web. The poor ass thinks he will trap me. What do you know of his plans?"

In great terror, King Ormul knelt. "Nothing, my lord Pyre. I know nothing."

"Really!" the great face said, staring at Ormul as if he were a poor excuse for a king indeed. Then the voice thundered down, "That is the wrong answer!" and all was darkness.

Through that darkness ran Naroka's king, without progress. He could neither see nor hear and yet he knew that *things* were rushing at him. He needed to scream but his lips would not move. On he ran, going nowhere.

The second bubble had burst into vanished fragments.

A screaming King Ormul opened his eyes to see that he lay sweating in his own bed.

The waiting servant obsequiously inquired, "Did Your Majesty have a nightmare?"

For a moment Ormul was content only to breathe. He ran his hands over the silk sheets, then the polished ivory of his bed. A bit reassured by the touch of familiar objects, he spoke in a tone that was unusually subdued.

"More than a nightmare, Elmry. It was portent, by my father's beard! I—I am tempted to cancel this year's Games of the Snare."

"I fear that my lord king will have to do that in any case," Elmry said, with less obsequiousness.

"What? What do you—why, pray, do *you* tell me this?"

"Because no victims are available."

"By the very Web! But my—*our* dungeons are full!"

"Lord King," Elmry said, with an unseemly smile, "they are not. During the night a host of Northish sea-wolves landed and ravaged the city. They emptied the dungeons and the treasury."

"Th tr—Name of the Spider! But my army—"

"—Could do little under the circumstances. Workmen arrived at the barracks with orders to nail shut all the doors. The soldiers were inside. Since the orders bore your signature—"

"Forgery!"

"—an excellent forgery of Your Majesty's signature, and the army is so well disciplined since the recent executions, the soldiers made no objection. Oh they set up a clamor when the barracks was set ablaze, but by that time it was rather late. The few who cut their way out were cut down by the Northrons. The Royal Navy is in no better condition. The barbarians fired half the ships. The others received orders to protect themselves from fire by scuttling their ships. It's *over*, Ormul."

All these disasters Elmry announced in a voice quite cheerful. So disturbed was his king by the news that he did not notice the servant's growing disrespectfulness.

"Summon Baron Tarnok and High Priest Hogrith! They can—"

"Little man, they can do nothing. The baron's scarlet robes have two new pearls and he is not expected to live so long as noon. That Hogface is not dead is a great wonder, since the High Priest now bears the full weight of his years."

It was then that Ormul looked at his servant's face and actually saw it. His eyes bulged and he started violently.

"Demon! How dare you come here? Begone!"

"Ah, but first you must answer my question," Pyre said

equably: "What is it that Ekron Toadface plots against me?"

"Guards!" Ormul bawled. "Guards!"

To his profound relief several men in bronze cuirasses and brass helms appeared at once. Their swords were drawn and they formed a ring of iron around the wizard.

"Do you not fear my spells?" Pyre asked mildly. Despite the armed men, he still spoke with mocking calm. His face was so pleasant it was almost sweet.

"Monster!" Ormul shouted, and paused, for his voice had broken. "The world knows you and your evil! But I am n—"

"A good thing for the world, else it would know a deal more of Ekron's evil," Pyre said conversationally. "That is a fact you would doubtless comprehend, were you blessed with a working brain."

Ormul trembled, waxed red while his mouth worked. At last sound came. "You—how dare you speak thus! You are surrounded by my men! See? Their swords are pointed at you, every one!"

"So it appears," Pyre said, without taking his black-eyed gaze off the king's face. "Do you want to give them the word now or finish your declamation?"

"I am not vulnerable!" Ormul ranted. "Every hair from my head and beard has been burned, with every fingernail paring. Burned! Without some part of me or what was once part of my body, you can cast no spell on me, sorcerer!" The king's tone sounded more hopeful than confident.

"I must remember to add that to my store of lore," the wizard all but purred. "Now perhaps I am evil, Ormul of Naroka. Certainly I have sinned against humanity by taking my ease when I could have improved the world by ridding it of such as you. Make no mistake, Ormul of Naroka! You are in my hand. The fire in which your hair and nails are burnt? That fire burns from ice, Ormul. It is my fire."

Aside from fearsome information he took as threats, the King of Naroka had just heard, three times, something he had not heard for many years: his own name, unadorned by preamble or suffixed titles. That was the final factor in his decision; that was too much.

"Guards! Take this man to the lowest dungeon and put him to a slow, mean death."

"You heard him, lads," Pyre said with a shrug, and the guards stepped forward.

They seized Ormul. Kicking and screaming, he was carried down and down into the darkness and blood-reek. The scent grew and grew and the darkness seemed endless and the hands that held him seemed more and more to be something other than human hands.

Ormul of Naroka screamed and screamed, but his voice made no sound.

The last bubble winked out of existence without a pop.

Ninth Strand:

HANDS OF THE SEA

It appeared that the burly black man was planning to entertain no less than three young women tonight. Professionals, Tiana assumed. Since he still wore his ornately brocaded lord's robe of heliotrope velvet, she saw no reason not to interrupt. She threw wide the door.

"Well father, I see you didn't mourn my death overmuch!"

Two of his companions squealed and departed with jiggly alacrity. The third was delayed. It was necessary that she pick her naked self up off the carpeted floor where Caranga had thoughtlessly dumped her on jumping to his feet. His roar of joy might have affrighted a lesser demon and given some pause to a major one. He rushed to clutch his adopted daughter to him. Crushed against that barrel-broad chest, she kissed his face and ran her fingers through the tight curls of his gray-tinged hair. The third damsel, unconsciously comparing bodies with Tiana —and frowning—left with more quiet than dignity.

Caranga was not a tall man, but his heavily muscled body housed strength beyond that of most. Frequently it was also beyond his realization. Tiana soon had to warn him to cease squeezing so hard lest her ribs become casualties. He eased his grip reluctantly and tried slipping into the role of stern parent. That might have been appropriate, had they not been in a pink-and-red-and-pale-blue room in a Thesian whorehouse. Tiana wondered about the fancy robe he wore.

"Daughter: what happened? I did not give up hope for you even though we had to break ourselves free. The remains we found in the Chamber of the not-so-Sleeping Demon looked suspiciously like a thoroughly burned pig."

She laughed. "That, dear old wolf, I have never been. But first tell me of you. Once I got back here to Port Thark, I learned soon enough that you and the crew were far from prisoners! What's this about your being . . . *Lord Protector*, of Port Thark?"

"Well now that's a bit grandiose. Actually . . ." Caranga paused to smile at pleasant memories. "Ah well, it would be closer to the truth to say that I'm 'Lord Protector' of all this sweet town's, ah, brothels. See, first there was all this excitement outside our prison. Soon enough we learned that Hartes and his nobles got their sweet selves fried. So the lads and I broke out. Some Palace Prefect actually had ideas about taking over Port Thark and probably all Thesia, can you believe it? We had to take his sword away from him and wipe his nose. Off."

"Along with a squad of his men?" Tiana asked, with a tiny smile.

Caranga gestured with a hand the color of sin. "Some of them didn't want to help us. After a while a lot of them contributed their weapons to our cause. By that time the news was out. With so many lords and lordlets reduced to ash, anarchy wore Thesia's crown. Various worthies—huh, *un*-worthies, by Susha's nether smile—were already struggling for power and even the crown. (The crown is slag, but Hartes had a spare.) A certain Mother Rinalay, proprietor of the House of Absolutely Astonishing Delights, asked for my protection."

Tiana shook her head. "Can't imagine why. Is that how you came by that lordly robe?"

Caranga looked down at it, almost embarrassed. "Ah, yes. She, ah, made this . . . nice offer."

"Doubtless."

He didn't quite look at her. "While we were moving in here we were accosted by a ridiculously ambitious General

Somebody-or-other. He'd likely be ruler by now, had he not tried to establish authority by re-taking us."

"He joined King Hartes and the court?"

"What? Oh, yes. Yes. Very imposing corpse, General Whatever-his-name-was."

"You and the lads have been busy while I was . . . wandering around."

Caranga shook his head. "Busier than you know. There was another one. Tried to gain power by uniting 'his' people against all us foreign devils in the House of A.A.D. We were forced to interrupt the very pleasant meal Rinalay had laid out, to go lay him out. Along with a trifling few followers of his, of course. After that we were left alone. About the time we were, ah, settling down, another Housemother came begging our protection. They have a guild, these . . . working women of Port Thark."

"You mean the city's whores."

"Um. And so they all have a protector."

"You. And is there more, aged but thoroughly vicious father of mine?"

"Don't be snotty, little girl. Actually, yes. There was a Minister of something—I forget—who hadn't gone to see your murder—ah Tiana I'm so glad to see you! Anyhow, this sweet fellow, Leroges, stayed home that day—plotting against King Hartes! A woman came flying to us to squeal out the news that a son of the king's uncle's wife's sister seems to be in line for the throne. Nice lad, about seven. This Leroges and a squad of his followers were on their way to imprison or murder the boy."

"Oh my. Wicked man!"

"Indeed," Caranga said with spirit. "My reaction exactly. And here was this dear lady asking *our* help. Well, we helped. Leroges is, uh—"

"—with his king," Tiana suggested.

"Just so. I've no notion what to do with his widow. He was in his sixties and she's a mere slip of twenty or so, and seems to've taken a real fancy to me. At any rate, little Baron Harved is safe and heir apparent. I think Mother Rinalay will make a fine regent. We've lost a good crewman, daughter. Ole Shen Dragonbreath is now Commander of the Royal Guard, with special responsibility for Baron Harved. Prince Harved, actually."

"Hmm! Well, I'm sure we can stand the loss—scores of Thesians must be longing to join the crew of the Lord

Protector, Lord Protector!" Tiana smiled satirically. "And if we-I-mean-you can keep juggling all these many balls you've, ah, picked up in Port Thark, *Vixen* will have another very friendly port, eh? And we shall have to see that we raid no Thesian shipping."

"The . . . thought had . . . crossed my mind, yes. But enough of that! My dear headstrong daughter—I want to hear what befell *you!*"

"That is a longish and twisty tale, dear father, and my throat is dry."

He slapped a hand to his head. "Ah! O'course!" He whirled to face the closed door. "HATHEDRA! *Hathe*—oh, there you are m'girl. Hath, do be at fetching us some wine." He glanced at Tiana. "Lots."

With wine-wetted throat she unspun the epic saga of her adventures, omitting no detail of her hardihood and complete fearlessness in the face of danger, not to mention certain death. Never once had she hesitated or known the slightest hint of fear.

Caranga shrugged. "Of course, *daughter*. As you know, I myself am without fear." Then he smiled. "Well, I said I wanted to hear what befell you, and what I hear is how you befell others!"

"Yes. Well, then I . . ."

The telling (and no few wine bottles) at last finished, she brought forth the ebony box and opened it to show her ebony foster-father its unhandsome "treasure."

In the House of the Owner, beyond the halls of darkness in the Room of Sun-brightness, a shadow again appeared on the image of the world. This time it was at Thesia's far southern port and capital, Port Thark. Exultation swept the ranks of the watchers. They contained themselves and remained silent, listening.

"Tiana," Caranga's voice drifted to them across the Gulf of Night, "I'm not sure I'm liking this, ah, treasure."

With the slamming of a box lid an infinite distance away, the shadow vanished.

"Tell the Master," the chorus rose from desert-dry throats long dead. "Tell the Master that the one He seeks is Tie-anna, in Port Thaaark."

Thereafter there was silence in the Room of Sun-brightness. The image of the world lay upon the floor and round

*about it stood half a hundred mummified corpses. Their
blank dead eyes stared at the map.*

Having returned the skull to the box, Caranga stared
at the flame-haired woman who now wore Hathedra's robe.
"Daughter, as I tried to teach you these many years, there
is enough clean treasure in the world for an honest pirate
to . . . find. Best you throw this accursed filth away."

Tiana's voice was edged. "No, father. Not after all the
trouble I went through to get it."

"Tiana, daughter," he began sharply, his own temper
rising. "I didn't raise you to . . ." Something very hard in
her green eyes gave him pause. Besides the night was late,
he was well filled with wine, and several playmates awaited
him. Doubtless they were anxious and desolate. ". . . stay
up all night talking when you so obviously need sleep," he
finished, only a bit lamely. "We'll talk more of this tomorrow."

He walked none too steadily to the door. "Do keep this
room," he said, turning back to look at her. "Before sleep
takes you, as a favor to your father, please give thought to
these two questions. First, this 'Owner' is obviously not that
fool on Riser Island, but . . . who then is he? Second, the
message on yon sweet skull's jaws. Why was it addressed
to 'Adventuress'? Think on those things, daughter. Mayhap you will see what a benighted business you're head-
longing it into."

With that he was gone. Tiana was left to ponder what
were, she reluctantly admitted, rather good if unsettling
questions.

For example, the Owner. Riser Island was a tiny dismal
place endlessly swept by storms. Yet its ruler gave himself
the grandiose title of Owner. It was his absurd conceit that
he owned all the world and that all kings must accordingly
pay him tribute.

Suppose there's the tiniest grain of truth in that claim . . .

Suppose the Owner had some hold on (the late) King
Hartes and the latter had been obliged to swear subservience and pay tribute. Would not the proud (late) nobles
of Thesia be fanatically determined to keep secret such a
shameful fact?

Yes; that *would* explain no little of what happened to
her.

As for her father's second question, well—Tiana made

an end to the winejug—as far as the translation was concerned, he was right and she had been in error. The message inscribed in silver above the skull's jaws began with a definite use of the female gender. Now someone had carved that warning long before she was born. Thus it/he knew not just that the skull would one day be stolen, but that the thief would be a woman.

It's almost as if that ancient writer addressed me by name!

She knew there were Powers in the world dwelling beyond human ken. Sometimes these powers involved mortals in the dark intrigues they fought against each other. Tiana had been (too) much involved in such ghastly matters.

She realized with a little shudder that Caranga might be right. Maybe she ought to sell this jewel-housing skull for less than its obvious value, just to be rid of it.

The morning brought fresh quarrels between Tiana and her foster father. Naturally he got around to reminding her of the past and what she owed him. That he was not her natural father did not mean he was not a parent. She had been a little girl, orphaned and outcast; the bastard offspring of a then duke of Ilan. Caranga saved and adopted her. He taught her the honorable trade of piracy. The former cannibal resigned his command in her favor and took the first mate's post, so that during his declining years he might give her the benefit of his accumulated wisdom. (His declining years still seemed not to have begun.) Now what use, he asked, were all his sacrifices and care if she insisted on entangling herself in some perilous web of darkest wizardry?

Tiana hotly replied that the political games he was playing were no less hazardous. All the prisoners freed from Dindroom Prison accepted him as their leader—for the time, at least. With that unstable force he was more or less ruler of this city, true. But all hung on ropes of sand. The whole realm teetered understandably on the verge of civil war. None, save only *Vixen*'s crew, owed him any real loyalty. (She omitted mention of the fact that he had *retired*, and upon his return to *Vixen*, bored with inactivity and lack of excitement, Tiana had been unwilling to give up her captaincy. Older men, she knew, had selective memories. Tiana was smugly grateful that such was not true of her.)

Their quarrel continued, and did not end. It lost force and wound down into a compromise between people who had shared much and loved each other. Tiana would make *Vixen* ready to put to sea on short notice. Caranga would ease out of his position as Lord Protector of Port Thark. He would resign as soon as his political fortunes either declined dangerously or improved enough so that he might transfer the contents of the Royal Treasury to *Vixen*.

Tiana was fretful in the days that followed. Delay and hesitation were not her way. Too, that unconscious logic called intuition told her that a noose of some kind was tightening about her. Nights were spoiled by dreams in which she saw the dying witchwoman gasping, *"And the Hands of the Sea shall rise against you."*

She spent much time in the (unmanned) office of the harbormaster. There she studied charts and records made by generations of navigators. The river Vervex widened to form the Bay of Sundoh where stood Port Thark. The bay was narrowly connected to the sea by the Strait of Qualise. So great was the strength of the tides that one could gain the bay only with the incoming tide and leave only with the ebb. This told her that half the time the bay was a trap from which a ship might not escape. That was a situation she liked not at all.

Neither did Tiana like the fact that in these days of near-anarchy no one bothered to keep watch in the city's lookout tower. Tiana posted one of her trusted men in the tower day and night. She was not able to tell them what to look for. They did not argue. They were pirates, wolves of the sea. Keeping watch was a good idea.

The precaution was rewarded. One day at twilight Chandak Keen-eye had the high watch; a brown sailor from the southern Yabazo Islands. He came running, yelling, from the tower to collapse at Tiana's booted feet. As she looked down at that tribally tattooed face, Caranga came trotting out of his room.

"Warships!" Chandak blurted. "The fleets of every nation on the earth have come against us! The sea throngs with them! It's—it's an assembly of might like unto none seen before in the history of the world!"

He said much more, too, but it was not heard. Tiana and Caranga were racing for the watchtower. As he chugged behind her up seemingly endless stairs, Caranga cursed the past weeks of soft living. Chandak would pay dearly if this was a false alarm!

It was not. His darling daughter was there before him, and she gestured at the horizon.

Below them sprawled the panorama of Port Thark's twisted streets and black-shadowed alleys. It gave into Sundoh Bay's sandy beach and water of shimmery green, and the white chalk cliffs that separated the bay from the ocean. Beyond, stretching to the horizon, were the troubled dark green waters of the Asmygorian Sea, now splashed with gold by the setting sun.

The great wide sea was cluttered with ships.

"Susha's Name and Eyes!" Caranga muttered, while his daughter voiced a mild, "Dung!"

Nearest in view were war-galleys of Sarch and Narokan Barracudas with their blue sails. Only a little behind were the triangular sails of Bemar. Then came the Men-of-War of . . . Ilan! There she saw even the pennons of Bashan, a land-locked nation. Caranga stopped counting. Fighting ships of all sorts and descriptions crowded the waters. They bore the banners and pennons of all the world's nations. And all had come to wage war on this over-brave child he called his daughter.

"Susha forbid," he said. "Tiana: all flags sail against us!"

"Not quite," she said judiciously, her hair snapping in the sea-breeze. "By my count it's only the nations with naval bases within seven days' sail of here."

This subtlety was lost on the reformed cannibal. He snarled, "But what are we to do?"

"Offhand I'm not sure, father. They have us like a fly in a bottle." She chewed her lip thoughtfully. *All the hands of the sea have risen against us,* she thought, and wished she had not. She sought the positive side: "Still, the tides are against them, so we've a few hours' grace."

Tenth Strand:

WIZARD-TRAP

The last bubble winked out of existence without so much as a pop.

A hand was on his shoulder, shaking him. His eyes opened. He saw his servant, Elmry.

"Your Majesty was having a nightmare."

His Majesty was shuddering and had to exert effort to avoid jibbering. The words of his servant were true. Yet Ormul must wonder if he was now truly awake, or if the nightmare continued. This concerned man who stood before him, one of many whose faces he never bothered remembering . . . might he not be or become some fearful dream figure?

One thing only was clear: the wizards Ekron and Pyre were at the waging of war one on the other and Ormul was caught in the middle. He was out of choices. He must go to that shuddersome Ekron and order him to abandon his attack on Pyre. In his great fear, Ormul overlooked one fact.

King or no, he lacked the power to enforce such a command.

Ormul dictated orders, partook of a snack that gave him no pleasure, washed it down with strong unwatered wine —facing up to Ekron was no nice chore—and had himself dressed. He chose hunting clothes. Doeskin leggings flowed smoothly into high brown boots; a shirt of yellow doeskin; and a long, heavy vest of russet-hued cowhide. The broad belt was secured with a huge round buckle of gold set with four handsome sapphires the color of kittens' eyes. He attached to his belt that multi-utilitarian tool called a dagger, of course; what man would go forth naked?

His orders had been carried out and fortune favored him in one regard, at least. His chariot, fresh painted and oiled just yesterday, was ready.

To carry out the king's sham of an early hunting foray, a tall boar-spear stood in its niche on either side of the car. Almost simultaneously with the king's emergence into his courtyard his driver appeared, still lacing his tunic and donning his close leathern helmet with the royal plume. The lean, powerful fellow was the best and knew it. Naturally he said nothing about being so early aroused, but he took his time in adjusting his leather driving gauntlets.

"A-hunting so early, lord King?"

"Straight to Ekron's," Ormul muttered, "and with all haste."

The pair of excellent white mares seemed as wide awake and excited as their owner. Scarlet harness creaked, brass rang and jingled, and Ormul hung on, trying to look tall and regally calm. Without creaking, the high yellow wheels rattled across the cobbled courtyard.

As he ordered the gate opened for his passage, dismay and confusion seized His Majesty's guards (called the Brassheads, fondly or no). All at the same time, three Brasshead officers attempted to explain something to their king. To silence the idiots King Ormul ordered one executed. He had never liked that cousin of his wife's cousin, anyhow.

While the others watched mutely, His Majesty rode forth—and saw the cause of their dismay. The night sky was painted with red flames. The seaside quarter of Shamash was ablaze and the wind carried the sound of arms ringing against arms and armor, along with the screams of wounded and dying men.

The raiders of his dreams had come in reality!

"ESSSS-cort!" Ormul bawled, as he rattled out of the palace grounds.

His mind filled with a single great fear that blotted out all other concerns. He seemed incapable of aborting this pre-dawn mission that should give way to the setting up of a command center and pretending to command his generals. Somehow he could do naught but scream at his driver to go faster, to whip harder the horses. The fellow applied the lash with exceeding skill and zeal. A peasantish carter foolishly got himself in the way, and panicked as he saw the chariot racing-rattling down on him. He and his mule screamed together and the cart went over while its driver splashed his brains against the wall of the Temple of The Sacred Web.

No recompense would be paid for that one, Ormul thought; all deaths this night would be blamed on the invaders. They would be beaten back into the water of course, the cold-country curs.

At breakneck speed the royal chariot raced down streets littered with the debris of battle preparations.

Ahead loomed the mouth of an avenue lined on both sides with burning buildings. Behind the king and falling ever farther back were his guards. Though custom demanded that a squadron of Brassheads accompany and protect their liege-lord at all times, their mounts could not keep this pace. It occurred to Ormul that some pale-haired giant from the world's top edge could pop up and kill him. Thoughtfully, Ormul drew his driver's sword. He had not attempted to use a boar-spear in a dozen years.

As they sped through the inferno, Ormul grew fearful that he had lost his escort. At least he saw no Northrons. He did have to beat out a fat yellow spark on his sleeve, and another on the back of his driver's jerkin. Still he saw no enemy. He heard them right enough, unless only Narokans were being hurt and slain.

The chariot came into view of Ekron's estate. Ormul glanced back. Thanks be; here came his plodding squadron of Brassheads. Vaguely he noticed that they seemed to be mounted on spanking fresh horses. That was odd but not nearly so interesting as the four big blond men in ring-mail who came running from one side, on course to intersect the chariot. Only one had a sword; another bore a spear and two carried truly hideous axes made the more ugly by the dark splotches on their blades.

From Ekron's estate came flapping an eagle big as a horse and a half, with wingspread enough to supply a large ship with sails. With a lot of yelling and flashing of blue eyes, the barbarians tried to fight the monster, then turned and fled. Once they had vanished into an alley leading directly toward Garrison Three, the eagle became a lark and flew back into Ekron's orchard.

Now the problem was the gaining of admission into the wizard's lair. Bad enough that Ormul had come here instead of summoning Ekron to the palace. The problem with that was that Ekron might well neither have complied nor replied. Even worse seemed possible, now: suppose the enchanter kept his (?) king waiting outside his gate like some tradesman! Ormul realized that had he considered a bit he would not have been so rash in rushing here. But now his guards were banging at the gate set between the likenesses of two enormous toads, each uglier than the other no matter how often one looked back and forth. Between them crouched a huge-headed dragon of wrought brass.

"Open in the King's Name!" the biggest-mouthed Brasshead bawled. "Open for Ormul, King of Naroka and the world!"

Ormul winced. Then he swallowed: it may have been illusion, but for an instant the brass eyes of the gate-dragon seemed to hold intelligence. Certainly the voice issued from its throat:

"Follow the path of the small white flowers."

With a click, the gate swung itself open. Revealed was a pleasant green sward of grass, shrubs, and flowers.

Now Ormul, as befitted a king of Naroka, was a connoisseur of traps. Hence for all his fear and haste one corner of his mind critically examined the garden. There should have been trees, he thought. That would have made the illusion perfect. Still, while he paced down the path faintly marked by tiny white blossoms that definitely glowed, the king had to admire the cunning and the workmanship of this trap.

Ahead of them there was a slight ripple as the ground settled less than a hand's breadth; behind king and escort the ground rose again, and the flowers lost their phosphorescent glow. Aside from these manifestations there was no warning. The path felt firm and normal. Yet Ormul knew that behind and before them was quicksand.

He had laid quicksand traps of his own; hence his admiration of the work of Ekron the wizard. It was trivial to build a trap that alternated between mud and quicksand. All one need do was sink pipes into the mud and force water up through it to quicken it. Maintaining the illusion of firm trustworthy soil, now; that was much more difficult and required careful design indeed. And the powers of one of the world's two great sorcerers.

Ekron's home was in stark contrast to his beautiful and treacherous garden. The building was of black stone, squat and ugly, windowless and of obviously prodigious strength. Its design and purpose were clear: Ekron had raised an invulnerable fortress as home.

The path of white blossoms led to a featureless stone

wall. At the approach of the royal troupe, however, a false section fell to cover a deep trap and a small door opened. Beyond the dimly lit entry stood a pale young man in ivory robes. Despite his raised cowl it was obvious that his skin was an unnatural dead white.

On the king's entering, the pale man genuflected.

"Your Majesty, I am Paramane, acolyte of the mighty Ekron. How may I serve the king of Naroka?"

Ormul knew that the mage referred to himself as "Ekron the Supreme" and appreciated the acolyte's circumspection. "Call your master. We have urgent business with him."

"Glorious Majesty, my master is not here nor do I expect him for some time. I am the king's loyal subject, be assured. Gladly will I serve the king with all the art Ekron has taught me." Paramane the pallid regarded the guards. "Come, let us confer privily. Your Majesty's men are weary. Do allow them to refresh themselves with wine from that cabinet."

Ormul would have liked to join them. Moments later, though, he was seated in a dark room. telling Paramane of his dream or dreams. "Thus," he concluded, "we must obtain Ekron's promise to abandon all plans against Pyre. I am king. We cannot and will not permit any of our subjects to wage a private war that brings ruin upon the kingdom."

"Alas, Majesty, I have no way to give Ekron your message. Nor do I know more than a trifling of his illustrious plans. I am but his acolyte, humble and unfinished. Still, perhaps I may be of service."

"How?"

"I shall give Your Majesty . . . something. Then, if the egregious Pyre sends forth his execrable soul to trouble Your Majesty, he shall be destroyed." Paramane's voice was the rustle of dry leaves—or cerements.

"Bait a trap for *Pyre?*" Clearly the idea appealed to Ormul, but his fears were too strong. "No, no, we dare not."

"Dare not? Thou art king."

"Will not. No."

"Oh, but you shall," the acolyte said, and for the first time without proper form of address or exaggerated oil. Too, there was something most disturbing in his voice. (Ormul started to rise from his chair. He could not. He tried to shout for his guards but remained mute as in his dream. When he bethought him of his dagger, the king discovered that his hands seemed made of lead or stone.) Paramane continued, "We shall bait a trap for Pyre, you see, and Your Most Glorious Majesty shall be the bait."

Though Ormul Searuler ruled a nation that held many wizards, he knew little of the black arts. A bit of light glowed on a round table and he saw without understanding them the strange objects Paramane was assembling. Among other things there was an oval of smoky quartz the circumference of a man's head. This the acolyte held before the king's face. Ormul felt a sudden sharp pain, but was unable to turn his head to see where he had been cut. He felt the touch of the acolyte's hand on his flesh. The hand was cold; cold as death.

Now Ormul remembered the story he had heard years ago: that one of Ekron's assistants was a long-dead corpse. Moveless, Ormul could at least swallow.

And he could see. He saw Paramane raise a hand stained with crimson and commence spreading the red over the great smooth oval of quartz. As he worked, the quartz cleared, seemed to become crystal. An image began to form, against a background of red. *My reflection*, Ormul thought—and then he knew horror. He saw that the mole on his right cheek was on the right cheek of the image. It was not a reflection. The sorcerous mirror held his true image. That meant—

King Ormul's eyes widened, then went blank, for his mind could not contain the horror of his fate.

Paramane chuckled, a sound dry as coffin-dust. "Yes, O High Majesty. The mirror that holds a true image sucks forth the soul. Your soul will rest comfortably in my mirror, O ruler of men. Soon Pyre will send forth *his* soul to question you about Ekron's plans. Easy as landing a fish, the soul of Pyre will join yours in the mirror, and I shall break it. Perhaps my lord Ekron will enjoy wearing a necklace of quartz beads—*small* quartz beads."

The dead man bowed in polite mockery to that which had been a king. "Now if Your Most Majestic Majesty will excuse me, I must tell my master of my good work."

As Paramane turned and strode away with a rustle of pale robes, the doomed king saw a shadowy blur following behind, silent as death.

*   *   *

Following Paramane with all possible stealth, Gray moved through the chill stone halls of the toad wizard's home. Ahead he heard a door. He reached it. The ebony slab was slightly ajar. Beyond, the dead man was prostrating himself in a pale lump on the floor before some misshapen . . . object. He rose to a kneeling position under the flickering light of three black candles. Unwillingly Gray listened to the singing of invocations, a mad, unstable sound, before an image carved in green stone. The likeness was that of a large and entirely repulsive toad. The eyes seemed to be gigantic citrine topazes.

The hair on Gray's nape stirred as he saw a subtle change creep over that figure. The eyes cleared, and were eyes. Words rumbled up from the stony throat.

"Worthless servant, why do you disturb your master?"

"My lord Ekron! The unexpected has happened!" Paramane babbled. "I have seized the opportunity to set a trap for thy enemy, Pyre—may his name be destroyed and forgot. King Ormul came here. He actually seeks to deter thee from the war with Pyre, blight his name. After I gave his guards poinsoned wine, I . . ."

While the dead man told his tale, Gray stared narrow-eyed, and he wondered. *Ekron is absent. How am I to give him Pyre's deadly present?*

The image?

Yes! And by Cud and Candence—that's why I have this goose grease!

The toad had heard out the acolyte. Now it rolled its eyes of living stone and spoke in a voice like the grumble of distant summer thunder.

"It appears, meddling fly-brain, that you have not done overmuch harm. Pyre will be taken and destroyed not by your piddling efforts but by the web I have been spinning for long past telling. His doom was sealed when first I pushed aside the veil of time and saw that mighty Pyre would make a fatal error. He has done it. He has bound himself to another, a mere woman, by swearing the Third Oath. But there is no need for you to know such things. Hear your instructions! Dispose of the bodies. Retain the mirror. And send Ormul the Inconsequential on his dullard's way."

The stone figure's wide mouth remained open, but the eyes became lifeless gemstones.

Scarcely had Paramane hurried from the chamber than

Gray rushed in. Never mind the sorcery and his fears. He had to act. He bore an object that burned bright as fire and yet was cold as ice.

The stone toad's mouth was slowly closing. The spell ended, it was slipping back to its normal state. Into that tightening vise of cold stone Gray thrust his arm, and pushed the glowing blue egg deep into the throat of the statue. Though the stone was flowing shut, squeezing him with mounting pressure, his greased arm slipped out with little discomfort or effort. It was his brain that hurt, and staggered.

During the brief moments of his touching that awful image, he sensed the thoughts of the monster the world called Ekron. The thoughts were utterly alien, for the wizard's soul was that of a toad. It worshiped God-Spider in its twisted way and kept as its familiar an aid in un-clean magic, a tiny spider. One day, when it had become greater than destiny, it would eat them both.

The clangor of battle came echoing along dank stone corridors to drive the ugly visions from the mind of the Gray Knight. He hastened in the direction of the sound. He knew that Paramane had met the supposed Brassheads —his own Northish raiders—and found them quite un-poisoned.

He reached them to find one man battling a wolf-pack . . . and faring dangerously well. Though Paramane had suffered fully a dozen lethal wounds, his unnatural virility continued undiminished. His bare hands flashed with deadly speed, breaking spears and ax-hafts—and men.

Shouting an ancient warcry, Gray raised sword and charged the undead foeman. Paramane whirled at the shout —and froze. His eyes widened as they looked upon the face of the charging knight.

The man recognizes me!

The acolyte's hand flashed up to point at Gray. His mouth opened to shout the knight's name—and an ax smote Paramane's neck. The big half-moon blade rushed on, trailing a wake of scarlet, while the severed head jumped into the air. It flew, lips still moving in futile effort to speak. It occurred to Gray that with quiet, he might still read those twice-dead lips.

"Wait! Hold! Silence!" he shouted, as another of his men swung up his ax to egg-splatter the head.

Meanwhile Paramane's body continued to fight. The

deadly bone-snapping hands slashed the air as men dodged and lurched out of its path. Their warchief squatted beside the head. The face he made was involuntary.

The odor that always lingered about Paramane; it was growing rapidly stronger. Long-denied corruption was claiming Ekron's acolyte. His flesh turned from fish-white to gray to a hideous green-brown and began falling from his bones in slimy lumps. The stench of putrescence filled the chamber and Gray's stomach lurched. And that horror continued fighting the air.

Now only a skeleton remained, with tattered rags of flesh clinging to its white frame like seaweed. It ceased its blind fighting. That which had been Paramane the acolyte charged through the open front door of its master's keep. Headlong though headless it ran into Ekron's garden. But a single pace off the path of white flowers it was claimed by the quicksand. The horror of impossible animate skeleton writhed furiously in its descent into a long overdue grave.

To his men the Gray Knight snapped, "After all this you'll be wanting a drink, eh? *Well, there's no wine here!*" he shouted, and lowered his voice: "Nor anyplace else we can drink safely except back on the ships. Get the wounded back as best you can." He well knew what happened to those men whose wounds were complicated, or in the guts. He would not see them again. "I'll join you as soon as I have dealt with King Ormul."

He was not questioned. He was sent them by Pyre. He was the Warchief into whose face no man could look. All they had to do was get back to the harbor, staggering under their booty. Blond, every last one of them, they left—to pace carefully along the path marked by the small white blossoms.

Their leader found Naroka's ruler still sitting in paralysis and horror, staring into the mirror that held his soul. How to free the wretched fellow? The mirror was fastened to the table by slender chains that appeared to be silver. Perhaps . . .

A stroke of Gray's sword rent the chains asunder. The mirror became a large piece of smoky quartz. Ormul groaned loudly. Then he was free to cower in his chair and plead incoherently for mercy.

"Calm yourself, King of Naroka," the Gray Knight said in a mild tone. "Do you wish to know what instructions

the mighty Pyre has given concerning you?" Even as he
spoke, Gray frowned. *But—how . . . I do seem to remember Pyre's saying something about this man, yet that cannot be. Pyre and I have met only briefly. (Haven't we?)*
Another puzzle—and one he knew he must set aside for
now.

He lifted the oval of quartz that contained the king's
soul. "Pyre said that we ought not go too far out of our
way to slay you. Your successor would probably be as
cruel a man and ruler as you, but might lack your saving
virtue of incompetence." He handed the mirror to Ormul.
"Do take care of this, King of Naroka. Break it and you
may have bad luck!"

Eleventh Strand:

JAWS OF THE RIVER

Vixen eased out of Port Thark before the city's people
realized that the approaching armada was more than a
garbled rumor. With the moon a pallid leer above the
twilight, wind filled the corsair's sails. *Vixen* plowed
through choppy waters. At the mast's top fluttered the
banner of her called Pirate Queen: a red fox's head on a
black field, seeming to laugh in the breeze. That flag of
Tiana seemed to proclaim arrogantly that if all the world
should pursue, she would lead it a merry chase.

She was more than half a league out into the bay when
the first fireball came roaring out of the crimson sky.

It crashed and instantly spread fire and destruction on
the docks. Others followed. Salvo after salvo hurtled in
upon Thesia's capital, huge earthenware jars filled with oil
and covered with burning pitch. Some few splashed harm-
lessly into the water. Most struck the city and burst asunder to spew furiously burning oil. While Tiana and
Caranga watched in horror the entire dock area was en-
gulfed in flame. Piers, pilings, ships great and small were

swept up in lambent fire. The conflagration's light outshone the waning sun and black smoke billowed up.

Though there was little they could add to what was begun, the fireballs continued to rain from the sky. Most exploded in black smoky puffs within the raging fire on the wharf. Only a few fell short or went wild to crash in other parts of the city. There they spread flaming destruction to places hitherto spared. The screams of people suddenly trapped in inferno carried across the water.

The fools, the obscene fools! Tiana thought in fury. *If they want to kill me, that's one thing. But they're firing blind—wasting an entire city.*

For all the bloodshed he had seen and done in his many years, Caranga's eyes were also wide with horror. "We must stop this!"

"Father, if I had the power, I'd gladly send that entire fleet into Drood's arms, but . . ."

"No," he interrupted, "I mean we must sail to the mouth of the strait and let the enemy see us. Once they know they're wasting their missiles, they'll stop."

He's right. That would save the city . . . and risk my ship—and tell me something more about the enemy I must fight.

"Helmsman! Hard by steer-board!" Tiana shouted.

Vixen swung rightward and sped across the bay toward the Strait of Qualise. Still her crew heard the city's anguish. The cries drifted across the fire-bright water, muted by the sound of the wind in the rigging and the groaning of canvas.

Tiana stood in the prow, peering into the deepening gloom of smoky dusk. If it was portentous, she ignored it. She yelled minute course changes aft to Caranga—for no other helmsman would either of them trust in this dangerous maneuver. Shallow and jutting rocks lurked to steer-board, and yet Caranga and Tiana edged the ship closer to that hazard.

Again she thought it, encouraging and reinforcing herself: *This is the only way.*

At the mouth of the strait, swift current would grasp *Vixen*, thrust her out into the ocean and the waiting armaments of their enemies. The current in the shallows was weak. By racing through, Tiana could build up the speed she needed to swing across and through the swifter currents in the center.

Now they were scudding through thick shadow. Ahead lay the mouth of Qualise Strait, bloodily bathed in the sun's last red-gold light. *All this trouble and risk is for nothing,* Captain Tiana thought, *if our foes fail to see us! Wait for us, sun!* She had ordered that every polished shield and bright sword be high and on display.

A vixen shows the hounds her teeth, Tiana mused. She was fingering her long bow, its cord greased against the sea-spray. *And if that's not enough, even those lackwits will have to take note of a few fire arrows in their guts.*

Then they burst into the sunlight and rushed into the very teeth of their enemies. Despite all knowledge that none could sail through Qualise against the tide, three war-galleys were rowing their way in. Tiana was forced to acknowledge: it was a heroic effort. Then *Vixen* was within bowshot of them for several heartbeats. Tiana had been expecting to make a few long distance shots for show. Now she plied her bow in earnest.

That bastard in the ostrich-plume helmet is likely their captain, she thought, and yelled, "Two more points to port!" even as she released her arrow and snatched the next.

As the first shaft sprouted like an extra feather from the man's forehead, she loosed again and stamped her foot; she'd missed. The missile whistled past a Sarchese officer in gold-chased cuirass to flesh itself in some hapless rower. Meanwhile her crewmen were twanging their standard shorter bows. For all the surprise, there were some among the enemy who managed to raise their bows and volley back. Scarcely had this running duel begun when it was over; the range became too great for short bows. Arrows from both sides dropped into the sea.

With her longer bow Tiana continued harrying the other ships. Several men were easy targets. They fell like fatted birds at a turkey shoot. As the range increased, she could still see the black-hooded slavemaster on the nearest galley plying his whip to force more speed from the rowers. Tiana could taste her desire to see a shaft buried in that fat gut, but thrice she loosed and missed.

With the fourth all-too-precious arrow in her hand, she hesitated. Then she nocked, sighted, elevated her left arm a trifle, and released.

Bull's-eye! By Drood's grin a perfect bull's-eye!

Vixen pulled steadily away from the trio of galleys. Two

continued to fight the swift current in the strait's center. One, thinking perhaps to follow *Vixen*'s example, pulled toward the edge. The watching Tiana marveled at the stupidity of that ship's master. *Likely some idiot noble has command, not the master. Even he should be able to see that in the strait itself the current is swift everywhere, and the rocks . . .*

With a slow crunching sound like that of a great dog crushing a bone, the galley was forced onto fang-sharp rocks. It was shortly broken and ground into driftwood. For fleeting moments its purple dragon banner fluttered valiantly aloft while the vessel was rent asunder. Then ship, men and banner were gone.

In *Vixen*'s bow, Caranga and Tiana held council.

"Those galleys are going to make it right through the Eye of Qualise," she told her First Mate. "That leaves us with no choice but to flee up the Vervex River."

"Aye," Caranga nodded, "but what after that? Aren't you merely backing deeper into this trap? How far can *Vixen* flee upriver?"

She shook her head. "The Vervex branches. We can sail up Bark's Fork and take the lower branch, the Vervex-Lubok, back to the sea."

"Unless your aged father's memory fails him," he replied, watching her closely, "the Lubok isn't navigable. Any ship entering it is smashed to kindling in those sweet rapids. They are rather famous, Tiana."

"True, dear father." She smiled cheerfully. "Many a canoe and other small craft have successfully run the rapids. Large ships that accidentally enter the Vervex-Lubok have invariably been destroyed, true. No one has ever *deliberately* tried to run the rapids in a ship this size. We surely have quite a good chance."

"The reason no one has ever tried it," he exploded, "is that never before was there anyone so foolhardy as my daughter! I knew white girls had no business commanding ships—"

"Stop that bigotry! No one has ever had the finest helmsman asea at the steering oar either, O finest helmsman asea! Look here, don't you see the advantage to my plan? We are going to take a seemingly suicidal route so as to escape by a supposedly impossible exit. Likely our enemies won't have wit enough to watch the exit and we'll be loosed hounds!" She amended, "or rather a loosed fox, *from* the hounds."

The black pirate did not deign to answer. He turned and went off to make the ship as ready as possible for the coming ordeal. The while he bemoaned his having raised such a foolish headstrong daughter. She, meanwhile, was thinking about all those other ships. Men! Who had ever intended that *men* command ships at sea? Obviously 'twas woman's work, and color had naught to do with it. It occurred to her that all sea-craft should be commanded by the more patient, cleverer sex, whilst men were loaded aboard to pull oars and wield ax and sword.

Still, now she was alone with no audience for her bravado. During those moments she thought on the fearful risk she was taking and her mouth felt dry as the White Desert. *The trouble is, there just isn't any choice!*

That was true, and they entered the River Vervex under close sail. From here she could see that the fires in Port Thark had at last been extinguished—except for those in the dock area. At least they appeared controlled. Fine— but Tiana was far more concerned with what she could not see. The enemy fleet. Unless *Vixen* gained a commanding head start, she would never reach the fork in the river. Not ahead of pursuing galleys with many oarsmen. Any sailing ship, even one so nimble as *Vixen*—was clumsy going upriver. The slave-rowed galleys would have the advantage. Should they overtake . . . Tiana shook her head. She'd match her crew against any fighting men in the world, but sheer numbers hugely favored the other side.

The last rays of sunlight revealed no sign of their pursuers. That meant nothing. They were there; the race was merely against an unseen foe. *Vixen* coasted, never out of danger, through waters bright with moonlight.

Tiana paced the deck, calling an occasional order while she chewed her lip. She was dressed customarily in a long cloak of black and tall boots of black leather. Beneath the cloak she wore a sleeveless silk shirt and short leggings— tight—both of the emerald hue of her eyes. From her black belt hung her dagger and the strange weapon she favored, a slender rapier. No way around it; she could not match the strength of most fighting men. She had skill, and she was swift. The rapier was a weapon for the swift.

Twice she ordered absolute silence while she listened.

She heard nothing. The third time she heard two quite different sounds. The roar of rapids promised that the river's fork was near; the insistent drums and creaking of bending oars told her that the enemy galleys were closer still. Caranga meanwhile was tacking as much as he could while still maintaining a respectful distance from the river banks. A quick ship designed for the ocean was doing quite well, really, on this narrower waterway with its disrupted wind.

With the next turn of the Vervex, she saw the point where the river split. The area was broad. Reaching that fork meant victory and Tiana shot evil looks aloft as if to affright and spur a too-gentle wind.

Rowing was not feasible; just that.

In the dark shadows behind them a drum changed its beat. It became a frantic throbbing sound like the heart of an animal running for its life. A galley captain had spotted *Vixen*'s goal, and had ordered attack speed. Now men would be straining at their oars, breaking their hearts with the exertion. It was that or be whipped to death.

The fork of the river tantalized Tiana. It was almost within a long bowshot when the galley, a Sarchese two-decker, burst out of the shadows. It came at *Vixen* in froth, fast as a hawk swooping on prey. Captain Tiana Highrider stared.

He means to ram us.

That was frightening, but she waited, quietly. Her eyes narrowed, darted glances that measured time and distance. She knew the galley's prow sprouted a great copper spike, sharp as a bull's horn. And she must dance with this bull. *Pray Theba and father's beloved Susha that galley's captain be a man of slow reflexes, and does not hand command to ship's master or even to the beater.*

Down it sped at her, throwing white foam high on either side, oars blurring, drum *thum-thum-thumping* frighteningly. A sleek monster to spear deep, or rake *Vixen*'s flank open. Her crew jittered. Closer . . . closer . . .

Tiana screamed the command: "Hard aport!"

For several heartbeats the other vessel held course while *Vixen* eased, then swung from its path. Too late the galley veered. Speed and momentum, Tiana knew, would carry the Sarchese past *Vixen* on the steer-board side. She smiled tightly. *A clean miss. Or perhaps even better . . .*

"Drop sail! Back off two points to steer-board!"

Men sprang to obey. Nearer the galley drew, carried by the resistless force of its own speed. And *Vixen*, as if weary, slowed, swung slightly, and lingered in its path . . . almost. And the galley kept coming.

"Is that Sarchese captain *blind?*" Tiana did not know she spoke aloud.

The drum maintained its frantic beat. Oars rose and fell at a pace to kill the men who pulled them. The wind stirred, shifted.

"Stand by for full sail!"

Impact was but a few heartbeats away when the awful boom of the drum ceased. Tiana heard the shout from the galley: *"Ship oars!"*

"Too late, numb-brain," Tiana muttered. Then, "Weapons ready for boarders!"

The galley's ram hissed past *Vixen*'s hull only a few sword-lengths distant. Next moment the two ships' hulls ground together and ran grating across each other. Oars splintered like twigs under a giant's foot. Tiana knew that the men on the other ends of those oars were being pulped. Yet she had no time to give them her sympathy. From the crippled vessel grappling hooks flew. They bit into *Vixen* while arrows buzzed angrily between the ships.

She saw an overenthusiastic boarder, saw Caranga's broad sword slice him nearly in two. Another Sarchese marine came swinging over to be cut down by one of Tiana's crewmen before she could stick him.

Two, three . . . four grappling hooks firmly in place. They've locked themselves to us past any hope of shaking them off. And already the enemy had a foothold. Others joined them to enlarge it rapidly. A man actually cut past those fronting Tiana and she was not displeased to meet him with her long, long tine of a blade. Then she shouted.

"Ahoy, the galley captain! I have the black box you want! Are you interested in a truce to discuss it?" To her crew she added, "Hold your positions. Belay any attack."

Her previous command to stand by for full sail had never been followed up; *Vixen*'s canvas remained down if not furled. Locked together, the two craft were drifting with the current. A shout from the galley: the attack stopped. One battle continued with the clash of metal until a man dropped, and then there was silence. Enemies faced each other in a moment of peace stable as a soap bubble. Into that tense air the galley's captain called.

"Ye may call me Areth Duke of Jinary, pirate. Truce will be on my terms!"

"I hear you, Duke. You may call me *Captain* Tiana, and I will agree when I have heard those terms in exact detail."

"Watch'er, my lord," she heard someone say on the galley. "She's a trickster!"

Men moved aside for the passage of two cloaked individuals, one with a very black mustache and square beard under a helmet of iron and copper with a sprouting of three impossibly yellow feathers. Tiana and Areth faced each other across their ships' railings and a scant swordlength of water. The pirate was swathed in her cloak black as Areth's shaggy brows and beard. He wore armor, she noticed. She quickly discovered that his terms, too, were armored in wads of unnecessary words. What he at last said was that he demanded unconditional surrender.

Tiana favored him with her sweetest smile. "As I promised, lord Duke, I agree to all your terms completely and without reservation. The only small detail still unsettled is . . . the price of passage on my ship."

"What? What do you think you are talking about, woman?"

"You heard me, man."

Areth got the message as to what a ship's captain was called, despite her occupation or her sex: "Please explain, Captain Tie-anna."

Tiana's head made a little bow. "Aye, milord Duke Areth. You have spoken long. Our ships have drifted into the Vervex-Lubok. Already the current quickens. It is quite impossible to turn back now—especially for you, with half your oars broken and all your rowers dead or hopelessly exhausted."

(In the stern Caranga looked ahead at the swift white water and the jutting, hungry-looking rocks. *Does Tiana know we're going downriver arse-end first?* Doubtless afterward—if they survived, and with a ship—she would claim it had been deliberate, that this way he could see where the ship was going and try to steer her better.)

Tiana had been speaking in a voice loud enough for all to hear; now she addressed the Sarchese marines directly.

"Do understand. Both our ships are going down the rapids and there is nothing anyone can do to prevent it.

The galley cannot possibly survive such a passage. However! I shall accept you as passengers—provided you lay down your arms." And she began to let her cloak drift open.

"Witch, you cheated me!" Areth exploded. "Zerth—get her!"

Instinctively Tiana sprang backward. She heard an angry whistle and an arrow thudded to quiver in the deck where she had stood. She did not pause to stare at the treacherous noble of Sarch. Her dagger flashed into her hand and flashed again in air to re-sheathe itself in Areth's throat.

As he staggered back and collapsed a man pounced at Tiana. Her left hand swept her cloak open while her right whipped up her rapier. For a moment the man paused to stare at the bulges in the tight green shirt she wore, and the cleavage above the unlaced V of its neck. Many another man had reacted just as he had. They had all been run through by a long slim blade, too.

While Tiana withdrew her blade, the clangor of battle erupted anew. On two ships rushing toward disaster that was worse than useless. Just as useless would be a call for peace. Tiana joined her men, and even used the cloak ploy —successfully—against the first enemy she faced. After that she plucked it loose and whirled it around her left arm—which she also armed with a dead man's dagger. An almost-dead man, anyhow. It didn't matter. He wasn't one of hers. There. Now he was a dead man.

She surrounded herself with flickering narrow blade, and with wounds and death. The Lubok's tide carried the ships and the tide of battle was running against *Vixen*. The decks were sloshing with blood as *Vixen* raced down the turbulent waterway. Steadily the superior numbers of the Sarchese were driving her men back toward where Caranga desperately tried to steer. The enemy bridgehead on *Vixen*'s deck expanded like some relentless cancer.

Ahead Caranga saw jutting rocks like a tiger's gaping mouth. He fought his steering oar to sling *Vixen*'s wrongway bow toward that boiling white water. And he yelled Tiana's name. She pounced at a man and as he fell back she cut another. Then she whirled and ran to pounce again. She looked forward—across the stern. Rocks. Insufficient room for both ships to pass. The Sarchese helmsman was fighting, not even trying to steer. The choice as to which ship passed was up to Caranga, and she saw that he had made it. *Vixen* was swinging her hind end—which was her fore end but never mind technicalities —at the rocks. *Vixen* would never touch them; between her and that tiger's mouth was the galley from Sarch.

"STAND FAST!" Tiana yelled in a voice that hurt her throat. "Hold the line—and stand by to hold ANY-THING!"

A dagger flashed past her. One of her men stuck its thrower, who had off-balanced himself. Another loomed, blade on high to exact instant vengeance for a shipmate, and Tiana erupted an awful yell as she ran at him.

Then the crash came. It was as though a stone-faced monster rose from the depths to devour the galley in a single crunching gulp. One moment nothing, no warning. The next, big rocky fangs smashed wood and men in a great ghastly thunder. The impact sent pirates and marines tumbling, rolling over each other, clutching at anything and each other. Amid a horrid grinding a section of *Vixen*'s railing was wrenched away by the Sarchese grapples. They went down even faster than the gutted ship.

"The gods fight for us!" Tiana yelled, and her crew echoed the shout. Some were still rolling about.

The warriors of Sarch saw all hope ripped away and smashed into kindling. A third of their number were gone with the galley. They yelled their death oaths and returned to the battle with a demonic fury. Meanwhile *Vixen* jolted, wallowed, half-turned, and was swept on too rapidly to overturn. She swung wildly to and fro in her race down the river gone mad. The gods surely had as much to do with her dodging jutting boulders and great fangs of rock as did Caranga. The burly black was knocked down again and again by his own rudder, and he would have bruises on bruises. He saw a big silver coin through a dazzling silver-and-white spray of frothing water, and realized it was the moon. He would not have risked much to bet that *Vixen* was not rushing to the moon. He'd have wagered even less that they were not rushing into Drood's Arms.

Even as she yanked her blade out of a man's chest Tiana felt the deck reel beneath her. She dropped her dagger to grab a trailing ship's line. The deck, slippery with river water and blood, turned at an insane angle. Crewmen and invaders alike wallowed and were slipping over the side.

Swinging out on the line, Tiana stabbed delightedly down at her foes.

"Push the dogs overboard!" she screamed. "Overboard with them!"

Soon men were wrestling, and bodies went flying into the water. At the stern, an aging black pirate looked ahead and murmured a prayer. It was just as described in those records Tiana had thought she wouldn't bother to read: a great whirlpool; a river demon's mouth capable of swallowing *Vixen.*

Canoes had run this section of the Lubok slowly, cautiously skirting the edge of the maelstrom. *Vixen* must go straight through the center. He must try to build up her speed so as to burst through the whirlpool in a single thrust. The thing was broad enough to feed directly into Hell.

The fight against human foes was over. Several Sarchese were begging to be signed on. Among the few others, exhausted and dazed, were several bearing wounds. Now Tiana shouted to them all. They started to lay down their arms and surrender even before she bade them.

Tiana smiled—and the world dissolved anew in roaring thunder. Again those on *Vixen* were tumbled thither and yon. Tiana, still hanging onto the thick rope, looked to see a vast sucking mouth in the water, frothing that its prey had escaped. Caranga had just run the maelstrom, and they were beyond it. Tiana sighed.

I really did mean to give my father a hand with the steering. Oh, but how well he did without me!

Ahead she could make out the broad expanse of the sea. To her that meant home and safety. She raised her blood-smeared rapier on high and ran to the stern.

"It worked!" she shouted. "My plan worked!"

Still wet with spray and cold sweat, Caranga greeted her with a tight look. "Your . . . plan."

"Yes! Oh, and your genius in ruddering, of course."

He nodded, continuing to show her that same tight, unsmiling face. Pearls of water and sweat gleamed on skin like moonless midnight. Then Caranga gestured.

"We're not quite out of it, daughter. Look yonder."

She did—and saw the four warships.

"Dung! *Rat* d— By the look of them, they're Ilani Royal Navy! It isn't impossible that our friend King Hower sent them to help us . . .'"

"Aye, not impossible," Caranga grunted. "But more likely, King Hower is our *former* friend."

"Yes," Tiana sighed. Her eyes scanned the waters in calm calculation. "I don't see much hope of either fleeing or fighting them, father."

"Much?"

"Any."

"Now we're in agreement. We have no chance of— Tiana?" He was staring, frozen, at the unbelievable. For an instant she saw nothing, save that one of the four vessels was riding rather low in the water. . . . No. It was not riding. It was going down!

"Susha's milky paps," he muttered low.

"Great Cow's Cud!" she said rather more loudly. "They're scuttling a perfectly good ship!"

Before her incredulous eyes, men were leaving the sinking ship in small boats. They were all in calm good order, as though at practice. Smallboats were departing from two of the others as well! Moments after their departure, all three vessels' decks were awash with flame.

"One sunk and two ablaze," Tiana murmured. She shook her head as though to throw off the mystification. The remaining ship was sailing to meet them at the mouth of the Lubok. Even at this distance she could hear the sound of axes. The sailors were methodically chopping their ship into a ruin!

"Ahoy, *Vixen!*" the call came over the calm sea. "Request permission to come alongside without arms."

"Granted, Admiral Voltadin!" she called back, having recognized the voice from Ilan, whose capital, Reme, was her home port. "And do tell me why you are sinking your own fleet."

"Hardly a fleet, Captain Tiana. But it is a ruse to fool the enemy."

Well, at the very least I'd say it will certainly confuse them!

"My orders come from Hower, King of Ilan," Voltadin called, even while his big ship eased in alongside *Vixen.* "The king ordered that I publicly join the armada that pursues you. Secretly I am to aid you. My lord king was especially urgent that I must get this letter to you. Once I saw the tactical situation at Port Thark, I contrived that my flotilla would guard this exit. None others wanted to

bother! Knowing you, Captain Tiana, Captain Caranga—
I guessed what the others could not imagine . . . that you
would attempt what no other mariner would dare. You
did! You have run the Vervex-Lubok! My congratulations
to you both on a remarkable feat of seamanship."

"My First Mate was at the rudder. Caranga deserves all
credit. But you still have not explained why those ships
are being thrown away, Admiral."

The ship from Ilan bobbed closer and she could see the
movements of Voltadin's white beard as he spoke, wheez-
ing a bit. "My failure must be explained, Captain. I am going to claim that my flotilla faithfully guarded this river
mouth, but that you forced past us by using powers
arcane."

Now the ships were close enough for Tiana to see the
admiral's cool blue eyes set in a face of aged marble that
vanished into that snowy beard.

She said with continuing incredulity at the sacrifice,
"That means three ships gone entirely and a fourth crippled. All merely to give color to a lie that will not long
fool anyone!"

"True, Captain. But when you read King Hower's message, you will see why time is so precious. It's in a whaleskin wrapping. Please stand back—it's also weighted for
throwing."

Tiana heard the admiral pass a quiet order, and she and
Caranga drew back. A few moments later a dark packet
thudded to the deck—and squished, in blood. Tiana was
glad for the waterproof wrapping of the message from
King Hower, who usually had about as much foresight as
a moth once it spotted a lamp. She assumed Voltadin had
thought of this, and too that he had planned for the care
of his men.

"We have lost perhaps a halfscore men with more
wounded," she said into the night, "and have Sarchese
prisoners aboard. I should love to hand them over to you
—but I can see that you couldn't hope to explain how you
came by them! You don't happen to have a few men
aboard who wish to depart the Royal Navy for a month or
several aboard *Vixen,* have you?"

No excitement-lover aboard Voltadin's ship was given
opportunity to express his enthusiasm. "No," the admiral
said.

Nasty old pirates, Tiana thought, *shouldn't ask for honest*

*naval men to supplement their nasty crews, no matter what
we're doing for king and country!* Aloud, she courteously
bade Voltadin thanks and farewell. The ships moved apart.
Vixen, wind filling her sail, swept away into an ocean
sparkling with moon-silver.

Twelfth Strand:

A PYRE IN AN ALE MUG

Under a snarly, storm-threatening sky the twelve long
ships rode at anchor. Their crews were gloriously drunk.
If the mood of their mistress changed they would sober
quickly enough; their mistress was Awairna. The sea.
Fickle Awairna, they called her. Her lover too was fickle
and a traveler, else she'd not at times be so sweetly placid
and at others so stormy and petulant.

On the deck of the largest ship paced a man in dull
gray surcoat and matching greatcloak over blue-gray mail.
His was the mission. His was the responsibility. He had no
name. He was not sure whether he had a face. He worried
for them all.

For the moment they were safe from Narokan pursuit. Of the warships that chased them off Shamash, only a
few had dared follow them through the Strait of Sytheas.
There turbulent white water fanged with rocks like the
jaws of a gigantic shark had smashed those ships to kindling. For the moment the Gray Knight was a hero to his
men; he was the warchief who led their blond horde in the
plundering of their ancient enemies. Were he to ask they
would gladly follow him to Drood's domain and wrest the
bracelets off that grim god's Thousand Arms.

The Gray Knight's problem was that he was their hero
and master but not his own. He'd no idea where to go or
what to do next.

The wind punished his face with salt spray as he bent

toward the last remaining barrel of beer. Other men were
finding solace, even answers, in ale mugs. While he did
not expect to accomplish that, at the moment it was as
good a place to look as any. He filled a jack and with a
sigh raised it toward his lips. Then he jerked, stared and
cursed. The reflection in the ale—beer, really—was Pyre's!

For a single long moment the wizard regarded the Gray
Knight in silence with his calm, calculating eyes.

"Did you not say," Gray demanded, "that you couldn't
give me any help, not even advice?"

"I did," the amber-hued image answered blandly. "Nor
have I any intention of helping you. You, however, may
help me by reporting on the progress of your quest."

Gray gestured at a puddle of sea water on the deck.
"Would you mind moving? I do hate to let this Narokan
almost-ale go to waste."

When Pyre obligingly stared up at him from that wet
wooden surface, Gray drank. "Thanks, mage-image. Progress: I've managed to learn part of what you should have
told me to begin with. You wizards can foresee the future
but once you've seen it you cannot change it. Too bad if a
mage were to learn when he was to die! Thereafter he'd
have no choice but to march down the road to that death
like a pig led to slaughter. Someone else's death, now . . .
that is a simpler matter. You could see precisely when a
man would go to relieve himself and be waiting with sharp
iron. Or you might see which of a thousand wine bottles
he may drink next year or the next and put poison in that
one bottle, long before the time. This is correct?"

"You are talking," Pyre said, eyes bright as those of a
bird of prey. "I am only listening."

"Hmph. Then such, my *dear* friend Pyre, is the snare
Ekron weaves for you. With the aid of his familiar, a
spider, he spins a web. It is in the hands of those Blind
Ones who weave the tapestry of the world. He arranges one
circumstance and then another into a pattern; an altered
destiny that will destroy you."

"Wait," Pyre interrupted. "That altered destiny you
speak of will destroy *us*. Make no mistake: our fates are
linked. We two form a sort of web also, you see."

"No, I do not see. I know only that you're the one who
blundered into this and dragged me after! You looked to
see what Ekron was plotting and saw too much, didn't you!

You saw either your own death or circumstances that imply it! That's why you are paralyzed and I have to do everything for you. For *us*. Isn't that so?!"

The puddle of sea water was only that, and yellow-bearded men stared rather anxiously at their leader. He shook himself as though he woke from a dream. He glanced around. *Firebird* rocked at sea-anchor. Her master was one of several staring at Gray.

"Warchief? You spoke with Pyre?"

"Yes."

Tall Northmen exchanged glances and a few knowing nods. Their leader—after the Gray Knight—spoke again. "The wizard spoke to you, Warchief?"

"Yes."

Blaze nodded. "He says we done well, Warchief?"

"*I* say we did well, Blaze Blazetop! I do not serve Pyre; I act for him." Gray peered into his mug. It contained neither ale nor beer nor mage. A man hurried forward.

"Let me fill 'er up for yourself, Warchief."

"Thanks, Skiller."

"Any orders, Warchief?" That was Master Blaze again.

"No. I've got to do some thinking, Blaze."

Blaze nodded and whirled to show Gray a back that looked broad as a door in its brass-ringed leathern armor-coat. Delighted to have something to do, he bellowed, "Warchief's got to do some thinkin' now, and you mules know how good he is at it! Everybody shut the blight up while the Warchief thinks!"

Gray turned away, but not to hide a smile. Already he was gone away into himself. From time to time, absently, he glanced into the mug.

He had not known those things he told Pyre, not before the wizard appeared! They had sprung into his mind during the conversation. Triggered by Pyre's request for a report? He did not know. He was sure he was an aristocrat, a man of birth and breeding and warlike training. How and why then did dark knowledge sometimes come unbidden, like a freshet from hidden corners of his mind?

What manner of man am I?

Angrily he dismissed the question. Whatever his lost memories might hold, they would not change *him*. He was a man who always did what was necessary, however grim that necessity might be. Just now what he had to do was find that gemstone woman: her of the ruby hair and emerald eyes. What he had seen in Ekron's thoughts made it plain that she was the key to this Drood-begotten affair. What he would do to or with or about her once he found her was an open question. It would be whatever the situation required.

Thirteenth Strand:
THE EYES OF THE SKY

The Sarchese captives were being "initiated" into *Vixen*'s crew. The ship's captain sat alone in her cabin and gave no heed to the occasional cries of agony. Later she would make whatever surgical repairs were necessary. Now she must study this message King Hower sent at the incredible cost of four good ships.

Within the sheathing of whaleskin she found a scroll within a scroll. She laid one aside and read the one from King Hower, whom she had served better than he ever had her.

Tiana, Captain of the ship *Vixen*, a Greeting from Hower, King of Ilan and your lawful sovereign

When you rescued my daughter the Princess Jiltha from such extreme and dire peril, I thought that I and the entire kingdom owed you a debt which could never be repaid. It now seems that I greatly underestimated your ability to inspire disaster; you have done a heavy deed which sends winds blowing across the world, winds in which monarchs in all their power are but leaves.

Howsomever, peradventure you have made trouble which should be, in your own words, treated as a boil: lanced and cleaned rather than allowed to fester. If in all the world there exists one who can bring a bright outcome from the present darkness it is yourself; accordingly I have decided to give you what help I may, probably at cost of my life.

No secret has ever been more diligently kept than that which shames all rulers: the fact that we are all slaves to the true ruler of the world: the Owner.

Inasmuch as the Owner cares neither for appearances of power nor for its responsibilities, we are each free to wear crown and royal robes and rule our domains as we choose; this is provided we swear subservience to him and pay tribute as he demands. With one exception these demands are so light as to be trivial; a bit of gold now and again, a few leaves from a sacred forest, and suchlike; nothing in crippling quantity.

I spoke of one exception. It is exceedingly heavy. With the advent of each season the Owner picks some nation and the king of that land must deliver up one hundred young women, all passing fair. So as to maintain the secrecy we and the Owner desire, seldom indeed is the entire tribute dispatched at once. One is not happy to employ that term "dispatched," Tiana; indeed their fate on Riser Island none can say; indeed again, naught is known of that dreadful isle so far south. Any merchant ship forced there by storm or other accident is never seen again. Whatsoever the Owner requires from the outside world is conveyed to Riser by his own black-hulled ships crewed by his fearsome servants, the Moonstalkers.

For no reason that I understand, during my reign the Kingdom of Ilan has been spared the payment of this unspeakable levy.

My father, Oorer King of the Remilani, had a mistress; a tender and gentle woman whom he loved truly; the Owner claimed her. My father wept for days, and sent her off never to be seen again by human eyes. That day, I, Hower, King not yet then, made vow that were I king no subject of mine should ever go to so vile a fate—whilst I lived.

Now I keep that vow.

The penalty for rebellion against the Owner is, of course, death. Even in that there is horror beyond death; some maintain that those slain by the Owner's devising return to serve him; revenants, liches. That is inconceivable and unthinkable.

The Owner's habit is to play cat-and-mouse with his victims, displaying his power to slay in many horrible ways before striking the final blow. Some monarchs have refused to submit sheep-like to their own slaughter; thrice to my knowledge and doubtless on other occasions, expeditions have been prepared in great secrecy and launched against that unknown which is Riser Island. Of these vast hosts of ships and men no trace was ever found; not so much as a bit of driftwood or scrap of pennon.

Thus though I command a great army and navy, they are powerless to help me and my life is entirely in the hands now of Captain Tiana Highrider of *Reme*.

Somehow you acquired a mysterious object which the Owner fears. Use it! Destroy him! You have fought blackest magic and unholy powers before, Tiana, and prevailed; do so again!

The details of strategy and tactics I leave to your decision. Such useful information as my spies have gained over the years I enclose. We all must live in the world, Tiana. If in you exists any love for your native land, strive; make an end to the Owner before he or it learns of my rebellion and slays me.

Hower, King of all the Ilani

Tiana stared at the scroll as it rerolled, seemingly restless. She was blinking, trying to decide if this was some monstrous joke or if the world at large had taken leave of its collective senses. (She had wondered about Hower's for years. But then she knew that she questioned all who ruled. Tiana knew of only two people in all the world who were fit to rule. Well . . . three, including that handsome Prince-now-King Eltorn of Collada! Of the other two, one was . . . Tiana.)

Certainly the handwriting must be that of Hower's secretary, and these were the king's own scrawled signature and pretentious seal. She made a face, toothing her lower lip, gazing at the scroll.

Within the Sun-bright Room a hundred dead eyes watched, unblinking in mummified faces, waiting for the

shadow to appear on the image of the world. The Master
was ready now, ready with deadly swift-striking power.

Tiana unfurled the second message from Reme. It was a
report from Duke Redlands, the king's master spy.
Thoughtfully she read its summary of the knowledge
gained from Redlands's years of patient observation.

The Owner, she learned, imported all manner of strange
goods. Minerals of no known use. Stones that had fallen
from the sky, or supposedly. Glass that had poured as
roiling liquid down the slopes of a volcanic mountain.
There were other oddities. No pattern could be discerned,
except that nothing preferred by the Owner was of the
ordinary or "normal."

With meticulous care the Spy Lord recorded the details of the Owner's demands for young women. Despite
storied tradition, he did not specify virgins. In spring he
might specify young mothers from the farming district of
Bemar; at summer's beginning "whores and mistresses"
from Port Silvar; as fall opened the group would be from
a different area. The record of horror spanned many years.
Many were the shams employed by monarchs to meet the
Owner's demands without their peoples' being aware of
this bleeding off of so many young females. Indeed, the
haphazard birth records some nations bothered to (try to)
keep indicated that Nature had compensated, as after a
mighty war; the female birth rate was slightly higher.

No one knew whether this was a natural phenomenon or
whether the Owner "repaid" his depredations. No one
knew who—or what—the Owner was. No one had seen
him—at least no one who had lived to comment.

Reading Redlands's dry, impersonal account of these
events involving thousands and thousands of innocent
women and girls, Tiana shuddered. She had to believe it.
So well had all this been covered up that not even she had
known or suspected!

Within the Owner's actions, milord Duke believed, a
pattern could be discerned. Those selected as tribute were
always either identified by name or specified in some detail as to place of birth and station in life. The Owner
knew. It was as if the Owner were . . . God. If one assumed that each woman had an astral sign corresponding
to the date of her birth, one looked in vain for correlation.
Redlands had persisted. If one assigned an astral sign to

her *position in the world,* it became evident that the Owner was acting in accord with the stars! How and why were unknowns.

If the stellar configuration at the solstice was Picarus rampant above Nevinia, the Owner's tribute demand was predictable: it was Nevinia who sent 100 women; 100 virginal nuns, for instance, to Riser Isle. If Sycore stood above Bemar, then that nation must be drained of all who might become the future noble ladies of that land.

"In advising you of the above, Captain Tiana," Redlands wrote, "One has obeyed our king. One does not share his hope that you will be able to accomplish anything useful in the present emergency. One wishes that you had not brought it about. (One ignores the fact that all was precipitated by the One called the Owner; no emergency existed until you . . . did what you have done.) Indeed our belief is that Ilan must look to its own resources, for there are none who might aid a man or a nation or a king.

"Some years ago one contrived to send a message to the dread mage called Pyre. It asked his aid against the Owner. Pyre replied that 'You know not what you ask'; that against such an opponent even he could do naught. Moreover, that mighty and arrogant wizard said, even if he could he would not! 'The present balance of power between good and evil in the world,' he said, 'is to my satisfaction.' Perhaps the Owner is that ultimate deity called God. Pyre is . . . godlike. Neither is easy to love or like.

"The great and powerful white wizard Sulun Tha is commonly accounted Pyre's equal and opposite. From Collada he messaged that he too is helpless before the power of the Owner. Certainly one did not make any such query or request of Ekron!

"As for what you, Captain, ought do. If you have aught that may be helpful, pray contact me. If not, the best advice would appear to be: Hide and preserve yourself as best you may! Women with beauty such as yours are all too rare.

> "Fare thee well, Captain Tiana.
> —R."

Tiana threw down the scroll and cursed fervently and with eloquence.

"Ilan's king is a sheep and his ministers are wolves,"

she muttered, slopping wine into a handsome mug once taken off a Zadakan ship. While that well-meaning old man cowered and begged her aid, Redlands let her know that he was handling the matter and she ought not to bother him. Or the Owner! *Ilan must look to its own resources!* Indeed!

My bet is that this means Milord Spy is preparing some secret assault on that blighted island! Great Cow, the idiot! Soon thousands, tens of thousands of men—young men—will spend their lives in foredoomed stupidity. Why can't the gatherers of "intelligence" be intelligent enough to stay out of tactics?

As she thought about it her hand quivered with anger so that she sloshed wine over her chin, and worse. It splashed coldly down into the cleavage between what Caranga called "a pair of melons—tahlequah melons." That startled her so that she dropped the lovely cup of thrice-dyed, thrice-fired clay. It shattered. Wine splashed over her bare feet and up her leg. In leaping up and dancing away she nearly fell; in stripping off her shirt of silk green as slawgrass, she tore it. Now the mounting rage of frustration sent the torn garment hurtling across the cabin. It seemed almost to swerve, and drop beside what she had begun to think of as The Box. She stared at it while her eyes blazed and her bosom heaved.

She snatched up the lid of the ebony box and yanked out the skull.

"It's all because of you!" she fair shouted. "I am a fugitive with the entire world in pursuit of me and my homeland in dire peril—all because I had to find *you!*"

At last the shadow appeared in the shadowless room!

Exultation rose in half a hundred parchment-dry throats, only to sink unexpressed. The identifying shadow was in the midst of the trackless ocean and moving rapidly. Would it remain visible long enough for them to learn its course and direction?

Avidly, the Watchers watched.

Still glaring at the ugly shell of human bone, Tiana snapped, "*All* this trouble is because of you! Every time I open this Drood-sent box I am *attacked!*"

She stopped.

By the Sacred Cud! That's true! On both occasions the

*timing was such that my attackers must have started short-
ly after I opened this blighted casket!*

Caranga tapped and entered her cabin just as she
breathed, "Sacred Udders of the Cow Whose Rumination
created the World!" He paused, staring, and nearly forgot
to close the door behind him.

"Well, that's an appropriate oath," he said conversationally, continuing to stare, "though those beauties would
look strange with four nipples each, daughter. I am sorry
I entered at the wrong time, Tiana. The initiation is over.
Three of our new hands need some patching; a stitch or
two here and there . . ." He trailed off as at last he raised
his gaze to her face. He saw the writhing set of her mouth
and the blazing green fire of her eyes and knew that he had
entered at an inopportune time indeed.

Strangely, she stared at him—not seeing him, he was sure
—and whispered.

"I found this thing in a specially designed room, a room
where it could not cast a shadow. Is there something strange
about its shadow? It would have fallen on that great map
or replica of the world." She held up the skull and seemed
to stare into its eyeholes, and then at the chart-table beneath. "Once Caranga fought shadows. . . . This one *is*
strange. . . . Rather . . . pale; as if 'twere only . . . half a
shadowww . . ." She held her other hand beside the skull,
so that the hanging lamp etched their shadows side by
side.

That made it obvious. She stared at a normal shadow
and a pallid one. And with that enormous gemstone inside,
the skull was more substantial than her hand! *By the Back!
That's it! It's* half *a shadow! The other half is . . . somewhere Else . . .* "—betraying our location!"

"Uh—daughter?" He raised a restraining hand as she
started to put the skull back in its box. "I'd like to examine
our friend a moment longer, please."

"Caranga! When did you come in? Oh, but—"

He plucked the skull from her hand and gave it a long
hard look. It was he who restored the grim object to its
container. Hurriedly Tiana snapped down the lid. She was
trembling, but no longer in rage. She had discovered truth,
and she was sure of it. Now if only she could know who, so
long ago, had placed the thing there along with a message
to . . . her?

I wonder how old Pyre and Ekron truly are, she mused.

At the same time Caranga was muttering, "Hard to imagine the face from the bone under it. Still . . . I have this strong feeling that some time in the past I *met* our late friend."

Tiana stared at him.

Joy among the dead! Laughter and mirth in the withered faces of corpses! The shadow had remained long enough before it vanished. The Master's Power was launched against a certain target, and how could they fight an attack from above?

"Father . . . how can that be? Whoever this He-Who-Sleeps was, he died . . . centuries ago."

Caranga shook his head. "All this is too much for an honest man of weapons. Pray Susha that we never learn the answers to such dark questions, my dear. And those things you muttered . . . we must talk of that. But now . . . if my daughter and the captain would not mind calling the ship's physician? The wounded are waiting."

"Wounded?"

She *had* been distracted. "Three initiates?" he said, in the tone of one reminding another of what should be known.

"Oh. Of course. Here, let me get my tools." She picked up the oilskin bag containing her superb surgical instruments and started for the door. "I need something to do right now."

By Susha's holy paps—she doesn't even know what she's doing. "Ah—daughter. They can wait long enough for you to get a shirt or tunic or something on. You're, ah, bouncing rather distractingly."

She turned back to stare blankly at him, then looked down at herself. "Oh! Why didn't you tell me?" Bouncing distractingly, she headed for her locker.

"Uh—"

"Ha! Don't bother formulating an answer, dear aged but lecherous father! Hate to see tahlequah melons stuffed into a sack, don't you!" And she slipped a plain homespun tunic over her head. "Gray's a nice color, don't you think? Gray." For a moment her eyes flickered, as if the color or the word meant something to her.

Caranga coughed. Tiana said, "Well come *on,* father!
Those poor men are *waiting.*"

The moment she had done ministering to the new crewmen, Tiana ordered a course change. She was obeyed by
men who frowned. The new course she mandated would
take them to the same destination, but not as directly or
presumably swiftly. If what she suspected about the skull's
shadow was true, danger might be seeking them on their
former heading.

To Caranga she was cryptic; she wanted him well rested.
Once he had retired to his cabin, she hurried from hers.
All through the night she paced the decks. (One of the
new men watched her, swallowing. Looked like a temptress
in a temple of Shamash of the Blood Arena, she did! *Walks
like a prowling tigress, she does.* And O mighty Back—
what claws that temptress-tigress-healer has!)

The new course and the old were not greatly different.
They could not be, without executing the ridiculous, which
would require a complete explanation. That, Tiana did not
care to do. Men had been known to mutiny when they
learned or suspected that their captain was deliberately
leading them into ireful danger. And the menace that
sought them upon the old heading might still find them on
the new. (Not, of course, that the fearless Tiana was worried about such things. She was merely watchful; cautious;
a good captain.)

When at last her long watch was eased by the first red
rays of dawn, she relaxed and breathed more easily. Deliberately asking one of the new men—he was from the Fanwood area of Calancia, not Sarch—for a bite to eat, she
hurried below to wash her face and get her boots on.

She returned to stare at the sky. While the rising sun
painted the eastern clouds with burning gold, the west remained the color of Caranga. Out of that Simdan darkness
a tiny yellow light was flashing. It appeared for an instant;
disappeared; reappeared. Cold fingers touched Tiana's
heart.

*Either it's getting brighter or it's coming at us at an im-
possible speed.*

The light, though low on the horizon, was definitely
above the water. Something fire-bright was flying toward
Vixen, over the sea, and it certainly was not a gull or even
a lost vulture. Tiana whirled to raise a shout.

"ALL HANDS ASSEMBLE! BOWS, BOWS—we're at-tACKed!" And to the first man who caught her eye: "Jemora! Fetch my longbow and quiver from my cabin!"

Men assembled noisily, looking this way and that. Their captain quelled their noisiness and their milling. The tiny yellow light was no longer tiny as Tiana spoke to her crew.

"This will be no ordinary battle. Every man on my right hand: string your bows and be sure your arrows are close to hand. You at my left hand: fetch buckets! Douse the decks, douse the sail. When that's done, start dowsing each other! Step lively you rogues, unless you want to swim home."

"Captain—what is it we face?"

She gestured. They looked. They scrambled. At the same time Tiana saw Caranga approaching.

"You know what we're to face?"

"Aye," he said, and his face was funereal. "We may have a chance—two. I have two harpoons aboard, remember? I'll fetch them."

Tiana accepted her bow and arrows. "Thank you, Jemora. Help Caranga now. First Mate: Do both harpoons have plenty of cordage?"

Caranga jerked his head in a single violent shake. "One has none at all and I was too damned stupid to bring any from Port Thark."

She considered. "In that case save the roped harpoon for the second pass?" She waited while he nodded, and she was grateful he avoided saying "If there is need for a second pass." She went on, "I'll try to give you a good shot the second time. We'll have to withstand one, that's all. It means we'll take some punishment, but that's not to be helped."

"I'll get the sweet little harpoons, Jemora," Caranga said. "I'm no weakling. You scare about and fetch every bit and piece of oilskin and hide you can find—anywhere!"

She looked aloft. The flashes were brighter now. The thing was closing fast. She must decide on a battle plan, and she must be fast. Oh, for a catapult or lance-flinger! Worse, the enemy was coming out of the darkness, nearly invisible, while it would see *Vixen* outlined against the eastward glow. It would soon be diving at them out of the dark. The wind was from the west. Likely the blighted thing would circle and come in from that direction on its second strike, also.

Men were banging buckets and sloshing water. They kept glancing up into the blackness. It didn't matter. Water was needed everywhere.

Chandak Keeneye came to the captain. He turned, stared into the dark, squinting. "Captain? Those flashes . . . rushing toward us . . . what is it? That—it is flame!"

"Yes. A dragon, Chandak."

"I thought they were all—yes. It is. Sorry, Captain."

"Take the helm, Second Mate. Bring us to a course just north of due east."

As he departed, Tiana saw Caranga again approaching through the melee. He was dowsed. The burly man neither smiled nor deepened his frown. The seaman looked frightened, until he remembered that the cap'n had ordered everyone well splashed. He'd like to get the job of throwing a nice big bucket of water on Captain Titsiana!

"Harpoons in order, daughter. Now a man can throw one just so far, and that thing can destroy us from just about twice as far."

"I know. I said I'd try to give you one good cast."

"If we survive this one, Tiana, I'm for throwing that blighted box into the sea!"

"First let's concentrate on getting out of this one, father," she said, touching his arm high. "But—that won't be necessary. All we need do is not open it anymore!"

He blinked. "Wonderful. As soon as I think of a good sensible reason to hang on to a big jewel that's inside a skull that's inside a box that we can't open without attracting fleets and armies and Firebreaths, I'll send you a message."

Tiana hastened to the stern. *Vixen* was running precariously with the wind; the pursuer was coming fast as the wind. It was overtaking. Now Tiana could see something above the yellow flashes: two dull green glows, not quite round.

Now I look into my enemy's eyes, she thought. *Soon it or we shall be dead*. And she called out anew: "ALL RIGHT! The sails are wet enough. Drench everyone aboard. Everyone." She glanced at a sailor standing close by, with a big wooden pail in his hand and a most uncertain look on his equine face. "I said everyone, Versin," she said with a tight smile, and she posed.

Versindoga of Bashan blinked, swallowed, nodded, grinned and hurled the contents of his bucket over his captain—as did two other men at the same time. Tiana staggered and spluttered.

"Enthusiastic lot, aren't you!" Thoroughly soaked, she pushed dark red strands of sopping hair out of her face and looked aft. "Now drench each other. FAST!"

Now a black face was outlined by each flash of yellow. A vast reptilian face, the glowing eyes green as moss above widely flared nostrils and powerful jaws studded and aglint with sharp fangs like daggers. With its every breath, yellow flame surged from its nostrils and mouth.

"Captain!" she heard, and hardly noticed as a former Sarchese marine hung a whaleskin stormcoat over her head and fastened it at her throat.

Tiana was staring at the oncoming Eyes of the Sky. It was very close, not beyond four or five bowshots. In a moment it would begin a dive like that of an eagle onto a rabbit. Slowly, thinking, she drew and set an arrow to her long Thunlandish bow. She held it high.

"Careful about slipping on that wet deck, lads! NOCK ARROWS! Wait as long before loosing as courage allows —and then don't run—watch for where the flame comes. Do NOT aim at the head. DO AIM at the hindquarters. Even a dragon will feel an arrow in its privates!"

She saw a few appreciative grins and heard even fewer chuckles.

Then the huge black form was rushing from blackness, rushing down upon them. Tiana yelled "Pull!" The dragon was upon them, looming too huge to be believed, wings like black sails that gusted a wind of their own—and it seemed to be sucking a deep breath. "Loose!" she shouted, and sent her arrow speeding at a nostril. A flight of arrows sped up into that gigantic animated cloud of darkness. Most were accurately aimed—the monster was hard to miss—for there was the sound of wood snapping, as if the shafts had been loosed against a stone wall. Tiana's arrow missed the nostril and drove through a wing, which was about as debilitating to the dragon as a savage gnat bite. The dragon exhaled.

Amid a horrid stench a cloud of flame gusted down to sweep over *Vixen.*

Men screamed and knots of them tried to dive and run in eight directions at once. Tiana dragged wet whaleskin around her and felt the searing heat just the same. She had to close her eyes; she learned only later that, like a lot of others on *Vixen,* she lost most of her eyebrows in a moment.

The dragon swept past the raised partial deck at the bow, and the big black man there. A harpoon was a clumsy weapon, but it sped from his hand as if it were a light spear. Caranga knew as he loosed it that it was a futile gesture. That didn't stop him from cursing when the big shaft splashed into the sea. Then the dragon brought its wings down in a hard flap to gain altitude, and Caranga was staggered. He did not quite fall, and cursed the more.

The dragon was beyond *Vixen,* outlined against a gold sunrise. Tiana was not heartened by this first view of the monster. The area of its wings was greater than that of *Vixen's* sails. The wings more resembled those of a bat than a bird. She could see little of the shape of the body, save for the long narrow tail. Contrary to some legend, there was no spear or arrowhead at the tail's tip.

The dragon was circling to gain altitude and soon, she knew, it would come hurtling at them again. She glanced around. Several men were burned, but none fatally. Others were rapidly extinguishing small fires and re-saturating the sails. Tiana turned to Chandak.

"Keeneye: stand by to come hard aport."

His face showed his consternation and doubt of her wisdom. "But—Captain, we daren't bring this ship across the wind. She'll jibe! You'll un-mast her!"

"You're right. We may well lose our mast. We must take that gamble, Chandak—the alternative is to lose the ship —and us all."

Slowly, he nodded. "You're the captain."

She looked steadily at him for a moment before lifting her face to gaze aloft. Again the dragon was become a yellow flashing in the darkness. As Tiana had expected, it had swung back so as to come at them again from the un-natural dark. It would pass to port.

"TAKE COVERRRR!" she bawled, and down the length of the ship her gaze met Caranga's eyes. He understood. He knew. It was up to him. Arrows were completely ineffective.

Again she stared at the oncoming monster. *It does not belong in this world,* she thought. *Dragons do not fit. Dragons do not bel—it must have been brought here from one of those other . . . existences, or "cycles of the cosmos" Pyre talked of. "There are those who were before Man,"*

*he had told her, "and they seek to re-enter this world from
which they are banished. There are dwellers in the cosmic
abyss of the eternal night. . . . It is the art of a wizard to
invoke these beings by spells and by deceit and guile, and
bind them to his will. But—there are others. These others
are non-beings, which are not part of this cycle of the
cosmos. Their presence is a violation of the order and har-
mony of the universe."*

Yes, Tiana thought, *like a flying reptile that is bigger
than a ship and breathes fire. Such a horror never grew in
this world—this "cycle of the cosmos!" How came it here,
then? The Owner? Ekron? Are they connected? Suppose
. . . Ekron? Could he have put that accursed box there for
me to find? But if so—why me? It's Pyre Ekron wars
with—*

The dragon was coming. Everything depended on timing. Any other thought was extraneous. Superfluous to
waste time speculating when she might be dead two minutes from now! Already it looked close enough to touch,
but that was an illusion caused by its immensity. Her
mouth was dry and her hand quivered and still a calm
voice at the back of her brain was whispering, *Not yet!
Not yet—Now!*

"HIT THE DECK! HARD APORT!" And she had to
skip away from Chandak Keeneye's violent putting over of
the steering oar.

In the moment before *Vixen* responded, Tiana knew
fear that she might have waited too long. Then the wind
grasped the sail and the boom swung violently. Every man
had dropped or taken whatever low cover he could; else
the rushing through the air of that huge pole would have
brained and hurled them into the sea. The mast groaned
with the sound of a wounded giant. It was a terrible thing
to do to strong, rope-strengthened wood. Could it withstand the shock and continuing strain?

It could. *Vixen* lurched drunkenly into the path of the
downrushing dragon. For an instant it appeared that the
Mesozoic monster would not be able to avoid the ship's
rigging. *Vixen* could survive such damage, but the dragon
would be an easy harpoon target. Tiana, like a desperate
spider, had set a trap of canvas and cordage to ensnare
an attacker bigger than a billion dragonflies.

Dismay struck her like a fist in the stomach. The enormous black wings twisted, flapped, and the dragon climbed

while Tiana squinted against the down-draft. Their attacker must pass directly overhead. At this range its horrid breath was a sword of fire that cut across the deck. Men screamed. Fire crackled. The air was filled with black smoke and the odors of burning wood and flesh. Tiana had failed. She had promised Caranga a good target and cast; promised that the enemy would pass at a favorable distance and angle. Instead the uncooperative monstrosity had passed dead overhead. That required an impossible throw, directly vertical.

The smoke cleared and she saw the thick black figure on its feet. His hands were empty. *He threw anyway. Our only real weapon is lost.*

Then she saw the rope, the huge coil attached to the end of the harpoon. That mass of oddly slim whale-holding cord was alive. Coil after coil, foot after foot of rope was spinning up into the sky.

"Right in his sweet soft belly!" Caranga exulted. "Noted ye the white patch there? My target! To me, to me, let's see if we can land this sweet fish we've hooked!"

The rope was light and more slender than a man's smallest finger. Yet it was woven of the silk of the spiders of Il-Zadok Marsh, which was stronger than hemp or any normal silk saving only the extraordinarily rare dragon silk. Most of those who stalked the monsters of the deep used pulleys and complex mechanisms, but the former cannibal was of the ancient Simdan tradition that placed all reliance on skill with knots. His cord was twined and twisted into a complex knot about the stout oaken post at the prow, a post thick as Tiana's torso though only half her height. In his right hand Caranga held one loop of that knot.

All the length of rope between harpoon and post had paid out. Now the cord was whipping about the post, through his hand, round the post—and up. Slowly Caranga began to snub in the loop. Friction increased between rope and post until they smoked. Caranga knew exactly what he was doing. His prey was easily strong enough to snap the rope with a single jerk. Caranga prevented that jerk. Slowly he would increase the tension on the barb sunk into the creature's stomach, until its agony would not allow it to pull harder.

At least that was the theory. The upward flow of the cord had slowed but had not stopped. Caranga was nearing the end of his rope. Now the tension in the line was extreme. Both the post and *Vixen*'s superstructure moaned under the stress. It began to appear possible that the line was *too* strong, that before it snapped, the ship would be torn to pieces.

Caranga's hands were as hard as his life had been but the rope was cutting and searing them as he pulled ever harder. Even amid the dousing of flames men cried out at a new source of fear; the ship's bow was rising from the water and *Vixen* was listing dangerously to steer-board. And still foot after foot of rope slipped away aloft.

Caranga did not have to look up to know that Tiàna was beside him. With but thirty feet of rope remaining, he heard her voice.

"I can see the dragon against the stars in that blackness. It's—it's not flapping its wings! It must be riding a powerful updraft—*Chandak!* Give me ten points to port. Eleven."

That was their joke; steering could not be so fine, unless perhaps Caranga was at the rudder and held it by strength alone. Caranga was not; he was pulling against the loop of weirdly slender cord with his full strength. Fewer than twenty feet of rope remained. Each inch came into his hand smoking hot. He had waved off the man with pail and ladle. The post gave off a steady pall of smoke. All would be lost if it burst into flame. Yet he dared not allow it to be wetted lest he lose friction.

With a scant ten feet remaining, the rope stopped moving.

Tiana's voice sounded almost hysterical: "We've pulled the demon out of that updraft!"

That was true, and *Vixen*'s rightward list was worsening. Horrible to slay the monster and lose the battle anyhow! With each moment of this life-and-death tug between men and monster, the steer-board rail dipped closer to the waves. No man needed orders; every one had put the weight of his body on the port side. Still the list increased.

Abruptly the rope went slack and *Vixen* righted herself so that men fell and rolled amid curses. Rapidly Caranga pulled in the loose line.

While it was vital to recover the slack as quickly as possible, care was necessary too; if his knot was disarranged the loop he held would not hold the dragon but would cut off his hand.

Without warning the line went taut and again he must bring the rope's paying out to a smooth halt. The force needed was less this time: Tiana shouted a swift command and Chandak took his ease. *Vixen* sailed after the dragon. The ship knifed swiftly into the darkness, pulled by the monster. Going home? After a moment Tiana ordered the sail struck.

Every fire was out and burned men were being aided by their fellows. Only Caranga had to continue to battle for life and ship. The battlefield was rope and knot.

Again and again he pulled in and paid out his line. He knew that each time he stopped the dragon he caused it agony and robbed it of strength—and blood, assuming it indeed bled. Soon must come the most dangerous part of the battle. After a time the creature's pain would become its own anesthetic. Panic would die and cunning return. Then what? The monster's strength would largely be spent by then, but it would use what remained with guile and a new will to do harm at any cost. The line remained taut. Somehow Caranga knew it was about to go slack—and it did.

"Take cover!" he shouted as cord looped down. "It's coming back!"

Caranga took no cover. The rope had to be hauled in. Peripheral vision showed him the return of the dragon. This time it was much slower. This time its flaming breath was reduced to a dull glow. The eyes retained their fierce emerald brightness, though, and seemed fixed on the big man it seemed to know for its tormentor. All heard the vasty canvas-like flap of its wings. All heard the harsh rasping sound as of a huge saw, and some realized it was the dragon sucking in a deep breath. Not to live; to kill.

"Caranga!"

He ignored the call. The black pirate would not abandon his rope. Yes, he knew the coming gout of flame would not miss him. Sweat beaded and dripped while his mind raced and the dragon came in and in—

Caranga heard the twang of a single bowstring. The dragon's howl of agony expelled its flame—too soon to injure Caranga or *Vixen*. He looked up to see the arrow that had driven itself deeply into the thing's right eye.

Tiana was yelling proudly; he could not distinguish her words for the louder howls of the plunging dragon. Fire spewed from it, into sky and sea. Caranga continued to pull in his rope—and found that it had been severed by dragonfire. The vast creature's wings were buckling. It was dropping into the path of the oncoming *Vixen*. Caranga let go the rope and grabbed the rail with both numb, bloody hands.

"Sails—" Tiana began, and the crash interrupted her. It also sent her two body-lengths along the deck to plow into a trio of her own men. Anger aside, she had to smile and admire the crewmen who had presence of mind to grab a goodly feel of his captain.

For a moment the ship pitched as if she were riding up a reef. Then she moved steadily forward, plowing sideward while from beneath her came a grinding sound. Caranga peeled himself off the rail and looked over the side. He saw fire in the water. Clouds of steam commenced to rise from the surface. The fire burst like lightning; *Vixen* reeled and boiling water gushed up on both sides of her. Then all was silence and darkness.

Tiana seized her foster father. "Father! We did it! We won!"

He smiled at her, and sweat dripped off him. His hands dripped blood. "Nay, daughter mine, by Susha's loins we have slain the demon-thing, but I have lost."

"Oh father! You're hurt? Lost what?"

"My best harpoon *and* my catch!" he said, and flashed white teeth in a grin. "For the rest of my life I'll have to talk about the big one that got away."

Hours later Tiana returned wearily to her cabin. Every fire was out and repairs nearly finished. Caranga was growling about trying to drink with two bandaged hands. Burned men were greased and bandaged and guzzling analgesic from ale-casks. One was drunk and unconscious and Tiana did not think he would live. Two men had joined the dragon in the world's largest graveyard. One had not been quite dead, but kindness had been done him. Dowmar Cliffcat did not seem to realize that his legs were gone, and Tiana sincerely hoped someone would quietly open his throat in the darkness, poor good man. The Narfese lute-player called Kascat (because he was hairier than a Simdan gorilla) was singed bald and in danger of being boiled as well, once sunlight hit that hairless new body of his! And Tiana was staggering in the weariness that follows relief.

"Why?" she snarled at the ebony box. "What's your secret that this Drood-begot 'Owner' seeks you so?"

The silent object seemed to mock her. Within the box, she knew, the skull was grinning.

"Or is he or it trying to destroy you? Certainly I'm marked for death, just for having dragged you out of that stupid room in that blighted cave. If I was *meant* to find you, you ugly misbegotten fugitive from a boneyard, why? Only so that I could be murdered? What sort of sense is there in that—and who could have known about me so long ago?"

Ekron, the suggestion crept into her mind. *Sulun Tha. And . . . Pyre? He looks . . . oh, a well-preserved fifty or just under, I suppose. Maybe less. How old is he?* That led to an unpleasant thought: *Could I be just a girl to him, a posturing juvenile? No, though; he did swear the king of oaths to avenge me if I . . .*

"Why, that makes him vul—that makes me make him vulnerable, doesn't it!" She gave her head a jerk. "I'll find the answer!" she flared at the casket she had once considered rather handsome. Ugly thing! "I'll *know,* if I have to lop off Drood's Thousand Arms one at a time and turn over every rock in Hell. I'll . . ."

Her eyes narrowed in sudden new thought. She stood silent, her hand frozen in the process of unlacing her shirt. The answer did not lie with Drood. The answer did not lie in the Underworld and probably not in Pyre's Other-world, either. The answer must lie in that equally grim place, Riser Island. It was far, far south, below Simda and far below Lightning Isle and Serancon's Isle—which was no longer Serancon's the Poisoner, thanks to Caranga!—and eastward even of the Temple of Cignas, where once she had been a sacrifice—temporarily.

Riser Island. And there was a way she could go there.

Fourteenth Strand:

THE HUNGRY APPLES

High carnival ruled the golden city of Palanigh of the kingdom of Orvar, that isle set like a great jewel on the bosom of the green Asmygorian Ocean. 'Twas the season of the Morning Rainbow when the sun climbed over mist-shrouded mountains to paint the sky with a thousand colors. By night, people burned ornate candles of many-hued wax. Every mind and body devoted itself to the Festival of the Lesser Turtle. During the heat of the day the Islanders disported themselves on beaches of pure white sand, or passed the time wagering on the turtle races. Now, in the cool of an evening soft as black velvet, was the time for love.

Couples made wanton in the mazes of well-tended shrubbery that were golden Palanigh's parks. By design they were filled with private nooks and grassy nests. Bare bodies were caressed by the ocean breeze and by each other, while laughter filled the parks like the songs of birds at courting time. They were poor, aye. But may happy folk in truth be called poor?

While they thus amused themselves, the wealthy in their great villa-houses feasted on tender island pig boiled in butter and sweetbreads baked in honey. They drank great quantities of pungent wine from golden melons . . . and, of course, they made great orgy. Thus did the wealthy seek elusive happiness.

Palanigh fair reeked of happiness and sensuality.

Thus the commons and the nobles; and what did the royal folk do?

In the palace, King Yemani was prodigiously busy. Not even he was exempt from the law of the land. It straight-forwardly stated that a man might keep only so many wives, and concubines, and mistresses as he could satisfy on this one night of nights. And all in the household of

136

Yemani were determined to be got with royal child before this auspicious night gave way to dawn! My lord king had little time for other matters. Pity the labors of those whose heads droop under weighty crowns!

If Yemani gave thought to his kingdom at all, it was to assume that everyone was as pleasantly busied as he. Never did that brain consider that any spent festival night waiting for an enemy to come aslaying!

One on Orvar Isle did just that.

Palanigh rose up out of leafy jungle: a realm wherein only death ended the constant cycle of hunter and hunted. Within the frond-deepened dark of that jungle, in a hut a league or two beyond the city, a man waited for those who would be his murderers. His patience was worthy of the Simdan warrior he had been, silent and moveless and nearly invisible.

A single entrance gave way to the hut's two rooms, one behind the other. The pirate had chosen to sit in the rearward chamber, where the moonlight was brighter. He was a motionless statue of jet among shadows and moon-paled darkness. His ears appraised and recognized every faint sound carried on the night breeze.

The hungry apples made no sound.

He had found the black round objects hanging in the trees of the jungle. By day, they gave off little buzzing sounds, and they quivered. If the perch to which an "apple" clung was not satisfactory, it would roll along the underside of that branch until a better site was found. The hungry apples of Orvar sought locations such that men and animals would pass beneath. The hungry apples were always hungry.

The reformed cannibal who waited in the dark had gathered the evil fruit that afternoon. The delicate process required the cutting of branches bearing the black objects from the very trees. Next he meticulously placed the branches within the hut so that the balls hung poised above doors and the single window. The last two he had contrived to hang from the ceiling of the chamber wherein he sat. There they were invisibly black against the black of night.

He sat silent. The hungry apples hung silent. Caranga waited, as did they.

Having prepared for the advent of the expected assassin, he waited. His eyes, blacker than night in sclera slightly yellowish, sent their gaze roaming continually around the room. His night vision was excellent as his sense of smell—and taste, for he was also a superb taster and identifier of poisons. Still, he knew that two of the apples were his superior. They could discern in total darkness. They sensed the heat of a body, whether human or beastly.

Man and "apples" waited.

From the jungle came a small scream of agony. An owl had caught its dinner. The waiting man did not twitch, though his muscles were going ever so slightly stiff. Once again he went through his statue exercises.

Without a sound and with virtually no movement he worked his muscles until they grew limber.

For all his alertness, a small portion of his mind wandered.

He remembered the hot words he had exchanged with his daughter. Tiana had told him of King Hower's message and the dire peril into which her recklessness had plunged them this time. The waiting man sighed. His lips moved, forming silent words: how often he worried about his willful piratic daughter!

How can Tiana possibly survive when I am no longer present to save her? For I myself am truly without fear, he reflected, with perfect seriousness.

Still, bad as it appeared, the present situation was . . . manageable. All the world was enemy to the one called the Owner. Great as that King-Demon's powers might be, they were surely incapable of staving off and manipulating all the world. Caranga deemed it a safe surmise that the Owner's repeated attacks on Tiana stemmed from fear; fear that she might somehow expose a hidden vulnerability. Already she had ranged half the world and laid low one great sorcerer, ridding all humankind of the menace of the demon in the mirror, and of that awful Sarsis. Now—if only she and her foster father could learn more about the Owner!

That problem, Caranga thought as he sat motionless in the hut, might well be solved were he able to capture and question one of the Owner's servants . . . one of the Moonstalkers.

Earlier this day, Caranga had gone about Palanigh playing the role of wine-bibbing boaster. By mid-afternoon few did not know that he claimed to possess a strange skull in a box of ebony and silver. Now he awaited the result. The enemy was unlikely to send a large force to investigate such a rumor, spread by a lurching man with considerable silver in his tight black curls. If that happened, Caranga would hear their approach well in advance of arrival. He'd simply fade into the jungle that had been his home long afore he walked the planking of a pirate craft. More likely they'd send but a man or two, and—

A little crackling and snapping arose outside, and Caranga congratulated himself on having sown the earth around the hut with seashells.

The pirate recognized the sound of a single set of footfalls disturbing his alarm system, and yet the sound was strangely . . . blurred. Though he also recognized that sinister sound and knew his doubled danger, he did not move. The sound of footfalls ceased. Caranga ceased breathing.

The enemy was just outside, before the invitingly open door. From there, only the empty front chamber could be seen, and that dimly. Caranga waited. After a moment he heard a single very quiet footstep. Immediately there was a *fump* as from the impact of a small falling object. Cries that were surely curses arose in a language unknown to Caranga. Little matter; the angry exclamations soon changed to wordless screams of anguish. Caranga's ears were able to follow the sound of breaking seashells, from the door. First the shells were cracked and shattered by running feet, and then by feet on staggering legs. Caranga heard the gratifying thud of a falling body. It was followed by a widespread crackling as a man writhed on the ground. The screaming reached a hideous crescendo.

Silence returned like a great black cloak thrown over all.

Caranga waited. A hungry apple had done its work.

Through it all, he had neither moved nor made a sound. Nor did he move now, in the returned silence. No noises came now save those sounds of the never-sleeping jungle; the wind moaning in the trees and the distant humming roar of the sea.

Caranga sighed—quietly. Time never passed so unconscionably slowly as in the hours close before dawn. It was no easy feat to do nothing while eternity seemed to exist and pass, eternally.

In this sort of small war, the chief foe was not the enemy outside but the one within. Nasty little ghosts of self-doubt crept from their hiding places and banishment to attack the mind, seeking to blur the attention. Those spectres came. Was he not ageing? Were not his powers declining? To protect his foster daughter he had insisted that this task be his. Was this the folly of a man with gray amid the jet of his hair; an old man's folly?

If I am slain, won't Tiana take suicidal risks in her quest for vengeance?

Aye! (She'd better!)

What if she were in danger at this instant? She had a knack for it, that so-shapely pirate captain only he dared call "girl." What if he were a foolish old man sitting alone in doom-thickened darkness, deluding himself that a deadly enemy was nearby and vulnerable to his brain and physical prowess—while elsewhere his truly heroic daughter was in prodigious peril?

The night dawdled on, dragging feet of unbroken darkness.

At last, when dawn approached with the color of pearls and fading fire, Caranga decided that the time was right.

To his right rose the straw wall that divided the hut into two rooms. He lifted his sword slowly, silently. He reached out as far as his long arm permitted. He set the point of the cutlass on the soft earthen floor of the hut, so that it touched at a spot two feet from the wall and six feet from where he sat. He twitched his wrist. The swordblade scratched the ground with the smallest of sounds.

Immediately a spear crashed through the wall and slammed into the ground.

For an instant the long leaf-shaped blade and haft stood quivering in the earth, less than the breadth of two fingers from where Caranga had scratched. Then the weapon was drawn back. Before the blade could be drawn through the wall, a stroke of Caranga's cutlass bit the haft in twain. Caranga's knees did not pop as he rose, fluid as water. He took a silent step.

From beyond the wall a voice spoke: "Well, Caranga, we meet again."

"You know me! Then you were fool to think I wouldn't know the disguised sound of two men carefully walking with one tread! I've been waiting for you. If we're old friends as you indicate, why not come in so we can talk over old times?" Again, silently and fluidly, the pirate changed position.

"And pass under another of your hungry apples? No no Caranga, that task I leave to my expendable friends."

As the Moonstalker spoke, Caranga's ears picked up another sound, nearly covered by that of the voice. "I waited all these hours," the Moonstalker said, "waited for you to make the first move and provide a target for my spear. You cheated me. How did you know I had a spear?"

"It was logical that you would bring a weapon to let you kill without facing me. Your kind has little stomach for a real fight."

"We seem to be at stalemate." Again beneath the assassin's voice came the faint second sound: a cutting? What was the devil cutting? "Tell me, Caranga, do you remember the last time we met? Do you recognize my voice?"

"Familiar, aye—but I place it not."

Caranga studied the wall. It was not a single piece, but many sections bound together. Aye, that accounted for what he heard. He stepped back and to the right. Now one ceiling-hung apple lurked between him and the cutting sound.

"When last we met," the Moonstalker murmured in a voice of contemptuous amusement, "you told me your name, and I promised to remember you when I came again."

Caranga knew the voice then. "LIAR!"

So he shouted, but he knew it was true. His nape prickled. Though he feared no natural enemy, this was nighted madness and horror. Long and long ago he had done death on a man, knowing naught about the fellow save that he needed slaying. Caranga did not flinch from the words: he had done murder. He and the victim were the only witnesses. And the Moonstalker knew of it—and spoke with the voice of that dead man!

"Naturally," the voice from the grave continued, "when you appeared in Palanigh, I volunteered to come for you. I want your heart; I hunger."

Caranga shuddered. The slicing ceased. The wall that divided the hut was made of panels lashed together with thongs. Several had just been sliced. One tall panel wavered, tilted and fell in. Caranga saw the assassin.

The Moonstalker was an uncertain form in the moonlight. Its only distinct aspect was the glittering knife in its fist. The blade's glitter blurred toward the point, and

Caranga knew that something coated the point—doubtless venom. The figure's hands and face were an uneven pale gray, as if smeared with mud or grease. A dull steel helmet protected the head and the body was covered with blackness that was not skin. It had the shape and form of loose clothing, but it was not the blackness of cloth or Caranga's body; he was looking at blindness and the pit.

The man-shape came half a pace forward. Caranga saw the eyes, eerily gray and calm to the point of near-lifelessness. They were without pupils. The moonlight was treacherous, he sought to convince himself; this was merely an illusion of uncertain light. . . . But no. It could not be denied: this was the man he had killed so long ago. In unholy, horripilating nightmare, the dead had returned. *I hunger,* it had said—for Caranga's heart! Caranga fought for control of his own mind. Time later to consider such horror; now he must battle his enemy—his ancient enemy —be it man or lich or demon.

For all his resolve, his mouth was dry and his hands wet.

The horror stepped through the opening in a cautious move. *Trying to guess where I concealed the hungry apples,* Caranga thought.

The Moonstalker smiled, and that was more horror. "I expected some sport. But look at you! Naked to the waist to blend with the dark—do you recognize my clothing?"

"Aye," Caranga said dolorously, "you wear dragon silk."

The stuff he named was lamentably rare, and commanded fabulous prices. Dragon silk could not be cut. A man in such clothing might be crushed by the blow of a heavy weapon, but he could be neither slashed nor stabbed.

"You have gone to a lot of trouble to have yourself slain, Caranga. Why?"

As he spoke, the lich moved a pace toward Caranga. Another step and it would be beneath the hungry apple, silent and invisible near the hut's ceiling.

"I want to ask a few questions of you," Caranga said, and shifted leftward to place the apple between them. "Mayhap once you're my prisoner, you'll do some talking. Just a little chat . . . old friend."

"So you thought."

"So I thought," Caranga said, and struck.

For all its suddenness, the attack was carefully planned. Caranga's sword passed beneath the apple; his hand and

arm did not. The sword's edge caught the assassin's arm—
and slid off the silken armor. A blow with a cudgel would
have been more effective, for at least it would have struck
solidly. Any fool could see that the stroke was clumsy as
well as useless; now his guard was down. Nothing easier
than for the Moonstalker to lunge forward and stab his
enemy.

So Caranga had planned, for such a lunge would place
his foe directly beneath the deadly globe hanging in the
darkness above.

The revenant began that lunge—and checked himself.
He sprang back. His eyes scanned the ceiling. Though
Caranga gave no sign, he cursed inwardly. A carefully set
trap had failed and his enemy knew the location of one
of the hungry apples. While he—or it—could not know
where hung the other one, logic would apprise him that in
a chamber of this size there would be more than one of
the deadly balls.

The Moonstalker circled the apple and Caranga shifted
to keep it between them.

Like two jungle cats they slow-danced the battle, a
pavane of movements and threats and feints without the
ring of steel against steel. The Moonstalker had only to
scratch his opponent to slay. Caranga's targets were his
enemy's bare hands. Their blades flashed in the room's
pallid moonlight as they lunged at each other, black hands
on black arms whipping from black bodies that dodged
and twisted. More than once, each missed what should
have been an easy hit, because of the ever-hungry third
foe: the apples. They were enemy to both opponents.

The assassin paused to stand still before the pirate,
while he tossed his long knife from hand to hand. The
temptation to knock the weapon spinning was great—but
the apple hung over the space between them and the distance was too great by a hand's breadth.

Dragon silk did not rustle when the Moonstalker
dropped to stab left-handed at Caranga's right foot. The
cutlass sped at the other hand. Wielded too swiftly, the
knife failed to bite into the old leather of Caranga's boot,
hardened by salt water and the blood of others. The sword
grazed the Moonstalker's right hand. It left a stripe of
blood without inflicting real damage.

The pirate had drawn first blood.

It was a trivial victory, psychological only. His enemy

was fast, too fast. Bit by bit, the revenant was forcing him out of position. Caranga knew that when the menace of the apple no longer separated them, the fight would change. Only the apple made useful the longer reach of the cutlass; at closer quarters the knife would swiftly claim his life. Clearly, Caranga faced an opponent who was faster, more skilled and, for a fight within a hut, better armed.

The choice was simple: Caranga must die or cheat.

No choice at all!

Rather than directly between them, the apple was now a foot to the right. A good broad cut would endanger Caranga's sword-arm, no matter how fast it was moving. In moments his swift opponent would force him completely off position and slay him.

The second apple was three paces behind Caranga. He retreated, with the Moonstalker pursuing. Pirate struck at lich with the full strength of his arm. The blow staggered the assassin—and the swordblade snapped against the dragon silk. Holding a ruined sword, Caranga took a swift pace back and another to his right. The second apple was *not* between them. Caranga tried to look like a man trying to look helpless. In truth, he was.

In the act of lunging, the Moonstalker arrested himself. Caranga's bluff had succeeded! The assassin began to circle the spot above which he surmised the second apple to be, while Caranga shifted to keep the same invisible—and totally harmless—spot between them. He could have been slain at any second. The Moonstalker shifted, shifted . . . was almost beneath dangling, awful death . . .

He stopped, looked directly into Caranga's eyes, and smiled.

"Clever," the damned clever revenant said in a murmur. "Very clever."

Stepping around the space beneath the apple into which Caranga had almost maneuvered him, the assassin advanced with poisoned blade held to gut. Now he knew the location of the apples as well as the unarmed pirate, who had no place to hide and no defense against death. Oh, of course he might well destroy the other even as he was stabbed, or scratched—but that scratch would envenom its wound, and he would be dead in minutes.

"I am faster than you," the Moonstalker cheerfully said. "That means that without a weapon . . . you are dead, Caranga."

Caranga knew that was true—and from the edge of his eye he saw that which the Moonstalker had completely forgotten. The pirate dived for it.

As the other lunged for him, Caranga rolled up off the floor with his hand clamped around the truncated haft of a spear. Spearhead and knife clashed together in ringing, scraping clangor—and the knife went flying through the air.

"I assume that this too is poisoned," Caranga said, and drove at the creature's face.

The disarmed assassin sprang back; Caranga was up and after him. While he retreated, the Moonstalker flapped his arms in an ever-shifting pattern of dragon silk, against which the spearhead would break. Then, for an instant his defense was holed, and Caranga had only to lunge at him—

"Die again, lich!"

With his arm just starting to uncoil like a steel spring, Caranga's instinct stopped the stroke in a way that would leave his muscle cramped. His whole body quivered with the effort of arrested violent motion. The Moonstalker had very nearly tricked him into stepping under one of his own apples!

Again they glided that weird dance around the death-ball's space. Now Caranga was on the offensive. Slowly he forced his opponent off balance and away from the apple's protection.

"Congratulations," the voice from the grave said in a tone of amiable mockery. "I must concede defeat."

"I am accepting no surrender." Caranga's tone was flat and deadly.

"Oh, I offer no such. I merely said that you have bested me. Beating my Master is a different matter."

With that he pounced backward, swung, and started into the night. At once he became part of the darkness. Caranga stared at emptiness. One moment a solid enemy had stood before him in battle; the next the lich was faded, gone. The knife lay on the floor as proof of—

The knife rose to come floating at Caranga.

The knife stabbed at him; dodging, he spear-thrust at it. The spearhead shattered against empty air and Caranga, over-balanced, fell. An invisible foe stood above him with envenomed blade held high. It stepped toward him—and under the second apple.

It dropped.

Leaving the ceiling as a solid black sphere, the deadly ball struck as a soft blob that spread rapidly like a strange liquid pouring itself over invisible contours. In a heartbeat it became the outline of a naked man. A statue whose medium was black dots on empty air. Perfect in every detail: eyes, face, arms, legs, genitals.

Despite the man-thing's screaming, the buzzing was clearly audible. The hungry apple was a colony of thousands of tiny blood-sucking insects. They swarmed and bit and sucked, and the envenomed dagger fell from nerveless invisible hands.

As Caranga rolled out of the way, the figure fell squirming to the floor.

Caranga rose and coolly kicked the dagger away. He stood watching the Moonstalker, now a visible man, a revenant. The insects gorged themselves.

After a few moments the convulsions ceased and the Moonstalker lay slowly writhing and moaning. Caranga stood over him and felt triumph and pity—and knew he could afford neither. This was but a small battle in what would be a long war. An overly close battle! Had his enemy realized that the apple could feel the heat even of the body of an invisible man . . .

"Belay your whining, dog," the pirate snapped. "I once fed one of those sweet things, and it's nothing a strong man can't endure. After a day or two they get enough and drop off you. I've medicine hidden nearby that will ease you considerably. The price is low: answers." He waited. The agonized lich did not answer. "To begin with, this cursed skull Tiana has—why is it so important to the Owner?"

From clenched teeth came the answer: *"Slay me."*

"What, and show the weakness of mercy? Nay; answer! Think not to lie, for I already know more than half the answer."

The Moonstalker made no reply. He—or it—stopped breathing.

A logical tactic, Caranga mused. A strong-willed person could hold his breath until he lost consciousness, at which point breathing resumed, automatically. In such a manner one might keep himself semi-conscious and, to a degree, protected from pain.

The Moonstalker did not resume breathing.

Was he turning blue? In the moonlight Caranga could not be sure. There was no mistaking the spasm, though, that shook the fallen assassin, or the stillness that followed. It was final. Man or lich, he had held his breath until he died!

(Again?)

For a moment, Caranga was too surprised to curse. He had failed. And that failure revealed something most unfortunate indeed: the Moonstalkers might be slain, but not captured! Dying to avoid being taken was logical and practical, for those who had indeed come back from death . . . and might again.

Damn! Tiana had a talent for finding trouble, but enemies like this . . .

When he emerged from the hut, carrying a hideously bloody knife, Caranga found the Moonstalker's "expendable friend." The nondescript man lay dead on the ground. The insects had not slain him; indeed, there was no discernible cause of his death and already those creatures making up a hungry apple had departed him. Somehow even such unnatural events did not notably surprise the pirate. From the little he had seen and experienced of the Moonstalkers, he knew they were not the sort to leave loose ends that someone else might tie together.

In no good mood, Caranga trekked back to the city. Its habitants had exhausted themselves in revelry while he had striven at great risk—and learned nothing of real value. Why was it that not all heroism was to any good purpose, much less known and lauded?

The only positive aspect of this night's labors was that at least Tiana had remained aboard *Vixen*. At least that's what she had promised to do . . .

No! He'd asked for such a promise, Caranga realized, but now that he thought on it . . . *she said only that she wouldn't interfere in my plans! Damn!*

Despite his weariness, Caranga quickened his pace. His red-tressed, green-eyed daughter from the pink-tan race, he thought, was about as trustworthy as . . .

As I am.

Fifteenth Strand:

THE MADAM'S MISFORTUNE

In the wine cellar of the House of No Tomorrow, House-mother Larine searched through the racks of dusty containers. The face of the solidly built woman showed her years along with the strength that had brought her through those years. Enormous gold loops swung below lobes elongated by long wearing of several ounces of gold. The tight curls of her hair were cropped quite short and cosmetics gave her eyes a bruised look.

The wine she wanted was in plain view and she didn't see it. Her mind was preoccupied with the troubles she knew were coming. Now that it was too late, she realized that coming over to Orvar had been a capital error. At the time it had seemed an excellent business opportunity. Love was free to and among the natives of this paradisic isle, and at Festival . . . ! Yet it was forbidden to foreign visitors lest they pollute the pure-blooded Orvarian "race." Of course what travelers did in the dozen or so brothels—all staffed with foreign women—was no concern to the proud Orvarians. So Larine established her House. Business was ever brisk. Her girls and "girls" were happy and well off and Larine had jewelry enough to purchase a duchy, not to mention her herds of hundreds and hundreds of pigs.

Now, with trouble approaching, the astute businesswoman from east of Lamarash realized that she and her "girls" were aliens in a land where all foreigners were considered slightly less than human. It had nothing to do with her color.

She jumped at the sound of footsteps on the stairs. She looked up to see a man and a woman approaching. He was a warrior of a glowing mahogany hue lighter than Larine's purple-black. He wore only a breechcloth, though his sword and dagger were far from primitive and the latter's

148

hilt was jeweled. His companion was flame-haired and fair of face as a lily. She hid her figure under a long black cloak embroidered with a fox's head in red on the right, near the shoulder. A *fine* figure of a man, Larine thought, who had moved beyond his primitive background just as she had. And Larine sucked in her stomach.

"We have need," he began amiably, "to ask you a few questions."

"Drood take your questions!" she snapped, and immediately found the smallish cask she sought. It contained the best of the best. Then, licking her lips, she reconsidered. She was carrying a heavy load of fear and while she didn't regret snarling at a handsome man who'd just spoken kindly to her, neither did she want to be alone. "If you are willing to sit and listen to my troubles, you are welcome to all you can drink. Otherwise, begone!"

Anger flashed briefly across the man's face, which was tribally scarred. Larine saw how the pale flamehair gestured to him before quietly seating herself on the earthen floor. High boots with heels, Larine noted.

"Our ears are at your service," he said. "Do let me knock in that bung for you, Housemother." And he opened the cask.

"We specialize in others' problems," the young woman said. Eyes like citrine quartz, Larine noted. Like her companion, she was not yet so old even as thirty. And what confidence she radiated!

Flattered, Larine was smiling, accepting the opened cask from the man's strong brown hand. *Odd,* she mused; *that slip of a girl seems in charge of this Yabazo (ex?) warrior!* She sipped. Ah yes, it was good, good. It had been worth saving back. Best not try to take it with her, and simply sinful to leave it behind. After handing a sack of more ordinary vintage to her unknown visitors, she settled herself with her back against one of the racks.

"It began last night," she said. "Five men came to my establishment. Dressed in some sort of loose black garment. Loose leggings. Not proper clothing at all. I and my girls've had bad customers. Sadists and worse! But never the like of these. At first glance they seemed normal enough. Slim, not truly handsome, even neatly dressed in that odd way of theirs. But then . . ." Larine shuddered, took another deep pull from the banded wooden cylinder. "When you saw their *eyes* . . ." Again she paused, or broke off to fumble for the right words. Her speech was a twangy drawl.

"Uh, they say that the eyes is the window to the soul. These *men* was like elegant tombstones. Handsome on the outside until you look into their eyes. You know? O Susha's eyeteeth—the souls in them are as dead and as maggot-eaten as a corpse." She paused to shake her head, remembering. And she drank. "They paid good, extremely good. All they done was look at all my girls, then they left. I knew they was shopping, making selections for later. I'm used to that. This morning I went to the harbor to arrange passage for all of us on the next ship out! What ship, where to, I don't care. It don't matter. By decree of the king hisself, no working girl can leave Palanigh and soldiers guard the port area to enforce that."

Larine sipped, and saw the black-cloaked girl take a hearty swig, too. She nodded understandingly, encouragingly.

"Over the years I've done lots of favors and made lots of gifts to several powerful nobles. Any of them could easily hide my girls and I until this—this darkness is past. Except I soon discovered that none of them can remember me now. You know? That's when I found out what desperate is! I was ready to seize on anything, hazards or not. Fate opened a door. I heard that the great White Wizard, Sulun Tha, had just arrived here."

Larine paused to see the effect of that revelation. Though the warrior gave no sign of understanding, the white girl's face showed dawning horror.

She spoke in a mere murmur. "Surely you didn't go to see *him?*"

"Oh yes, dear." Larine took a deep pull of wine. "That's exactly what I did. Not all the wine in this cellar will wash away the memories of that . . . interview!"

The man was staring at her. His puzzled face was all the encouragement Larine needed to detail her meeting with that enigmatic fellow Tiana had once met up in Collada, Thesia's western neighbor.

"Sulun Tha received me graciously. He listened real sharp to my troubles. But he explained that he could take no overt actions against those fellows in black—Moon-stalkers, he called 'em. If I wished, he would come stay here in my House and ward them off just with his presence." With a shudder she added, "He has a lot of *that!*

'Twould be easier to have ole Drood Hisself for a house-guest!"

Her male visitor shook his head, the black hair of which was bound back to dangle in back like a switch. "You tell us you're in grave danger, but when a good man offers to keep you safe you *refuse?*"

Larine shuddered in remembering. The *eyes* of that man, looking down at her! All her life naked to that penetrating gaze! "The presence of such an upright, such a rigidly righteous man is . . . uh, *uncomfortable.* Especially to those of us who ain't all that virtuous, you know? I mean, since I was nine years old I have, uh, well . . . I can't explain. But you'd understand if you ever met Sulun Tha!"

He looked ready to pursue the topic, but at a gesture from the white girl he subsided. She said quietly, "I have met Sulun Tha. I understand. No one is ever more naked than before that man's eyes, right?"

"Exactly!" Larine burst out. *She's no aristocrat,* she mused, *giving orders to a strong man by virtue of title and birth or husband . . . no! She commands and he obeys because she's his warchief—maybe his superior in battle? A white girl of true beauty and fighting skill—she has to be that adopted child of my old friend Caranga! Susha— she ain't no girl, neither!* Abruptly Larine smiled.

"The important thing, by Susha's sweet gourds," she said, deliberately employing a favorite oath of Caranga's, "is that I couldn't accept the White Wizard's help. So my problem remains. Captain Tiana, I need a ship bad, to take my girls and I away from this city."

The woman gave no sign that a dangerous secret was out. The brown man flinched ever so slightly. "We should," Tiana smoothly answered, "have introduced ourselves sooner. This is Chandak Keeneye, and you know who I am."

And you don't fool me, Larine thought; *you've been hiding your identities! That means that if the authorities know you're here in Palanigh you'll be in the same trouble as me. As me is? As I, then!* She had been working on her speech for a long, long time, Larine had. She nodded to Chandak and said, "Captain Tie-anna, since we're both in trouble, surely we ort to help each other. I'll keep my mouth clamped about you being in Palanigh and you . . ."

The pirate queen's pretty green eyes went hard and deadly. Larine knew with another shiver that she had gone

too far. It would not be in the character of a "daughter"
of Caranga to yield to blackmail and she was all too ready
to do violence. For a frozen moment both pirates stared
at the aging whore and she knew they were deciding; her
fate rested on a sword's edge.

The only way out of the cellar was up the steep stairway. Larine was acutely aware that they were between it
and her. She heard a little noise. She thought *rat,* and reminded herself that she no longer had to care about this
place. It seemed to attract their attention, though. She
watched the man Chandak's hand move in a swift complex
gesture. Tiana's nod was barely perceptible. She rose all
sinuous and sinewy like a she-lion. With a careless toss
of that glorious sunset mane, she turned toward the stairs.

"It's time we were going, Chandak."

"But—" As they went to the stairs and up, Larine
stared after them in puzzlement. With a casual motion the
regal pirate captain let her cloak part. She revealed armaments: a dagger and a skinny sword. *And a lot more,*
Housemother Larine's practiced eye noted with envy and
some avarice. Then she saw the stairway in a new light. It
was a perfect place for an ambush! Had that been a rat?
At the top one turned and had to go down a narrow hallway that was always most lamentably dim. Because of the
stair's high railing, one could not see from below what
might be hiding up there in the darkness.

Is that beauty so blandly walking into a trap?

That made no sense. Neither did any other explanation
Larine could imagine. *Should I say something?* Now she
was sure Chandak's gesture was a signal to his captain.
They must know.

As she reached the threshold of the ambush if one existed, Tiana paused and half turned. "Housemother: if I
could give you and your whores passage on my ship, how
much could you pay?"

"My savings are small," Larine lied promptly and automatically, "but I can offer you twice regular fee. And
anything your crew wants, you know?"

Again Tiana took an upward step. Seeming to think better of it, she descended a step or two, quietly. "How many
passengers are we discussing?"

As they haggled, Larine could scarcely concentrate on
what was being said. All this was a pretense, she realized
now. An excuse to allow Tiana to dance on the edge of

the trap, tantalizing her hidden enemies by dangling herself before them! *Clever bitch!* Maybe it was just a rat, though. On the other hand, if it was those awful men in the black cover-everything outfits, they might be getting frustrated, impatient . . .

As Tiana intended. Before the black brothel-mistress was sure that such a deadly game was indeed being played, it ended with horrifying suddenness.

Giving Larine a wicked little smile, Captain Tiana eased her sword and then her dagger from their sheaths. The drawing made not a sound. At last then she climbed the last few steps to the top—and instantly fell flat.

The masked bravo who lunged at her slashed his long-knife through empty air and, tripping over her unexpectedly prostrate form, fell headlong down the stairs. As his hurtling form passed Chandak Keen-eye there was the briefest contact, but when the man crashed to the floor almost at Larine's feet, he gazed up at her with dying eyes. His throat was neatly cut.

She looked up from what would soon be a corpse to see that a battle was in progress. Tiana and Chandak fought a dozen or so masked assassins. Would-be assassins! It was like watching a match between a pair of tigers and a flock of sheep. The killers had come here to do quiet murder and showed small appetite for an honest fight. Those closest to the door leading from the hallway were engaged in a scrambling match to be first through that narrow opening. Others sought with equal panic to avoid the storm of edged metal the pirates loosed on them. There were few clangs but many *chunks* and *thunks*.

Theba's gourds, what a fine show! Pity I can't wager on the outcome!

Larine's wish died with the realization that in a way she had placed a very large wager on this struggle. If the masked raiders prevailed, they were unlikely to leave behind a live witness.

A sudden chorus of new screams made her look up to see something on the far side of the doorway. The men who had been fighting to get out now could not retreat in time to avoid its advance. They were shoved aside as though they had been rag dolls. (Kicking a bloodied man down the steps, Tiana did not hesitate to slash her dagger across the mask of a man turning from the thing at the door—and run another through the back.)

Whatever it was, it was coming. The head alone seemed to fill the doorway. Its scale-armored shoulders were too wide to pass through. It thrust its massive bulk forward anyhow. With the sound of an avalanche the oaken doorframe splintered and the stone wall crumbled.

Huge paws knocked men aside. As if they had been children they were smashed back into the wall or onto piratic blades or sent flying over the railing. One struck a rack of wine with enough force to smash it partially, along with himself, amid a frightful racket. From beyond the doorway a voice was shouting.

"Kill, Kragg, Kill!"

Having cleared the way, the monster advanced on Tiana. One man barred the way, although he certainly did not want to. He was lifted at the end of one huge arm and slammed over the rail—to fall directly onto the lamp that was the cellar's only illumination. In utter darkness, Larine heard the sounds of battle and pain and death. She felt trapped in a nightmare without reason, sanity, or equal.

When silence came it was total and just as frightening.

Larine waited, listening hard enough to wear her ears out. She knew a candle lay nearby, with flint and tinder. She dared not light it lest she attract most unwelcome attention to herself. With some unknown enemy all too possibly lurking in the darkness, she felt it prudent to breathe most quietly indeed and make no other sounds. Tense with fear, Larine stood motionless. Constantly she told herself that this utter silence was not awful; it proved that all danger had ended. Left. Departed. Ended. *Please.*

When she was half convinced and was too impatient and scared to care, she found and kindled the candle.

She was alone. After a moment of combined relief and trepidation, she began ascending. Along the stairs she had to step over masked men. Some were dead of sword and dagger wounds inflicted by the pirates. Others were . . . smashed. A ragged hole marked where the narrow doorway had been. Stone and shattered pieces of oaken timber were scattered about. Larine trembled. She had hoped the monster would turn out to be only a trick of the uncertain lighting, or her wine-befogged wits. Illusion, even.

It didn't look that way. She had seen it. Now she saw its deeds.

She passed through the hole, stumbled and stepped over another corpse—oh dear Susha, it didn't have an arm!—

Despite their roles of captor and helpless captive, a close observer would have noted that it was the man who was drenched in cold sweat. His tone when he whispered was one of mixed anger and fear.

"I still do not understand the purpose of this mad scheme of yours."

"All you need understand is that Chandak Keeneye is close by, watching you along the line of a nocked arrow. You bought your treacherous life by agreeing to do this little bit of play-acting. Continue. Chandak has not missed with an arrow in all the years I've known him."

He swallowed audibly. "But if we go through with this we are both doomed! Why you want these Moonstalkers to carry you off to a nameless fate I cannot imagine. But . . ."

"Oh stop starting every other sentence with 'But.' You sound like a bad taleteller—ah! Here comes our . . . welcomer." Raising her voice Tiana said, "Oh please my good lord—" After a moment she murmured, "Well at least say 'Shut up, wench' or *something*."

"Shut up, wench," milord Duke instantly said, but his heart was not in it. He was staring at the tall gaunt figure. It came toward them from the ship Tiana knew was the Owner's. He wore a long-sleeved black tunic, long and loose, over equally loose leggings of the same drab color.

"You are late." Its voice was cold and almost a monotone. "And instead of the twelve extra girls you promised for my purposes, you bring only one."

Murtud struggled to speak. Fear held him mute. Tiana did her best to look frightened. She was sure that was impossible, but she also fancied her acting ability.

"You surely realize," the dark figure continued, "that the hundred girls I convey to the Master are already aboard, and I have been waiting with little patience for you to keep your promise. Our bargain was that I would do you a certain favor in return for which you were to bring a dozen females for my personal use." For a tiny moment the Moonstalker's gaze fell on Tiana. She shuddered under that obscene caress of its eyes. "This girl," it continued, "is admittedly unusually fair, but that is no excuse. Our agreement is for quality *and* quantity."

Pig, Tiana thought, *just how many "girls" do you think your personal use requires, anyhow? Besides, who could want more than one, when that one is Tiana?*

She watched the Moonstalker with a dry mouth despite her thoughts, and a feeling of coldness possessed her spine. There was something most unnatural about this shadowy being with a voice as animated as a stone. Now it was extending a hand to the duke—no; *toward* the man. Its fingers moved rhythmically, steadily contracting and almost-opening, contracting . . .

"No, please!" the terrified noble gasped. "Please!"

The movements of that empty hand reminded Tiana of a pulsing heart. Watching the fingers moving in and out, she could almost imagine the Moonstalker held an invisible heart in his palm.

"You," it said in a voice the more dread for being so calm, "are a traitor to your people and now you betray me. You are guilty of *annoying* me, little man."

The fingers suddenly constricted and squeezed tightly. Duke Murtud clutched his chest. His cry never emerged and was hardly so much as a groan. He collapsed and lay crumpled on the pier with a thin stream of blood trickling from his gaping mouth. His blank eyes stared at the night sky. The moon shone full upon them. The pupils did not contract.

The Moonstalker looked at Tiana and gestured. "Come."

Her leash rose and stretched to meet his hand. He turned and Tiana moved fast so as not to be jerked off her feet. As he led her onto the mastless ship that would carry her to Riser Island, she knew that the first stage of her plan had succeeded. She had second thoughts about it now, this most dangerous plan of her life. From what she had just seen she was not likely to survive this, her latest stroke of genius. It was also too late to turn back.

Sixteenth Strand:

THE MADAM AT SEA

As Caranga trotted into the secluded cove that concealed the anchored *Vixen,* he breathed a little easier. He saw no overt sign of trouble. His relief evaporated when he saw the people who now ambled about *Vixen*'s deck. Caranga hastened aboard, stared a ridiculously bosomy, gutty girl out of his way, and made for the Second Mate.

"Chandak! Where's the captain? What are these whores doing on our ship?"

"Sir," Chandak answered cautiously, "if you will go to your cabin, you will find someone there who can explain better than I can."

"Young whelp! I'm asking you!"

"Yes sir, but—"

"Never mind. Check stores. I want garments on those harlots. Voluminous garments, you understand? Whores on a ship!" Far too impatient to waste time arguing, Caranga hastened to his cabin. There he threw open the door—and stared. After a gape-mouthed time: "Larine! What are you doing here?"

"Waiting to give you this." She handed him a pair of waxed tablets.

He took them as if they were a venomous serpent. With a stare at Larine, he unlatched the tablets and read the message incised in their wax.

Dearest father,
I know that you would never approve of what I am about to do. In the present emergency it is the only course open to me. Perhaps you can understand when I remind you of what you yourself taught me: there is no safe way out of danger. A brave warrior takes well-chosen risks and generally escapes. The coward

161

refuses to take any chances and thus betrays herself into disaster.

Given our present extreme situation, half measures are doomed, father. Our only hope lies in facing great hazard. We need far more information about the Owner than could ever be extracted from a single captive.

Tonight I went into Palanigh and found one of the swine who were collecting girls to deliver to the Moonstalkers. In exchange for his life, this Duke Murtud will deliver me to them. I go to Riser Island on their ship, as one of the Owner's intended victims. There, gods willing, I'll spy out the Owner's secret and escape. The risk is not as large as may appear at first glance, father. The measures this King Demon takes to guard terrorized women are not likely to hold *me!*

Besides, if the Owner is like every other lord of great domain, he must have enemies within his own household. I plan to find such and seek their aid. Whatever happens, wait for me on that island where I celebrated my sixteenth birthday. If I do not come in two months, mourn me as you would a son fallen in battle, and do not endanger yourself seeking futile vengeance.

Instead live on my behalf, beloved father who *chose* me rather than gained me as accident of birth!

Whatever revenge my death needs, the Arrogant One will supply. Remember that he and I fought a fearful thing of darkness, called Derramal. My tactics were much too reckless for the August One and in a moment of exasperation he predicted that I would die. He vowed by the Fires Which Will Destroy the World that he would avenge my death. That unbreakable oath still bonds him. If the Owner slays me, he who swore will be obliged to destroy him, whether he wishes to or not. If you would help the dark wizard in this task, give him the skull but do not waste your life. I go only to save the whole world. It isn't worth both our lives!

Calm seas to you, father.

All my love,
Tiana

In fury Caranga hurled the tablets from him. Even in writing this message she had been fearful of discovery or interception, and so had not mentioned Pyre by name, or the island she referred to.

"We will go into Palanigh and recover my daughter if I have to tear the city to fragments!"

Larine touched his brawny arm with a hand just as black. "Tiana was on the Moonstalkers' ship when it sailed some hours ago, Caranga." That stopped him cold while she continued, "I know it seems to you that your daughter is being grievously reckless, old friend. But she believes she is taking a prudent, well-calculated risk. It may be that you underestimate her. From what I saw she is . . . singularly formidable."

"You wouldn't say that," he exploded anew, "if you'd met the monsters she goes to face! Against such horrible powers mortal courage is, is . . ." Caranga broke off. He took a deep breath before continuing slowly, "It is a grim thing to say, but I doubt that Tiana has any chance against such foes."

"All my girls would have gone with them. Many others did." After looking at him for a long moment, Larine went on softly, "The Moonstalkers' ship has sailed and is long gone, Caranga."

"Aye," he said heavily. "My daughter is now somewhere on this trackless sea and there isn't a thing I can do about it."

Seventeenth Strand:

SHIP OF THE DEAD

Yawning, Tiana stretched luxuriously on the silken-sheeted bed and reveled in its softness. For all her hard life and ability to live in ascetic sternness, the queen among pirates loved comforts and luxury more than most. This bed with its gleaming posts of Colladan mahogany and sleek, flame-gold sheets and pillows, for instance.

I'll say this for the Moonstalkers, she mused, luxuriating sinuously. *They keep their captives in style!*

Not a whit more than is my due, of course.

She had been able to see little of this cabin last night, when she was locked into it. Now the morning light revealed a room, rather than a cabin, and one furnished in style to please a queen. From the superb bed she surveyed matching table and chairs on a plush rust-gold carpet surely hand-woven in far Narf and those fabulous color-swirled drapes that were obviously of Il-Zadoki spider silk dyed in Ilan.

She slid from the bed to prowl to the table. Helping herself to a pastry from its burden, she eyed the drapes. Somehow, before this was over, she simply must steal those drapes.

Tiana munched. There was no way she could make away with a supply of this excellent pastry. Such delicacies would not keep. Pity! These fine grained cakes with little crunchy nuts were especially good. Pausing to stretch tall and bend ten times, knees straight, to rake the carpet with her fingers, she nibbled another. It washed down nicely indeed with wine from the golden carafe. Though on the tart side after the pastries, it was an excellent Narfish vintage.

Stretching supine, she sat up ten times, to keep tight her stomach's startlingly firm musculature. Then she flowed to her feet with a warrior's suppleness.

Well now. Should I loll here in comfortable captivity until this ship reaches Riser Island, or shouldn't I be slipping out for a bit of exploring?

It seemed unlikely that she could learn anything of value by shipboard spying. There was the risk that she'd be caught at it. They would guard her more closely thereafter, and take away these wonderful luxuries. On balance then, best she just . . .

Wait! What's the matter with me?

Such timid thoughts were entirely foreign to her nature. This was sufficiently strange as to demand explanation. So did other things. Why, for instance, did the Moonstalkers provide their prisoners with accommodations worthy of royalty?—or at the very least the duke's daughter she had been born? And something else. That big ugly padlock. She was alone in a ship's cabin whose sole door, a massive oaken slab, was fastened shut with a heavy iron padlock . . . which was impossible.

She was locked in a spacious cabin that was locked from the inside.

Now how, by the Great Cow's Cud, could the Moonstalkers accomplish such a thing?

Whatever the answer, she'd not learn it by standing here! From beneath her hair she plucked an ear pendant. It was attractive and decorative, wasted under all that hair. It was also a picklock, an instrument with which Tiana Highrider was expert. She plied it now. In short order the lock yielded and the door opened. Tiana stared.

She was gazing into another luxurious bedchamber! While the color scheme was different, bright warm hues replaced with soft dark tones, the basic furnishings were the same. That included another door, padlocked from the inside.

Grimly Tiana strode across that chamber to pick the second lock. Thrusting open the door, she revealed another bedchamber. A third padlocked door stared at her in silent challenge.

This ship is not *this large!* Angrily she whirled to return. The door she had just come through was . . . gone.

This chamber, like the first one, had only one door. How she had entered was without explanation. For a horrible moment she saw an endless series of chamber-like cabins and her picking open lock after lock to rush from one to another. A frantic running to nowhere on a treadmill, like prisoners turning great millstones as their contribution to the society they had offended. Their product was flour. What was hers? The whole situation possessed an unreal quality. It was as if she was a helpless spectator watching herself doing these footless things. Whether it really happened while she was in blind panic or occurred only in her frightened imagination, Tiana could not say.

I'd as soon be a victim of Eidar's Disease or on a Calancian Lion's Tooth! She was exhausted and still in that selfsame cabin. She forced back the fears that crowded her mind, forced herself to reason. There seemed no way out of this Drood-sent box. Or . . .

Suppose all this is merely illusion? She remembered that awful Bear, animated by the Eye of Sarsis, and clamped her lips against a shudder. It had held her aboard a ship of illusions. Perhaps . . . perhaps if she just shut her eyes and trusted her other senses . . .

The instant her eyes closed she felt as though she was losing her balance. Up and down seemed to swim, as if unable to make up their minds to be the one or the other. The floor seemed to revolve under her very feet. *If I don't open my eyes I'll fall and bust my*

BANG.

She did fall, although she broke nothing but her dignity. Stretched on the floor, she cursed softly—with her eyes still tightly closed. *Now why did a fall onto plush carpet hurt like that?* Her questing fingers sought to explore the floor. The sensation was blurred, as though she felt through a sort of tactile fog. The temptation to open her eyes was almost overwhelming. She resisted. She must not rely on her eyesight. Now she felt sure she was on the right course.

The carpet was definitely rough, more coarse than it looked. She felt a hard ragged weave with the texture of . . . wood! Unfinished wood!

There was no carpet. The floor was nothing but bare boards.

Her hands traced it to right and left. She encountered the walls. What had seemed a luxuriously large bed-chamber was in truth but a tiny cubicle. The great bed proved to be but a heap of straw. The golden decanter of wine was a clay pot filled with brackish water. She crumbled one of the delicious little cakes. It was not; it was stale bread. One of the tasty little nuts tried to crawl out of her hand. Her stomach lurched.

Maggots! Oh by the very Back! Rotten food and foul water and a stall the size of a cattle pen! Oh, for this I owe a debt! Furthermore . . .

She fought her nervous stomach and clamped her lips. It was food. She needed food. She was a prisoner in just the kind of stall in which cattle were kept to fatten them for slaughter. That hardly boded well for her future. *Oh, when I reach Riser Island I'll . . .*

If I reach Riser.

She had almost forgotten the conversation between Murtud and the Moonstalker. She was not part of the regular quota of women destined for the Owner. She was an extra, intended by the Moonstalker for his own . . . use. What that grim word might portend for her Tiana pre-ferred not to think upon. It did seem safe to assume that she was to find out before this ship reached Riser. Therefore she was in immediate danger. She met it by keeping her eyes studiously closed.

She felt along the wall until she found the door. At her gentle push, it yielded by a thumb's width. *The overconfident lackwits didn't even bother to lock me in!* She pushed some more, and listened. Nothing. Ship sounds, none of them human. The usual creaks and groans of wood and cord.

Only when she was out of that cubicle of illusion and the door shut behind her did Tiana dare open her eyes. She was in a corridor in the hold of a large ship. It was lined with stalls identical to the one she had just vacated. At its far end, a ship's ladder led up into bright sunshine and her first impulse was to rush up into that daylight. Still, each stall was equipped with a peephole and morbid curiosity—meaning Tiana's inherent nature—impelled her to peer within. And then into the next, and . . .

In each cattle pen was a young woman. They were uniformly attractive. Each was as placidly happy as a pampered princess. (Or a cow chewing her cud, Tiana thought, and wished she hadn't.) This one was brushing her long brown hair—without a brush. That one and the next were prettying their faces with nonexistent cosmetics. An exquisitely formed blonde posed naked, as if admiring herself in a mirror. She stood before a blank wooden wall. While Tiana watched, the poor Northish idiot went through the motions of removing one expensive gown and carefully donning another. Naked, all the while naked.

So much for vanity! Tiana scornfully thought, not without self-righteousness.

Toward the corridor's end she looked into an empty stall. On the plain planking lay a gown, a blue cape, the separated legs of leggings, wadded, and a wig, long and curly. The prints in the filthy straw were those of a man with big feet. Booted feet. Tiana stared, trying to make sense of that array.

Puzzled or no, she thought at last, *'stime I was moving along.*

At the top of the ladder she paused with her head just below deck level. She closed her eyes and listened, opened them and listened. She heard the normal sounds of ship and sea. Nothing else. With infinite caution, she raised her head enough to peek out. She was looking at an empty deck. Again she was reminded of the ship of the Sarsis Bear. Well, it was gone, and perhaps things went in patterns. Was it part of some plan? Perhaps. Meanwhile . . . *Apparently the Moonstalkers are what their name implies —sleepers by day. Nightwalkers, only.* Asea on a sailless galley. And at the oars . . . ?

Slowly and very quietly she crept forth into sunlight. Logically some few of her enemies must be up and about. Someone on watch. A helmsman. One who counted herself a consummately skillful thief ghosted forth onto that deck of mystery. She advanced with care and in bursts, scurrying from hiding place to hiding place like a mouse. At each stop she gazed about and listened with all her ability. She detected nothing to indicate that she was not alone on deck. There wasn't even the thump of the drum, setting the pace for the galley's rowers.

There may be no one else, but there has *to be a helmsman!*

She knew where he must be, and saw a loose pile of heavy rope. From behind it she would be able to see the man at the steering oar with small chance of being seen. Getting there without exposing herself required no little squirming. She did it. From the vantage point of coil upon coil of rope she peered out and . . . erupted into gooseflesh all over her body.

The thing at the helm stared back at her with empty eye sockets.

Some of its brown skin had turned to leather and clung to it, mummy-fashion. In places bare bones gleamed through in sickening ivory whiteness.

For a long while she crouched staring, waiting for it to move. Well Tiana knew that dead things could be given a false semblance of life. It did not move. Nothing happened. It must be what it seemed, she decided; a long-dead corpse and nothing more. That was quite enough. It was ghastly. Even so she had an icy feeling that the unmoving dead man held this ship more accurately on course than could any living navigator.

Another thought occurred to her. She kept the dead helmsman in view while she moved to the rail. She looked over the side. The galley's oars were amove and their rapid rise and fall told her the rowers were being driven at a frantic pace. Dragged along by her curiosity, she moved stealthily to the rowing pit. It was unnaturally silent. There should have been constant thumps, even a few groans and grunts—and certainly a drum to set the pace for the rowers and keep them together. Save for the sounds of the sea, everything aboard the black galley was quiet as a tomb. She reached the rowing pit. She looked down, and wished she had more fear than curiosity, rather than the reverse. Tiana did not care to see this at all.

She looked down upon half a hundred corpses sitting rigid at their oars. Among them stood another skeleton with a whip in its fleshless hand. A dead taskmaster ruled a little kingdom of the dead. The pacer sat beside his drum, seemingly mummified in the midst of his drum-beating.

Drood's demons! I can look over the side and see those oars rising and falling fast as a heartbeat—and now I see only motionless corpses at their handles! Magic . . . sorcery . . . *necromancy:* conjuring with the dead!

As she watched the blasphemous necromancy a shudder took her and the sun felt less warm.

At first glance this was horror. Looking deeper revealed something far worse to her excellent mind. The Owner was telling a lie. The truth was that this galley had inert figures at her oars and could not move. He lied, the dark master who held the world in thrall. He declared for any to see that the dark ship raced across the ocean. By his unholy Power he forced the very fabric of reality to unravel a bit to accommodate the lie.

And who was she that she should dare set herself to spy on this demon-god? He or it had in times past crushed whole armies under his feet as if they had been the tiniest red ants. Desperately Tiana shook her head as if physically to throw off clutching fear. No matter the odds, no matter how mighty the enemy. She was committed to this venture. She had no hope of turning back. Her mouth was dry and her hands were sweaty and she pretended not to notice.

Tiana moved forward to see what else this ship of the dead might hold.

She considered the normal arrangement on a galley, especially a slave carrier. Two separate sections belowdeck; a cargo hold and an area of cabins for crew and ship's master. Obviously that would be the most rewarding place to investigate. *Also the most dangerous,* she thought, and moved to it. She was Tiana; curiosity overcame dread.

Moving with the grace and stealth of a cat stalking a

bird, she crossed the deck and slipped below. She descended into another narrow, door-lined corridor. Choosing a door at random, she pressed her ear against it and listened.

She heard nothing. Perhaps it was empty and she could safely enter. Perhaps it was not. With great care against the slightest sound, she pushed the door open a crack and peered inside.

In the large chamber of bunks were a dozen men in the loose black clothing she recognized. They lay in the positions of sound sleep. Very sound; she saw that they were not breathing and their faces bore the pallor of death. Such creatures were seen only at night. In a few hours, she did not doubt, these would rise and move about with counterfeit vitality. Stalking, under the moon.

Behind her the flooring creaked.

Her imagination filled with horrible visions and she spun about, dropping into a combative posture to face anything. She faced nothing. Staring up and down the empty corridor, glancing back into the room of the sleeping undead, she wondered. Had it been only an old, warping plank moving under the strains of the sea?

Perhaps. Certainly this tiptoeing among corpses and sleeping enemies was accursedly hard on the nerves. Cold little worms were crawling up her spine and her bone-dry mouth badly needed wetting with wine. Beer. Anything. Every moment she spent exploring increased the danger of discovery. *The thing to do is get it over with quickly. If this corpse-ship has a log like any normal ship, it will hold —something. Worthwhile secrets I'd surely be better off knowing, at least.* Again she glanced up and down the corridor.

One door only was fitted with a handle of brass. It seemed logical to assume that beyond that door lay the quarters of the master of this floating tomb. There she would find the ship's charts and log—and greater danger still. The fact that the unnatural crew slept by day did not guarantee that their captain did.

Tiana sidled along to that door. Caution made her go down to peep through the crack betwixt door and flooring. She heard nothing and she saw nothing that moved. Good signs—but the light within had an odd silvery quality rather than the usual yellowish of lamp or candle or yellow-white of sun through a port. This reminded her of moonlight.

Most unnatural. Most disturbing.

Tiana rose and set both hands to that brass handle. Stealthily she opened the door. She saw the furnishings of an austerely aristocratic good taste. The polished oak furniture was of simple design and fine workmanship. The velvet drapes were red as blood above a green carpet of movalock wool.

All this she gave only a glance. There were two men in the chamber. On the floor an armored knight lay moveless with a dagger standing from his back. A man dressed in shapeless black clothing hung from the ceiling by the rope tied about his neck. He or it hung there suspended, swinging gently this way and that with the movements of the galley. Since its back was to her, Tiana could not see its face. Nor did she want to.

She had had this feeling before: that she was failing to notice something of importance. Her gaze roamed—and fixed on the porthole. In utter violation of all that was rational, bright moonlight streamed through that opening.

Tiana perceived a sort of nightmare logic. The servants of the Owner were creatures of darkness and the night. It appeared that the Owner or one of them used arcane means to make this important cabin a place of perpetual night-light.

The dangling corpse was starting to rotate, ever so slowly. A voice in the back of her head seemed to scream "Run! Flee!" but Tiana stood still, in the slight crouch of the weaponeer, watching in horrified fascination as the figure turned gradually to face her. She wanted to flee. It was as if some external force held her to the spot. She stared. Watching, waiting.

The corpse came around. It was most definitely a corpse. *Another one.*

The face was but a piece of old off-white leather stretched over bone. The eye sockets were empty as those of the helmsman.

But this one's were different. Within those twin voids an unnatural fire seemed to smolder. Did smolder? The hanged thing appeared to be looking at her. Seeing her.

Then the mouth opened to reveal rotting teeth and the hanging old corpse said, "Welcome, fair child, to my parlor."

Eighteenth Strand:

FROM PYRE WITH LOVE

Tiana had failed to move when she was able. Now she was unable to move. The undead creature held her in its cold gaze as effectively as if she were weighted with iron chains. She struggled—without moving. The veins in her temple stood out with strain and her heart raced at a terror-driven pace.

"I fear I cannot let you go," the horror said; "not until I have had my pleasure with you."

She could imagine what grotesque fate this thing planned for her. Its pleasure would hardly be hers. And she was utterly helpless, unable to move a single finger. Fear fought insidiously to overwhelm her reason. She fought back. She was determined to keep her head, to do her best to outwit this hanging . . . man. She forced her voice into a tone of casual banter.

"Do you usually sleep that way?"

A hand rose, leathery skin stretched tautly over bone. It grasped the rope. With an effortless gesture the thing extracted its neck from the noose and lowered itself to the floor. Surely it was dead and had somehow returned. A revenant; a lich, not a man. An *it*, not a he.

"It is more convenient," it said, "than lying supine in a coffin. Is there aught else you would care to know, fair child?" It was coming toward her step by slow, inexorable step.

Desperately Tiana tried to make her mind formulate a question from the horror that swirled in it. All she came up with was, "W-hy do you need twelve extra . . . people? I remember your anger with Duke Murtud when he brought only me, and . . ."

"It is twelve days' sail from Palanigh to Riser Island, in a ship that is not prey to the vagrancies of weather." The answer came in words as dry and dead as the throat that

172

spoke them. An impossibility stated by the impossible. "It is a pleasant luxury to dine each evening. But just now I require something else of you." A skeletal finger pointed at the fallen knight. "Tell me, who was this fool? How did he come to be on my ship? For ages none dared approach Riser. Now *two* of you have the temerity to come spying. Why?"

There was rage in the horrid voids that served this undead thing in lieu of eyes, and a fearsome urgency behind its questions. Tiana had no idea how to answer. She had no idea of the identity of the man on the floor and assumed she had never seen him before. Yet if she failed to speak she would provoke the revenant to some unspeakable action. She decided to try to buy time; perhaps some opportunity would suggest itself and she could break the shackles on her mind and muscles.

"You're asking me for valuable information. What will you give me in return?"

"Dear sweet girl!" The revenant's bony hand came up to brush her cheek in an obscene caress that was worse than walking through a cobweb in the dark. "If you cooperate, I will eat you." It paused to show her a horrible smile. "If that seems no reward, consider your alternative. Since there are one hundred and one girls on this ship, I could invite one of the others to dinner and include you in the necessary hundred for my Master, the Owner of the World. That would be a fate quite beyond anything you could imagine."

She had little doubt of that, but now she spotted the opportunity for a fine lie. "In that case," she said confidently, "you can't count and you are just going to have to go hungry. The total *women* on this ship, including me, is one hundred. Precisely. That poor brave gentleman there on the floor came aboard wearing a wig and a gown!"

"Impossible!"

"Well I should know," Tiana said, as if she did.

The horror of a skull-as-head shook. "No. That man is tall and bearded. Such a disguise could not fool . . ." It trailed off as if considering.

Tiana pushed. If only she could shake him, make him lose this awful control over her limbs! "You never truly saw him. You saw what appeared to be a hundred women because that is what you expected to see."

Empty eye sockets stared at her. "Have you only hit upon that or do you know of the spell?"

Tiana had no notion what the revenant was talking about. Spell? She said, "Of course."

"That jackal Pyre?" the thing said. "In past he has placed men under an enchantment . . . they could be seen only as what the viewer expected them to be, rather than what they were. Such a spell is even better than invisibility! It renders the most superficial disguise completely effective!"

Tiana, astonished that she had lied her way into an explanation and knowledge as well, nodded wisely. Truth could be found in the strangest ways and places!

The revenant's chuckle was not at all pleasant. "So. It seems I am to miss a meal. But then I shall have the pleasure and satisfaction of having slain one of Pyre's assistants."

"You aren't thinking this matter through," Tiana pushed on. "You stabbed that man in the back and expected that he would fall dead. Therefore that is what you saw happen." Given the illogical premise, that seemed to follow logically. Tiana was proud of it, especially since she had not the faintest notion what she was talking about.

Oh, and look at the effect on old skull-face! Ah Tiana, Tiana, she congratulated herself, *what a mind is yours!* She was only just able to keep from smiling, for abruptly the grip of cold, sorcerous paralysis relaxed its hold on her. Just a little. The revenant's manner was apprehensive, and that distracted it from the force it exerted on her.

"That is no illusion!" the revenant said angrily, and it pointed to the prone man with the dagger in his back. "That dog is dead as a side of beef."

It had always intrigued Tiana how it was mainly dogs who called others dogs. Just now she was not amused. Just now she could move. Knowing that, she remained wholly still. She had struck doubt into whatever served this undead *thing* as a brain, and doubt was a long step toward fear. If she could thrust it along and then play on its fear, perhaps she could trick it further. Perhaps she could bring about a lowering of its guard as well as its paralytic powers.

Then I'd have a single brief chance to slay it. If it can die. Again.

But how?

She said, "Dead as a side of beef, is he? That's the way

it appears to you, is it?" She forced a smile. "Do continue believing that, O Moonstalker, while he awaits the chance to destroy you!" Ah by all the mud on the Turtle's Back, how she wished that were so!

Its occult grip was dissolving even as the revenant spoke so violently: "Nonsense!" She knew why that word had burst forth so—it wanted to believe that she spoke nonsense. *That must mean it can't control us both,* she mused, doing her best to ignore the tic in the muscle of her left calf. *The other illusions on this floating tomb must be the Owner's, then, not this lich's!* And mentally she added, *All it has is the power to slay me in an instant . . .*

"I am not vulnerable to any man, much less that corpse," the revenant said. "Common weapons cannot harm m—"

"Then look at how you are vulnerable!"

Tiana's outburst was a sudden inspiration that proved inspired. The animated dead man just had to swing and look anxiously at the porthole.

Of course! *Moonstalkers, they are called . . . the artificial silvery light of the moon by night . . . of course!* Her ruse had worked. The horror had told her what she wanted to know, and Tiana leaped toward the cabin's sorcery-bound window.

If I can smash through that port and let the sun shine into this cabin. . . . It was between her and the porthole but she had taken it unawares. Its hideous arms reached to grasp her—too late! She was past it and free and now she was going to—

Tiana hit the floor hard, not understanding how it had contrived to trip her. She rolled over and tried to dodge and a bony foot came down on her chest. Again the icy paralysis held her frozen. She looked up to see that skincovered skull grinning down at her, nodding slowly.

"I must commend you on a clever effort. Everything you said was an ingenious lie designed to distract me— me! You nearly succeeded! That makes you no girl, and too dangerous to continue living." Its smile was an appalling obscene act. "And also too delectable to pass up—"

"You can't!" Tiana shouted. "You cannot return to the Owner one woman short of *his* quota!"

"Minor shortages," it whispered softly, bending toward her, "can always be explained."

From the edge of her eye Tiana saw something. Though

she remained frozen, tension drained from her and she relaxed.

"In that case," she sighed, "I might as well resign myself to being eaten. There is just one little thing, though . . ."

The skull-face was quite close to her, but the revenant could not bear to let that provocative half-statement hang in the air. *"What?"*

"Well, all that I said about that man's not being dead and illusion and all that—that was meant to be a lie just as you said. It seems that I happened on the truth. Look at the porthole now!"

The revenant sneered. "Do you think that you can deceive me twice with that same trick? Me?"

And down came that repulsively smiling face, and there was the ripping slash of a fist driving through a cobweb of illusion, followed by a thump as the wooden outer cover of the porthole was knocked violently open. Bright sunlight splashed into the cabin, filled it, and fell upon the skeletal creature.

It disintegrated.

The leathery skin changed in texture to that of a fragile ancient parchment. A moment later it crumbled into dusty flakes. The white bones lasted only another moment. Then they came apart one from another, to fall to the floor and to break into countless fragments—and dust.

Tiana escaped the worst of that disintegration, but she busily dusted herself as she got to her feet. She was cursing under her breath. She turned to the knight, who still stood beside the port he had smashed open.

"You, sir, could have timed that better."

"Why Lady Tiana," he replied mildly, "those are scarcely grateful words to speak to your rescuer. Besides, how could rescue be timed better than to come at the last moment? Also, it seemed best to wait as long as possible, lest he reveal a bit more information to both of us."

"Rescuer! You're forgetting that I did all the work! *I* held the enemy in play while you punched through that illusion-web over the porthole and opened the port itself!—and that at my suggestion, too! *I* made that—that thing betray his vulnerability! If I hadn't been utterly calm and totally without fear throughout the whole of this horror—"

His impatient gesture seemed to slice off her angry words. "It's done with. We've no time to talk of such trivia. Though we must talk of other, important matters, this is scarcely a safe place to do it. Come!"

As though there was no doubt of her obediently following him, he turned and walked away.

Outraged, Tiana stared at his back. *Men!* Had she found another arrogant clod of a hero like that blight-ridden Bjaine of Northland? She drew breath for a yell that would wake the dead . . . and let it out quickly. On this ship it was quite possible that any loud noise might do just that.

She hurried after the man in metallically rustling mail. He was leading her back to the slave stalls! Opening a door, he bowed and gestured for her to enter. Tiana stood where she was, staring at his face. That was a weird experience. It was as if her gaze was a physical object that kept somehow *sliding off* his face before she could see him.

"What's wrong with you?" she demanded. "Your features are—blurred."

His only reply was to raise a silencing finger to his lips and make a more urgent gesture for her to enter. Tiana, who had not survived this long by trusting strangers, politely indicated that he should enter first. She was mildly surprised when he did so. She closed the door behind them both—and the stall was instantly transformed into a luxurious apartment.

"I think," he said quietly, "that in here we are in no immediate danger." He lifted a decanter and filled two gem-set silver goblets with rich red wine. He offered Tiana one. "I've a longish story to tell and we may as well be comfortable."

She ignored the proffered goblet. "Suppose you begin that story by telling me who you are and why I should trust a man whose face won't let me see it."

His laughter was harsh and bitterly ironic. "Tiana of Reme: I call myself Sir Gray. The truth is I have no idea who I am. And for all I know you should not trust me."

"What?"

"It's as true as the Sacred Cud. The same spell that robs me of all my memories also makes it impossible for others to see my face. You can see the logic in that, ugly as it is. I can't remember who I am and no one can recognize me and tell me."

Tiana gazed at him, blinking, her head cocked. There was something disturbingly familiar about the knight's voice, especially the sardonic way in which he laughed. Frowning a little, she stepped toward him.

"Sir Gray: let me feel your face."

She shut her eyes tightly and attempted the trick that had freed her from the other stall. Her questing fingers discovered that his beard was small, just enough to cover his chin. His features were sharp, angular, almost hawklike. *Why, I know this man! Sir Gray is really . . .*

Involuntarily she opened her eyes. On the instant what she seemed to know of him vanished like the memory of a dream.

"I almost did it!" she told him. "Another try and I'll free you from that spell."

Again she heard that harsh, maddeningly familiar laughter-without-amusement. "I fear not. It is a well-known law that one always gets what one wants as soon as it is too late for it to be useful. I began this quest wanting to break this Drood-begotten spell and regain my memories more than anything in the world. Now though . . ."

"You need the spell," she finished excitedly as she realized, "for it serves you well as a disguise!"

"Exactly." His tone became bitter. "And I have a feeling that when I learn who I am, it will be no pleasant surprise. Therefore as I said . . . perhaps you cannot trust me."

"Perhaps, but I think I will because you say that." With that decision made, Tiana relaxed. "Now what about this so-called wine and these other furnishings? Are they to be trusted, Sir Gray? In my 'cabin' I found—"

"Yes, I know," he said, and she heard the bitter smile she could not see. Maddening! "But for no reason I understand I find that I have the ability to see at will through these illusions. I've seen to it that my wine is honest clean water in—" he paused to tap the gleaming goblet so that it rang like a gong—"a good tin cup. For getting drunk it will serve as well as any other vintage. Also," he said, gesturing to the red-silked, canopied bed, "that is clean straw. And the food" (pointing at the table where lay piping hot roast pork, salmon in lemon sauce, buttered leeks, potatoes smothered in sour cream dusted with tarragon and various flaky pastries, all filling the air with their delectable aromas) "is dried beef, dried fish, and stale bread."

"Without maggots?"

"Without maggots or mold. All quite nutritious, Tiana my ally."

Too hungry to worry about philosophical problems, Tiana immediately fell to eating and drinking. He said it was nourishing and it tasted better than that. That was enough for her, under the circumstances. Her mouth was quite full before she noticed that her more-than-mysterious host had remained standing.

"If you will excuse me," he said quietly, "I believe I will change my clothes. While this armor turned aside an enemy's knife while he thought he saw it go in, it is scarcely comfortable or suitable for dinner."

A snap of his fingers and he was clad in a dark green dressing gown, richly plushed and with a scintillant silk trim. Tiana stared.

"Will that work for me?"

Without waiting for an answer, she snapped her fingers. Instantly she wore a black lace gown, very decolleté. A quite immodest garment—exactly as she desired. *Fine wine, superb food and a mysterious knight, tall and broad of shoulder—and no Bjaine Nor'man, at that! He just could* not *be homely! Fortune has indeed turned for the better, Tiana you lovely darling!*

After a sip of the wine/water, she said, "Now good sir, I am glad to give you my undivided attention." She couldn't help wishing that the black lace was a bit tighter about her full breasts. Immediately, marvelously, it was. *Oh, it's that simple, then!* she thought, and added a chain of gold that vanished provocatively into her cleavage.

"First," the faceless man said, "there is a gift I ought to be giving you." As she smiled prettily—ready to kick herself away from the table, for she was never trustful of gifts—he put an object into her hand. "It is from Pyre."

"Pyre! This—you are his work?"

He nodded. At least she thought he did. She opened her hand and stared at what he had put there. "Just what does the *great mage* expect me to do with a *walnut?*"

"I'm sure I don't know," he said mildly. "You see . . . at the start of my . . . adventures, Pyre gave me a chest filled with various, ah, needful objects. Each was in a drawer that would not open until just before I needed it. Only last night the final drawer opened. I found that inside." He gestured at her palm. It was a large walnut, at least. Maybe it had a nice fat jewel in it?

"But—how do you know you're supposed to give this to me?"

"Why, by the inscription, of course." He pointed. She looked and turned the walnut over and over. It was a walnut, covered with a walnut's natural striations. "Right there," he assured her. "It says, 'For Tiana, with all my love—Pyre.' "

Tiana said, "Oh."

She stared at him quite sharply. Apparently he was sincere. He had actually read a message where there was none. *More cursed magic! Oh if one could only get away from such obscenities and stick to honest work such as theft and piracy and an occasional combat!*

But he just couldn't *be ugly!*

"It's scarcely a sentimental gift," she murmured as she examined the nut. She noticed a small hole. It was not a worm hole; it had been bored through the shell. The nut had been removed or allowed to dry up and become dust. In its place there was something else. *A nice fat emerald?* She could not quite make out what—ugh. It moved.

"I took the liberty of examining it, Lady Tiana. You have twenty or so dead flies and one small, live spider."

"Oh." She wondered what use she could possibly make of this weird gift. It was hardly decorative. Nor was she anxious to wear an old walnut shell containing a live spider, as a pendant! She rather imagined that its intended use was not to be anything pleasant.

"Sir Gray: I should tell you that I am not *Lady* Tiana. It's true I am the daughter of a duke, but he didn't get me on his lady wife. I do have my own ship and crew. The ship is *Vixen;* I am Captain Tiana. Since you are most obviously nobly born and trained, and my ally as well, do please just call me Tiana. Not Tee-ahna; it's Tie-anna. I should know. It's my name."

"I am glad that you have one," he said dolorously. "I wonder if I have heard of *Vixen?* I wouldn't know, would I? Anyhow, thank you, and do just call me Gray without the 'Sir.' "

She smiled rather wistfully. "I am looking at you, Gray. Are you looking at me?"

"Most definitely. And I can see you looking at me."

"Well I can't," she said, and not without a pout she upended her jeweled goblet of gleaming silver. *A tin cup and a man without a face. How wonderful. For all I know I'm naked.* She sighed.

"As for my story," Gray said, interrupting thoughts

better left unthought. "Since it is a long one and I don't want you to become impatient, I'll start by telling you the ending." He took a deep draught and a deep breath. "I regret to tell you, Tiana, that you are in a death trap, the most dreadful one in all the history of the world. Though I came here to rescue you, that was a mistake. As far as I can tell, we're both doomed."

Nineteenth Strand:

TO SHOUT DEFIANCE AT THE HEAVENS

For a long day *Vixen* lay like a paralyzed fish in the waters of the secluded cove. That day Caranga drank, for his mood was no good one. His daughter whom he loved above all the world was worse than dead; doomed, and beyond his ability to do anything about it. The crew lounged in enforced idleness; nothing could be done without Caranga's orders and none dared approach him. The big black man's frame of mind was too close to that of a wounded tiger.

At nightfall he emerged from his cabin like a hurricane. He spat orders furiously. He would be back soon! When he returned he wanted everything shipshape! Straighten up there! Then (having given no clue as to where he was going or when he might return) he departed, at the stride.

Caranga did not go alone.

Larine insisted that she must talk to him. If he would not wait, then she would follow for as long as it took her to have her say. They were scarcely out of earshot of *Vixen* when she began.

"I know who you're going to see."

He did not interrupt his stride, but grunted, "Well? And what of it?"

"It's suicide." Her voice was full of disapproval. "Even if your body survives, your mind will be destroyed."

He merely repeated his last comment.

"Caranga! No—please!"

"Woman, you exaggerate. It will be no more than an unpleasant experience. My daughter is worth far more and I have withstood worse."

"I KNOW!" she screamed. "I came within a hair's breadth of losing my mind! And believe me, it will be far worse for you than it was for me!"

Caranga continued pacing down the trail. Stopping, he turned to face her.

"Larine, I appreciate your concern, but there's nothing you can say to change my mind. I met Sulun Tha once, years ago. I remember. The experience still gives me an occasional nightmare. I well know the danger you're warning me about. I don't have a choice. It is the only way I can help Tiana."

His obstinacy turned her pleas to anger. "If you suppose I'm going to cry for you, then you've already taken leave of your senses!"

He sighed and regarded her contemplatively. "There'll be no occasion for tears. But, Larine, I'd take it as a kindness if you'd share a jug with me, later."

Her only reply was to mutter obscenities about *men*. Then Larine turned and fled.

She'd have liked the way Caranga gazed after her before he resumed his trudge toward Palanigh.

He had heard that the legendary white wizard had taken up residence in an abandoned monastery on the city's outskirts. (The demigod once worshiped there was as long forgotten and out of fashion as the monks and the virtues they had preached.) Caranga's best route was through sparsely settled area. Thus he traveled in solitude and silence, scarcely thinking. His course was set. He saw no point in torturing himself with fears or regrets. He had to try. Only when he saw the marble ruins before him, white as old bones in the moonlight, did Caranga pause to reflect. What he was about to do could be accomplished in a far easier and safer manner. Sulun Tha was famed for his wisdom. Many consulted him, and were wise enough to do so by messenger.

I could have done that. Chandak Keeneye would gladly have come in his place; indeed he would have counted it a favor, a privilege. He whom Caranga thought of as a boy was curious and ever eager to learn. He was unable to comprehend what could be so terrible about meeting a truly good man, one whose eyes could see all that one was and all one had done. Nothing could have been simpler than for Caranga to shirk by sending Chandak.

At least that's one bad mark my soul won't be wearing! With that thought, Caranga moved on.

Firelight gleamed from the one section of the desolate once-monastery that was still more or less intact. Caranga entered and found himself face to face with an old man in flowing robes of white.

It was a terrible anticlimax. He had steeled himself to meet a mage worse than demons, and here was this pleasant-looking old man making a vegetable stew for his dinner, the same as any elderly person the world over. Yet Caranga was sure that this was the nigh legendary Sulun Tha.

"May I help you?" The voice was soft, aged.

Do my memories betray me? Caranga blinked several times. *Have the years exaggerated a bad experience into something worse?*

"My daughter is in grave peril," he said, "and I come to beg your aid."

"Beg?" Sulun Tha's serene countenance was flint weathered by decades unnumbered and his eyes were the bright blue of the sky—and seemingly as limitless. At first glance he had seemed merely a tall man. Now, possibly because of his extremely erect posture, he almost towered above the black pirate. His reply seemed to come from on high.

"You know, Caranga, that I cannot assist in any selfish endeavor."

Those vast blue eyes saw and knew him. Under their infinitely penetrating gaze old memories, long comfortably buried, rose within Caranga. Ghostlike they came up from their graves to point accusing fingers at a man who had been a cannibal but given it up for the piratical life. He prided himself on being a true friend—and all too many times he had misled and betrayed those who depended upon him. By thoughtless indifference to their safety he had failed them, with the result that they had paid in bitter coin. More than once his own courage had failed so that he was not the man he and others thought him, ever brave. And he had lied . . .

Lies. Broken promises. Red rages and spilt blood. Fighting on the wrong side because the pay was better. Overlooking humanity for booty. Countless little arrogances that made him a daily injury to all around him.

All of it welled up and rushed through his mind. No penance could ever be adequate for all his . . .

Stop! No! I cannot forget my purpose!

He squeezed his eyes shut, shook his head violently, reopened his eyes. The great seeing eyes of the mage were all he could see. They filled the sky like the very Powers of Judgment. Still he was able to shout up at them:

"Surely trying to save my daughter is a righteous cause! Surely it is a cause worthy of the aid of Sulun Tha!"

Down from the heavens the answer thundered, and the logic was awful: *"Many men's daughters are in peril. Yet you wish to save only one, your own."* The eyes had merged into a single great orb; a ball of blazing blue light in whose illumination each and all of Caranga's dark sins burned in accusation. He felt they were a hot iron pressing into his soul, and yet he answered; he pleaded in the only way he was capable.

"Then we'll save them all!"

"That would be less selfish," the words reverberated from on high so as to shake his very soul, *"but still unacceptable. Know this, man. If you are to serve Good you must do so without qualification or reservation."*

Knowing the agony of the damned, Caranga shouted in defiance of the very heavens. "I have a box with a skull in it and in the skull a vast red gem! What is its price? What will you offer for it?"

"Nothing. It is far too important to have a price. In the ultimate conflict between We Who Truly Are and the nonbeings, it is the key." The crushing words rolled over Caranga like great stones off a mountain. *"Know, Man, that I may not take it from you by force or bribery, and that you must give it to me of your own free will without any thought of reward or recompense. Indeed there can be no reward. For if I attacked the Owner, it would save your daughter from one set of perils and expose her to other and far greater hazards."*

The great blazing Eye was more than he could stand, for darkness could not abide light and man remained ever an inseparable compounding of good and ill; darkness and light. Caranga had the awful thought that in another moment this illumination of truth and Good would consume

him, as sunshine destroys the hapless earthworm once it
is trapped above ground.

It is what I am, Caranga realized. *A worm standing in
the light of the very gods themselves.*

And still he stood upright, an arrogant worm that shook
balled fist at the heavens and bellowed his challenge.

"If you'll not help Tiana, then DROOD TAKE YOU!"

Almost as though they had wills of their own, his legs
spun him about and sent him in headlong rush from the
stark ruins. Down the jungle trail Caranga sped until his
wind was spent and every breath was an agony. The pain
was a distraction; thus it was a small blessing. Despite the
increasing distance between him and the crumbled monastery, he dared not look back. He was sure that if he did,
the whole sky would be a great Eye staring at him.

Twentieth Strand:

SHADOW OF THE SKULL

Despite what she had shouted in the anger of frustration,
Larine stood and waited and watched for Caranga, and
she waited long. From *Vixen's* deck she saw him and the
heart went out of her. Caranga was running as though all
the demonic guardians of Drood's underworld pursued
him. He came bursting out of the trees to sprint across the
strand and hit the water without pause. He swam to the
ship leaving a trail of frothing white water.

.He seemed to see nothing as he scrambled dripping and
panting onto *Vixen's* deck. He spat orders furiously. Where
they were bound he did not disclose. That they must sail
within the hour was abundantly clear.

To Larine, who had so tensely waited him all this while,
he said not a word. Completely ignoring her, he strode
to his cabin and slammed the door tight shut.

That bit at Larine like teeth. Yet she was not surprised
that he behaved so bizarrely. The important thing was that

after the ordeal he had just passed through, no one should be alone. She followed.

Chandak barred the way. "Sorry, uh, Housemother. Caranga gave orders. No one's to go in there under any circumstances."

"Surely," she said, seeking to brush past him, "he couldn't have meant me." But a muscular brown arm blocked her.

"He mentioned you by name, uh, Housemother."

"For mercy's sake call me Larine—and let me pass! After what he's been through, being left alone is the worst possible thing. And look!" She pointed at the bottom of the door. It was black. "He doesn't even have a candle alight! He is shaken, and sits alone in total darkness!"

"The First Mate," Chandak said, "commands, and does not act without reason."

"His reason's unbalanced!" She knew this lad was trying to take refuge in formality and pretentious ship's rules. Her voice rose close to a scream. "He's had a horrible experience and he needs my comfort! Stand aside there— I'm going in."

It did not work. "Woman! After the captain and Caranga, I command this ship. I say that you may not, and I do not want to hurt you."

"No, boy, you command the *men* on this ship. My girls outnumber them considerably. Furthermore, those boys won't fight hard if I order my girls to rape them!"

While the young warrior stood looking nonplussed, deep-throated laughter gusted from the other side of the door. "Chandak!" Caranga called. "Maybe we should let her try. It could revolutionize combat!"

Chandak continued frozen, shocked; Larine said unsmilingly, "It could end war, you mean!"

More laughter from Caranga. Then, "Larine, I'm as sane as I ever was. You may come in if you insist. The catch is . . . the worst part of my interview is yet to come."

He heard her sharp intake of breath. "You are . . . all right?"

"I said I was. Would I lie to you?" Caranga's voice flowed around the statue that was the Second Mate.

"Yes!" Larine said. After a moment she almost whispered, "You promise to talk to me afterward?"

"Aye, old girl. Sure as sunrise."

With a last scathing glance at poor Chandak, Larine

turned away—and whirled. "Yah!" she said, lunging. Then she turned and departed in truth, feeling a bit better for his jerk.

Caranga listened to her footsteps fade into the distance. He said, "Go on up and see to the getting under weigh, Keeneye. We must be firm, but do be careful not to call her names. We must be patient with her, for she is a sweet girl, Larine is."

Chandak glanced at the securely closed door. It wasn't the application of the word "girl" to that hefty harridan that disturbed him. For once Caranga sounded as if by the adjective "sweet" he meant . . . sweet. Shaking his head, Chandak went to command the crew.

Caranga meanwhile returned to his work. It was grim work and he was grim about it. The darkness was not total in the cabin. Here and there a bit of light crept through this crack or that. Methodically he sealed each, unable to escape the thought that perhaps she was right and he was indeed, mad.

Still, there was a logic even in the nightmare of a lunatic. Tiana had deduced that the skull was under a spell. When it cast a shadow, its location was betrayed. Thus the Owner knew where to attack, whether with all the navies of the world or a dragon or a squadron of swift light cavalrymen. Therefore the only safe way to examine the skull was in absolute darkness.

Such an examination might provide Caranga with the clue he needed. Much was clear already, though barely comprehensible. Both the Owner and Sulun Tha represented powers vast beyond imagining; forces now locked in cosmic war one against the other. In that which Sulun Tha had called the "ultimate conflict," the skull was somehow immensely important.

The why of it was a mystery.

Yet Caranga was sure that the evil being who claimed to own the world, perhaps literally owned the world, feared the fleshless head of . . . someone. Sulun Tha, too, both wanted and needed the skull. So he had admitted, and well he should! The interview with the white wizard had confirmed Caranga's ridiculous suspicion of the manifestly impossible.

The skull in the casket of ebony and silver and the skull he had seen underlying Sulun Tha's face were one and the same.

Such a thing should not be. Such a thing could not be. That such a thing *was*, was a monstrous violation of reason. Yet it was and Caranga knew it for the truth. Just as surely he knew that such obvious explanation as a twin brother was false. No, the explanation for this darkest of mysteries had to be . . .

The chain of his thoughts broke as he gazed about and saw—by not seeing—that the cabin's darkness was now total and absolute. The last trace of light that might betray him to the Owner was gone. In the safety of this improvised blackest night, it was time to open the box. As he did so, he was horrified to see that light streamed forth from the raised lid!

A crimson light burned within the skull, making the eye sockets glowing red coals that seemed to send forth illuminating rays the color of blood.

Upon the image of the world a diffuse shadow fell, a dark blur that betrayed no location. The watchful dead saw and knew that this strange shadow portended some event to come. Tensely they waited, watching.

Caranga stared into those furnace-red eyes . . . and then he relaxed and let go his breath. Strange as the light from within the skull was, it was safe. Illumination from such a location could cast little or no shadow. Gingerly he lifted the fleshless human head out of its container. It was only cold bone. Slowly he examined it. Aided by its own glow, he contemplated the morbid red grin, gazed into those glowing eyes that were not eyes. (They weren't, were they?)

Tiana had been right in one regard: the skull did indeed house a massive ruby. Aglow by some internal fire, the jewel was a piece of crystalized flame. *Was* it a human skull? Consider. It was impossible for anyone to have placed a solid object of such size inside a seamless, unbroken skull. He had to smile at the absurd thought: unless whoever-it-was had been born this way! A creature not of flesh and blood, but solidified fire. That was no more possible, and yet it possessed a sort of logic.

Abruptly he ceased smiling with a clamp of his teeth.

It was not impossible! Not if one believed the ancient legend that claimed the Flames Which Will Destroy the World could and sometimes did take on human form and

walk about in the guise of men. With their true nature
thus concealed, the Flames went about among humankind,
unknown to humankind . . . inspecting the world, judging
whether or no it was ready for the ultimate burning. All
knew the grim myth concerning the city of Moshida. The
inhabitants of that ill-famed place had made it their custom to make perverse *use* of any passing stranger. And
when they were visited by the Flames . . .

Of course there was no evidence that the tale was true;
none save that waste of sand and rock melted into glass.
The Shining Plain: Moshida. Perhaps those ruins had once
been a city. But . . . perhaps not. Who could be sure?
Sometimes believing legends was simple stupidity. Sometimes it was stupid not to believe.

Abruptly Caranga's hands were chill and slick with
sweat. He set the skull down. No. The story was incredible.
His own opining was impossible!

Yet it explained much, which lent the feeling of truth.

For example, why should the Owner of the world fear
the skull? Answer: Any property owner fears the fire that
can destroy his property!

*Am I simply piling speculation on opines on speculation
—or am I dealing with great power of the utmost danger?*

There was no ready answer to that one, either. For an
awestruck moment he wondered if he had any right to
tamper with such fearful forces. Could any mortal man so
dare? It was tinkering with destiny itself. The consequences
of error were beyond calculation or even speculation.

These were the thoughts that assailed Caranga. He
sweated. And suddenly in that cabin of darkness he stood
tall in determination.

*I am going to save Tiana. If that puts all the world at
hazard, that is the world's problem! Doubtless all-good,
too-good (and potential monster?) Sulun Tha would regard
such an attitude as hopelessly selfish. So? Who expects
altruism from a pirate?*

Thus Caranga argued and wrestled with self and conscience, and for all his courage and resolve his hands trembled. His mouth was dry as this dread skull and his spine
no less chilly. His logical next action was all too obvious.
The skull's jaws were held shut by a silver plate whose
polished surface bore the ambiguous warning: *"This is the
skull of one called He-Who-Sleeps. His jaws are bound*

that he may not wake. Unbind them not, unless you would hear what He-Who-Sleeps will say."

Caranga nodded, and spoke aloud to that weird red-glowing skull.

"Well, my sweet smiling friend, there is no other I can ask for help for my daughter. *My* daughter! Tiana's white on the outside but any fool should be able to see what a lovely black soul she has! Since that is my problem, I do indeed want to hear what you have to say."

Bit by bit his nervous fingers undid the silver wires.

Bursts of darkness burned in brief furies upon the image of the world. The darkness was so black, so brilliant that it seemed almost to reverse the state of things. What was happening within the chamber wherein a hundred dead eyes Watched that meticulously detailed likeness of the world? Was it brilliantly lighted and now subject to flashes of darkness? Or were the flashes light, in a room in a state of darkness far more intense than the mere absence of illumination? Whatever the true state of things, the dead Watchers trembled and wails of foreboding wheezed from their mummified throats.

The last of the silver wire was loose. If there was to be second thought, now was the time.

Without pause or hesitation, the man acted. Caranga of the Simdan tribe and pirate of the Asmygorian Sea pulled off the silver plate and freed the jaws of him called He-Who-Sleeps.

Upon the image of the world the shadow of a skull appeared; a brilliant blackness of blinding intensity. From the chamber's ceiling a likeness of the sun still shone in a bright cerulean sky and for a moment the light of the sun-image warred upon the darkness of the skull-shadow. Abruptly the war was lost. Appearance shifted as suppressed truth burst forth. The image-sun shed unnatural darkness and always had. Under the burning light of the skull the false sun was withering. Half-a-hundred dead saw this whelming of their ancient black light and screamed their consternation.

"Master! Come to our aid!"

In despair and frenzy they howled in unison for help that was not to come.

*The skull opened its eyes and stared upon the dead that
were not dead. As it saw them and knew them, they could
no longer escape the truth. They were dead. Knowing
themselves to be dead, they ceased to move. Ceasing to
move, they crumbled into the decay they had so long unnaturally evaded. In moments nothing remained save dust;
the dust found in ancient tombs. The Watchers Watched no
more. The Watchers were no more.*

*With none to watch, the skull changed. It swelled, grew,
and became the shadow of a man. At this manifestation
the very stones of the chamber's walls aged and weathered
as if under the pressure of eons of desert sand and wind.*

*The shadow of Sulun Tha watched while the weight of
ages descended upon the Room of Sun-brightness and
crushed it into a ruin.*

Its work done, the shadow faded and was gone.

Caranga knew naught of the Watchers or the Room of
Sun-brightness. As far as he could discern, nothing at all
happened on his unstopping the jaws of bone. He knew a
mingling of relief and disappointment.

Having invoked a great magic without result, what did
he do next?

The furnace-red eyes drew his attention. With horrid
fascination he saw patterns in those burning eyes; things
he could surely see if he but looked more closely. *Something* had happened as a result of his releasing the jaws.
The skull was indeed speaking—with its eyes!

To see what it was saying Caranga must set his eyes
directly against the thing's empty sockets and gaze into the
interior of the skull. He disliked such necromancy. He
hated such an unclean act full of deadly possible consequences. He had vowed and would not swerve; thought
fathered deed, and he bent to the unpleasant task.

For a moment his dark-accommodated eyes must squint
and strain in the sudden bright light, however that it was
red. Then they focused and he stared out onto bright sea
sparkling like a myriad gems in the sunlight. In the distance he saw an island. It was a place whose like he had
never seen. He had heard grim tales. Despite the sunny day
and the placid sea surrounding it, the island was shadowed
over with thick black clouds that rendered it a place of
perpetual night. From myth and dread legend, Caranga
knew it.

Riser Island.

Citadel of the Owner. It was a stronghold against which several armies had launched attacks. Every assault was without result—except that those stout hosts, with their ships, had vanished without trace.

Riser Island.

In the depths of his despair, Caranga had not considered going there. Now the skull showed him the way. The skull bade him invade Riser Island.

21st Strand:

ISLE OF DARKNESS

Slowly the cabin door swung inward, and the Gray Knight tensed. A corpse appeared, dry and shriveled as a twice-ancient mummy, and did a slow glide into the captain's cabin.

"Mas-ter," it croaked, "it—is—time."

Time for what? Gray wondered. He was dressed in the clothing of this ship's late captain and, thanks to the See-The-Expected spell, the Moonstalker saw him as its ghastly master. That did not stop the imposture from being signally dangerous. The slightest violation of the role Gray played, any word or act out of character, and this monster would see him as he was. So would its horrid fellows, and no man could be a match for so many, already dead.

His gesture was a curt wave of the hand that could have meant anything. The thing took that sign as dismissal. It turned and walked slowly away. It did not shamble, or lurch, or quite shuffle. Yet to describe that gait as a glide was to insult the word. Since it left the door agape, Gray assumed that he was expected to follow.

Gray followed, feeling rather like a rabbit hopping on spikes through a nest of serpents. Down the dark narrow corridor, up the steps and onto the moonlit deck they went. The entire crew of walking dead was gathered there. Blank eyes were fixed upon their supposed captain, waiting and expectant. To Gray a lovely moon became a luminous skull riding high in a sky full of menacingly twisted clouds like skeletal hands.

I am walking on eggs. I've got to give them the order they await—or be exposed and die obscenely. And I haven't a clue as to what that order might be.

Their silence was gruesome. The night wind moaned sepulchrally. The Gray Knight's mouth was cotton dry and his hands were slick with sweat. He forced himself to pace slowly among them, austerely checking this and inspecting that. It was in character for a ship's captain, even one as weird as the monster he and Tiana had destroyed, to take his time, ever re-establishing his captaincy.

Nothing he saw gave him a clue. He heard only that mournful breeze. Was he expected to order some routine operation, something that might be done on any ship? Or was now the time when some special obscenity was performed on this vessel of the dead? Fifty helpless women prisoners languished belowdecks. It was too easy to imagine them as victims in some vile ceremony.

Gray tried to swallow but couldn't get past the boulder in his throat.

Propelled by dead rowers who sat motionless at their oars, the ship scudded over waters bright with the spectral silver of moonlight. On deck *waited* the host of walking dead, wizened dry things indifferently clad in dirty gray remnants of what might once have been colorful finery. They watched the lone knight, and hunger haunted their revenants' eyes.

Not that that tells me anything—the monsters always look hungry.

Well—I've no choice. Doing nothing is sure exposure and giving some stupid order is only probable death. It's my best gamble, then. And standing tall, Sir Gray shouted a crisp command.

"Proceed as usual!"

Instantly the ship slowed as the oars that impossibly propelled it became still. The dead oarsmen, who had sat at their locks like so many wooden figures, rose. Those on the left stepped rightward while the steer-board complement moved to port. Each group sat in the places just vacated by the other.

Brilliant leadership, captain, Gray told himself, and locked knees that wanted to let go.

"Rotation completed, Captain!"

With a curt nod, the knight strode unhindered back to his cabin. He felt chilled, as the air stirred by his own passage evaporated the sweat of apprehension and tension.

Once he was inside with the door firmly shut, he devoted several minutes merely to breathing. He had just edged sidewise through the latest of many crises in his masquerade. How long could he continue this dangerous game without disaster? *Of course it might not last much longer. And it might go on and on—I've no way of knowing how long before this awful ship reaches shore.* He did know that arrival would convert a risky situation into an almost certainly disastrous one.

His laugh was part irony, part true amusement. That Tiana woman was a magnificent fool. He had explained to her the hopelessness of the odds against them . . . and she remained arrogantly confident. The fire-haired beauty was certain that her wit, strength, and skill would bring her out victorious! *If vanity and confidence were gold,* he mused, *it's she who'd be the owner of the world!*

Stop thinking about her, he bade himself, and took out the ship's log. He opened it to resume his studies. Though the late monster had kept it in a language long dead, Gray was able to puzzle it out. He was not sure how, but felt it must be some clue to his identity. Selective—or selected— memories remained. Meanwhile the facts he had gleaned from this great ironbound tome had prevented the immediate failure of his imposture. So far, however, it had revealed nothing that would help him when he reached Riser.

Gray sighed. As he worked, occasional stray thoughts distracted him like harmless but pesky insects. Or like strands of rich red hair. . . . So many details! Any one could go awry, with deadly results. Tiana, for instance. Would that willful doer remain in her cabin? Upon his explaining why she must not leave it she had reluctantly agreed that the risk would be excessive—and promptly added with an inviting smile that at least he could come visit her.

Of course if any of the Moonstalkers were to observe such a suspicious act, the result would be fatal. And some of the things were active for brief periods during the day.

Trying to explain that to the vastly desirable and inordinately confident woman had been not so much disaster as catastrophe.

So she doesn't like being alone. Candence, neither do I!

Gray smiled wryly at memory of how he had been forced to flee her reaction. Then he pushed his attention back to the book and the strangeness of its revelations. Oh, he still saw no hope. Still, he meant to make the most of whatever chance the fates gave him. He concentrated . . . and another stray thought brought a grim smile to his face. With a singularly beautiful—and presumably willing —woman not many yards away, few men indeed would be probing a dusty old book!

The greater fools they, he mused. The eve of battle was a time to sharpen swords. Legend told of a pair of doomed lovers who whiled away the hours before a great conflict in passionate embrace. Next day brought them defeat and death. Gray had no taste for a similar fate.

This word here . . . what did "wh!atar" mean? If it was similar to the ancient Narokan "wh!etier," then. . . . Yes, that seemed to fit . . .

What would it be like to make love to Tiana? The world might have seen many women as beautiful, for the world was a large place. But he doubted that any woman had been so vividly alive. Gods, to be with her . . . ! How long since he had allowed himself a moment of peace and shared joy? While he had no memory, it seemed to the nameless knight that he had been at war for long and long. And a woman with a body like Tiana's could . . .

Drood take these thoughts! I've got to concentrate!

For what seemed the hundredth time he forced his attention back to the book. The phrase "wh!atar shz' mark!t" should mean "my ship/boat . . . landing/marking . . . Riser!"

Candence disrupt all Dark! This page describes what happens when this ship lands at Riser. It's forewarning! I'll be able to carry off this charade and get safely ashore!

The while, an enchanted cabin of that same vessel contained—only just!—a woman boiling with frustration. How dare Sir Gray neglect her this way? How dare he? Not even a word from him for days!

Yet despite her anger Tiana understood and reluctantly agreed. The eve of conflict was a time for preparation, not romance. Were Gray to come knocking at her door with amorous intent, she'd damn him for foolishly risking both their lives and slam the door in his face. (Face? He had none, damn him!) That he gave her no such opportunity considerably contributed to her anger. It was natural that men should be irresistibly drawn to her! After all, she was Tiana. *What makes Gray a sudden exception?*

Why should he have the interesting role, all the danger that makes living worthwhile, all to himself while I am stuck here like a princess amid her finery—a captive *princess?!*

Her frustration was the more intense because furious as he made her, she could not bring herself to dislike the man. *The dog! The dirty d—no, he isn't!*

No, she was forced to respect him highly. In that one brief interview he had shown himself to be bold, cunning, and more worldly-wise than any man she'd met save only Caranga. Here was a warrior who fought with his head! A better man than Bjaine the giant Northman, or Prince Eltorn, or even Bandari Highrider. He even possessed a fine sense of humor, even if it was twisted toward irony. Strong, brave . . . and yes, in his backhand way, even noble.

All of which means he shouldn't be able to resist coming to me, damn him!

To keep such thoughts from driving her up the cabin wall, Tiana attacked the only enemy to hand: the illusions that furnished her cabin. Gray's art of seeing through illusion would be handy and perhaps even decisive in the coming struggle, if only she could master it.

Slow, careful, methodical work was hardly to Tiana's taste. Still, she was quite capable of it when necessary. The art of *feeling* things as they were came rather swiftly. It was a matter of shutting her eyes, giving no heed to what she heard, and concentrating on the sensation reported by her fingers. Refocusing her ears was much harder. The cabin wanted to fill itself with the myriad sounds of a royal palace in high celebration. By practice and force of will she became able to pierce these illusions, to hear the sounds of the sea and the wind and the steady beat of oars.

Then the sound of Gray's voice would come sneaking in from somewhere and she'd have to curse and start all over again.

Seeing was a different matter. Though she assaulted known illusion with the full power of her prodigious will, the yield was but little. Her surroundings admitted their illusory nature by blurring and becoming translucent—but not transparent. Not enough to let her see the truth. A grungy cabin on a horror-ship crewed by the dead.

And that ship fled on, while Gray's necessary nearness-while-so-far heightened his desirability and fed Tiana's fantasies. Faceless and absent, he became daily more attractive.

There came a day when she thought she had lost the hard-won talent for true hearing. She could no longer discern the familiar rhythm of the oars. Another moment and she realized what had happened—she heard no oars because they had ceased to move!

There! Now they resumed thump-scraping, but at a different beat . . . which changed to a third tempo even as she stood frozen listening. The ship was maneuvering.

Praise the Back—are we approaching port at last?

Oh what I wouldn't give for a porthole! Hmm . . . why not? These illusions respond to my will, at least to some degree.

Promptly the desired viewport appeared. First it was blank. Then it filled with a view of the sun setting into a calm crystal sea. In the center of that tranquil scene was—blackness. A single, low, utterly black cloud squatted toad-like over the sun-bright waters. The foreboding veil was far from normal, hovering below a sky of red gold laced with high clouds of wispy white. Never had she seen the like of this . . . and she recognized it at once.

If she could believe the grim myths and old sea-tales, the blanket of thick black covered an island where the sun never shone; a grim place indeed of unending night.

Riser Island.

Urgently she wished that the porthole could show her more. She *willed* that she see the inner nature of that dark lair of the Owner. After a few seconds, the pattern of the cloudscape shifted and congealed. Briefly she saw through the veil of dark mists into the core. It was black. Tiana stared, unpleasantly reminded of the temple of evil she had once discovered up in Woeand; that bat-dominated place of the Sisters of Death.

Riser Island *was* a bat. A gigantic thing, taller than mountains. Its baleful head vaulted arrogantly up toward the heavens while vast wings beat out waves of hatred upon the world.

For a single moment of horror Tiana saw the monster flaunting its power and its contempt for all that lived. Then the scene vanished. So did the porthole, and all the other illusionary furnishings of the cabin. Tiana was alone in a rough wooden stall with a pile of molding straw in one corner. There was the mingled reek of ammonia, feces, and . . . herself.

Tiana hardly noticed. She did not notice the tremblor of her hands. Her awareness was filled with the evil she had just seen, and the greater horror it implied. Yet surely the vision was not literal truth. She had wanted to see the true nature and had viewed a symbolic representation: the Owner was a malign Power vast beyond reckoning. Before him she and the Gray Knight were mere insects; creatures the Owner could destroy with a casual gesture.

And I just blundered. The use I made of the porthole could easily attract his attention.

Likely no harm was done. She must be more careful just the same, particularly in view of what Gray had told her. They had exchanged accounts of their recent adventures. Naturally Tiana's saga was far more glorious and exciting, for she omitted no detail of her hardihood and absolute fearlessness in the face of peril. Nevertheless Gray's quietly told story was of considerable interest; it did explain much of their present situation and how they had gotten into it.

It was the knight's gloomy deduction that all was the result of a nightmare war between the wizards Pyre and Ekron. Long had it endured, and now it seemed approaching the final confrontation. True, Pyre was not vulnerable to any attack the toad-souled Ekron might launch, and he had proven it. But in a moment of haste and anger he had sworn an unbreakable oath to avenge Tiana's death. In that vow, Gray opined, the Narokan mage had seen his opportunity. Not even Pyre, wizard of wizards, had any hope of victory against the Owner. Therefore Ekron had plotted to arrange matters so that Tiana would die at the Owner's hands. Pyre must move to avenge, and thus his doom would be sealed.

It was the most hideous admission Tiana had ever had to make: *I am considered unimportant; merely a tool!* At that unacceptable assault on her pride she had bitten unwittingly into her lip. It was still sore.

Perhaps the toad-souled one had somehow tricked Magistrate Ishcon into acting as he did. Perhaps the late jurist had been offered some irresistible bribe. Either way, he had served his purpose, and he had been rewarded. Ekron's murderous familiar, a tiny spider, had hanged Ishcon at the end of a single strand of its webbing. All that had been an elaborate ruse to get Tiana into the arena-cage. Her resourcefulness was without question. The means of her escape had been present; naturally she had employed them. And even that was a part of Ekron's plan. Ishcon's words and her escape were part of the ruse to trick her into stealing the casket of ebony and silver. The box that housed the skull of He-Who-Sleeps. That too was predictable, knowing Tiana; she was, after all, a thief.

Her theft had flung the fat into the fire, Gray had said, and Tiana had winced, thinking of the pig that dropped into her place in the burning "temple" of the Sleeping Demon. For some reason her taking the skull had challenged the Owner—*frightened* the Owner? Thus he was provoked to attack her. The Owner had mobilized the armada against *Vixen*. The Owner had sent the supposedly legendary dragon against her. The Owner had sent Thunlander troops to find and slay her near Cave Run Falls in Thesia. In each case, she had provided unwitting aid by opening the box and taking out the skull, which somehow apprised the Owner of her whereabouts.

"Somehow," Tiana said slowly, staring at the cabin wall rather than the faceless knight, "that skull is the most important object in the world!"

He had nodded. "Since the Owner of the world seems to fear it—yes, it must be."

"Wonderful," she had sighed. "And here I am, a captive, without that Drood-grasped box!"

Together, they had continued outlining the master plot and its consequences—to now. While Ekron was marching toward victory—having manipulated Tiana and, in a way, even the Owner—Pyre had not been asleep. Yet he had been in the paralysis of some occult restriction. The future was there. How could he avoid it without knowing what it held? Yet if he knew what it held how could he avoid it, given that restrictive aspect of prescient magic? This Gray had attempted to explain by pointing out that if one saw something, it was there. How could it be changed? This hand, for instance. Very well; substitute the future. If one saw it, obviously it existed. How could it be changed, altered, avoided? Tiana had given little heed to that involved metaphysics-complicated-by-sorcery. Enough to know that Pyre was unable to take action on his own behalf. The best he could do was impress some hapless man of honor and gallantry into his service. Thus; the Gray Knight, rendered nameless and faceless. Sir Gray. And he was sent forth without instructions as to what he was supposed to do.

"Now I realize it," Gray had said sadly. "My mission is to save you, obviously."

"Hmp! As if I—hmm. Perhaps your mission is to destroy the Owner?" She liked that concept far better than his, which made her the oft-told-of squeaky "heroine" in need of rescue by a big strong clod. Even as she was reminded of that big strong clod Bjaine Nor'man, her mind provided an even more complimentary concept. "Or to help *me* destroy the Owner!" she said excitedly, and almost immediately carried it a step further, into suitably satisfactory importance for Captain Tiana Highrider: "Or to provide me with the means to combat Ekron and Owner!" *Which makes you Pyre's messenger and my assistant,* she had thought, but then she had begun to gloom again.

All this trouble to bring her and Gray together so that he could hand her a junky walnut shell stuffed with a spider and some dead flies?

Still, she clung to that disgusting object. The spider obligingly remained within. Munching flies, no doubt.

It was infuriating to discover that Ekron had manipulated her; that he *(the toad-nosed lackwit!)* actually chose her as an expendable pawn in a dark game whose board was the entire world. The latter fact did not make her feel more important, she told herself. She was both insulted and furious but able to deny being slightly affrighted. That was comforting.

Gray had to be wrong, she decided. She told him so.

"You're right that we're in a death trap, dear. But you're wrong in saying we're doomed. We're far from doomed! Look here, Gray. By my own bold actions I have reduced the trap to a—half-clever scheme! Who could possibly predict *Tiana?*" She had slapped her chest, which at the time seemed to be mostly visible above the gold-purfled "neck"-line of her mentally created gown of royal purple all asparkle with pearls. (Atean pearls, of course, each worth several pieces of the best gold.) "That frog-begot Ekron thought I'd go all squeaky and run and hide like a scared mouse. Ha! In that case I'd have been destroyed by the entirely-too-great Power of this man or thing or toadstool called the Owner. But instead he is dealing with Tiana, that doubtless fly-catching Ekron Toad-butt. I am attacking! Such daring must surely take our enemies by surprise!"

Never mind that she was a helpless captive in a pen rowed by dead men who probably took their nourishment from the veins of such as she. She had taken action! She was attacking!

Thus she argued with Gray and thus she convinced herself throughout endless days asea on a ship she did not command. It was necessary that she argue thus. She must convince herself that she was in control and that all would be well. She knew that if she yielded to despair she was as good as dead before the battle.

Now all I have to do is make sure there is a battle—

Her reverie was interrupted by sounds from without. The ship's oars commenced making loud splashes as though they were being stroked against the galley's motion. The ship, she knew, was slowing, turning slightly. She held her breath during a few moments of silence. Then there came the wooden banging of oars being shipped, followed by the grumbling dull roar of the galley's hull scraping against a pier.

"We have landed at Riser," she said aloud. "Soon I'll have my chance."

As soon as she got her heart up out from between her toes.

Her chance was coming and she was determined that odds did not matter. She would fight this one, as she had fought all the other battles, to the utmost of her considerable ability. What matter that the vile toad-wizard had built an elaborate scheme on the assumption that she had no chance in such a conflict? He was only a man! The world was full of foolish men who had grossly underestimated her—to their pain and worse. Surely rather more than half of them no longer tenanted the world.

Footsteps sounded.

A company of men coming for her and the other women.

No. Though they walked on two legs and in step, those who paced toward her stall were anything but men. Tiana stood waiting. Chin high, arms folded, eyes haughtily staring. She would not admit to herself that she was afraid. Yet for all that high resolve and her stance she trembled in dread of the shuddersome things that were coming for her.

There was a fumbling at the door of her prison and her armpits prickled. With infinite slowness that door crept open.

Tiana gasped at sight of the being standing in the open doorway.

He was a smiling, pink-faced, plump man clad in cheerful green velvet with wide lacy frills like feathermoss on a crentree. A royal chamberlain! He beamed at her.

"Joyous tidings, Princess Tiana! Our ship is at last arrived in our homeland and your adoring subjects await you."

He made a bowing gesture that she should follow him and in a trice Tiana was the center of a glorious royal procession. She walked upon a soft, plush red carpet while pages in powder blue livery scattered rose petals at her feet. Somehow she wore a regally flowing gown of marmoreal white, in diaphanous samite within which the beauty of her body was concealed or revealed depending upon the lighting and the length of her steps. A circlet of gold studded with a multicolored blaze of gemstones circled her brow. A necklace of fiery rubies and emerald-encrusted bracelets glittered at her neck and wrists. The scent of rose petals filled her nostrils and her dress swished just marvelously. From her necklace and bracelets trailed long strands of fine gold chain, their ends borne by darling little girls with childish faces oh-so-solemn on this momentous occasion.

Tiana walked straight, head high, her shoulders so well back it almost hurt. Her brows were regally arched. Soon the royal procession was off the ship and onto the flowerflanked road leading up to her father's imposing palace of marble. Pennons fluttered on high. Adoring throngs lined the road, cheering their lungs out with ecstasy at the return of their beloved Princess Tiana. Flowers were tossed into the roadway for her royal feet.

It's no more than I deserve, of course, but still I don't quite believe it. For all that she watched the flattering illusions with disdain, their appeal to her vanity was great and passed into the main room of the House. She had furnished this reception chamber with an elegance none of her competitors could match. Now her belly turned to lead. A trail of smashed and torn finery spread from one end of the chamber to the other. A big boulder could have rolled through and left no more wreckage.

Of the door at the room's far end there remained only shattered kindling. Forgetting that she had planned to abandon this place she had created, Larine could only gaze in horror on the destruction of her property.

In a corner, one of the masked invaders was coughing great gouts of blood on her brand new Morcarish carpets. His chest was crushed.

"Here you," she stormed, "stop that! That rug cost two months' profits!"

He rolled dazed eyes at her. "Name of . . . the B-Ba-a-ack . . . mercy," he said, in a hideous strained voice, and continued to befoul the rug.

What to do? Cutting the dog's throat would just make more mess and even smothering him with one of her beautiful Aradotish cushions would soil the sky-blue silk irreparably. Snatching up a brass spittoon, she propped it against his face.

"Here," she urged, "do be kind enough to cough into this."

Even as the dazed man stared at her, there came a tremendous thundering crash. The sound of striking lightning came from beyond the shattered door. Larine shuddered at the thought of more damage to her property.

Passing out into her garden, she moaned at the destruction. The trail of smashed bushes and crushed and uprooted shrubs might have marked the passage of an elephant. The tracks, however, were those of a large bear. Where the earth was moist and soft in the shade of a big crentree, she found more prints—high-heeled boots. Here and there the boot-prints were *in* the animal tracks.

That wolf-bitch is chasing the monster!

Her eyes stared along the path of destruction. It wound so that she could not see its entire length, yet still she saw its end. The garden was surrounded by a high stone wall of which Larine was most, most proud. In one place it was now blasted asunder. She understood the crash she had heard. Unable to stop herself, she crept to the breached wall. And found Chandak Keeneye remonstrating with the wolfish bitch.

"You promised your father to stay out of trouble, Captain!"

"I made no such promise," Tiana replied evenly.

"Well, he thinks you did. If aught befalls you, he'll hold me responsible. Look!" He gestured at the scattered fragments of stone and the jagged hole. "That beast did this as easily as a man knocking over a cricket cage—and you were chasing such a creature!"

"Of course I was—and I expect my Second Mate to have sense enough to know that if I had *wanted* to catch it, I'd have caught it. I did not."

"But Captain . . . why?"

"I had to chase it," Tiana said sweetly, "or it wouldn't have run away."

That fellow's got a lot of restraint, Larine thought. *I'd wring her smarty neck!*

"Why would a creature of such great power run away at all?" the poor fellow asked. "What did you do to it?"

"I scratched its nose."

"What?"

"Chandak, that was just an overgrown bear. When I flicked the point of my rapier across that big soft black nose, it *hurt*. Stung like fire." Tiana paused, looking at his right arm. His bronze body bore many red splotches. Only the red stain on his arm was his own blood. "That," she said judiciously, "won't require a stitch, but we had better go back so I can wash and bandage it."

Abruptly Larine noticed the man's boots. *The fool went running through my compost pile!* Her own voice and words surprised her, but here it came, as if she had been tapped on the knee: "You're not tramping into my House until you clean those boots!"

Puzzled, he looked down at his own feet and Tiana's boots. "Captain, why are your boots clean and mine dirty? We ran along the same path—right to and through the dung-heap."

"Compost pile," Larine corrected.

"I used a stepping stone," Tiana replied cheerfully. "Come, I'll show you." She turned and began walking; they followed. "Housemother . . . I know little of the noble symbols of Palanigh. Would you tell me what three red ostrich features signify?"

"The Royal House," Larine told.

"Ah. And a red lion on a field of gold?"

"Rampant or crouching?"

"Rampant."

"That's a chief Lord of Justice—a magistrate from whose word there is no appeal."

"Aha. And lastly—a silver bar on a black field?"

"Black and white are for the priests, Captain Tiana. If pale, then the wearer is a High Inquisitor."

Tiana smiled. "Ahhh. Then a man wearing a silken hat with three large red feathers, a cloth-of-gold coat with a lion and black velvet leggings with a silver bar trim would be . . . ?"

"Duke Murtud! Member of the Royal Family, Highest Lord of Justice, Chief Inquisitor. After the king, the most powerful man in Orvar." There was more than a hint of alarm in the voice of the proprietor of the House of No Tomorrow. "Wh-why do you ask that?"

"Yes," Chandak said, "who's this Duke Murtud and what is he to us?"

Tiana made no attempt at concealing the wicked glee in her voice. "Why, he's the man in the dung-pile. I didn't befoul my boots because I used him as a stepping stone." She laughed at their consternation. Poor Larine hurriedly made the Sign of the Dagger, the means by which the Orvarian demigod Yorimagua had been slain. "The gnat-brain stepped directly in front of the bear," Tiana advised. "I had the thing lumbering along in blind panic, scampering on all fours. Old Murtud stepped right into its path. He shouted 'No, Kragg, back, back!' It ran right over him and stomped him into the, ah, compost."

They had reached the source of fertilizer for Larine's table-spices and her beauteous garden. In it wallowed a man dressed in what had been blatantly elegant clothing. Three sets of tracks crossed his body. He was only now regaining consciousness. Up came his pointy-bearded head.

"I'll have that cowardly beast skinned alive," he mumbled. "Such disloyalty—"

"I doubt that you gave it much reason to be loyal," Tiana observed.

"What! How dare—" His voice trailed off when he saw who loomed above him, with the point of her rapier a hand's breadth from his potatoey nose. It was a very narrow blade, profoundly nasty-looking.

"Why did you try to have us killed?"

"I—I—you dare—uh!" The swordpoint approached. "It was a mistake!"

"Of *course* it was. Perhaps your last mistake. I asked why."

"Ahhh . . ." As he hesitated, the point of the sword advanced almost to his nose, forcing him down into the stenchy cess. Murtud commenced to babble. "It wasn't my idea! The others said that as long as we had to raid the joyhouses to get the girls for the Moonstalkers, we might as well despatch the proprietors and confiscate their property . . ."

"Murder the honest businesswomen and take all the loot you could carry, you mean. So. You serve the Moonstalkers who serve we-both-know-who, eh? It may surprise you, dear duke and priest and judge, but I've been looking for someone like you! What's your quota?"

Larine was mumbling away to Susha, Cud, Yorimagua, and several others. Chandak Keeneye was looking from his captain to the mighty lord in the pile of manure.

"A dozen . . . extra girls," Murtud replied, in obvious fear and puzzlement.

"Well, my darling lord, you are going to meet that quota! Oh not with that absurd *quantity,* but with quality that is the same."

"What!" Larine's shout was one of horror. "You mean you're going to help deliver innocent women into this monstrous evil?"

"No," Tiana said equably. "Not innocent, and not *women* either. *A* woman. A single person of such wonderful surpassing beauty that she alone fills the quota. A woman worth any twelve others."

Chandak stared at his surpassingly beautiful captain first in puzzlement, then in dawning horror.

Palanigh's harbor was empty save for one vague dark shape in the ghostly moonlight. The black galley rode at the end of the longish pier. Along that planking a man and a woman came walking. Her hands were tied behind her back in a way that tightened her tight blouse across her chest in some strain. Another rope circled her neck; the man held its other end. Her tight silk shirt and short snug leggings displayed a figure just as beauteous as her face.

and Tiana fought the temptation to forget that all this was a lie designed to beguile her every sense.

The Bear, the Bear, she thought. *Think of the Bear of Sarsis, Tiana! This is all standard illusion and you've been here afore.*

Ah but the beauty, the glory, the vanity . . .

Her new sandals were especially pleasing. Completely open save for a few ruby-laden straps, they provided excellent display of her beautiful feet. *(But if my boots are gone so is the dagger I hid there back in Palanigh.)*

A frightening thought, that—and there was worse. As massively pleasing as it all was, she could not help noticing the unpleasant odor. It kept fighting its way past the scents of perfume and rose petals.

Something was rotten. *The Bear,* she tried to tell herself; *the Bear* . . . but wasn't that another illusion altogether? When was she?

Amid a smashing mental blow she perceived how deadly it could be to lose touch with what she knew had to be reality. She was supposed to be sucked into this sweet quicksand of illusion. She was being sucked in! *No!* But could she do anything against it? Perhaps not. Yet perhaps too these illusions were so very pleasing because they were weaker than those which had filled her cabin, able to prevail only against those at least partially willing to be deceived. The skill she'd developed at cost of great frustration might now serve her. Perhaps . . . Fear spurred her to fight. Urgently she desired, *willed* that she see things as they were, beyond this wondrous appearance.

My father's a handsome pirate and so am I and I am captain of a ship, not a soft princess, and this isn't seemly! I will know what is the true state of me and my surroundings! I will I will I will . . .

She was a participant in a wrestling match taking place behind her eyes, trying to break a hammer-lock grasp on her mind—and then she broke free.

All about her matter shuddered and a host of subtle changes took place.

Her gemmy necklace and bracelets became a black iron slave collar and heavy manacles. Rather than gold chains carried by pretty little girls, her bonds were connected by heavy iron chains to the collars and manacles of other girls and women in a line of bound and helpless captives marching in grim coffle toward . . . no castle. The squat building of black stone crouched in darkness on a hill under a leprous moon. The chamberlain was indeed much as he had initially appeared. The difference was that he was a few weeks dead. Putrefied flesh hung loosely from his bones and occasionally fell in dripping gobbets onto the muddy ground.

All this Tiana saw in a flash, for a greater horror demanded and possessed her attention.

A crowd did indeed line the roadway. They were not cheering. They were dead, some freshly so and others like the chamberlain while still others were withered parchment-dry mummies. Though the mob of corpses was widely varied, in one hideous respect all were the same.

Their eyes.

They watched the procession of attractive young women, flaunting their beauty as though they were in truth princesses, with avid eyes filled with unnatural hunger.

Tiana Highrider, pirate! She wanted nothing so much as to scream her terror to the skies. Her spine crawled with cold worms and she was drenched in chill sweat. Her legs quivered and she clenched her teeth against their chatter. And she strove. She imitated her companions in preening before the obscene watchers *they* saw as loving subjects. Devoutly she hoped that the decaying horde would see her as merely one more in a procession of a hundred; and that nothing would attract their horridly fervid attention to her.

Sir Gray had promised that as soon as he was able he would secure a disguise of some sort for her, come and find her in captivity, and free her.

Never before had she depended so much on the promise of a man.

As her escort approached the black stone building, Tiana realized that it was not atop the hill, but just over the apex. Thus when the line of chained women passed over the top, she had a few moments in which to survey Riser Island. It sprawled below—a great necropolis.

Under the light of a moon that seemed a grinning skull sprawled a vast shadowy panorama of tombs, crypts, and mausoleums. The buildings of the dead stretched as far as she could see through the semi-darkness.

To her right, in neat orderly rows like bushes in a large well-tended garden, was an army of men in full armor. Each was impaled on the sharpened top of a wooden post. She could only wonder at the purpose of this cavalry

"I know this about myself," the faceless knight said gravely. "Mine is a twisted fate and no lesser oath could bind me. And—I do wish to be bound to you, Tiana."

Even as he spoke, she was distracted at sight of what lay ahead. The first of this long single file of squatty night-mares was marching through a gate that glowed a dull red. Furnace red. It was a furnace. In the inferno beyond the gate, the . . . things burst into bright flames and shriveled like leaves in a fire. Tiana's shudder communicated itself to Gray, who gripped her legs strong enough to hurt. It did not hurt. It reminded her that she was alive. Too, she and this man had just accepted formal permission each to lay hands on the other in reassurance, and otherwise as well.

Two become one, they watched those ahead of them stride into the flames to be *gone,* without shrieks or flinch-ing. Each fiery disappearance brought Tiana and Gray a step closer to the same oblivion.

At last, that thing said, Tiana reflected. *Final, ultimate death, "at last." That's hardly my view! Perhaps the de-tails of my future, this oversworn marriage, all of it—all of that seems less important than whether I shall have a fu-ture at all!*

So far as she could see, the worshipers of death were making the final homage to their god without an audience to applaud their piety. So far as she could see . . . but her instincts shouted that the opposite was the truth; a great and fearful power Watched everything that happened here. Abruptly the patterns of shadow and fireglow and ghostly moonlight shifted. For an instant she glimpsed what was above the fiery gateway: a single watching Cyclo-pean eye.

A vast unnatural beast, she realized—and the gate must be its mouth!

Only four of the things remained in the line between Tiana/Gray and that dreadful mouth. Now three. She could actually feel the edacious hunger with which the horror watched them. Suddenly her breath caught. Until now she had paid no heed to the odd loops of stone that surrounded the gateway. Mere unusual conformations of masonry? Oh no! No more than the ceiling-scaling serpents in the temple of death! She was looking at tentacles; the tentacles of the monster whose mouth the gate was . . . tentacles that completely surrounded her and Gray. And the last of the three before them vanished into the fiery mouth.

The two adventurers were alone in front of it. The mouth yawned. The fires leaped within.

Turning to the black thing behind him, Gray spoke in his usual soft, polite tones. "I believe you are entitled to go before us."

The thing stirred, started past. Then it halted. *"Us?"*

Tiana was not sure what happened next. Perhaps the demon went ahead into swift incandescence; perhaps Gray tripped it. In either case it was gone and the pirate queen and nameless knight were alone on the threshold of flame-death.

"By my count," Gray said blandly, "you have received your full quota."

No, Tiana thought, *no—that one you slew that vanished . . . but then it was different . . .*

The eye opened wide to glare down at them with fearful intensity. Tiana heard Gray's soft whisper: "I am merely what you expect." Over and over he repeated it, and she joined him, matching her words to his, their words and tone blending while the stone tentacles quivered in a threat to lash into malign life. The doubled whisper droned on, a chant from two throats bound by the Third Oath.

Gradually that ireful Eye dulled. The stone became again inert. The great infernal mouth slowly closed, and they stood before a blank stone wall.

23rd Strand:

CAPTIVE HONEYMOON

Outside the small building of white marble that seemed to house the sunshine itself, Gray paused. "Well, beloved, this seems a pretty place to spend our honeymoon."

He was jesting; yet the words and trace of mockery in his tone might as well have been water hurled on a cat.

Her green eyes flashed as Tiana spat her reply. "Wedded or no, we are companions in battle and no more! Mates of necessity and just that! Once this is over I'll be the one to say what happens between us, and when—if ever!"

She could not hear his expression. She could only hear that quiet sad murmurous voice that tended either to calm or to instill guilt. "When we were together in your cabin on the ship that bore us here, you did not take that attitude. However, my lady wife, it shall be as you say . . . in the unlikely event that we survive."

"The ship—that was loneliness and desperation and nothing else and you're cruel to mention it!" Then she pointed to the door and hurriedly shifted the focus of their attention. "What do you make of that lock?"

"The same as you. A good but common enough lock, one I am sure you could pick with ease. However, the lock is the only barrier keeping us out of this treasure house, and that is most suspicious."

"Right. Give me a boost up. I want to check the roof. And don't *fondle!*"

"Who could resist," he murmured, and hoisted her high. From atop his shoulders, she stretched, strained, grasped an ornamental carving. After a moment of struggling for hand- and footholds, she vanished up onto the roof.

The Gray Knight was left alone with his thoughts.

Why did I act that way? That marvelous woman is as nervous about this so-called marriage as I—and too vain to admit being afraid. There's no reason for me to take pleasure in reminding her that we're likely to die. She's bright and eager, like a girl when I'm more an old man—could I be?—burning with hope. Merely because I cannot share that hope is no reason to quench it. Why, I've probably no right to wed! 'Twill be a Drood-knot indeed if it turns out that I already have a wife! Even if I do not I surely have a position, responsibilities, probably a betrothal; duties I can't neglect. How will all that fit with marriage to a wild, utterly free and such a girlish woman?

He could not cage her; that would be worse than murder! On the other hand to live with this woman on her own terms meant the destruction of his quiet, well-ordered life . . . assuming he had used to have one and could return to it.

Such a change—particularly with such a woman—seemed as radical as birth!

The phrase *quiet, well-ordered life* had come easily into his mind, Gray realized. Strange. He had no trouble remembering what kind of person he was—in general terms. *Is the spell wearing thin?* It might soon be gone! That was exciting, yet . . . Much as he needed his memories, wanted his identity and complete sense of self, Gray dreaded regaining them. What he learned about himself would, he suspected, be nothing pleasant.

Why was that continuing suspicion there?

Damn blast and blight Who Am *I?!*

He did not know. But he knew what was part of him, or rather who.

Abruptly Tiana dropped from above, flexing legs absorbing her impact in the manner of a big cat. "I've found something extremely important! Listen . . ."

"Wait. You listen, Tiana. First I must say something. I . . . find," he essayed, and hesitated for these were words that did not come easily. "I find that I love you and that I want you for my wife more than anything else in the world."

She regarded him—or rather did not, but showed him a soft gaze. Slowly she said, "That doesn't mean our living together would work, you know. The gods know I'm drawn to you, but . . ."

"I know," he said quickly. He was as uncomfortable in this as she was. He moved, clasped her to him, felt himself hugged in turn, and loved the feeling. What he knew was that he was being used, without knowing exactly why. And he did not know who he was. Caring for her and about her and knowing she cared about him; embracing her and being embraced; these were to Gray what six fawning haremgirls might have been to another man. No, more. Gray's need was deep, and it was broad.

At last he eased his hold, and she did. "I know, beloved," he repeated. "We can sort out all that later. Tell me what you found."

He saw her sigh, and he was gratified by that. Then he saw the old excitement leap into her eyes and animate her face. She was again the reflexive, almost pure sensation Tiana of Reme: Pirate Queen and bane of wizards and demons.

"Nothing! she said. "Absolutely nothing! I was sure I would find some kind of alarm on the roof. There is *nothing!*"

Gray nodded thoughtfully. "Umm. That makes this smell all the more like a trap. The question we have to decide is . . ."

His voice trailed off. Tiana, not waiting to discuss the problem with him, had already begun picking the lock. Of course she was right: there was no way they'd accomplish their mission without taking some large risks. Still, life with this beautiful headstrong creature would never be dull and never easy, the faceless man mused . . . if he could in fact get the magnificent woman to live with him. (*Or if I could live with her*, the thought came, but he pretended that it had not.)

With a nice little click, the lock yielded and the door opened soundlessly.

Before them lay what had to be the treasure trove of the Owner; He Who Owned All The World. They gazed upon a single smallish room empty except for a crude iron table. Upon that table, arranged in a neat row, lay six skulls. They appeared totally human and their jaws were wired shut with silver. Both disturbers of this room's strange tranquility were squinting. Together the six skulls glowed as though they were the very sun.

"Six," Gray's soft voice murmured, with reverence. "And the one you stole makes the seventh. A perfect set."

"*The* seventh? What do you know about these shining uglinesses that I don't?"

"Tiana . . have you heard that the Flames Which Will Destroy the World are seven?" He put a hand on her shoulder, pressed without quite squeezing. It was more a touch than a cling; more a sharing than possessiveness. "This explains much—I think. The—like any prudent property-owner, the Owner sought to protect his property. He imprisoned six of the seven Flames, that they might never destroy his property: the world! Since the seventh Flame was hidden beyond the realms of men, even the Owner could not find it."

Tiana knew when to listen. Still, she was nervous about her and Gray. "We'd best stop staring into this glare, darling. Here, look at me while you t—oh *Dung!*" She kept forgetting. Her gaze slid off him as heated oil slid off a polished swordblade. *Wed!* she thought in some anguish, but she touched his arm. "Please go on. It makes a sort of sense—more sense than most of what has happened to us, and we know it *has* happened!"

"How Ekron succeeded in locating that seventh Flame when the Owner failed," he said, "is a mystery. Perhaps for some reasons of its own the Flame was willing that Ekron should find it, even imprison it. Once he learned its location—or put it there?—he began constructing a complicated web of events that resulted in your stealing that Skull—and thus starting the deadliest of quarrels."

"Between Owner and Ekron?"

"Pyre is involved."

"Well, so are we," Tiana burst out, "and what are we going to do about it?"

No sooner had she spoken than her eyes widened in the horror of knowledge most unwelcome.

She sees it too, Gray thought. *We are in a win-or-die quarrel with the Owner and the only way we can win is to unleash the Flames and put the world at hazard! Blight and Candence . . . I have just begun to enjoy living in it! What an exciting world, with Tiana ever near!*

He said, "I don't know." He gestured at the orderly row of shining skulls. "Perhaps if we examine our smiling friends we'll find some clue."

Both of them turned toward the iron table and its eerie burden. "I'd love to know why it is we feel no heat and can even bear to look at all this brightness," Tiana said, but still she and her husband had not become quite suspicious enough; had not noticed quite enough.

Gray did, too late. Those objects of awesome power were close enough to touch and—Gray's eyes narrowed. Something was wrong. The skulls were somehow fuzzed at the edges; ever so slightly blurred. Like an imperfect image, each and all of them. He reached out for one—and cursed explosively when his hand passed through it.

"Tiana! Flee! It's a trap!"

Her reaction time was incredible. Surely no heart could have beat between the time he shouted his warning and that of her whirling to leap toward the open doorway—only to rebound as if she had struck a solid wall.

While she was scrambling up from the floor, making vicious noises from a vicious face, his sword flashed through the air in a broad arc. Sparks flew where the stout blade scraped upon the stone wall, and also where it scraped seemingly empty air.

"Drood's Thousand Arms—I can see that door we came in by, but it isn't there! It's shut like—"

"Like the mouth of some monster that's swallowed us," Tiana said, and her voice was grim. Or perhaps it was defeated, wretched.

Standing helplessly before a doorway that was in truth a solid wall of stone, the Gray Knight cursed himself. He should have guessed. The Owner had guarded his property against theft; it was only natural that he would also bait traps to catch thieves. These skulls on the table were merely a seeming! A damnable illusion used as as bait to lure would-be thieves into this cage. The devil had thought of everything! Doubtless the Owner did indeed possess the skulls they thought they saw here. They were not here. They must be infinitely well hidden and guarded somewhere altogether else.

"Gray! You're sweating and so am I!"

Such a distraction annoyed him. "Of course we are! We're both tense to the crowns of our . . . skulls." His mind was busy with another problem. A slight not overly pleasant odor rode the air. He could not quite place it . . . yes he could! Recognition, realization hit him with the force of a blow. The room seemed cool. It was not. He and Tiana were sweating profusely and the fact could not be attributed solely to tension. The odor he smelled was that of roasting leather! Their boots were smoldering because the floor was red hot under their feet.

It was a blasphemy against deified reason and logic. His mind reeled; he *knew* that although this room appeared entirely normal, it was a disguise for a huge oven. As he desperately set his brain to seeking some escape from the infernal trap, the floor rose beneath his feet.

Even while he fought for balance, Gray discovered that he was suspended in mid-air. So his eyes told him; yet it felt as if he was resting upon a ragged row of enormous, sharp teeth. He heard his own scream and struggled wildly while the upper jaw descended toward the lower. For the moment his armor was holding; otherwise he'd have been multiply pierced. He was just able to wrench free, leaving behind a jagged piece of his gray cloak.

What he and Tiana saw was that bit of cloak floating on air while slowly being shredded into smoking smoldering fragments.

An unseen tentacle seized him and Gray struggled against madness. It was trying to force him back into the invisible teeth.

"We're in the mouth of a Fire Elemental! It's trying to chew us to pieces!" Again he tore himself free of the tentacle he realized was the demon's tongue. "Tiana! Here! It's escape now or perish!"

She whirled in a wild spray of fire-red hair and leaped into his outstretched arms. As he lifted her swiftly upward she sprang away with a recoil of strong legs that staggered him the more. Still, he was more than gratified to see her sail over the invisible tongue. She landed in the rear of what Gray still saw as a bright-lit room—illuminated by the glow of six skulls that were not there.

Legs and arms flying, Tiana vanished into the floor.

Gray was on the tongue, fighting it, floundering in the air, battling his way up and over an unseen barrier that squirmed like a vast snake. The only way out of the demon's mouth was to crawl down its throat, he knew. To be swallowed whole deliberately before he was chewed to pieces. The task seemed impossible, like climbing a moving mountain of slime. No sooner did he force himself up by a hand's breadth or two than his slippery adversary hurled him back down. The heat remained. Though his armor had at first afforded protection, now it threatened to roast him within a carapace of iron links.

Looks like I'm dead. Glad I threw Tiana down the thing's throat, at least. To die without ever knowing who I—

A sudden spasm seized the invisible tongue. It swallowed. Lifted up and over, Gray flew through the air to fall toward the floor that was not there. He plunged into darkness . . .

For a heartbeat he was falling blindly through a void. Then he landed with a chime of hot armor and a bone-shaking impact. His teeth clacked. Lying still on his stomach, he was content simply to gasp his breaths and be glad that he lived. He lay in total blackness, and it erupted a voice.

"Gray?"

"Darling! I'm here. Are you all right?"

"You don't mind if I don't answer? I think you saved us from the frying pan but I fear this may be the fire."

"Look on the bright side, Tie. We—"

"I can't look on anything! Open your eyes and you'll see we're in pitch blackness!"

"A stomach, yes. But I was about to say that we came to

Riser to learn the Owner's secret—to discover what he fears—and we've succeeded."

"Oh yes! But by the Cow's udders! The *great secret* turns out to be trivial. Anyone with any sense could have guessed that the Owner would fear the World Fires!—a *stomach!* Blight and dung, you're right! Ugh!"

"By the Cow's Udders and Candence, woman, anyone with any sense would never be here in the first place."

He heard her sigh, and when she spoke it was with uncharacteristic softness. "That's true." She was silent, but as he started to speak, she said in a child's voice, "I wish I knew who this Candence is you swear by."

"My dear, I haven't the faintest fogbound notion." The moment he had spoken, though, he did know the answer. "Wait! It isn't a 'who,' Tiana! Candence is light! Light is what the Owner fears most, after the Flames."

"Well, I wish we could meet him and curse him with it," she said, and he felt her hand touch his gauntlet. He squeezed.

This time Gray sighed. "It's normal enough, I'm afraid, this not realizing the obvious until it hits us in the head. Most great secrets are painfully obvious. Men ignore truth that is staring them in the face until they die or are bashed in the head with it."

"Why dar-ling! That's positively philosophic! You have depths I'm still discovering."

He squeezed her hand. "I wish I could believe we were going to have time to explore each other's depths, beloved. We just—" He forgot to finish the sentence as he stared. Somewhere, seemingly far in the distance, a pale, opalescent light appeared. It was moving toward them. "I think," Gray said in a whisper, "that we will soon learn whether you are right—whether this is indeed the fire."

"Gray . . . what do you see?"

"Light."

"Gray? What do you *see?*" she repeated, and it hit him so that together they said, "Candence!" And hope soared.

Gray was sure that Pyre's spell could afford no protection in this situation. Anyone finding them would expect thieves and see them accordingly! As that pallid light came slowly, silently toward them, Gray searched his mind, desperately seeking some trick that might save them from discovery. He found none. And then he could see the source of the ghostly light: a great round moonstone, all

aglow with a cool silvery luminescence. It seemed to float
through the air—until he realized that it was a globe that
rested atop a black rod. Someone—or something—approached, bearing that rod.

Walking calmly through the stomach of a Fire Elemental?

No; now Gray could see that they were in a corridor
hewn from living rock. The approacher seemed to be
merely a man dressed in concealing dark robes . . . except
that rather than walking along the corridor, it was a shadow that glided along the wall of stone.

A living shadow.

Perhaps; but its voice was flat and cold as death. *"You
are to be congratulated. Not in an eon have any thieves
made so skillful an attempt to steal the Master's treasure.
Accordingly you have earned the honor of being questioned
by him personally: the Owner of the World, prior to your
destruction. Follow."*

"Suppose we just don't wish to follow?"

That bit of truculence from Tiana, naturally. There was
no reply. She, like Gray, merely felt her body rise to its
feet without conscious will—indeed, against all conscious
will. The adumbral form turned and walked away along
the wall. Tiana was forced to pace like an automaton after
it, Gray at her side, obviously equally unable to resist the
occult compulsion.

*I really should have settled down years ago and birthed
five or nine babies like any sensible woman,* Tiana thought
(and Gray wondered why she made a retching noise. Unfortunately he was busy walking and could not speak).
*Better still, I should have stuck to robbing ships asea. Or
just robbing ashore in Reme under the tutelage of Bandari
the Cat! Why, I even had opportunity to be queen to a
handsome king and pretend to rule sprawling Collada.
Tiana m'girl, you lackwit dolt, why didn't you do that?
What a lovely country it is . . .*

How easy it was to walk along thinking when one did
not have to think about walking!

Their outré guide led them through a maze of tunnels
until at length they emerged onto the surface of Riser
Island. Before them loomed that familiar vast, hideous
mausoleum guarded by armored dead men monstrously
mounted on one-legged horses. Citadel of horror: the
palace of the Owner.

As the gliding shadow led them through that fatally mounted host, Gray wondered if this would be his and Tiana's fate. *No,* he decided. *For us, surely something worse. Those must be men who sought to invade and attack. We did invade, and sought to steal!*

He had removed a gauntlet and tucked it in his weapon-belt. That bared hand held Tiana's and was held by it. Her fear was all too evident, though he knew better than to refer to it. She would only deny, with heat. That one so beautiful and so very much alive should be doomed filled him with helpless anger. Aye, it was love; he grieved more for her than for himself!

Before them now was the entrance to the palace. The mammoth gateway was filled with darkness so complete that it was as if solid, and gave the eye a feeling of blindness. Feet turned traitor forced the two to follow their shadow-guide. Gray and Tiana entered that uncanny blackness considerably against their wills. The glow of the moonball seemed to shrink back from the dark. It showed only their immediate vicinity and that wanly. From the way their footsteps echoed through the darkness, Gray had the feeling that they were as insects walking down a vast hallway in a realm of titans.

To their left a seamless stone wall was just visible. At intervals it was set with torches that burned with a cold, pallid blue flame. More than strange, Tiana noted; it was utterly unnatural. The torches were invisible until they were closely approached by the glowing moonball. The "torches" warred against its light as though they emitted not light, but darkness itself.

It seems, Gray thought (and thought he said), *that here darkness is more than just absence of light. I suppose that's only fitting . . . this is the realm of Death, which is far more than a mere absence of life.*

The shadow stopped before a small doorway that was little more than a hole in the wall of stone. *"Enter."*

Gray started obediently forward. *Wait! My feet obey this blighted shadow, but my hands are my own, by Candence!* As he passed through the doorway, he angled close to the umbra. Abruptly his hand shot out.

"We'll be needing this, thank you," he said equably, as he snatched the black rod with its bright ball of moon-glow.

Before the umbral guide could respond to that theft,

Tiana said, "And we'll be needing some food and water, too!"

For an instant the shadow-thing looked at them after they had passed through the doorway. Then the hole contracted. Behind them was only dark stone. Tiana and Gray were alone in a small, entirely featureless chamber.

"To be personally questioned by the Owner, no less," Tiana muttered, looking about. "It's just another damned prison. Moss on the Back, but I've been in a lot of damned prisons."

"Never with me," Gray said, and brought a canteen from the back of his belt. "Here. You asked for water and who knows what you might get from an animated shadow!"

"Ah!" She whipped the little container from his hand and squatted to pour a puddle on the floor. As he moved to protest the insane waste, she said, "We need help! Pyre appears in mirrors and this is the only way I know to make one." Firming her mouth, she straightened. "Except that I really don't care to talk with him!"

Gray saw no point in telling her that clever as her effort was, it had to be futile. This was the very stronghold of the Owner. They were deep within the citadel, which was undoubtedly protected by the most potent of magicks. Even the mightiest of wizards could not project a sending through such barriers. Still, she wanted to try this forlorn hope, and was at least entitled to his cooperation. Gray handed her the rod as he squatted over the puddle. Standing on its opposite side, she held the glowing moonball low.

Gray looked down into the puddle . . . to see Pyre!

"Are you newlyweds enjoying your honeymoon?" the mightiest mage asked sardonically.

"Likely it's going to be much too short!" Tiana snapped, standing aloof above the moonball. "Can't you tell us what the Owner is and how we can put an end to him, preferably without destroying the world?"

"Failing that," Gray said, recovering from his surprise at seeing the wizard, "is there any chance we could strike a bargain with the Owner?"

"The Owner is a non-being," Pyre said. "The term means little to you and I can explain but a small portion of its significance. Men . . . gods . . . demons, even they that dwell in the night and the formless void . . . all share the common property of existence. They are beings. They do evil to gain what they desire, or to gratify their egos, or for some other *reason*. Beings, then, with purpose. By contrast, the non-beings do not truly exist. They are nonetheless vastly potent at the working of evil. It is their nature to love destruction for its own sake—and to work ruin is their chiefest joy."

"Non-joy," Tiana muttered, "from non-beings."

"Thus the answer to your other questions," Pyre continued, "is that there is no possibility of your destroying the Owner. The only bargain to be made with him would be one involving a monstrous service to the cause of evil."

Tiana made a rude noise. "That's no help at all!"

"True," Pyre calmly replied. "That is because you asked the wrong questions."

"Damn you!" Tiana snapped. "Are you playing with us, and us about to be eaten or fried or *something?*"

"Something worse, actually," Pyre told her. "But I assure you that I am not playing any sort of game at all, aside from what is called a very dangerous one."

After a moment of silence in the empty chamber, Gray spoke.

"What are the right questions? And assuming that we were to ask them, how would you answer?"

"The right questions pertain to the future and the dangerous art of seeing it. It is quite hazardous, because the future once seen cannot be changed. That makes future seeing a business in which too much knowledge can be disastrous."

"We didn't ask that because we already knew it!" Tiana flared.

She was ignored; Pyre continued in the same dry, even tone.

"Despite this hazard, Ekron chose to use his talent for future-seeing in his plot against me. In imitation of his god, the Spider, he spun the trap as though it were a web. He arranged a circumstance and looked beyond time's veil just enough to see the result, then set up the next logically necessary event and checked again to learn the effect. This he did many times. Naturally it was a procedure with considerable waste effort. When Ekron saw that his carefully planned actions would not have the desired results, *he still had to carry out those fruitless actions.* Yet at length my toad-souled enemy saw that he would be able to bring us to our present position—which is a perilous one!"

Tiana's satirical "Oh," was quite ignored.

"Now Ekron was emboldened to look forward to the final outcome of his laborious scheming. At the same time, he knew he had to avoid the risk of learning overmuch! He decided to invoke the Oracle of Tarrek, and journeyed to the ruins of the Temple of Sismar. There he summoned the Oracle. That is not difficult, for some; the hard part is gaining proper answers while maintaining some sort of control over the Oracle! Ekron cast spells that bound the Oracle to silence if the answer to his questions would tie his hands—his paws—in any major decision. With that done, he asked whether he would succeed as he desired.

"There was no reply. That told him something, but precious little. He asked then if he would destroy his enemy Pyre and 'Pyre's whore,' the girl Tiana."

"Girl!" Tiana burst out, and Pyre's image faded as she lowered the moonball. Hurriedly Gray lifted a hand to push it above him so that he could see. Pyre continued present.

"Again," the wizard said, "there was only silence. Ekron's third query of course must be his last. He chose it well. Continued silence to his first two queries proved that some decision he had yet to make would determine the outcome of events. Ekron had gone to much effort to arrange my destruction at the hands of the Owner! Still, there was naught he desired so much as that he should personally be my bane. Perhaps the Oracle's silences indicated that such could be. Accordingly he phrased his final question. What action if any, he asked, must he take so that Pyre and Tiana must fall helpless into his power. These are the exact words of the Oracle:

" 'There is nothing further you need do. The flow of events already in place will inevitably place both Pyre Magus and the pirate Tiana in your power as two flies in the mouth of a toad. Their struggles to escape will be futile. Notwithstanding your oath to Pyre, you shall be free to do with them as you please.'

"Upon hearing this, Ekron rejoiced greatly! If you and I, Tiana, were utterly in his power, he was certain to have only one significant decision to make: whether to grant us mercy. He knew how he would settle that issue! I need not tell you, Tiana, of how merciful Ekron plans to be with us."

Tiana did indeed know, and she was filled with dismay by the entire grim recitation of the wizard's image. Her voice rose high:

"By the Cud, Pyre, why don't you use your powers? Break this accursed prophecy!"

Gray added, "Why did you let this happen to begin with? Why did you not destroy Ekron long ago?"

"Questions, questions." In that same tone of amused detachment Pyre said, "The words of the Oracle of Tarrek are unbreakable exactly as is a wizard's oath upon his power. Indeed, merely by knowing of this seen future I have placed myself under severe restrictions. I can take no direct action! I can't take any *indirect* actions save those the two of you accomplish on my behalf. As for why I did not destroy Ekron years ago . . . the answer is obviously that I never could! The toad-souled one and I had . . . certain business dealings some time ago, and we exchanged pledges in the form of sworn oaths. Upon his power Ekron vowed never to take any action that would directly injure me. It was the best I could get from him. I swore a similar vow to do naught that in any wise, direct or indirect, affected him . . . saving only that I could help *complete that which he chose to do* of his own free will."

"But Pyre," Tiana said, "those oaths—"

"Yes. You learned some time ago that a wizard's oath upon his power is always kept with literal truth and a maximum of bad faith. Accordingly, as soon as Ekron swore not to destroy me directly, he began his efforts to achieve that same end by indirect means."

The image in the puddle from Gray's canteen was beginning to blur. The voice of Pyre became muffled. It grew difficult to understand, though the tone maintained its irony:

"You both know that I swore the ultimate oath to avenge you, Tiana, if you are slain. Hence Ekron has striven very very hard indeed to see to your death—and you have proven remarkably hard to lay to rest!" Did that murky image smile? "One is sorry to give you newlyweds all this entirely bad news but I maintain confidence in you. I'm sure you will manage. Indeed you shall have to, if we are to survive."

Tiana fair shouted, *"Rat* dung!"

"No doubt," Pyre said equably. "And now I must—ah yes. Gray: you were quite correct about its being impossible for me to project a Sending into the palace of the Owner! I am appearing here by purely natural means."

The image was gone.

The newlyweds were alone in their little cell. In its dryness, the puddle had all but evaporated.

Gray continued squatting over the dark stain on the floor. He was dazed, striving to take in all the strange and unwelcome news Pyre had borne. Tiana meanwhile assaulted his ears with some most imaginative obscenities, among them various physical impossibilities involving various improbable partners and obscene gods known only to Simdans—and one who was a Simdan's stepdaughter.

She finished with, "Half of what that arrogant genius said was a prediction of utter doom and the rest was self-contradictory! I'm beginning to wonder if my l—regard for him has been misplaced all this time! Maybe I am just an impressionable g—no!"

Her husband looked up at her, blinking, but she could not see that or his expression. She did see the dilation of the wall behind him. In the opening appeared that adumbral guide. He was not bringing food and drink.

"The Owner will see you now."

24th Strand:

SUNRISE AT RISER ISLAND

The shout was bellowed from *Vixen*'s crow's nest: "Island ahoy!"

From the prow the acting captain half-turned to roar his response: "Where away?"

"Three points to steer-bo-oarrrd!"

Caranga strained his eyes but saw only a mass of black clouds rampant against a sky burning red-gold in the setting sun. He knew that Riser was an island buried under thick black clouds. The visions he had seen in the skull's eye sockets had promised that the northwest corner of the isle would be a safe harbor bathed in bright sunshine.

Would that be true? It seemed impossible—yet the perpetual cloud was just that, and it existed. Caranga swallowed as he easily ruddered *Vixen* toward that motionless cloud. To have crossed the wide ocean on a fool's errand—! *No! It will be there! We shall land.*

He had spent most of his time in his cabin, these past days. In utter darkness he had sought to learn whatever strange things the skull of He Who Sleeps could teach him. The running of the ship had been left to Chandak Keeneye. That faultless, polite young warrior most probably believed that his commander was a bit mad.

Of course I am, Caranga reflected. *We all are. It's madness and horror we've all been caught up in for the past two—nearly three years!*

Larine had been concerned and solicitous, constantly willing to listen to his woes and his uncertainties. She, too, was puzzled by his mysterious actions. He knew she feared that he might have broken under the stress.

Of course I could have explained what I was about. Almost, he smiled. *That would have removed any doubt that my mind was gone!*

Wind gusted through the crumpled black-and-gray curls of his hair and his loose tunic rustled. *Vixen's* sails snapped and white water furled back on either side of her bow to bubble and spread in a widening wedge behind her. The tangy scent of salt was a constant fact of life, and the ocean seemed bent on accepting sunset with waveless calm. The breeze drove *Vixen* without disturbing her medium. Now Caranga could see the island toward which he and his strange shipload of crew and Orvarian whores moved at good speed. Or rather, he could see the cloud—the Cloud —that entirely blanketed it. Of the sun-drenched harbor promised by the skull there was no hint.

In but a few moments he must give orders of some kind.

What would he do? Admit that he was a worried and deluded old man, driven out of his wits by loss of his daughter who wasn't truly even his daughter? To save her he would gladly pay forfeit of his life as well as his pride. But how—LIGHTNING! He squinted hard and shook his head.

Silent, blinding brilliance split the sky and sundered the black clouds. A great section of the dark blanket was abruptly ripped away to reveal the land beneath. For a brief instant the squinting man saw something beyond description.

A comparison came to his mind, and it was not welcome. What he saw was as though a great stone had been turned over and all manner of vile slimy creatures were scurrying for cover.

Before he could be sure of what he was seeing, it was over. All motion ceased. The unidentifiable and unspeakable objects dried and bleached white and slimeless under the blinding brightness of the sun. Soon they were dust that the wind blew away.

Before his eyes Riser was being transformed. The coastline of grim threatening rock dissolved into white sandy beaches while barren hills lost their somberness to become green, tree-covered vistas. Again, it was accomplished before he could be sure it was happening. The northwest section of Riser was a verdant tropical eden, exactly as the skull had foretold. Also as predicted, the rest of the island remained a realm of darkness brooding beneath opaque black clouds.

"Prepare the small boat! When we're a bit closer in I mean to row in alone." Caranga turned to Chandak Keeneye. "Hold *Vixen* offshore. Wait three days for me. If I don't reappear in that time, consider me dead."

"But—"

"You heard me, Chandak." Caranga stared grimly at the brown man.

"And—the captain?"

"Obviously if the captain appears within three days, Keeneye, she's in command. If not, consider us both dead and don't be foolish enough to try to take vengeance!" And the black pirate turned from his Second Mate.

He returned on deck carrying the skull in its box of ebony and silver. The boat was ready, and soon Caranga was rowing toward that inviting shore.

As his oars clove through the muddy gray waters, he saw for the first time the beauty of the island that was his goal. Waves of sparkling turquoise splashed in bubbling white foam upon the diamond-gleaming sand of the beach. It ran up into jade grass and cinnamon-brown trees laden with emerald leaves. Every color was vivid, intense be-

yond any he had ever seen. By contrast, the surrounding
sea and sky seemed drab and tarnished. It was as if all the
world was only a pallid shadow of this island's glory. He
approached a realm that tingled with the very force of Life
itself. His heart ached at the sight of such loveliness. It
drew him as the flame draws the moth and . . .

And he knew that he would be an intruder in this place
of supernormal vitality; a drab shadowy ghost at a joyous
wedding feast.

He did not question that odd and lyrical analogy that
filled his mind. Caranga questioned only his actions. *Am
I wise to come trespassing where no mortal man belongs?*

He steadied the boat while he shaded his eyes and
scanned the boundaries of the superhuman realm.

Clearly he could make out the region in which the dull
gray of the common ocean was gradually transformed into
the splendor of brilliant azure. That region of transition
stretched across the sea, perhaps fifty yards from the
strand, and then turned inland. Part of Riser Island basked
in the light of a day more glorious than the earth had
ever known—and part lay trapped in unnatural and perpetual night. Between the two was a twilight zone that was
part of the world he thought of as normal; the world of
men.

Caranga angled in toward the portion of the beach that
was part of the twilight zone. For now, at least, it might
be prudent to avoid the unknown.

Once he had hauled the little rowboat up onto the
sands, Caranga took up the container of the skull and
drew his cutlass. He was well aware that the second act
was more for the comfortable, weighty feel of the sword
in his fist than because he expected to meet any foe against
which it might be useful. He turned from the boat and
gazed thoughtfully around.

Since he had no wish to enter the realms either of
Night or Greater Day, he was constrained to walk a narrow line between them. He did. With the box carried
against his chest and his sword ready in his other hand,
he left the beach and moved inland.

He rounded a low hill to see a marble building set
athwart the strip of twilight. One end was bright within
the region of supernal Day; the other nearly vanished into
the area of darkest Night. That was not all. Along its
length the structure changed! In the ultra-brilliant sun-

light it stood majestically tall, stately columns forming a
gleaming pearlescent forest. As it slid into twilight it became a simple building of ordinary marble, well carved
and yet showing signs of the decay of age. Where twilight
shaded into Night, however, the building fell into crumbling ruins.

Caranga cursed under his breath. "If there's one thing I
don't want now, it's another mystery!"

Still, he had come this far in pursuit of a forlorn hope.
There was no point in stopping now. He continued, slowly,
warily.

He saw that to reach the structure's entry that lay in the
twilight zone, he must cross a section of Day. In a burst
of impatience he forgot a pirate's caution. He strode into
brightness.

The grass beneath his feet changed to become a brilliant green that threatened to burn his squinted eyes. Impossibly, it was hard and strong. It scarcely bent under the
pressure of his feet. Worse, his boots were being cut! Each
blade of this unnaturally bright grass was as a razor-edged
knife.

Or was he seeing things backward; misinterpreting? Perhaps it was not that the grass was abnormally strong, but
rather that he was merely a pallid shadow, so weak as to
be cut easily by common grass?

The terrible beauty of the grass and trees grew more
awesome still. It became a sensory assault that threatened
to overwhelm him. He was beginning to perceive the dreadful truth, which was an alternate reality. The world—that
one in which he had been born and lived all his life—was
but a dreamy shadow; a blurred copy of the real and
original. Now he was in the presence of the original; of
reality.

No law, natural or unnatural, stated that reality had to
be pleasant.

In this instance Caranga knew that reality was to be
avoided!

Thinking was not easy. His brain was only just able to
move his body. A stride; another . . . and he was back
within twilight: the safe ordinary world he thought of as
"real." Leaning against the marble wall, he strove with
labored breathing to catch his breath and mental equilib-
rium. He had just had a narrow escape and knew it. Another few moments in that realm of eye-searing hyper-

colors and incredibly vivid sights and sounds and he would not have survived.

He was still panting when he stepped into the building. Within, he saw two massive chairs. Thrones! One was of ivory; the other ebony. They faced each other and between them was a parti-colored table. On it rested a strange game board.

The black throne was empty. The other was not and Caranga's attention was entirely consumed by its occupant. He was a very, very old man, stern of face and robed in sublime, marmoreal white. He did not speak. Caranga did.

"Sulun Tha: I have suspected that you were behind the events that led me here. But nothing has changed. I will help you if and only if you promise to help my daughter Tiana." Caranga felt a small child shouting defiance at a vastly wiser and more powerful adult, but he felt he had no choice.

Sulun Tha's voice was the whisper of wind through dry rushes. "I cannot make promises. My actions are wholly determined by what is Right. By the same token I may not steal, even to wrest from you that which is rightly mine. These are matters beyond your comprehension, I know. I cannot explain."

"Drood seize it all! Can't you—"

Without thinking, black pirate had stepped toward White Wizard and thus entered the realm of Light. He broke off speaking for immediately he knew what he was; a tiny unclean insect crawling before the Judgment Throne of the very gods. Sulun Tha's face grew and was vast and filled all the chamber and the heavens. Behind Him the awestruck Caranga saw six other faces, and all were grand and vast and terrible.

The man's steps were driven by panic. Hurriedly he departed that unbearable Light. Again the mage looked to be no more than a man and was—at least seemingly— alone. Suddenly Caranga pointed, and his outstretched finger seemed an accusation.

"I know who you are! You and those six Others . . . you are the World Flames!"

As the words burst loudly from him, he knew they were true. Sulun Tha and his six companions—invisible companions, now—were Light, and Caranga's world was made of shadow. It was simply that he could not endure their presence. They were more than righteous; they were the Right. No man who was a mixture of good and evil could stand before them. *Thus no man can stand before them,* Caranga thought, for what man—what person, could be all good with no evil thought or act on its conscience? They were Truth and Right. To a dishonest world their very presence was all-consuming fire—the fire that was destined to destroy all the world!

By . . . these, had Pyre sworn to avenge Tiana! O unwise mage, to believe that such a One as Sulun Tha was only a mage—and to swear by such a force!

Caranga's heart was the drum of an attacking galley and his mouth had gone dry as sand. First he must muster and bolster his brave front. He was Caranga; he did.

"Great as you are," he said accusingly, "you still need this box!" He held high the silver-bound casket of black, and rattled the skull within it. "And hear me: You'll not have it unless you promise to aid my Tiana!"

Only by shouting thus a challenge to a force of evil, rather than good, could a man have proven more brave than Caranga at that instant.

Slowly the mage shook his head. "Only because I understand love do I repeat: that is impossible. You may refuse an act because you will not; in this wise I *can not.* Time is slipping away, Caranga of the Simdans. Unless you give to me that which is mine, and very soon, it will be too late."

"Can you not see that *I* cannot? I have said that I would not, and—"

Sulun Tha waved a hand. That brief gesture equated human pride with dung and consigned it to the middenheap. He need say nothing, and did not.

By Susha's Own curls and all the Mud on the Turtle's Back, how is a man supposed to haggle with a very god?

Caranga had nothing to say and strove still to be strong and firm. "I know you have some sort of war in progress. We are caught up in it! I demand that you explain it to me."

The figure of stainless white shook his head. "I can only tell you a story." As if he were making a momentous decision, he said, "I shall." He extended a finger as if to fix Caranga's muscles and his attention.

"There was a certain country whose people had wealth beyond understanding and they had—call Him Enemy.

There was danger that this Enemy would come to dominate a neighboring land whose inhabitants suffered in the direst poverty. The wealthy could relieve this agony by sharing their riches, and never notice loss. Sadly, 'twas clear that the gift of vast and sudden wealth would destroy all but the most worthy of the poor. Accordingly, the rich land chose seven of its citizenry to be emissaries. They were to travel in the poor land, to learn what in wisdom should be done, and then, of course, to do it. So as not to disturb the poverty-suffering, these seven stripped off their glory— or rather their wealth—and hid it. Ah, but the Enemy was crafty beyond all expectation. The Enemy contrived to steal the hidden wealth of six of those seven. Thus he held them captive. The seventh escaped—in part. Perhaps you have already heard this part of the tale: the legend of the skull lost in the domain of Theba's daughter Hella? Well, the seventh . . ."

The White Wizard spoke on and his mild, gentle voice filled the pirate with awe. Caranga had indeed heard the store afore, and given it small heed. Now he listened anew and shuddered. Sulun Tha knew whereof he spoke and his wisdom was beyond that of mortal men. To hear him spin a parable was to gaze upon a veil behind which lay mystery. The hidden naked truth was too terrible and wonderful for humankind.

Caranga shuddered as he spoke: "And what was the ending of all this?"

"That cannot be said, for the event is still within the womb of time and 'twould be a violation to gaze upon it before its birth. I may tell you only how matters stand at present. It is thus: the seventh emissary is at last free and must do battle to liberate his comrades. Once all seven regain their freedom, the situation and the Enemy's past actions will leave them no choice. They will be obligated to share their wealth with the poor even though very few will survive the receipt of such bounty."

For a time after that man and Worldfire stared one at the other, and the silence was heavy and portentous. Caranga feared to break it; Sulun Tha did not.

"This was merely a story, you understand. I cannot attempt to explain the truth, Caranga, for that is much beyond your comprehension. Nor need you feel insulted by that. It is enough for you to know that you must now give me that small casket you clutch so tightly, and the skull that lies within it."

"Damn your All-seeing Eyes—what if I don't?"

"Then," Sulun Tha replied emotionlessly, "the Owner will defeat me and gain absolute suzerainty over your world. He will be its overlord. Though I am attacking him, my hoarded powers will soon be exhausted. At sunset—which is near—he will gain the victory. Now of this you may be sure: that will mean certain death for your daughter."

Caranga swallowed but stood firm. "And if I do? What happens then?"

"Then the battle will continue, outcome unknown. Your daughter is and will continue in the most extreme peril, but her death would not be an absolute certainty."

Caranga had been known to take frequent heed of logic, and for a moment he wanted to squeeze shut his eyes and moan. The larger significance of what he had just heard did not escape him. In the back of his mind the truth was vivid: this was the ultimate battle between cosmic forces. Victory for either side meant destruction of the world! That, however, was the world's problem and beyond human conception anyhow. Caranga was a father. His proper worry was the saving of his headstrong daughter. Given Sulun Tha's revelations he had small choice: the greatest danger was better than certain death.

"Here! Take the cursed thing!" With that anguished cry, he thrust the box toward the enthroned mage.

As he started to open it, the casket became abruptly lighter. It was as though it was suddenly empty. An instant later the wood crumbled in his fingers like so much ancient parchment. Even as he looked down at it the box disappeared into powdery fragments that were no more than pollen.

At the same instant the face of Sulun Tha blazed with incandescent wonder.

That glory was apparent but for a moment. Then it was veiled. Still an aura remained, an aura of power that burned about the white-robed man-not-man who turned his gaze from Caranga to stare at the game board set before his ivory throne.

At first glance, Caranga had thought it was simply a playing surface composed of squares of white, black, and gray, each square containing one or another strange playing piece. Now he recognized his error. The board was of many white, black, and gray *windows*. Within each a strange object was visible. One gray square caught his attention. It held a tiny black figure. It was Caranga.

As he raised his right hand to point, so did the tiny figure in that window.

Something in Sulun Tha's manner made Caranga shelve that mystery within his already overladen mind. The mage raised his hands and lifted them above the board. His tone was one of solemn invocation.

"Let the Game begin."

25th Strand:

THE OWNER OF THE WORLD

"Follow me," the ghostly shadow bade Tiana and Gray, and it took back the moonball.

Treacherously obedient legs gave them no choice but to obey. Pirate and knight were led in a twisted course through dank and narrow passageways. Eventually they emerged into a vast darkness. The feeble radiation of the rod-mounted moonstone carried but scant feet. The way her footsteps echoed hinted to Tiana that they were in some great hall. An enormous audience chamber, perhaps —probably the throne room of the non-being who owned the world.

For all her fearfulness, Tiana burned with curiosity. She wanted to see this place and—was it only her imagination or was the darkness opening to eyes eager to pierce it? For an instant a vision filled her mind:

A cavernous hall endarkened by eerie blue-green torches that radiated cold and devoured any trace of light. A feasting hall lined with tables where vague obscene shapes sat consuming unclean food with horrid pleasure. At the end of the vast hall rose an exalted throne of utter night. It was Darkness. On it sat an unseeable Unknown, an entity

*whose very presence was madness; One whose voice could
blow out the hearer's reason like a huffed candle.*

The vision was gone swiftly as it had come and Tiana
was left in a cold sweat. Repeatedly she told herself that
what she seemed to have seen was a mere daydream, a
creation of her overwrought imagination. She stood only in
impenetrable Darkness that she fancied she could *feel*,
crowding around her.

From out of that Darkness the Silence . . . spoke. It
destroyed all sound as darkness destroys all color and
vision. It deafened the ear and blasted all thought from
the mind.

Tiana screamed at the top of her lungs. There was no
audible result. Nor did she know what she was doing until
the Silence ceased to speak. As she choked off the scream,
Gray turned to face the Silence.

"I'm sorry," he replied mildly, "but if you speak so
loudly, we cannot hear you." And strangely, the knight
sounded a whistle that was a dull, steady sound.

Again the Silence spoke, more softly this time. Its voice
obliterated only a portion of the droning and thus formed
strange inside-out words.

"She is Tiana called Highrider, of Reme," Gray replied
as if to a question; "a justly renowned captain of the
Oceansea. I have no name. That need not concern you,
since I serve the wizard Pyre."

Again Gray hummed so that the Silence could be heard,
voiding parts of the sustained note:

"I am curious as to how such trivial creatures as the
two of you could cause such inordinately great trouble.
Accordingly I have delayed your annihilation long enough
for you to explain. You will be brief." Those words of the
Owner contained no hint of anger or indeed any emotion
at all; only calm, utterly impersonal intellect.

*"The first move is mine," Sulun Tha murmured, "since
Light precedes Darkness." His hand glided above the
board to pause above a gray square. Within that window
Caranga saw six tiny skulls prisoned in a cage. At the
White Wizard's touch the gray square burst into brilliant
light. The cage dissolved. All six skulls were instantly free.*

Under Tiana's feet the floor reeled like a ship's deck in
a storm. Her ears were filled with such a bass as she had

never known. That awful thunder counterpointed agonized shrieks, as if massive buildings of stone were suddenly collapsing upon their inhabitants. And all Riser shook.

The resounding clamor of tumbling masses of rock ceased as abruptly as it had begun. The cries of pain and shouts of confused anger did not. They continued to build to a mad crescendo.

All sound ended when the Owner's silent voice destroyed the shouting confusion of his minions. What orders the Owner gave Tiana could only guess. His rule was total: the chaotic babble swiftly became only a tense susurrus. His creatures suffered almost in silence.

Suffer, Tiana mentally urged. *Oh, do suffer!*

Strange as the circumstances were, Tiana had no doubt as to their cause: the Owner of the World was under sudden, massive attack! Who might have such power she could not imagine—nor did she much care. Attack and battle meant confusion. Confusion was opportunity for her and Gray to escape.

Her feet were fixed to the floor as if rooted. She had just enough freedom of movement to twist around and gaze anxiously at the shadow guard. In this Darkness there should be no shadows. It was there. Whatever thoughts might lurk in that ill-defined shape, what it might intend, she could not guess. Nor did it matter, if she acted swiftly. The shadow-thing, she was sure, was invulnerable to orthodox weapons. She was also sure enough to wager her life that it could not stand bright light. Light!

All I have to do is make a fire. Light!

Her black cloak was dry and old. It would burn well enough, if stenchily. She had her knife and a bit of flint in her belt. Metal and flint and old cloth should be all she would need, if only she could manage to work unnoticed.

Slowly, calmly, she set about the task of making a fire unseen. Nevertheless her calm was brittle, like a thin glass bottle filled with the murky liquid of palpable terror. She was surrounded by the unspeakable and knew it. The slightest error would betray her into obscene death. Or, horrible thought, worse.

There! The first tiny spark glowed in the shredded cloth of her beloved cloak. It was strange, to have struck sparks without a sound of scraping. She had, in this Darkness and Silence, and in another moment or two she would have a burst of bright flame. If she could . . .

"It appears that the Master is too busy to interview you two." The dull voice was that of the shadow-guide. "The danger that you may escape amid this confusion is not large, but perhaps it is too large to be acceptable. Therefore," it said, absolutely dispassionately, "I order you to stop breathing."

The horror was the worse for the umbral nightmare's having delivered sentence of death in a voice devoid of all emotion. The deadly words all but blasted Tiana's reason. If she could have made it suffer for a decade, she'd have done it. She could not. She could only refuse to panic—while she died. The tiny spark she held in her hand was her life—almost literally, now. Fanned into bright flame, it would aid her. If it died, so would she. She was wholly unable to disobey. She did not breathe.

Gray meanwhile was using sign language in an attempt to argue with the shadow. Tiana noted it almost absently. Argument was plainly futile—but it might serve to direct the guard's attention from her. Without breathing, using all her skill at fire building, she waved the tiny spark. The cloth only smoldered. Her lungs began to ache for want of air. Then the spark brightened, only to flicker and die.

Sulun Tha was watching the black throne as if it held his opponent in the outré game. At first Caranga could not imagine what the White Wizard saw. Then he realized that the darkness had somehow metamorphosed, congealed into an absence; a dreadful Emptiness that was as easily overlooked as it was terrifying when noticed. Thoughts seemed to radiate from the dark throne. Vast, incomprehensible and utterly alien thoughts bespoke a mind evil beyond description. Even Caranga was shocked at such malignance. It was there, as if he could reach out and touch malignity and evil. Then the darkness/Emptiness flickered. Something happened on the game board and Sulun Tha spoke in the murmur of one in deep concentration.

"My opponent has made a very interesting move."

"You are fortunate," the shadow said. "The Master summons you to his immediate presence. Follow." It waved the luminous moonball.

Tiana sought to follow. Her head was filled with a dron-

ing wind and her air-starved lungs were afire. For all this
agony she was only an automaton who commenced to pace
after that shadow . . . unable to breathe. The world was
beginning to spin around her and she staggered drunkenly.
Then she fell to her knees and at last the guide seemed to
take note.

"Oh very well. You may breathe."

Tiana's body convulsed. The air her starved lungs drew
in was sweeter than the finest new wine. Relief at being
allowed to breathe was like release from Hella's domain . . .
except that she was still a captive in the palace of the
Owner, a place far worse than Hell.

Her brain began to show signs of returning to function.
As her chest heaved and the ache in her lungs subsided,
Tiana's mind returned to escape. Yet she raised her head,
and frowned.

Had something happened to make the Darkness less
deep, less totally absorbing of light? For whatever reason,
the light from the moonball seemed to carry farther; to
penetrate what had been purest Darkness. Now she could
see the enormous empty throne of the Owner of the World.
It was a chair of such imposing size that it seemed larger
than the very palace; larger than the building within which
it rested.

At the approach of Tiana Highrider and the Gray
Knight, however, that enormous throne dwindled. When
they had drawn near they saw that it was no bigger than
a common chair. It was not empty.

In that chair sat a . . . a void, a vaguely manshaped
Emptiness. Gazing upon it was akin to looking down a
deep well.

*Caranga watched in awe. He knew that cosmic forces
were at work upon the many-squared board before Sulun
Tha. The mage pulled thoughtfully at his cloud-like beard.
"The Owner chooses to play a defensive game. Logical
enough; he knows that after sunset I shall be at a great
disadvantage and even now the sun dies. He forces me
to mount a maximal attack." And his ancient hand moved
across the board's surface, touching it with blinding light in
dozens of places.*

The Darkness of the throne room was struck and sundered by dazzling illumination. In the moment that Tiana

thought she was being struck blind, the shadowy guide flickered against a diamond-white background and winked into nothingness.

The supernal light disappeared as swiftly as it struck. Its effects remained. The throne room now stood in eerie half-light. A host of ghastly beings was revealed. They were things of Darkness, screaming in horror at being thrust into even the dimmest of illumination. Squinting though the original flare was over, blinking, Tiana looked at the overturned tables and the unclean feasters. It was no pleasant sight, and yet it drew her staring gaze by its very horrid eerieness.

Before she could see them in the detail she at once wanted and dreaded, the floor trembled beneath her feet like a woman in ecstasy.

Gray's hands were suddenly upon her shoulders, striving to force her down. He crushed her to the floor. She was flattened, nearly buried under his body before she could protest. Though angry words rose in her throat, they died as the rockfall began. Again that awful sustained *bass* accompanied an avalanche of stone.

Stretched full length on the cold stonework floor, she felt the world quiver as though mountains of rock were marching past. The sound of their rolling thunder was deafening. Twice she felt Gray's body quiver with the impact of ceiling-stones and she could only hope, even pray that his armor would protect him. She knew he was saving her from death or at least severe injury, and knew that no one had ever done more for her.

At last it was over. Gray rose with a grunt and a sigh, and bent to help her up. Apparently he was unhurt, for which Tiana was more than grateful. Her ears hurt so that she could scarcely hear his voice. She and Gray were alive, and presumably unharmed. Dust eddied about them.

The palace of the Owner, however, was totally destroyed. What had been a vast complex edifice of myriad proud columns and vaulting arches lay all about now, in broken fragments. Dust was thick and Tiana sneezed. She realized that Gray's valiant effort had saved her from two impacts, but had they not been in such proximity to the throne of the Owner they would both be dead. She saw none of the Owner's servants alive and doubted whether any had survived. She and Gray had survived the masses of falling stone from walls and roof because they had somehow been deflected by the Owner's throne.

The palace did not exist. Tiana had an unobstructed view of the sky, and she stared in wonder and awe. The sky was—was split asunder!

To her left Riser Island was as she had seen it before: an island of darkness dimly visible in the ghostly light of a leprous moon. A few yards to her right was an incredible boundary. A line sharp as a sword's blade ran across sky and sea and land as well. That impossible line separated Night from supernally bright Day.

Tiana stared at luminous glory, and she blinked hard and rubbed her eyes. She could not believe what she saw. The land of Day was a place of rolling grassy hills and flower-bedecked trees whose vivid color and terrible beauty swept all thought from her mind. Inhuman loveliness drew her so that she knew how a moth felt as it was drawn into an infinitely attractive candle flame. Only by exerting her will strongly was she able to turn her eyes downward. She concentrated on driving all thoughts of that unearthly splendor from her mind.

Escape! She must think only of escape. Now! Their guard was destroyed—far too quickly, she thought—and the Owner was concerned with far larger matters. She and Gray had a single priceless opportunity to get themselves gone from this place.

Why . . . I'll bet the best course is to walk away calmly as though there's no reason anyone should even consider stopping us.

Besides, this is battle, and no battle is without risk. With that thought she turned to her husband. She gestured and took the first step away from the throne of Darkness. Before she could move another pace, however, a voiceless command snapped from the Emptiness occupying that dreadful throne, and her feet were again rooted to the floor.

Caranga knew that what he saw on the game board of Sulun Tha determined the fate of his daughter and indeed of the entire world. And now, except for a black square or two, the board was a shining mass of white. That brilliance clearly foretold Sulun Tha's imminent triumph. Such a victory, Caranga realized without joy, would be as much a disaster for all he valued as would victory for the Owner.

And the sun was going down. Despite the awe-unto-terror that gripped him, Caranga was no man to be an idle spectator. For a moment he looked at Sulun Tha. Then Caranga whirled toward the dark throne occupied by that Emptiness.

"Fool!" he shouted. "Can't you see you're going to lose before last light! If you had the wit of a ship's cat you'd play for a stalemate!"

The Darkness quivered. Caranga saw that something was happening upon the playing board. The tiny figure of an armored weaponeer had quitted the last black square and was racing desperately across the burning white. It was a faceless gray knight.

"Another interesting move," murmured Sulun Tha.

Destruction and ruin were all about. Rock-dust eddied. The continuing crumbling of Riser Island's structures was a rolling thunder. That sustained sound was cloven by the sound-annihilating voice of the Owner of the world.

"Little beings! As you can see I am under attack and soon to be destroyed utterly. That is inconceivable! There is a way in which I can retreat with relatively minor losses. Accordingly I offer you a bargain: do me a small service and I will spare your lives."

"I am told," Gray said blandly, "that any service to you would be a monstrously evil act."

"By your definition of this concept you call 'monstrous evil,' that is true," the silent answer came. "However it is in your own interest to prevent the Forces of Righteousness from gaining a total victory. Such a victory would have all manner of unpleasant side effects. For example: the destruction of the human race."

"I am well aware of that. I also noticed—" Gray gestured toward the shining realm of Day—"that there are six skulls resting on a grassy hill yonder in sunshine country. No doubt you wish me to fetch them here. But since we are discussing an evil bargain—how can I trust you? What is to prevent you from slaying us once you have those skulls?"

"Pyre is fortunate," the Silence answered, "to have such a servant as you. The problem of trust is—"

Tiana and Gray cried out at shattering brilliance. A bolt of purest Light struck at the dark throne. For an instant the blackness that was the Owner quivered. Then the light was gone and the two humans stood blinded.

The Silence continued. "The problem of trust is a mutual one. If I release you to run this errand, I must trust that you will not simply run away. This I can do since the woman will of course remain with me to insure your return. When you do, you must trust me not slay you. This you can do, since I am in grave danger. Obviously when I have what I need I will leave instantly. The small delay necessary to effect your deaths would obviously be a pleasure I could ill afford."

"Gray—" Tiana began, bent on urging him to accept the bargain. What other hope was there? The Owner would not submit to destruction without taking them along. Besides, another such blast of Light might well blind them both. But her husband was already replying:

"Very well, *Owner*. It is a bargain on one condition! When I am returning with those skulls, you must release Tiana as soon as I cross the boundary of Night and Day. As I approach you, I want to see her running away. That way neither of us can cheat."

Does he think I'd leave him to this . . . monster? Run away and always remember that I did? "Wait!" Tiana shouted. "Why should you have the more important role and I be merely a hostage? I can—"

"I agree to your terms," the Silence interrupted.

Released, Gray whirled and raced away with much jingling of his armor.

"But—" Tiana only began, but broke off to watch Gray's dodging among tumbled chunks of stones, zigzagging from what had been the palace, even leaping some stones. That was most impressive to Tiana; she had tried armor, and much preferred freedom of movement and speed. The Gray Knight obviously combined those attributes with the weight of his mail!

Why, I really had not realized how superb he is! My husband!

As she watched Gray approach the boundary a new fear struck her: what might happen to him in the brilliant realm of Day? Could an all-too-mortal human bear and withstand those blindingly vivid colors and inhuman beauty?

The running man in gray mail reached the boundary,

plunged past it, and . . . disintegrated. Tiana's shriek was wrested from her.

Through that uncontrollable, sustained cry the Owner's voice cut. "Look more closely and you can still see him."

It was true. When she strained her eyes, Tiana could still discern Gray's fast-moving form. He was now but a shadow. She could see through him and could overlook him, as if she were gazing through a filthy window.

The comparison did not please her.

"What . . . what happened to him?" As silence now surrounded her, she thought to whistle a single long note, as Gray had done. The Owner's voice was Silence. It destroyed sound. Within her whistled note, then, she heard the voice of Silence; of Emptiness; of the Owner of the World.

"Nothing. He is as he has always been. It is only that you see him in contrast with the realm of They Who Truly Are. Compared to that realm, your world is but a mist."

And yours the ultimate Darkness, Tiana mused. *Why— all our lives we live in twilight!*

That concept did not complement Tiana's ego or the ego of the human race and thus was less than cheering. On the other hand, neither alternative was pleasant.

With her thoughts and gaze riveted on Gray, Tiana did not notice the spider until it had completed the looping of its second strand of silk about her legs. On the point of brushing it aside, she froze. No common insect could have found its way to this place! Nor would any normal insect or spider devote itself so assiduously to enwebbing a human being. This nasty black dot speeding around her bare legs must be Ekron's familiar! The tiny monster that had hanged High Magistrate Ishcon!

Though she still had her dagger, Tiana greatly doubted that it would be of any value against such a foe. No natural arachind served Ekron and hanged humans! Her best tactic would be a polite request, she decided. Controlling her voice, she spoke casually.

"Owner, a bothersome insect or something is crawling about my legs. Would you mind being a good host and killing it for me? I am *only* a human."

The Silence laughed evilly. "As we both know, that 'insect or something' is a spider, and nothing less than the familiar spirit of the wizard Ekron. While I have no great concern in your quarrel with the toad-souled one, it happens that you are beautiful. As a matter of general policy I do enjoy the prospect of the ugly's destroying the beautiful."

Alas, my irresistible beauty has been my bane all my life! "The fact remains," Tiana snapped, "that you have to kill this spider and free me from its web or your bargain with Sir Gray will be void."

Again she was aware of that sickening inside-out, sound-destroying laughter. "That will not be a problem," the Owner said. "For though there is good chance that the knight's body will survive and he will return here with that which I need, there is no chance at all that his mind will survive the blaze of Light. When and if he returns from its realm, he will be an automaton and unable to notice whether you are here or gone."

(Staggering in clumsy haste across rolling fields, Gray felt as if he had been plunged into a blazing green furnace. The vivid color of the grass was as the most blinding of flashing emeralds. It seared his eyes and the scent of its moistness was a heady perfume that assaulted his senses like the fumes of too much strong wine. With every step the ironlike blades cut at his boots. Twice a gentle breeze had struck him with enough irresistible force to toss him onto the ground. His armor saved his life and his vitals, but here and there he bled.

(Ahead he could see his goal. Six skulls lay on a hillside like scattered silver coins. Cursing his weakness, he stumbled on toward them.)

Tiana did not waste her breath to curse the Owner's treachery. She bent, legs bound, and extricated her dagger from her boot. For an instant the spider was poised on a jagged shard of stone, a good target. Small though the demon was, she hit it squarely—and her blade shattered.

Before she could recover, a strand of silk snaked around her right hand. Swiftly that arm was bound to her side. The silk of this unnatural arachnid was like iron. Her struggles were futility. Swiftly the spider ensnared her other hand and began to cocoon her.

At first she struggled furiously. That was useless; this unnatural creature's webbing was like dragon silk. Tiana stopped moving and began to use her mind. Most obviously, events were rushing toward a climax. If she could only fathom the answers to several murky riddles, she might be able to do what was needful in time. (Never mind that she was being mummified by an implacable spider weaving silk strong as iron.)

Otherwise, she reflected, *Gray will at last be right—all will be lost!*

"I regret," the Silence murmured, "that I shall not be able to remain and see the conclusion of this drama."

"Why?" Tiana snapped. "Can't you see the time-to-come?"

"Of course, if I chose to," the answer came. "But I make it a rule never to practice that art. It is dangerous. A seen future is but a tiny portion of all that will happen. Far too often it proves true but nastily misleading."

Interesting, Tiana thought, but she was distracted by echoes of sundering Light flashing about the rocky fragments of what had been the throne room. From somewhere nearby she heard crashing thunder. Another huge building was going down to disintegration. *Maybe this time it was the temple of Death,* she mused. Still, that would not account for the lurid red flames she saw dancing against the night skyline.

Whatever the details, she could be sure of one thing. Whoever was attacking the Owner meant to bring about the utter annihilation of the non-being and its habitat, root and branch. Apparently the attacker would not stop until it had done everything short of sinking Riser Island into the sea. From the ominous way the floor trembled under her, even that seemed possible.

Best not to think about that!

Shutting her ears to the continuing destruction, she tried not to feel the spider that shuttled across her body, weaving her ever more helpless. Tiana allowed only one thought in her mind: *Who was in truth the knight called Sir Gray?* Some instinct told her that was the key to this whole dark business, and she had enough clues to solve the riddle, surely.

She'd have ticked off points on her fingers, but the spider had immobilized her arms and wrists, even several fingers.

Gray was someone she knew. A man whose face she would recognize could she but see it. He was tall and broad of shoulder. He seemed to have a nice small backside and good legs. Her fingers had told her that he was rather sharp of features, almost hawk-faced. He had no beard save the small one on his chin, and his lips often curled in bitter irony. That was hardly a full description of her husband, but it was all that was necessary to her seeking the solution to the riddle of his identity.

Pyre had given two extremely revealing hints. He had promised that once Gray had completed his mission, Pyre would treat all the poor fellow's problems as if they were his own. (This Pyre had sworn by his power, and Tiana had learned long ago that such oaths were always literally true and highly misleading.) The other clue was the way the image of the wizard of Ice always appeared when Gray looked into a mirror. Add to that Pyre's claim that his appearance here on Riser was accomplished by entirely natural means.

Now that is obviously impossibility, unless . . .

26th Strand:
PYRE AND EKRON

It was with a sense of triumph that the faceless knight struggled up the hillside and bent to grasp the first of the six skulls. He made his cloak into a sack for the carrying of the grim objects—the Fires Which Shall Destroy the World! As he began gathering them he realized how vastly more difficult the second portion of his mission would be. At once wonderful and ghastly, purest sunLight was washing his body, passing into and through his body, washing away all his experiences and previous thoughts. They were so few! And now they, too, were going! His few new-gained memories, his very sense of self were being bleached out of existence like so many impermanent stains on his brain. Already why he was about this task was a mystery to him. He remembered only that it was extremely urgent.

With the mystery of the Gray Knight's identity solved, Tiana saw how other events tumbled into place. At the outset of this whole nightmare, Pyre of Ice had found himself in a grim situation. His enemy and fellow wizard Ekron of Naroka had gained a seen future that guaranteed his own victory; Pyre's defeat! The means toward that end involved both Tiana and the Owner of the World. The Oracle of Tarrek had said that the toad-souled wizard would have Tiana and Pyre in his power "as two flies in the mouth of a toad." However twisted, that prediction *must* come to pass. Pyre's only option was to manipulate circumstances so that the oracular words could have more than one meaning; would take on another meaning.

That, Tiana speculated, would almost constitute the changing of the future—the *seen* future. Therefore it was impossible. No—one use of "almost" led to another. Almost impossible, then. Such a task required the most subtle and indirect of means.

Enter the subtle: an astonishingly equable and valorous knight, cruelly robbed of face and memory. Enter the indirect: that Gray Knight would act for Pyre! Robbed of self and memories and identity and sent forth on an unnamed mission!

She who had sailed the seas and flown the air and trod the earth and beneath it; she who had been the bane of royalty and of wizards and demons now had no way of knowing whether Pyre's effort had succeeded. Was Gray a success? (*Of course! He's wed to me!*) But at his *mission?*

She did not know. If he had failed to accomplish what Pyre hoped, then Gray and Tiana were simply doomed. Exit Tiana, exit husband, exit Pyre!

While that possibility was terribly real, there was definitely no profit in thinking about it, and Tiana did not.

On the other hand: if Pyre had succeeded and there existed two possible futures, two paths that might be taken to doom or . . . some form of triumph, it was a damnably limited success. Pyre could do nothing to influence which future came to pass! Therefore Tiana assumed that the whole responsibility fell to her. *This time we are truly partners, in every way!* Unfortunately, she had not the foggiest notion as to what to do. With only her wits to guide her she must try to guess. And then, somehow, she must act on her guess.

And to think that once I could have married a handsome king and avoided all this! Why, I remember that I was

almost flattered by Eltorn's suit. Oh but no! My suitor's
suit didn't suit me!

While she racked her brain thus, the little spider methodically continued its business, which was winding her up
like a Stigilatan mummy.

And again Light struck the throne of Darkness. Devour-
ing brilliance ravaged its occupant and blasted fragments
out of the black stone seat. For a brace of heartbeats the
Owner writhed under the assault; then the brilliance disappeared. Damn and blight; the non-being had survived
again! The silent voice proclaimed that:

"If your lover does not hurry, you will have no need
of worry about your other little problems. We shall all
be destroyed."

"Why don't you just surrender and end all this punishment of your doubtless aching self?"

His answer was laughter that came and went as sound-
unsound; silence-unsilence.

That was answered by another tremor of the very
ground beneath Tiana and the Owner. Above, even the
moon was melting. That leprously speckled sphere, set on
high to rule an outré perpetual night, dissolved into riven
fragments. Had it been no more real than the "moonlight"
admitted by the porthole on the Owner's ship?

And all the while the busy little spider went on with its
task, all untroubled by larger events. It belonged to Ekron.
In a way it was neither being nor non-being. In a way
Ekron served it and it served him. Now that symbiotic
toiler tugged one strand of its web to bring the helpless
Tiana smacking onto the stone floor of what had been a
palace. This time the flashes of light she saw were entirely
behind her eyes.

With its victim in a conveniently prone position, Ekron's
familiar began the next step of her cocooning.

(Burdened by his sack of skulls, Gray ran with failing
strength through a land of cruel beauty. Though his armored boots were more or less intact, he winced at every
stride. The balefully glorious sunlight that passed un-
dimmed through his body had washed from his mind all
thought and memory save one. Ahead he saw the realm
of Darkness and toward that goal he struggled with a
fixed, mindless purpose.)

Tiana struggled to squirm her right foot out of her boot
while the sky crumbled over her. Like a worn out gar-

ment of black, Riser's unnatural Night was ripping and collapsing in rot. Through the tatters was visible the splendid sapphire hue of Day, and its appearance was further destruction upon the firmament of Night. The end of everything was near. Dreadful cliché and dreadful truth. She *had* to get her blighty boot off! Inside was the hollow walnut Pyre had given her. She still had no idea as to how it was to be used, but it was her only remaining weapon. *It has to be ready for use!*

The playing board of Sulun Tha was a dazzle of coruscating white. Sulun Tha smiled. The faintest hint of triumph tinged his voice:

" 'Twould seem that my opponent has taken your advice, Caranga, and is indeed playing for a stalemate. 'Tis an effort at which he will succeed at greater cost and pain than he expects."

Just so he succeeds, Caranga thought. If he wins, he will enslave the world. If you win, you and the other six Flames will destroy it!

Gray crossed the boundary. What had been the dark realm of Night had seemed to have contracted leprosy. It was a strange spotted landscape, its black now splashed with the white of flaming Day. Where had sprawled a vast necropolis now remained only crumbled fragments becoming the dust of dead stone. Of the mighty palace of the Owner nothing remained save the throne where sat dark Emptiness. Before that throne a fire-haired woman lay prostrate, helplessly bound in the pallid gray of spider's silk.

Gray did not heed her plight because he did not notice her. The one thought remaining in his mind was to finish this important task and finish it correctly. One thought and one only had come to him the moment he gathered the skulls, and it and only it remained in a brain wiped anew.

He was close. He stopped. He rested his cloak-sack on the ground and folded it back to reveal six skulls. They looked human. They were not. Gray *felt* the fearsome eagerness that radiated from the throne of Darkness. He did not allow it to hurry him. He worked with the calm deliberation of a thoughtless genius. Up he straightened, a skull in either hand.

He took aim and hurled one; tossed the other into that hand; hurled it; bent for two more. One by one he threw the skulls into that Emptiness that was lack of existence, lack of being; non-being. The effect was that of pitching bright coins down a deep black well. Each skull struck the Emptiness and fell into an infinite black void.

Except the last.

It represented the faceless, nameless, mindless Gray Knight's volatile volition. It was the entirety of his single thought. It was his mission. That mission was not dictated by the Owner of the world, but by decision and command given long ago.

As his left hand tossed it carefully underhand, his right pulled the silver plate off its jaws. It spun through the air as an incredible ball of blue-white lightning.

Though the Emptiness recoiled instantly, it was too late. Instantly was not soon enough.

The skull, burning like the sun newborn at dawn, was within the Emptiness and there was no escape. The non-being called Owner writhed in agony on his dark throne.

Silence was awesome and absolute. Tiana realized the reason, and she was able to smile. The voice of the Owner was Silence. This unwavering transcendent absence of sound meant that he was bellowing his agony and anguish! She stared at the desperate movements of that dark Emptiness . . .

Then the throne itself changed into a long black tunnel. The Owner of the World fled the world, into the depths of infinity, and pitiless white light still coruscated in the center of that fleeing non-being. When the last echo of its silent screaming died, sound returned to the world. The dark throne of the vanquished Owner changed subtly. It showed itself as no more than a time-ravaged block of stone. Even as Tiana stared at it a crack flashed through that block, and a section slid off to shatter into fragments and dust.

It was a beautiful sound.

This world wanted no owner. Now it had none.

To the world, it meant freedom. To Tiana, it meant the possibility of success, even triumph. To Gray, it meant only that his one task was accomplished. He stood unthinking and unmoving while about him the landscape altered. It became an ordinary island of rock, standing barren in the last light of a setting sun that painted it gold and orange and red.

The Gray Knight knew no triumph. He looked down, blinking, at the spider entwining his mailed leg.

"Done!" Sulun Tha said with the satisfaction that served him for delight, and the game board before him turned to common gray. "This game ends in victory for human-kind, because it ends in stalemate for the Owner and Us. This battle is over. While the war will never end, the next battle will likely be ages hence."

"But my daughter . . ." Caranga broke off, for he spoke to empty air. The White Wizard, along with the thrones of Light and Darkness and the temple itself—all were gone like figments of a dream. Nothing remained except the game board. Through its window Caranga could see a tiny Tiana, bound and helpless as a trapped fly . . . and— *Susha have Mercy! No!* A giant misshapen toad was approaching her gray-shrouded form.

The Owner of the world was not a being or an owner. The Owner was gone. It had been an enemy and yet it had not been *the* enemy. In a manner of speaking, it had been a tool of the true enemy, as had Tiana and Pyre and Caranga and much of the world. The real enemy was he whose soul was that of a toad and whose god was the Spider.

He stepped now from behind the jagged spire of a sundered pillar. His bow to Tiana was the cruelty of mockery. As he bowed, Ekron's smile overflowed with malice.

Tiana stared. This mighty wizard seemed nothing more than a small ugly man dressed in flowing green robes designed to form a tent about a body better unseen. There was much about him, especially that ugly smile, that suggested a toad. Tiana was hard-pressed not to shudder. Even so, her voice was hard and she managed a passable sneer.

"I've been expecting you, Naroka's Shame! When the battle is over the buzzards always come skulking to pick the bones!"

"Silence, trull, else yours be picked while they still wear your skin!" The little wizard frog-puffed with pride. "Buzzard, is it! I have just proven myself the greatest of wizards by defeating that vulture-faced and oh-so-mighty

Pyre! All, all is as I planned! All has come to this! You
ought to address me with more respect."

The spider familiar was busily enwrapping the motionless Sir Gray now, and Ekron turned from Tiana to in-
spect that work.

Tiana was still and yet she sweated with effort. She
had almost slipped her foot out of that stubborn boot
and—

There!

The boot was off and Pyre's walnut was under her toes.
Within it was the spider of Pyre and, she assumed, very
few indeed of the twenty flies-as-food the mage had so
thoughtfully provided. Now her problem was how to go
about unleashing the little creature. If she tried picking it
up with her toes, she risked crushing an ally! On the other
hand . . .

Oh. She froze. On the other hand, something was crawling up her leg. The second spider had not needed her aid
to depart the walnut. It was now free and about its business. Assuming that she was right as to its sex and its
purpose, her task now was to distract Ekron. That proved
easy.

The toad-souled one was happily murmuring, "It is only
fitting that Pyre should witness these momentous events!
Especially . . ." He turned to favor Tiana anew with his
loathsome smile. "Especially considering what, my lovely
one, I am going to do to you. Poor little Tiana! You were
placed in this world to please ruttish men and feed . . . unusual appetites with that spectacular trull's body, not to
attempt to match wits with such as *Ekron!*" He slapped
his chest and his hand slipped into that flowing slime-green
robe. "Yes, I do think Pyre should watch while I enjoy
you!"

From within his garment the Narokan wizard drew
forth a scroll. He shook it; it unrolled to stiffen and become a mirror. He set it just so and within it he could
see the face of his mortal enemy. Pyre, now precisely as
helpless as the bound Sir Gray; as a fly cocooned by a
spider.

Tiana's mind was racing. She could see a tiny ambiguity
in the oracular prophecy; the words *could* carry an obscure second meaning. True, both obvious and obscure
meanings alike doomed her, but Tiana could not passively

wait for death by the one. She was Tiana. She would, if she could, take the extreme risk of shifting events into the alternate course. She glared up at Ekron while he positioned the mirror, and she sneered.

"Cute. I've seen better magic at cheap carnivals, frog-face."

Apparently the little wizard was thin of skin. The smile slipped from his face. "I begin to find your insolence annoying."

"That makes us even," Tiana told him, "for I find your stupidity a considerable annoyance! It's not the soul of a frog you have, is it, but the brain! You actually believe you have defeated Pyre! You lackwit! The truth is that while you cowered in craven safety with the world itself in dire peril, Pyre fought the greatest of battles. And he won! Even though he himself fell, the world was freed from the Owner and saved from the Fires That Shall *Not* Destroy the World! Only now that Pyre is helpless does Ekron the frog-hearted appear, coming like a jackal onto the field of battle . . ."

"Silence!" the Narokan stormed. The robe rustled and Tiana was kicked. "I am the better wizard! That I am pre-eminent in the world is no longer in question! Behold! The proof is that I live and soon you and Pyre will *die!*" That final word Ekron drew out with great relish.

Beyond him Tiana could see that the second spider, Pyre's spider, had made its way to Gray's body. Ekron's familiar had met it partway there. The two furry little arachnids were now . . . courting. Mating.

"Proof?" Tiana showed Ekron a satirical smile. "I can give you proof! Pyre is by far the greater wizard. Even in death he has defeated you, for he has robbed you of your precious possession."

The little wizard stared. "Explain!" The hint of fear rode his voice and spoiled the imperiousness.

"It is painfully simple." She drew out her words so that while she held Ekron's attention, the very thing he feared would happen behind his back. "Isn't it true," she drawled, "that a wizard and his familiar must agree in gender?"

"Obviously. But get to—"

"Your familiar is a male spider."

"One that has bound you as it slew that dolt Ishcon *and* re-wove the tapestry of the Weavers of Destiny! Aye!"

Only triumph rode Ekron's voice now, for his confidence returned at thought of his accomplishments.

"Pyre sent a female spider, Ekron, to provide sweet company to your male. She must be a most attractive wench, in spiderish terms! True to the nature of his kind, your familiar submitted to her charms. They have mated."

"What? So?" But Ekron started to turn—

As Tiana said, "Your familiar has just been eaten."

Ekron whirled and staggered as if he'd been struck with a poleax.

Tiana gave him no chance to recover. "I'll tell you something else that proves what a pathetic little fraud you are, toad-mouth. The prophecy is that you are to have me in your power as 'a fly in the mouth of a toad.' So what do you do? Have me trussed by a spider, and kick me. What now, stomp me to death? Any real wizard with pride and a sense of style would fulfill that prophecy literally, for once . . . by changing himself into a great big toad and actually eating me! You are not going to because you cannot. Your relationship to a toad must be limited to that wart on your alleged nose. You do not possess the *power,* Ekron!"

"I Will Show You My Power!" Ekron thundered, and he Changed.

The transformation was the more horrible because it was gradual and logical, a smooth transition from one object to its proper equivalent. Tiana stared and her eyes went huge—but not so huge as Ekron's. The squat ugly human form of the wizard impossibly melted into something utterly inhuman, a nightmare clad in slimy green, warted skin. Enormous eyes glared and from a yard-wide mouth a red tongue flickered like a serpent.

Her reason overthrown by horror, Tiana could not remember that she had been at the business of tricking the wizard into doing exactly this. She screamed uncontrollably.

Far away, in the kingdom of Naroka basking in evil; in the black stone building that was Ekron's lair; there stood a stone image carved in the likeness of a toad. Into the maw of that statue a smoke-blue gemstone had been thrust. Power poured from statue through occult channels to wizard—and the stone flared into a living radiance. Thus

*it added its ancient occult Force to the flowing Power.
Why else had Gray put it there?*

The red tongue wrapped around Tiana. It caressed bare
flesh with a warm slimy embrace that burned like acid.
Cocooning spider silk smoked. As the saliva dissolved the
webbing, Tiana was hauled, madly kicking and yelling,
into the air. Lusterless toad-eyes, large as dinner plates,
regarded her avidly and with hunger. Slowly, despite her
efforts to drive her booted foot into one of those eyes, she
was dragged into that door of a mouth. Vile toothless
jaws closed about her—and instantly spat her out.

Dazed by surprise and impact, she lay where she fell,
gazing up at the monster toad.

*Merciful gods and Gray's Candence! The thing is a
toad! It spat me out because it doesn't like the way I taste!*

The frog flop-whirled to Gray. The fallen knight was
pulled into the same huge mouth—and spat forth in the
same way. The vast toad looked about, throat working.
Seeing nothing that might be edible, it hopped away with
audible thuds. Mindlessly, Gray stood and stared into the
mirror.

Staring after it, Tiana lurched up to a sitting position.
Still in the grip of hysteria, she waved a balled fist. "And
don't come back!"

"It won't."

The familiar ironic voice spoke from the mirror.

As she turned to face him, Pyre went on, "Our erstwhile
enemy Ekron is now only a large but otherwise quite ordinary toad. We have both been as flies in his mouth—but
we were *not* flies. Hence it spat us forth."

"He's still dangerous! An animal that size—"

"No no," he said with smiling reassurance. "Can't you
see; the proper food of *toads* is flies and suchlike. As a
giant toad, the *former* Ekron is no menace to people. He
must instead search for giant flies. Where he is to find
them, I'm sure I do not know. But that of course is his
problem."

"Pyre—are you—are you all right?"

"I have put a long night's rest into the past few minutes,
and am well slept, Tiana. I am Pyre. All this I had seen
before, and knew just how long I had before the stone
we will not discuss—once it belonged to Sarsis, as part of

the Jewels of Ullatara—the stone I . . . arranged to be in the mouth of Ekron's power-source was needed."

Tiana heard that sentence, swirled it around her mind, chewed on it, tried to digest it. She sighed. "Yes, you are Pyre all right." She lifted one eyebrow as she stared at the image in Ekron's mirror. "Perhaps it is because I have seen you only in mirrors . . ."

"What? What?"

"I was wondering why I find that hatchet-carved face so attractive."

"Oh. Perhaps you prefer not to see a face at all?"

Tiana chuckled and did not answer. Taking a deep breath and letting it out slowly, she relaxed. Green eyes stared fondly. "Dear Pyre . . . however did you manage to set such an elaborate and thoroughly nasty trap?"

"It had to be nasty, dear Tiana, or it never would have pleased you so!" Woman and image smiled. "If you will recall, my *most* loyal but nameless servant led a group of Northmen in a raid on black-walled Shamash. By a rather clever trick—mine—entrance was gained to Ekron's stronghold. There squats a huge toad-icon absolutely vital to Ekron's power, which is not of this earth as mine is. Within it my faceless but *most* loyal servant left a spellstone. Once," he added with a very small smile, "you wanted it as an ornament."

Since that last wasn't worth discussing, Tiana hurriedly said, "Wait! Weren't you oathbound to do naught to Ekron save help him?"

"Ahh," purred the most powerful wizard in the world. "But that is exactly what I did. Voluntarily, of his own free will—and ego—he chose to turn himself into a toad. I merely helped him to make that change perfect and complete." After a smug pause while Tiana chuckled, Pyre went on in a more sober voice. "Now that my victory is won, my foe's fate seems somewhat harsh, or might to some who would excuse everyone! Still, considering the needless evil he did—massively—his punishment is woefully gentle."

Tiana, who was hardly Sulun Tha and had always been too sure of herself to be a do-gooder, nodded vehemently. "Agreed! Oh but wouldn't he look good in the clutches of a Calancian Lion's Teeth!"

"Or the one-legged horse he himself favored," Pyre said drily, and then that wizardly image bowed in manner courtly. "Of course my lady Queen of Pirates, I do owe you great thanks. In this affair I gambled heavily on your courage and wit, Tiana. Well have you rewarded my confidence. I was hampered by the occult restrictions of working against a seen future. Because of that I could give you only the barest clues and still you did the right thing at the right time."

"Thank you, my beloved monster." Tiana smiled prettily and batted bright green eyes in a ludicrous mockery of a member of any royal court. "But now—isn't it time to let my husband have back his rightful mind and face? One cannot embrace a mirror, you know."

All this time the Gray Knight had stood erect before the mirror, presumably staring from a blanked mind. Like a man awakening from a long sleep, he staggered and Tiana knew he was blinking. The vision of Pyre in the mirror jogged his memory and on the instant there was nothing pitiable at all about the Gray Knight.

"Wizard!" he said with strength. "You promised to tell me my identity."

(Tiana smiled at that strength, and knew that she did indeed love him/them. Nor was it that silly romantic infatuation that was always getting normal little people into such trouble. She respected the Gray Knight above all men; she respected Pyre above all humans. With the natural exceptions of her beloved self, of course, and Caranga. . . .)

From the mirror came neither answer nor acknowledgment of Gray's demand. He turned toward Tiana with a little frown, and then his eyes widened.

"You—you are looking at me! You are looking directly into my eyes!"

"Why so I am. I am looking into the eyes of the two men I love most." She nodded to indicate the mirror. "That is only a mirror. That is your reflection."

The frown vanished from the face of the Gray Knight, who had a face and a name as well, and knew it as Tiana's words keyed his memory—his reunion with himself. Then he was laughing.

"Of course!" Gray/Pyre laughed, charmingly, boyishly amused by the joke on himself. "The only way I could battle a seen future was to make it *un*-seen, by placing myself under a spell of forgetfulness. Mirroring surfaces were to key helpful or soothing words, what few I could vouchsafe me under the circumstances. As for my recovery —that was to be keyed by your saying what you just said."

Tiana smiled. "I know. I knew. In my heart I knew it was you that day on the ship, when I touched your face. You must know that, too. We both know I would not have wed a man I had not sensed was the one man worthy of me—or nearly so."

Pyre marveled at the perfectly sincere hypocrisy of the woman he loved doubly; both as Pyre the intellectual and Gray the intellect-less warrior. Though he concealed a chuckle, he was not displeased. What other woman could possibly be worthy of him—or nearly so?

"You are not to look at our future, my lord husband."

"I am vowed never to do, my lady wife. Now come, let us get from this place."

And arm in arm they wended from that place, and the past, into a better future . . . a future unseen.

The gameboard went blank before Caranga's eyes, and was only a slab of wood. Fine mahogany from Collada, he observed professionally.

Well, perhaps what he'd seen was enough. His daughter was safe and wed. If the marriage was tranquil, she would return in due course to show him his grandchildren. If— as was far more likely—the marriage was a stormy sea, she might steer her way back to him even sooner.

Tiana married! Caranga heaved a sigh and mashed his chin to look down at the hair on his huge chest. He saw black hairs, and gray, and . . . white. Two. He plucked them.

Caranga began walking from that place.

Well and well. Perhaps it was time to end his own long career asea. Funds should be no problem. He had this and that laid aside here and there, and all about him lay the ruins of the Owner's domain, almost begging to be looted. *(Looted? Salvaged. Liberated. Picked up!) A bit of searching by a trebly seasoned expert will beyond doubt discover horded hoards of gold and jewels and even a bit of silver to pay the help!*

He had been ambling back to where he had left the small boat. Now, as he topped a long granitic rise, he had a view of most of the island. As far as he could see in the deepening twilight, an utter desolation greeted his gaze;

crumbled buildings and vagrant chunks of stone. All emblems of once-was. Except for one building.

He focused his attention on it, puzzled. Not for long. Of course! Sulun Tha would have spared innocent bystanders. That included hostages and captives. Tiana had come here as part of a shipload of one hundred . . . business women. It was a safe guess that that host of whores was in yon building, sorely in need of rescue and guidance.

I shall be rescuer and guide. Tomorrow. Caranga, the Black Knight!

He smiled, then frowned. Where he would put that gaggle of girls was a problem: *Vixen* was already overcrowded with Larine's . . . business women. Their presence hardly made for a tranquil crew and—a hundred more!

On the other hand . . . still . . . yes. A few days' sail from here there was a singularly beautiful uninhabited island. Caranga sighed again. Perhaps . . . if a man was going to retire . . . the time might have come to organize a . . . a harem? A small kingdom, perhaps, or something like. After all, half of those Orvarians were beautifully black or brown at the very least. Hmm. A man had to be careful how he went about such a project.

Probably the first step is establishing a good and trustworthy headwife.

He'd have to talk to Larine about that.

And thus it came to pass that as the sun set next evening the black pirate Caranga sailed into the cliché aboard a ship laden unto danger with jewels and gold and beauteous whores. Whether or no his adventures were indeed at end, and what came of the marriage of his foster-daughter Tiana to the dread enchanter Pyre . . . those things are another tale, and an unseen future.

endit

GLOSSARY

Places in the War of the Wizards trilogy are listed separately in the *Gazetteer* section. Here we include everything and everyone else.

In laboriously making this compilation during the Dog Days of August 1980, the writers were soon aware of a profoundly high body count. We decided to indicate non-survivors with the standard tombstone inscription "R.I.P." This does not necessarily mean the usual; in many cases it should be translated as "Rest In Pieces, You Dirty Dog."

The numeral after the subject indicates in which book it/she/he appears: *Demon*(1); *Eyes*(2); *Web*(3). An (R) after the entry indicates a subject referred to in the text, without appearing. Drood and Theba, for instance, are never seen. Avan has always been; Alpheg, presumably, was always a crewman of *Vixen*.

Those readers unable to resist the compulsion to peruse the glossary *before* reading the book might well skip those entries that indicate a novel they have not yet read.

We love Tiana. We loved creating these accounts of the adventures of her, Caranga and Pyre. We love this glossary—now that all the labor is ended. Be advised that whichever of us you apprise of an error or oversight will immediately blame the other.

—RKL/AJO

Aldavar(R)—supposedly king of old Moshida
Allato(2)—thief of Reme and old friend of Tiana
Alnick(1)—murderous bandit of Dark Forest, until he attacked Tiana. R.I.P.
Alpheg—lean crewman of *Vixen*
Ap(R)—ancient warrior-hero of BEMAR. His blessed beard is a swear-by.

Areth(3)—Duke of Jinary, SARCH, until he challenged Tiana. R.I.P.

Argarf(2)—homely prince and suitor of Princess Jiltha. "Froggy."

Arms of Drood(2)—a forbidden cult dedicated to the Lord of Death—and to murder

Arond(2)—former pirate become blind beggar in the *Wayfarer*. A victim of the Eyes. R.I.P.

Ashina(3)—captain of a murderous Thunlander cavalry squadron—until he met Tiana. R.I.P.

Astorloth(R)—anciently, a dragon slain by Ullatara

Atean pearls—each is worth several gold pieces; ten will buy a good ship

Avan—long-dead sorcerer/hero/warrior, now demigod. A few of his tools remain; his Sword is a weapon for Heroes

Ball lightning creature(2)—a web-making . . . thing, of Lightning Isle. Aggressive only when its web is endangered, at which time it becomes swiftly dangerous unto burn-death

Bandari(1)—"the Cat"; former thief of Reme and Tiana's tutor; now leader of the Stromvili riders of the thunder

banner—Tiana's is a laughing red fox-head on a field of black. Pyre's, if he had one, would be a cold green flame on a field of icy blue-white

Bardon(1,2)—second Second Mate of *Vixen*. This morose-because-penniless noble of BEMAR, thanks to Pyre, proved himself as Hero, married a princess, and has even been called a demigod, as Bardon ca-Lionhight

Barkis(2)—"the weasel"; a corsair captain out of Reme

Barracuda—generic name for one type of Narokan warship

Barrenton(1)—of Lieden; murderous bandit of Dark Forest unwise enough to attack Tiana. R.I.P.

Bealost(R)—Tiana's murdered younger half-brother; would have been Duke of Reme

bear(2)—particularly dangerous host for the murderous Eye of Sarsis. R.I.P.

Berrock(2)—Ilani marine sergeant assigned to temporary duty on *Vixen*

Bjaine(2)—huge handsome blond Norther who believes that luck and force overcome all obstacles, including women. Recruited to oppose Tiana, he became her ally

—as long as she could bear him. Later called Demonbelly

Bjork(3)—Northron in the service of the Gray Knight on *Firebird*

Black Sword(2)—ship of Mandias, pirate captain of Tiana's acquaintance

Blaze Blazetop(3)—shipmaster of *Firebird;* a Northron of course

Blind Ones—the three who weave the tapestry of the world and all human affairs; the Weavers

Brassheads—the royal bodyguards of NAROKA. The name probably derives from their helmets. On the other hand, it may describe their heads

Bratch(3)—captain of security, Dindroom Prison, THESIA. Just one of Tiana's many jailers

Brehar(1)—Nevinian count who saved but tried to murder Tiana. R.I.P.

business woman—any proprietor or toiler in a brothel. Tiana prefers the more familiar term

Candence(3)—that by which the Gray Knight swears, without knowing why

Cartro(2)—proprietor of the Wayfarer tavern, former pirate haunt in Reme

Chandak(3)—"Keeneye"; third Second Mate of *Vixen.* A brown warrior from the far southern YABAZO Islands

Chervian Cross—an x-frame formed by two beams and several bolts. A prisoner bound here is open and terribly vulnerable. History forgets whether Cherv was the inventor or first victim, or both

Chotor(1)—twin of Sotor of Aradot; a murderous bandit of Dark Forest, until he tried opposing Tiana. R.I.P.

Cignas—variant of Signas; see *Temple of*

clammer—auctioneer; front man; shill

cliffcat—a dangerous denizen of the Mt. Erstand area

Clearspring, Countess of(1)—Colladan noble who is an admirer of Prince Eltorn and definitely not of Tiana

Colla Long-arm(R)—long-ago founder of COLLADA

Colla, Sons of—Colladans; people of Colla

Cormer(3)—young Northlander artist/cartographer on *Firebird*

corsair—any pirate. Also shark; sea-wolf

creba—man-eating fish from one of the Kroll Islands

cren—a large-boled tree; usually "crentree." Often festooned with the lichen called feathermoss

crown—COLLADA's is of coral, and belonged to Colla's son. NAROKA's is a silver web surmounted by a golden spider. THESIA's, as of *Web*(3), is . . . slag

cutpurse—the ill-advised wear purses or wallets thongslung from their belts. A cutpurse is that street-thief later called pickpocket

Dagger, Sign of the—religious ward-sign of the Orvarians. Yorimagua, resurrected demigod of ORVAR, was slain with a dagger

dancegirl—the best are trained in Shamash, and they are not, either, harlots! The aftermath of their temple dancing is a religious experience

Darganda—mugger and cat butcher of Reme, who tried for the wrong cat. A victim of the Eyes. R.I.P.

Dark Guards(1)—special corps detailed to guard NEVINIA's Tomb of Kings, when there was one

Darvra(1)—toiler in the House of Delightful Women, Reme. For her aid to Caranga, Tiana made her rich with the gift of a single jewel

Davri(1)—an apprentice highrider of Stromvil

demonflower—a large sentient bloodsucker whose tendrils act as tentacles

Derramal(1)—wizard who conspired with Arcone and Palance to overthrow Hower, nearly twoscore years ago. They failed—but murdered Tiana's father and carried off his infant heir, her half-brother Bealost

Despan(2)—northern provincial who is captain in the King's Own, Reme

Dinharu(1)—runaway niece of Ct. Brehar of Calencia, and the name used by Tiana for her funeral and interment in the Tomb of Kings.

Disciple—Tiana's pack-mule in *Demon*(1)

dithba—a liquid poison best used in something spicy, to disguise its flavor. But see Sweetbird!

Dorbandura(1)—venal, patron-murdering innkeeper of Escallas. R.I.P.

Dowmar(3)—"Cliffcat;" crewman of *Vixen*. R.I.P.

dragon silk—see *silk*

Drood(R)—"of the Thousand Arms"; Lord of Death; Lord of Demons; the Grasper; a satanic figure

Dung!—Tiana's explosive expletive, us. uttered in the anger of frustration. cf *Rat Dung!*

eagle—big silver coin of BASHAN, good the world over

Egg of the Phoenix(2)—cut and polished gem of ten thousand facets, egg-shaped and large as a man. Stolen by Caranga—to no profit

Eidar's Disease—a highly communicable affliction whose sufferers are feared and shunned. It lingers entirely too long before it—enough. We don't want to talk about it

Ekron—the Toad-souled One; one of the two most powerful wizards in the world. He is implacable enemy to the other, Pyre of Ice, and thus to Tiana. When something horrible happens, assume Ekron!

Elmry(3)—manservant to HRM Ormul of NAROKA

Eltorn—"the Fair;" handsome ruler-Prince of COLLADA and a suitor of Tiana. Long live Eltorn Bihal!

Eyes of Sarsis(2)—a pair of huge diamonds, part of the Treasure of Ullatara. They were much more, however, than gemstones

feathermoss—a plant-imitating lichen that festoons trees in long fringes and spiderweb traceries

Feho(1)—torturer of Calancia, until he tried his trade on Tiana. R.I.P.

Fersen(1)—a general of COLLADA

Festival of the Lesser Turtle—occasion peculiar to ORVAR, marked by turtle races by day and orgies at night

Firebird(3)—Northlander ship commanded by the Gray Knight as Warchief

Firebreath—Simdan term for (supposedly extinct) dragons. see *Picarus*

fireplant—a decorative plant that is prettily welcome until it pollinates. Dehiscing seedpods hurl agony; the victim looks burned to death

flourbean—starchy legume whose seeds are used in making a thick staple soup

Forfis(1)—physician to Eltorn the Fair of COLLADA

Games of the Snare—a truly sadistic spectator sport of NAROKA. The chief participant is known as the King's Victim. Gray was an entirely unwilling participant—or was that a dream of King Ormul?

Garnis(2)—crewman of *Vixen*, and victim of the Eyes. R.I.P.

Gerenna(1)—murderous bandit of Dark Forest, until he attacked Tiana. R.I.P.

glim-flower—one of Turgumbruda's more gently useful creations; a light-yielding plant goblet—Caranga's favorite, liberated from a Sinchorese ship, is of beaten silver set with garnets and a rather nice emerald

Golub(1)—happy, chubby, two-wived priest in Stromvil, a nice fellow shocked by Tiana

Goriarch(R) "Blackbeard;" hero; pirate-become-Duke of Reme 200 years ago. Patron of weaponeers and conquerors—who should remember that he was slain while abed with a woman

Gormansot(R)—clever fruit merchant of Reme who deters barefoot urchins with jacks strewn in the alley

Gray(3)—"name" of the Gray Knight

Gray Knight, the(3)—also Sir Gray; Gray. A tool from whom Pyre stole his face and his name, and who remained shockingly calm and competent—and attractive to Tiana Highrider

green—the color of the cold fire of Pyre

green—the color Tiana's eyes, and her favorite color. She likes it best when it marks that type of beryl called an emerald

grub—a pejorative term, used much the same as "dog" or "plagul" or "S.O.B." or "bastard." (Tiana, being a bastard by birth if not by nature, does not use that term pejoratively.)

Gunda(1)—Second Mate of *Vixen* slain by the power of the Demon in the Mirror. Thought to have been a Northlander—?

Hangman(1)—only known name of a murderous bandit of Dark Forest. R.I.P.

Hartes—(var. *Hertes*) King of THESIA, self-styled "Conqueror of Bemar, Paleran, Narf and Thunland," and patron and friend of Ekron. R.I.P.

Hathedra(3)—one of the Absolutely Astonishing Delights in the House of that name. A friend of Caranga, of course.

hawkwitch—any of the poisonous seers of THESIA. Powers are believed to derive from the serhawk, parts of which are woven into a hawkwitch's home.

Hella(R)—daughter of Theba. "Theban Hella" is ruler of the land of the dead. She is not inimical, does not truly desire more company or subjects, and is no friend of Drood.

Hertes—variant of *Hartes*

Highrider—an earned sobriquet of Tiana, having nothing

to do with her arrogance. Well, almost nothing. see *Mt. Erstand; Stromvil*

Hogrith(3)—High Priest of THESIA

Holonbad—HRM Hower's cousin, once "Lacklands." Now Duke of Reme. Also called Holonbad Lackwit

Horgarrav(R)—an ibscene idol from which Tiana once stole a ruby she claims was its eye

House—not necessarily a home, and never so when capitalized

HRH—Her/His Royal Highness: offspring of royalty

HRM—Her/His Royal Majesty: reigning queen or king

hungry apples(3)—horrors peculiar to ORVAR, we hope. They are not apples, and they are hungry

Illdabar(2)—advisor to Milord Holonbad of Reme

Irinda(2)—toiler in the House of Seven Delights, Reme

Iron Maiden(R)—reputed torture device reputedly employed in NAROKA

Ishcon(3)—Lord High Magistrate of THESIA, captor of Tiana, and entirely too clever for his own good. R.I.P.

Jemora—a crewman of *Vixen*

Jiltha(2)—flighty teen-aged daughter of HRM Hower, as anxious to dispose of her pesky virginity as Tiana is to preserve it. HRH Jiltha eventually prevailed, and Hower became thereby grandfather to twins

Kandor(1)—young genius of a Colladan admiral who slew the invader Lokieto

Kanja(3)—Thesian who bears the ugly title Painmaster in Dindroom Prison, where Tiana once sojourned on her way to execution

Kascat—of Narf; a crewman of *Vixen*

kascat furs—popular product of the Gray Lands

Kathis(2)—superb warrior of Reme and former agent of HRM Hower and Milord Holonbad. A victim of the Eyes. R.I.P.

Kensh(3)—Thunlander cavalry sergeant, until he met Tiana. R.I.P.

Kerreas(3)—streetfighter turned Thunlander cavalryman making war on villagers—until he met Tiana. R.I.P.

king's cord—a napped luxury fabric, usually woven in very dark hues

King's Ears, the—HRM Hower's intelligence gathering force

King's Own Guardsmen, the—HRM Hower's personal guards and police force of Reme kinkoo—a large hand-leafed bush found throughout most of the SW

Klain(1)—of Port Thark; crewman of *Vixen* slain in Killiar by shadows. R.I.P.

Kragg(3)—simply a kill-trained, armor-wearing bear of Murtud of ORVAR

Labyrinth, the—another name for Shamash, sinister capital of sinister NAROKA

lackwit—a favorite term of Tiana, indiscriminately applied

Largumdurga—"Durgy," a crewman of *Vixen*. His name identifies him as a Bash

Larine(3)—Simdan proprietor of the House of No Tomorrow in Palanigh, and a very special old friend of Caranga

league—our translation of *'rigul*, the standard measurement of distance: .89769589 km

Leroges(3)—plotsome minister of HRM Hartes of THESIA

Lion's Teeth—torture device invented in Calancia; "even the Narokans were impressed"

Lokieto(1)—Ducal brother to HRM Hartes of THESIA and invader of COLLADA, R.I.P.

Longo Stromvilo(R)—the first highrider. All he did was leap off a cliff with arms, legs, and cloak horizontally spread. It almost worked. R.I.P.

Lord Fortune(R)—of the Snows, personification of luck, in NORTHLAND

Luquila(R)—sister of HRM Hartes of THESIA, with a face her mother couldn't love

Machelen(1)—an admiral of COLLADA

mahogany—the best comes from COLLADA, though those few in the know claim there's better in TSC, which will someday make someone rich and show those dam' Colladans

Maltar(1)—of Banarizur; "Lord of Dark Forest." A murdering bandit chief who attacked Tiana. R.I.P.

Mandias(3)—corsair captain of the *Black Sword*, out of Reme

Marcon(R)—Prime Minister of THESIA, 70 years ago

Marderun(1)—"the Wise;" a most unfortunate old potter and seer of Escallas who aided Tiana when she was Pyre's enemy. That was not wise. R.I.P.

marrin hound—once a superior breed. Now the bloodline

is played out and a marrin is good only as a rather dull pet

marrin hound—Insulting slang; the scion or last member of a once-important family now at its nadir. A nickname of Bardon, q.v.

mastiffs—big vicious beasts of Stigilata, BASHAN. Excellent watchdogs unless a friend drops over late one night

Militor(1)—a sergeant of the Escallan nightwatch. One night he wisely elected not to notice a very suspicious-looking Tiana. He lives.

Misnavella(2)—a toiler in the House of Seven Delights, Reme

moonstalkers(3)—black pajama'd servants of the Owner; most sinister indeed, they are said to be liches, revenants; i.e.: returned from death. R.I.P.!

Mordabot(1)—widow who puts up pilgrims passing through Woeand. Bad things happened to such guests until Tiana stopped there.

Morna(2)—kidnap victim rescued by Tiana from Mother Vorgia's House in the Krolls. She gained a mighty husband and a splendid gift from Pyre. Current presumed residence: NORTHLAND

Mother—term applied to the person foremost in a convent of Theban nuns or a brothel, where it is also "Housemother"

Murtud(3)—Duke and Lord High Inquisitor of Palanigh, ORVAR, doubling as servant of the Owner—until Tiana's visit. R.I.P.

Nadya(1)—lithe and very lean highrider of Stromvil who considered Tiana . . . large. Tiana called her boy-girl and they fought. Later they became friends, as fellow Highriders

Nagranda(R)—great TSC warrior who built an empire and established Killiar as its center, over five centuries ago

Narokan gift—slang, meaning "Watch out—it's probably lethal (or worse)!"

Narota(1)—crewman of *Vixen* slain by shadows in Killiar. R.I.P.

Narthur(1)—a general of COLLADA

Nestor(R)—long-dead king of the Neviari tribe and founder of NEVINIA. His honored tomb became a temple for ghouls, until Tiana's visit.

Nired(3)—uncle of HRM Hartes and servant of the Owner who tried to set Tiana up. R.I.P.

Noff—crewman of *Vixen;* a tippler. (Or is that redundant?)

non-beings—(var. *nonbeings*) dwell neither on the earth, in Hell, nor the gulf of Night; they do not exist and yet *are*. Voice, appearance, and speech is an *absence* of light, sound, words. They do evil with relish, loving destruction for its own sake. We don't understand them either.

Nor'man: Norther; Northman; Northron—person from the NORTHLAND(s)

nuns—women who use Theban worship and service as an escape from the world. As they tend graveyards, they are of some use.

Old Ones—the ophidian predecessors of humankind. A few survive, in TSC

Oorer(R)—king of the Remilani and father of HRM Hower of ILAN

Orgar(2)—an Arm of Drood who sought to be First Arm, in Reme. He failed. R.I.P.

Orld(1)—chief counsellor to Eltorn the Fair of COLLADA

Ormul(3)—"Searuler;" king of NAROKA. Also Ormul Heartless and eventually Ormul Soulless

Osogar(R)—"the Incinerator"; long-ago king of THESIA

Owner, the—of the World! He exists, in Drood's name!

Paramane(3)—a most distasteful servant of Ekron, presumably a lich. R.I.P.—twice

Parsh—a crewman of *Vixen*

Picarus—a zodiacal sign; the Firebreather

pirates—corsairs; sea-wolves; sharks. There are many, and many of those harbor in Reme. Less accommodating ones hang about the Krolls

plagul(R)—a pejorative, after an unpleasant little beast not recommended as pets or even food, and about which no more need be said

Pyre—(He has said that what we say here of him will vanish, but):

Quarmos(3)—murderous Thunlander cavalryman so ill-advised as to attempt Tiana's rape. R.I.P.

Radev(1)—murderous bandit of Dark Forest, until he attacked Tiana. R.I.P.

Rarn(1,2)—beloved ship's cat of *Vixen.* He firmly believed that he was a person, but ran afoul of foul sorcery. A victim of the Eyes. R.I.P.

Rat Dung!—a strong expletive of Tiana, usually shouted

redbush—it is, in fall and all winter

Redlands, Duke of—master spy of ILAN; called Milord Spy

regal—major coin of THESIA, in gold and in silver

Rinalay(3)—proprietor of the House of Absolutely Astonishing Delights, Port Thark. A friend of Caranga's, of course

Rushil(1)—aide to Eltorn the Fair of COLLADA

Saint Theranos(R)—ancient hero in the War against the Snake, first ruler of the earth

Saint Tiana—legendary(?) savior of Lieden, City of Light

Saphistran(R)—philosopher able to "prove" almost anything, including his susceptibility to strong drink. His thoughts later influenced Aristotle, Jefferson, Sartre, and Rand

Sarsis—the ancient Great Snake. Assumed dead, until *The Eyes of Sarsis*

saytree—a tallish evergreen with a pungent wood and mildly poisonous berries

scepter—that of COLLADA is, traditionally, a reed from the bank of Lake Belanda. NAROKA's is spider-surmounted; NORTHLAND's is an ax!

Serl(1)—of Port Tilonbi; murderous bandit of Dark Forest, until he attacked Tiana. R.I.P.

Shadow War—ancient conflict unto species-death between the descendants of the Snake, first rulers of the earth, and of the Ape: humankind. The final combatants became Sarsis and Pyre

Shen(3)—"Dragonbreath;" crewman of *Vixen* who made good in Thesia

Shibenhar(R)—Nevinian nobleman at Tiana/Dinharu's funeral

Shorbanthuda(1)—murderous son of innkeeper Dorbandura of Escallas. R.I.P.

Signas(2)—(var.: Cignas, Ssigniss) an ancient non-human god of sacrifice

silk—much that is excellent comes from the accommodating spiders of Il-Zadok Marsh; its best weave comes out of NARF. "Dragon silk" appears to be enchanted, and its origin is uncertain; the non-beings?

Sinhor(R)—master swordmaker of Banarizur and national asset of COLLADA. Sinhorish swords are few, excellent, and prized

Skiller(3)—Northron in the service of the Gray Knight, on *Firebird*

slawgrass—pallid green, broad-leafed spray with fringy yellow blooms. Wonderfully edible

soap—most favored is the potted, fragrant variety from Tashol

Sondaman(R)—Duke of Reme; Tiana's murdered father

Sotor(1)—see Chotor. R.I.P.

Spider, the—god of NAROKA

spider—a normal-seeming one is Ekron's familiar

"—Those of Il-Zadok Marsh produce the finest silk in the world

"—A seemingly sentient giant one endeavored to destroy Tiana, in Reme. Its possession of antennae marked it as no arachnid. R.I.P.

spikebush—particularly nasty large plant with long, curving thorns

Star of Avan(2)—earring belonging to but not belonging to Pyre. It is of occult properties, and made of ice metal

Storgavor(2)—so-called King of the Kroll Pirates. A victim of the Eyes. R.I.P.

Stormfury(2)—Narokan ship captained by Bjaine the Norther

Swallow(1)—Kandor's racing galley, used against Lokieto on L. Belanda

sweet—Eng. translation of the Continental word *striss*. Oddly, the identical sound in Simdan means "Godless sister f—ing__." Such coincidences still occur; cf "Black Hole" in Russian and to "knock up" in British and in American

Sweetbird—a virtually undetectable and thus expensive poison that is a product, of course, of NAROKA. More commonly used is dithba

Sword of Avan(2)—an enchanted weapon for heroes; also a sobriquet. See *Avan*

Sword Oath—an ancient and honorable form of becoming wedded. It was enough for Princess Jiltha and, later, Tiana Highrider of Reme

Susha(R)—sensuous fertility goddess of SIMDA—and Caranga's swear-by. Susha does not, fortunately, mind semi-obscene oaths in Her name

Sycore—a zodiacal sign; the Crab

Syrodan—a merchant who achieved enormous wealth, long ago; Saw The Light, became a hermitish holy man, and left his estate to the People of Reme: the Grove of Syrodan

s—third and thirteenth letter of the Tianan alphabet

tahlequah melons—large sweet ones. Legend has it that Tahlequah was mistress of a long-ago king

Tarrek, Oracle of—it is up in Narf; it has to be cajoled or forced to reply; its reply is a seen future and *must* happen, but the words are subject to any interpretation possible, and still may surprise

Tarnok(3)—a particularly cruel baron of NAROKA, whose robes are trimmed with eyeballs—human, of course

Ter-Gon(1)—werehawk and acolyte of Pyre, ere he attacked Tiana. R.I.P.

Theba(R)—goddess of death with powers, presumably to prevent it. Thought once to have lived, she is also patron of women. Her growing following includes Tiana. Theba's nuns are called Sisters of Death and tend graveyards.

Thetoora(2)—arrogant and ill-fated acolyte of Ekron who excavated in the Grove of Syrodan for the Eyes of Sarsis. He found them. R.I.P.

Thor-Nack(1)—werehawk acolyte of Pyre, sent to stop Tiana. R.I.P.

Tiana—Highrider of Reme, Hero of Dark Forest, Wizardslayer; Demonslayer; Pirate Queen; She Who Ran the Lubok; Bastard of Reme; Savior of Lieden; Saint Tiana; Tomb-defiler; etc etc etc. After her apothesis into a similarly named goddess ages later by the credible and god-needing, she was eventually doubted to have existed

totatten—a tall lean tree with smooth bark and waxy tricorn leaves of a pungent odor. Nevinians drop just one on a grave, at each visit. Later it was thought to be a bane of vampires and other revenants

turkey bush—low bristly wildplant whose showy, variegated, droopy red flowers resemble wattles. Even turkeys don't eat the lovely smooth berries, which are strongly emetic

Turgumbruda(1)—wizard and "Dark Gardener of Escallas." A genius at evil botanical devising until he tried to murder Tiana. R.I.P.

Ullatara(R)—long-dead wizard and slayer of dragons and wizards

" Jewels of(2)—included the Tears of the Gods (pearls); Blood of Astorloth (rubies); the emerald Sky Island; the Crown of Aldavar—and the worse than deadly Eyes of Sarsis, big handsome diamonds

Uldrood—First Arm of Drood's cult of murderers in Reme, until he tried to sacrifice Tiana. R.I.P.

un-—of; as Tiana un-Reme; Pyre un-Ice; Caranga un-Simda

Urga—pirate who rebelled against Storgavar—and then met Tiana. R.I.P.

Varban(1)—murderous Graylander thief of Dark Forest until he attacked Tiana, Hero of Dark Forest. R.I.P.

Versindoga(3)—of BASHAN; crewman of *Vixen* and The Man Who Dowsed The Captain

Virakoka(3)—"Koka" of Nevinia; cook on *Vixen*

Vols(1)—murderous bandit of Dark Forest, until etc. etc. etc. R.I.P.

Voltadin(3)—Admiral, Royal Navy of ILAN. Oddly, a respected man of competence

Voomundo(2)—a later hero in the ancient War against the Snake

Vorgia(2)—venal brothel proprietor in the Krolls. Victim of the Eyes. R.I.P.

"walk naked among tigers, to"—an expression meaning to go forth despite known danger

Warchief(3)—Northlander title. Applied to the Gray Knight by Northrons who, because of "Runemaster" Pyre, accepted him as absolute leader.

weaponeer—any warrior; later "weapon-man"

Weavers—see *Blind Ones*

Windsong(1)—Tiana's horse, a chestnut

wine—a choice one is an export of NARF, in leathern sacks. The famed sup-wine of COLLADA is, of course, brandy; but like "pajama," the word has not yet been invented. A problem in the careful writing of period pieces

Woodlings(1)—painted cannibalistic aborigines of Greenwood, up near Mt. Erstand. A band once captured Tiana and the Hand of Derramal. R.I.P.

Yemani(3)—King of ORVAR, with many wives and concubines. A busy man, esp. at Festival time

Yorg(R) (R)—"the Mad;" King of THESIA, a century ago

Yorish(R)—HRM; son of HRM Yorg of THESIA

Yorimagua(R)—slain and supposedly resurrected demi-god of ORVAR whose shroud may be viewed in tours of Palanigh. cf *Dagger, Sign of the*

Zark(2)—Painmaster of THESIA who ran afoul of Bjaine and his own devices. R.I.P.

Zerth(3)—Sarchese archer on Duke Areth's galley, who sought to feather Tiana. R.I.P.

Zohar(R)—ancient king of NEVINIA who instituted the Tomb of Kings

Zolgis(2)—proprietor of the House of Heavenly Pleasure, Reme

Zud(R)—Caranga has the finery of this Narokan sea-captain whose ship fell prey to *Vixen* immediately before the opening of *Demon in the Mirror*. R.I.P.

GAZETTEER

Place Names in the War of the Wizards trilogy
A few preliminary notes: The two major continents seem
to have borne several names, leading to confusion beyond
cartographic. Accordingly reader may assume that any
place not otherwise noted exists on the main and so-called
"civilized" continent. The sprawling but sparsely populated
Southern Continent was called just that, and will here be
identified at TSC.
For convenience and as a courtesy to various rulers, nations are here rendered in all caps, as: BASHAN.
The words following the descriptions indicate inhabitants
and adjective, respectively. Reader might remember that a
county was once the domain presided over by a *count*, as
a *duchy* is a *duke*'s domain, not a dukedom, and that a
House is not a home.

Aradot—capital of BEMAR; Arads favor tall, big-boned
women
Arcone—a duchy of ILAN. Arconer, Arconish
Asmygorian Sea—the Ocean: true home to Caranga and
Tiana. Also: the Great Blue Sea
Atea—a pearl-rich area off the NW coast of TSC. See
Atean Pearls
Banarizur—a nice farm-surrounded citylet of COLLADA
Banavinbonro—a smallish city of SARCH
Bark's Fork—connects the Vervex R. (THESIA) with the
R. Lubok
BASHAN—a feudal inland nation in which the king is no
more than paramount among ruling lords. Bashanese;
also "a Bash"
Bash-an—old form of BASHAN

Belanda, Lake—on the COLLADA-THESIA border. Surrounds Lieden on three sides

BEMAR—an inland nation. See Tashol; soap. Bemaron; Bemarish

Blood Arena—in Shamash of NAROKA. A place best not visited or thought on

Calancia—capital of NEVINIA. Famed for its Tomb of the Kings—until Tiana's visit in *Demon*. Also as common variant: Calencia

Cave Run Falls—older—and local name for Sanna Falls, THESIA.

Cignas, Temple of—a grim sacrificial place on TSC, where Tiana once sojourned, briefly, in *Eyes* (var: Signas)

Clearspring—a county of COLLADA

Castle Ice—the abode of Pyre. It rises in an impossible area of idyllic lushness tucked amid a northern wilderness peopled with savages

COLLADA—a lovely inland nation plagued by bad neighbors and ruled by the most handsome of princes, an enlightened absolute monarch. Colladans; Sons of Colla. Its forests provide a fine mahogany prized the world over.

Dark Forest—a danger-fraught virgin forest in NEVINIA and ZADOK

Dark Land, the—Simdan name for TSC; also the Dark Continent.

DEROT—("DEE-rot") a sort of nation of TSC. Derotese

Dindroom Prison—a warren beneath Port Thark, THESIA. Tiana sojourned here as an inmate—briefly—in *Web*

Erstand, Mt.—a peak in ZADOK where Tiana earned the sobriquet *Highrider*—by flying. Erstanders; highriders; idiots

Escallas—"capital" or more properly major city of BASHAN.

Fanwood—a barony near Calancia, in NEVINIA

Gray Lands—not much is known of this sprawling easternmost area of the main continent. Its emigrants are closemouthed. The world loves its fine Kascat furs. Graylander

Great Blue Sea, the—the Asmygorian

Green Woods—a vast forest to the far NE

Hangtree Road—an excellent E-W road across MORCAR into ILAN. Both nations guard its broad length

House of Absolutely Astonishing Delights—a brothel in Port Thark, THESIA. Prop: Mother Rinalay

House of Heavenly Pleasure—a brothel in Reme, ILAN. Prop: Mother Zolgis

House of No Tomorrow—a brothel in Palanigh, ORVAR. Prop: Mother Larine

House of Seven Delights—a brothel in Reme, ILAN

House of Delightful Women—a brothel in Reme, ILAN

Ice—Pyre's abode; see *Castle Ice*

Ig—a beautiful city of NARF, surrounded by dairylands and rich pasture

ILAN—wealthy SW maritime kingdom with vast coastal expanse and extensive riverways, misruled by HRM Hower and enriched by its policy of offering open port to Pirates. The broad Syrodey R. splits ("EYE-lan") from the NE to the sea, forming Reme's huge port area. Birthplace and home port of Tiana

Il-Zadok Marsh—a most unpleasant and dangerous expanse of THESIA, N. of L. Belanda. Its spiders spin a passing valuable silk used in the making of fine fabric—and cord

Injana—Island kingdom southeast of Naroka. Noted for sacred bulls, a Veiled Queen and unique funeral customs.

Inn of the Smiling Skull—a watering-hole in Reme, favored by pirates, and scene of the events that set in motion the adventure called *Demon in the Mirror*. R.I.P.

Inn of the Wayfarer—a watering-hole in Reme, favored by pirates after their loss of the Smiling Skull. Scene of the events that set in motion the adventure called *The Eyes of Sarsis* (Tiana and Caranga are fond of inns). Not quite R.I.P., but business has fallen off sharply

Inn of the Ram's Head—a hostel in Taromplexis, ILAN, scene of a major confrontation between Tiana and Pyre. Here he—or his image—swore the dread Third Oath that set in motion the events of *Web of the Spider*

Iramar—a nation-state in TSC. Iramese

Isle of Red Stone(R)—Who cares? Nobody ever goes there

Janarizur—a temple city of NARF. A product is a superb white wine

JARSHOF—native name for the far N. continent called Northland or Northlands, cf. The Northlanders call themselves Jarls

Jinary—a duchy of SARCH

Jo—a barony of BASHAN. The growing townshippers call themselves Jorinnes

Killiar—a presumably dead city of TSC

Kla—a teeming barony-unto-city of MORCAR. Klamen

Kor—a duchy of BASHAN and, confusingly, a town in COLLADA. The fine cage-grip swords come from Bash-Kor. Korese

Kroll Isle—central and largest of a group SW of ILAN and NW of TSC. A pirate gathering place, still. Kroll-ites; pirates; sharks

Krolls—general name for island group dominated by Kroll and Teardrop Isles. Unassailable; a nice place to buy. Krollites

Lamarash—city on the middle-W coast of TSC. The black city is an important trading center and port tending to mercantile domination. Lamar; Lamarish

Lieden—("LIE-d'n") the City of Light. Lovely capital of COLLADA, on L. Belanda. Saved by Tiana, in *Demon*

Lightning Island—a most strange isle in the Sea of the Cow, N of the Yabazos and S of the Krolls. Home of ball lightning creatures, crystal(?) worms of giant size, Lightning Mountain (most of the isle), and no native humans. There are no settlers, either

Lower Continent, the—another name for the Southern Continent

Lubok, R.—its rapids are infamous. Connects with the Vervex via Bark's Fork, THESIA

Lugania—N. province of COLLADA. Medium wealth; good fighting men, but first province taken by Lokieto the invader. Luganians

Marazon—capital and largest city of NARF. Marazone(s); Marazonish

Martania—inland city of THESIA with too many priests and too many spiders. Good leatherworkers

Mesa Longo—the flat top of Mt. Erstand, where lies a salt lake

Mor—capital city of MORCAR. Morian; Morman; Morian

MORCAR—E. neighbor of ILAN. Sheepherding lands, grassy plain, absolutely wonderful, intricately patterned carpets. A perpetual treaty with ILAN grants the Mor-carish free access to the sea, via the Syrodey R.

Moshida—a most, most wicked old citystate. R.I.P. (See *Shining Plain*)

Mound of the Great Snake—a most unpleasant burial (?) mound in the far S. of TSC

Mt. Yazira—Thesian site of the Temple of Drood and the Chamber of the Sleeping Demon, a torture-murder site with spectators' boxes. Charming

Narakan—a tribe and citystate of TSC. Narakanese

NARF—a small nation bounded on the N by the absolutely awful White Desert and on the other three sides by greedy neighbors. Its paper is the best; its vines produce surpassing wines; its weavers produce superb shining silk. See THESIAN EMPIRE. Narfman; Narfer

NAROKA—nation known for poison, spiders, sinister arachnopriests, mazes, sadistic and often mad rulers, and extraordinarily beautiful dancers. Not a nice place to visit, but you wouldn't want to live there

NEVINIA—small nation bounded by barbarians and Dark Forest (supposedly inhabited by all sorts of unnatural creatures, including bloodthirsty outlaws). Nevinians tend to be cautious, mistrustful, and good traders. They also tend to emigrate

NORTHLAND, NORTHLANDS—(cf JARSHOF) non-native name for the large island or small continent up in the North Sea. During its brief crop season its women and children strive to lay in food for the long winter, while the men sail south to steal everything else. Good, loyal warriors with a love of braggadocio. Nor'men; Northrons; Northers; Northmen

ORVAR—paradisiacal island kingdom in the S. Sea of the Cow off TSC's W. coast. Home of the boisterous Festival of the Lesser Turtle. Orvarian

Palanigh—the Golden. Lovely seaport capital of tropical ORVAR. Home of the far-famed Festival of the Lesser Turtle. Its king survived Tiana's visit, though he lost a minister thereby. Palan; "orgyboy"; Turtlehead

Palance—a gold-rich duchy of ILAN. The Duke does not leave his estate

PALERAN—a lamentably small S. coastal principate. (See THESIAN EMPIRE) Palerani; -ese

Port Thark—multi-domed capital of THESIA and an important world port. Tharkman; Port Tharker

PORT TILONBI—an anachronism: an independent merchant state nestled on the S. coast between SARCH and BEMAR. Portilon; Tilonbi-ish

Qualise, Strait of—connects Sundoh Bay (THESIA) with the Asmygorian Sea

Queen Ina Street—avenue in Escallas of BASHAN

Ravenford—duchy-become-citylet of NEVINIA

Redlands—duchy of ILAN; home of Milord Spy

Reme—capital of ILAN and a chief world port. Home port of Tiana and Caranga—and a lot of other pirates. Reman

Riser Island—S. even of TSC, a grim isle of unnatural perpetual night—until Tiana's visit

Sanna Falls—in Thesia; separated from Shamash by Mt. Yazira. A scenic attraction whose beauty was not appreciated by Tiana when she went over the falls

SARCH—("Sark") a S. nation with a nasty coastline and good navigators. Sarchese; Sarchish

Sacred Swamp of the Mud Turtle—ORVAR

Sapour—an inexplicably ancient city of TSC. Sapourese

Scarba—capital of PALERAN. Scarban; Scar

Sceptre—citylet of MORCAR, home of a rich corundum mine and honored by having been named by MORCAR's first king, a fan of rubies and emeralds. Sceptran

Serancon's Isle—Long the home of the infamous poisoner, just off the coast of TSC. Many were saddened and as many gladdened by Caranga's visit there. It is still called Saranconis, sans Serancon.

Shamash—sinister capital of sinister NAROKA; a twisting maze and a sadist's dream. Major product: poison. Shamasher; Shammer; Spiderlover

Sinchore—(SIN-KORE) capital of SARCH and about its only decent port. Sinchorish men favor tiny fragile women and strong-hulled ships.

Sonul—the so-called "well-managed city" on TSC. A place of horror for its inhabitants—who aren't aware of it. Sonulman; Sonulese

Shining Plain—the site of the supremely wicked city of Moshida, after a visit by one of the World Fires.

Sim—capital of SIMDA

SIMDA—more a sprawling tribal area than a nation, this TSC locale is the birthplace of Caranga and an unseemly number of intensely hairy gorillas. Within recent memory the gentle priests of sensuous Susha ended cannibalism here—almost. Simdan

Siren Bay—below Slippery Hill on Kroll Isle. Peopled by murderous mermaids?

Slee—Oddly, a rather pleasant town of NAROKA, full of totatten trees and trailing feathermoss. Also fireplants and Sweetbird. Sleeman; Spiderlover; Second-sippers

Slippery Hill—*steep* hill atop which stands Storgavar Castle, on Kroll Isle. Smooth rock covered with rootless slime weed, it is a chute into Siren Bay

Stigilata—city formed as the result of a baronial alliance in far NE BASHAN. Famed for huge mastiff dogs and women in baggy drawers. Stigil; Stigilman; Hardhead

Stymnalia—inland city of ZADOK, full of fine tall nut-trees, pines, constant duels, and goats

Stromvil—a settlement clinging to a cliff overlooking Mt. Erstand. The Stromvili or Highriders ride the thunder; they . . . fly

Sundoh Bay—weirdly tide-protected, strait-protected inlet on which fronts Port Thark

Syrodan, Grove of—a charming holy place on Reme's outskirts, ILAN. By ancient decree and gift, it belongs to the People of ILAN

Sytheas, Strait of—a tight squeeze not too far asea from Shamash

Taromplexis—a small city of ILAN practically owned by retired merchants (read: pirates)

Tashol—a particularly odoriferous city of BEMAR, whose fine fragrant soap makes it famous. Tasholer; Soaper

Teardrop Isle—northernmost of the Krolls, named for its shape

Temple of Cignas—(SIGNAS) supposedly abandoned edifice to an ancient non-human god of sacrifice, where Tiana was slated to die in *Eyes*. She didn't. Located on that spit of leprous land called Ugly Point

Temple of Sirsinn—Thesian monument to Sirsinn Dragonslayer of long ago

Temple of the Sleeping Demon—a subterrene "arena" and chamber of murders in charming Port Thark where Tiana was slated to die in *Web*. She didn't

THESIA—long powerful nation whose well-sheltered Port Thark is a major world port. Its inland "capital" is ruled by a viceroy

THESIAN EMPIRE—THESIA, with viceroys in Scarba of PALERAN; Marazon of NARF; Martania of THESIA; and a prince of the blood in THUNLAND's Yathune

THUNLAND—a narrow S. nation with no good port.

Thunland's Thimble Mountain provides nice protection from NAROKA; nothing protects it from THESIA. Good warriors, but see THESIAN EMPIRE. Thunlander

Towar of Vargan—a luxury high-security prison in Naroka

Turbanis—R. of Calancia, in NEVINIA. Diverted by Tiana

TYREL—an area of two united tribes in TSC. Tyrelese

UGLY POINT—large spit of land W. of TSC in the Sea of the Cow

Vervex, R.—runs from THESIA into Sundoh Bay; connects with Vervex-Lubok via Bark's Fork just NE of Port Thark

Wayfarer Tavern—see Inn of the Wayfarer

Wharfrat—Street, in the old warehouse district of Reme. Its real name is Wortrav Street

White Desert, the—a totally inimical expanse bounded N,E,S,W. by the nameless land of the northern barbarian tribesmen; that little-known sprawl called the Gray Lands; NARF, and BASHAN

Woeand—ILANESE hamlet 50 leagues N. of Reme. A grim place in the grip of terror—until Tiana's visit

Yabazo Islands—a tiny cluster in the W Sea of the Cow, S. of Lightning Isle. Yabazo Islander

ZADOK—a NW land best known for Mt. Erstand and the legended Dark Forest it shares with Nevinia. Zadoki; Zadokish

Zed—coastal capital of ZADOK. Zedder

Zubaboogatooga—a joke; where one might wind up if one tunneled through or sailed off the edge of the road. Unlike Timbuktu, it is fanciful . . . presumably